Faith on the Run

By: Ron Francis

Acknowledgments

I received a lot of help that I am thankful for during the process of writing this book. I would like to thank my sister Laurie, my dad, and my friend Juan for their valuable input. I would also like to thank Mike of Mikebone Designs for a fantastic cover and Kevin of Kevin Horgan Media for his superb editing skills. Most of all, I'd like to thank God once again for the gift of creativity and the desire to write stuff down.

Chapter 1

The clouds were dark and foreboding, holding the promise of torrential downpours. The gloomy sky was in sharp contrast to the festive nature of the football game being played at Tottenville High School. Tottenville verses Wagner was always a highly anticipated event, and today was no different. Like most of the games these bitter rivals played, this one came down to the last drive.

Only two minutes remained, and Wagner was down six. Peter could smell the freshly-cut grass on the Tottenville field as the quarterback called the offense in for another huddle. With the exception of the clouds, it was a perfect day for football: late autumn, fifty-two degrees, and a light breeze blowing from east to west across the field. Peter loved every second of it. He stood in the circle and waited for the quarterback to call the next play.

"Seventy-eight yards to go and we're in first place," the quarterback said. "Peter, do you think you could get open down the sideline?"

"I don't know, Mark. They've been doubling me all game."

"No worries. Terrance is gonna pick one of them off you."

"Fire away then," Peter replied with a gleam in his eye. The huddle broke and Peter took his position on the outer edge of the formation. He was widely considered the best receiver in the city and right now he had to show it.

The breeze was beginning to pick up as the clouds grew darker and the hometown fans chanted, "Defense, Defense," loud and clear from the stands. He looked at the Wagner section and focused when he saw his sister, Dani, standing and cheering. He knew that she loved his games almost as much as he did. The ball was snapped and the play was on. Peter glanced at the scoreboard as he began his route.

The game clock was ticking down.

One forty-two.

One forty-one.

One forty.

His stomach was tight in anticipation and several beads of sweat escaped his helmet to run down his face. He was running full tilt towards the middle of the field where Terrance was waiting to block the cornerback. He turned abruptly and made a break for the sideline where a tight spiral waited for him to make an over-the-shoulder grab. He made the catch to the roar of Wagner's fans at the forty-eight yard line without breaking stride. Two defenders converged on him and he hurdled the first attempted tackle, while spinning away from the second. He was now at the Tottenville thirty-one and he sprinted another eighteen yards before finally being brought down from behind at the Tottenville thirteen-yard line.

The roar of the crowd filled the air as he picked himself up off the ground. Terrance met him with a high-five and pulled a chunk of grass out of his facemask. The rest of the team hustled down the field as the clock continued to wind down.

One eighteen.

One seventeen.

One sixteen.

This game couldn't be any better, Peter thought, as he waited for the team to huddle up again. First place was on the line with only one game to go, which made this year's matchup between the Tottenville Pirates and Wagner Falcons that much more exciting.

"Great play, man!" Mark yelled as he approached the line.

"Thanks, now let's bring this home," Peter replied with a confident grin. He unlatched his helmet strap to tuck away some stray locks of his brown hair before lining up for the next down.

The next two plays were running plays that brought Wagner down to the seven-yard line and brought the clock down to twenty-nine seconds. Tottenville was out of timeouts and couldn't stop the clock. The coach called in a pass play because they were getting nowhere on Tottenville's run defense and they lined up for third down.

"Let's make this count, Falcons!" Mark shouted as he looked at the excitement on his teammates faces in the huddle. "Let's do this!"

The huddle broke and Peter lined up in the same formation. The crowd was draped in anticipation. Charlie snapped the ball to Mark and Peter took off. Everyone in the entire stadium knew who the ball was going to. He started the same route he had run earlier, but instead of turning back towards the sideline, he cut across the end zone. Mark threw the ball high to Peter who, at six foot two, made the leaping grab over the defenders. Both feet hit the ground in bounds as the Tottenville linebacker hit him hard in the midsection and knocked him out of the end zone. On his way to the ground, Peter watched the official's hands go up, signaling a touchdown.

Peter pumped his fist in the air as the Wagner fans went wild again. Terrance and Austin helped him up and he tossed the ball to the official before running off the field. The extra point would win them the game and he would be in the newspaper again. *Another article for Dani's scrapbook*, he thought. The kick was good and the Wagner Falcons had taken the lead twenty-eight to twenty-seven, with fourteen seconds to go.

After the ensuing kickoff, the Pirates had time for one desperation play. Tottenville lined up with five wide receivers and the quarterback was slow to start the play. Peter looked on from the sideline, kneeling with the rest of the Wagner offense, and hoping there were no miracles left for the Pirates. The center hiked the ball and the quarterback performed a seven-step drop. He then fired the ball as far as he could. The stands were silent as the ball landed in the midst of a dozen players vying for position. After being tipped several times, the ball landed harmlessly on the grass, and the visiting Falcons celebrated with their fans on their rival's field.

"Great comeback, guys! You should all be proud of yourselves," Coach Bailey barked in his usual gruff manner. "But that doesn't mean there aren't things we need to work on, so don't get big heads. We need to be ready for Port Richmond next week because we haven't won anything until we've beaten them, and they're no walk in the park. I'll go over the good and the bad in practice Monday. For now, enjoy the rest of your weekend." He dismissed the team to the showers and, as they were walking off the field, he called out to Peter, "Donovan, get over here for a minute." Peter stopped his conversation with Austin and jogged back over to the coach.

"What's up, Coach?" he asked as he absently swung his helmet from hand to hand, still riding high from that last catch.

"We had a tough break with Jackson going down in the first half which means we're down both of our starting corners." He handed Peter a playbook and continued, "I need you to study the defensive playbook this week because you'll be pulling double duty for the next couple weeks. Think you can handle it?"

"Yes, sir," he replied as he tucked the book under his arm.

"All right, get out of here. We don't want to keep your ride waiting." Coach Bailey began to walk towards the assistant coach and Peter turned around to jog into the locker room. The sky finally opened up and the rains caused the remaining fans to scurry for the shelter of their nearby cars.

"What did coach want?" Austin asked as he took off his shoulder pads.

"He gave me the defensive playbook and said I might be pulling double duty playing corner next week."

"Makes sense. You catch anything coming your way anyway. Why not see if the other team will throw you the ball?" He smiled and added, "Do you think Hailey will be at the party tonight?"

"No idea, Austin," he replied with a shake of the head. "Why don't you just ask her out already and end my misery?"

"Come on, bro. Just because you don't feel like dating anyone—"

"You've been asking me about her since freshmen year, it's time to take the leap," Peter added as he walked towards the shower.

*****

Danielle had found an awning to wait under while the rain pattered hard off the cement around her. She couldn't wait for her brother to get out of the locker room. She knew he'd be in a great mood. This was a big win and he had caught the winning touchdown. While she waited, a couple boys approached her. One of them handed her his phone and said, "Hey, why don't you give me your number and I'll let you know where we'll be celebrating tonight."

She smiled politely and handed the phone back to her would-be suitor, "No thanks, I've already got plans with my brother."

"Who's your brother, maybe I can talk to him?"

"Peter Donovan." She smiled again as the boy took his phone back and then he and his friend were on their way. She had to admit, she liked the attention. She was average height for a girl her age, but she always felt short next to her brother. She had always considered herself to be a regular girl, but the way guys looked at her long, light brown hair and commented on her "beautiful", brown eyes she knew she was cute. Enough guys asked her out to confirm her suspicions, but she didn't really like any of them.

She preferred to focus on school instead of boys. She loved art and she could text with her best friend for hours, while watching romantic comedies on her iPad. She thought she was a pretty well-rounded teenager. She knew she wasn't super-popular, but that had never been a goal for her. She preferred sticking up for people that were getting picked on, and she would always rather be nice to people than be popular. It was exactly that attitude that first caused her to cross paths with her best friend, Laura, freshman year.

Now sophomores, Danielle and Laura had been best friends for over a year and Laura had recently talked Danielle into coming with her to her church youth group. Danielle had loved the group right from the start and had now been a regular for just under three months. Friday night quickly became her favorite night of the week and reading the Bible that the youth pastor, Nate, had given her had become somewhat of a morning ritual.

Danielle had never owned a Bible and, after reading the book of John, had decided to become a Christian much to Laura's delight. Her brother was quick to notice she was happier and began asking her questions. She was really excited because Peter had finally agreed to come to church with her next week. Her eyes lit up as Peter emerged from the school and she met him with a fierce embrace.

"You did so good today, Petey. You guys are gonna win city this year, I know it." She released her hug to grab hold of his arm as they began running toward Austin's waiting minivan.

Peter smiled at his excited sister and put his arm around her. "Take it easy, Dani. Let's just try and win next weekend first. If we beat Port Richmond, we'll be Island champs and we'll get a good seed for the city playoffs. That's the most important thing right now."

"What took you so long today?"

"Coach needed to talk to me. No big deal."

"About what?" She asked as they both hurried into the minivan's open side door to get out of the rain.

"Classified team stuff," he teased and then laughed at her reaction.

"Fine. If you don't want to tell me," she crossed her arms and feigned indifference, before taking her seat and fastening her seatbelt.

"He gave me the defensive playbook and asked me to be ready if neither one of our corners come back next week. Like I said, no big deal." He may have been acting like it wasn't a big deal, but his brown eyes said otherwise. Lightning crackled followed by the roar of thunder, as the rain continued its assault on pavement.

"Does that mean you wouldn't be a receiver? That doesn't sound like a good idea."

"No, it means I'll do both. Now enough about me, what are you and Laura up to this weekend?" Peter slid the door shut and fastened his seatbelt as Austin flicked the windshield wipers on and pulled into the line of cars waiting to exit the parking lot.

*****

Vinnie hated going to Brooklyn. It always took so long with all the traffic and the fifteen bucks he had to pay to cross the Verrazano Bridge didn't help either. Once he was in Brooklyn, however, he didn't mind it. The pizza was great and he always saw people he knew. He parked his black Mercedes behind the Drop and Go Laundromat. He and his three associates stepped out of the car and looked up and down the alley. He needed to make sure no prying eyes or working cameras saw them as they entered through the back door of the establishment. As soon as he opened the door, the scent of laundry detergent hit him and he wrinkled his nose for a moment.

"You can't be back here," a heavy Brooklyn accent called out. A moment later, an angry Italian man came into view. The expression on his face turned from anger to shock as Vinnie and his men all pulled their guns on him.

"Come on now, Marco, is that any way to greet a friend?" Vinnie replied in a stone cold voice. "You know why we're here, open it up."

Marco trudged across the small room to the wall that held the stainless steel safe. "Vinnie, you know Gravano will kill me if I give this week's take to you."

"Not my problem. Your boss owes Mr. Barbarelli a lot of money and he's tired of Gravano's excuses. He wants his money." He pointed to one of his enforcers and said, "Go check the rest of this place, make sure we're alone." Then he turned to another enforcer and said, "Make sure there's no surveillance in here and, if there is, take the hard drive. Remember gloves if you're gonna touch anything." He looked back at Marco and said, "Open the safe."

Marco knew that the gloves were a bad sign, but he continued his protest. "This is everything from his book for the entire weekend. There'll be hell to pay if you take it all."

"I got my orders, Marco. Now shut up and open it."

Marco looked at the three guns pointed in his direction and knew Vinnie wouldn't hesitate, so he did as he was told. He briefly thought about pulling his

10

own piece, but didn't like the odds of that ending well. He punched the last two numbers into the keypad of the safe and heard a metallic click. He turned the handle and the heavy door swung open, revealing several large piles of cash. Each pile was made up of many wrapped bundles of money. Mostly twenties, but several bundles of fifties and hundreds could be seen. Vinnie picked up two stacks of hundreds and asked, "How many per bundle, Marco?"

"Fifty," Marco bit out the terse reply.

Vinnie quickly put twelve bundles of hundreds in a black bag that had been sitting on the floor next to the safe. He grabbed another eight bundles of fifties. He finished by taking twenty-four bundles of twenties and two bundles of tens. He looked at Marco and said, "This is the hundred thou Gravano owes plus a five thousand collection fee. We ain't robbing you; we're only taking what your boss owes."

Marco looked inside the safe and could see it was still half-full. Part of him was relieved, but part of him despaired. He looked at Vinnie and said, "Make it look good and maybe Gravano won't kill me."

"No hard feelings, Marco. It's just business." He closed the safe and then hit Marco hard just above the eye with the butt of his gun while two of the men held him. He watched Marco's eyes roll into the back of his head as a gash opened up at the corner of his eye. Blood began to trickle down his face onto his shirt and his body slumped in the men's arms. They laid him on the floor of the office before leaving the same way they entered.

They jumped back into the Mercedes and drove away. Vinnie knew they had just started a war with Gravano. The big boss was not going to be happy that two of his Capos were going to war.

*****

After enjoying an early dinner with his sister, Peter was on his bike and heading to Barbarelli's restaurant for his delivery job. Thankfully, the rain had stopped, but he was going to be dodging giant puddles all night. As a kid, he would have preferred to ride through the pooled water, but now, going on eighteen, he knew that there were probably potholes beneath each of the tempting puddles that would throw him like an angry bull if he were foolish enough to try it. He had been doing this job since the summer following his freshman year. He was an excellent bike rider and Barbarelli paid him well for his services, so he thought it wise not to show up soaked and dirty for no reason.

He wasn't a typical restaurant delivery boy; in fact, very few of his deliveries were restaurant related. He was more of a personal bike messenger. He did deliver the occasional chicken parm hero, but he mostly delivered for Barbarelli's other business. He didn't know what it was called and never asked, but his boss told him it was more of an "antiques and difficult to procure items" business. Sometimes he delivered wrapped packages and sometimes he picked up payments. Tonight's schedule was payments. Barbarelli liked using him on a bike because it attracted less of the wrong kind of attention.

He entered the restaurant through the back and Barbarelli was waiting for him with a smile. "Great game today, kid, if you didn't catch that last touchdown, I'd be out ten grand right now." He handed Peter the schedule of pick-ups.

"Glad I could help." Peter's dry tone caused a deep laugh to erupt from Barbarelli's stomach.

"That's why I love you so much, kid, you always make me laugh. Keep catching those passes." His smile faded and it was down to business when he continued, "Remember, back here after each pick-up. The envelope goes right in the slot on top of the safe, got it?"

"Yes, Sir, Mr. Barbarelli." He knew the routine, and Barbarelli knew he knew the routine, but still, he said it every week on pick-up night. Before he left, a man he recognized from the restaurant walked into the back room with a black bag in his hand. He whispered something to Mr. Barbarelli and handed him the bag. Mr. Barbarelli immediately began to put the contents of the bag into the safe. Peter couldn't see what it was and knew not to ask because it wasn't his business. The whole exchange seemed a bit shady, but Peter just looked over the list one more time and then he was out the door. The sooner he finished, the sooner he could go home and get some sleep.

All of his friends were celebrating their big win right now, but he was stuck here working. He liked his job, but sometimes he felt like he was missing out on his high school years. All he could think was, *the party tonight won't pay the electric bill.* He pushed the thought out of his head as he pedaled through his neighborhood, careful not to let any passing cars purposely soak him. It was dark out, but he wasn't wearing reflective gear; the whole point of his job was to not attract attention. He arrived at his first pick-up pretty quickly.

He laid his bike down on the sidewalk and climbed the steps of a mansion on Todt Hill Road. Some of the priciest homes in all of New York City were located in this neighborhood and he seemed to do a lot of pick-ups and deliveries around here. He approached a fine oak door that cost more than everything his family had ever owned. He looked at the intricate stained glass patterns in the door as he lifted the oversized door knock.

Everything about this home screamed,"We're important and you're not." He had been here before; this house actually had a heated pool inside the house. There were seven bathrooms and three kitchens and, as far as he knew, only three people lived here. The outside was no less impressive with white marble columns facing a manicured lawn and a three-car garage. He released the door knock and then repeated the knock twice more. A moment later, he could see the maid moving near the door. She recognized him and without a word turned to let her boss know Peter was there.

A short time later, a middle-aged Italian man wearing an expensive purple silk shirt opened the door and handed him an envelope. "I heard you had a nice game today, Donovan."

"Yes, sir. I caught the winning touchdown and we're alone in first place now."

"Keep it up, kid. You're making a lot of people happy." He handed Peter an extra twenty dollars and began to close the door.

Peter pocketed the tip and added, "Thank you, sir. I'll do my best," before turning and descending the slate stairs. He was happy for the tip and it wasn't uncommon. Barbarelli paid him very well, so he was able to put the bulk of his money into the bank and keep the tips for himself.

His next pick up was right around the corner, and he was tempted to go there next to save time, but that would be breaking one of Barbarelli's cardinal rules and he didn't want to risk getting mugged with two payments. Barbarelli wouldn't be able to forgive that. Peter dropped the money off in the safe as instructed and took the same route back to where he had been a half hour earlier. He pedaled straight up Victory Boulevard, making the right on Manor Road. He crossed underneath the highway, passed the red brick, housing projects he lived in, and found himself once again in the nicer neighborhood for another pick-up.

He laid his bike down in front of another mansion and, while this was easily a two million dollar home, it was not nearly as well kept as the other homes on the block. The light blue siding was in serious need of a power

13

washing, the brick front of the house had been recently repaired with bricks that didn't completely match the color, and the lawn would be giving new meaning to the term urban jungle if the owner were to let it go any further. There was always a car being worked on in the driveway, and the once pristine pavers were now covered in oil stains.

He had picked up from here before, but not often. If the interactions he had witnessed the last time he was here were any indication, the people who lived in this home were not well liked. Peter shared that sentiment. He checked the schedule again and saw the name.

Sal Gravano.

Gravano had never tipped him and, the last time he was here, he left without payment. He had never delivered anything here, so he was unsure what Gravano was paying for. Before he could ring the doorbell, the garage door started to raise, the whir of the motor protesting as if the door were too heavy for it to lift. Still, it continued its painful ascension until the owner of the home emerged.

"I could check out that motor for you if you like. I'm pretty good with machines," Peter said with a friendly smile as Gravano was emerging from the garage.

"Or you could mind your own business before you wind up in the river," he threatened as he approached Peter. "Do I look like I need help from you?" He seemed to be in a bad mood. Peter thought it best not to reply as Gravano removed an envelope from his Armani suit jacket. Gravano was a walking contradiction. As messy and unkempt as his property seemed to be, his appearance was immaculate. His jet-black hair was impeccably styled, his fingers were manicured, and his suit was pressed. He didn't even have a five o'clock shadow. He stood six foot two and his suit had to have been tailored to fit and show off his muscular upper body. Peter couldn't imagine a man like that letting his expensive home get this run down. He held out the envelope with a wicked grin that sent a chill down Peter's spine.

He took the envelope and said, "Thank you, sir." He scrambled to pick up his bike and then he rode away. Something about Gravano was truly frightening and he didn't want to be near him for a second longer than he needed to be. He didn't wait to see if a tip was offered before he had started riding. He even thought he could hear Gravano laughing as he rode away, making him pedal even faster.

He finished the rest of his pick-ups without incident and wolfed down the two slices of pizza that Mr. Barbarelli had left out for him. He was weary by the time he reached home, foregoing the end of another victory celebration at Mark's house.

While he pedaled up Manor Road for the sixth or seventh time that night, he wondered if Dani had gone to the party. His question was answered when he arrived home. He took the elevator, which always felt crowded with his bike inside. He rolled his bike down the shadow-filled, narrow hallway. Reaching the door he took out his key and unlocked it. He opened the door and pushed his bike through, finally home. He looked to his right and saw Dani sleeping on the couch, which meant his father had come home intoxicated again. He put his bike in his room and came back out with his Giants blanket and gently covered his sleeping sister. He kissed her forehead and smoothed out the blanket before returning to his room. He shut his eyes and dozed off. Tonight, sleep came easily; it usually did on Saturdays.

*****

He awoke to the sound of his father yelling at his sister about not having any food in the house and he knew it was going to be a bad day. He was slow to drape his feet over the side of the bed; he tried to keep his temper in check as he listened to Dani calmly explain why there wasn't any food in the house. His father seemed to take her explanation as an affront to his parenting skills and began yelling again. Peter had heard enough. He threw his bedroom door open and interjected into his father's tirade, loud enough to make sure he was heard. "It's not her responsibility to make sure you have food, Jim. You're supposed to be the adult here. It's your responsibility. Leave her alone!"

For a brief moment, there was silence as his father turned to face him. "What did you just say to me?" His disdain was evident and his anger was building. He decided he was going to take out his bad mood on his disrespectful son.

"What, did all that drinking clog up your ears? You heard me. It's not her fault. You haven't bought us any food in months, Jim."

Jim couldn't believe what he was hearing from his son. He crossed the room in two strides and got right in his son's face, but Peter didn't back down. "Who do you think you are to talk to me like that?" He yelled, inches from his

15

son's face. "Who do you think keeps a roof over your head? Who do you think keeps the lights on? If you're so unhappy, there's the door." He thrust his hand in the direction of the living room as he continued to hover in his son's personal space.

"Dad, Peter, it's all right. I'll go buy some food right now. Please don't fight," Danielle called out in a voice that seemed small; and she knew wasn't heard.

"Who are you kidding, the only reason we have a roof over our heads is because the rent comes right out of your check. And when was the last time you paid an electric bill, Jim? I paid last month, and the month before, and the month before that." Peter was in his father's face now as he continued, "As for leaving, if it wasn't for Dani, I'd be long gone, but someone has to look out for her. Someone needs to make sure she has food and clothes, and it sure hasn't been you."

He had heard enough from his son. He shoved him and yelled, "Get out! Get out and don't come back 'til you can show some respect! I'm your father. I'm in charge, not you!"

Peter shoved his father back and yelled, "If I had to leave 'til I could show you some respect, I'd never come back." He looked over and saw his sister in tears and realized he'd gone too far. As much as he hated the man, he knew his sister still loved him. *She didn't need to see that*, he thought.

He went back into his room, slamming the door, and emerged a few minutes later, fully dressed. He brushed past his father and sister without a word, not meeting his sister's eyes as he left the apartment. His father wasn't going to calm down until he was gone and Dani wouldn't leave for church until she knew he was okay. Peter wanted to kick himself for picking a fight with his dad on a Sunday morning. Church was one of the few things Dani did to escape this nightmare of a life and it was one of the few times he knew she was happy. He walked out of his building, silently hoping she would still be able to go. He walked down to Saint John's and sat on the rock wall outside the old brick school. Almost forty minutes later, he noticed his sister walking down Manor road, and she was wearing nice clothes. He smiled, pushed himself up off the wall, and made his way over to her. He wanted to kick himself again when he noticed the dried tears on her cheek.

"Dani, I'm sorry," he started, not knowing where to go from there. "I just couldn't sit there and listen to him blaming you for stuff that's his fault."

"Peter, why can't you just be nice to dad? Why does it always have to be a fight with you two?"

"Because we don't like each other, Dani, and because he hasn't been a dad to me since elementary school." He shoved his hands in his pockets and kicked a stone as they walked.

"Maybe if you were nicer to him, he'd remember what he likes about you."

"Dani, I love you, and I love that you really believe that can happen. Because I love you, I'm even gonna try, but trust me; it'll never work. His hatred just runs too deep."

She looked like she was going to cry again, and he regretted that last statement. "But why? Why do you think he hates you so much?" She pleaded with her eyes for him to have an answer, but he didn't; at least not one he was willing to share. She composed herself and looked up at her big brother with a hopeful look in her eyes. "So, are you coming to church with me then?"

"No, I just figured I'd walk you to the bus stop and then get an egg sandwich from the deli. Are you hungry?"

"Yeah, but I don't have time—"

"Of course you do, I'll get yours first and you can eat on the bus. How are you gonna hear God on an empty stomach anyway?"

"Are you making fun of me? That's not cool, Peter. I really do believe in God."

"You're right, but you know how much I love teasing you. I have no choice." He looked at her and smiled, and she smiled back as she hit his arm. They made it to the bus stop and Peter ran into the deli across the street. A few minutes later, he came out with an egg and cheese sandwich with salt, pepper, and ketchup on it, along with a small orange juice. He gave them to his sister and kissed her on the cheek before running back across the street for his.

"Thanks, Petey," she called after him and was rewarded with a wave before he entered the store. She could see her bus waiting for the light at Manor and Victory to turn green, and she knew she'd be gone before he was back with his food. The bus pulled up to the stop with a high-pitched squeal, even though it wasn't traveling very fast. She smelled the diesel fumes as the door swung open, and she climbed the three stairs. She quickly swiped her metro card and, returned it to her pocket as her left hand balanced her Bible and breakfast.

She sat down on the almost empty bus and took a bite of her egg sandwich. She knew that if this had been a weekday it would be standing room only, so she was thankful for the seat because it allowed her to eat her food. She had put her Bible and juice down on the seat next to her while she ate her sandwich. She was almost finished when the bus reached her stop. She picked up her belongings and exited the bus with a smile and wave to the driver, and then she crossed the street to catch the bus that would take her down Clove Road to her church.

Peter was on his way to Austin's house after he finished his sandwich. He didn't want to go back home until he was sure his father was gone. He walked down Victory and turned onto Austin's block, Mountainview Avenue. When he arrived at the house, Austin met him at the door.

"Another fight with your dad?"

"Yeah, it's getting worse. Every time we're in the apartment together, it ends up in a fight. Anything I say sets him off." He sat on the edge of Austin's porch and looked out at the street.

"Dude, come stay with me for a while. We've got a finished basement and my parents won't care. They love you." Austin sat down next to him.

"Thanks," Peter paused and looked at his friend. "It's just that I don't want to leave Dani alone with him. That wouldn't be fair to her. Plus, I don't trust him."

"You think he'd hurt Dani?"

"I don't think he ever has, but if he got drunk enough, who knows." He took a penny out of his pocket and began twirling it through his fingers.

"I honestly don't know what to say to that."

"He probably knows I'd kill him if I ever found out he was hurting her." He hated even thinking about that. He hurled the penny into the street and just sat on the porch with Austin for a while.

Chapter 2

Danielle stood in front of the old wooden pew next to Laura and her parents as they sang a chorus she didn't know. She was still new to this whole church thing and she didn't know most of the songs they sang, but she seemed to like a lot of them. Every week, she would find out what the songs were called and then download them onto her phone so she could listen to them all week. Laura called them praise and worship songs, Peter called them weird religious songs, but she just called them songs. Like any other songs she liked, she wanted to sing along with them.

Laura had told her the songs could help her get closer to God. Danielle wanted to believe her, but she just wasn't sure how a song could do that. Maybe it wasn't the song itself that could help her get closer to God; maybe it was the act of worshipping him and the song didn't matter. She decided she was going to ask Nate about it.

She looked around and realized that she loved everything about the old church. She especially loved the gothic-style cylindrical lights that hung from the cavernous ceiling, the wooden pews, and the large cross that dominated the pulpit area.

Following the service, most of the congregation would stay after and have bagels and coffee. The church called this fellowship time, but Dani thought of it more as eating-bagels-with-Laura time. While they stood off to the side eating their bagels, Danielle heard "Hey, Laura! Hey, Danielle!" She turned to see Hailey approaching with a big smile.

You could see her Norwegian heritage in her blonde hair and blue eyes. Her cheeks had just a tinge of pink to them, and her friendly smile showed off her flawless white teeth. Cheerleading kept her in good shape, but she was always modestly dressed.

"Hey, Hailey," Laura replied, while Danielle just smiled and waved. She had taken too big a bite of her raisin bagel and couldn't yet speak.

"I caught you with food in your mouth, didn't I," Hailey began with a sympathetic frown. "I hate when that happens," she added with a laugh. "It's good to see you. You've been coming to a lot of Sunday mornings lately."

By this time Danielle had swallowed her food and answered. "Yeah, I want to learn as much as I can so that I could explain it better to Peter and my dad. They don't seem to understand what I'm talking about when I talk about God. Peter teases me about it, and my dad yells at me, but I really want them to believe what I do, you know?"

"I do know. My dad doesn't believe either, so my mom and I spend a lot of time praying for him."

"So do we," Laura added. "One day, Uncle Dave will come around."

"Yes, he will," Hailey added with a smile that touched her eyes. "I'll see you guys in school tomorrow." She left with a wave and Laura felt encouraged.

"I wish I was as sure about my family coming around as you and Hailey are about your uncle," Danielle said, before finishing off the last of her bagel.

"Just keep praying for them and let them see how God has changed your life. It's all you can really do." Just then, Laura perked up a little as it looked like she remembered something. "Hey, my mom is taking me to the mall in a few minutes. Do you want to come?"

"Sure," Danielle replied. It normally meant taking two buses to get to the mall, so she didn't go often. "I could really use some more art supplies."

"Great, then maybe we'll get dinner." They left the church basement in search of Laura's mom so they could hurry her along and get to the mall faster.

*****

Barbarelli was exiting Mass when he saw the Don sitting in the back of a black stretch limousine. He knew exactly what Mr. Catalano wanted to talk to him about. Catalano stepped out of the back of the limo. He placed his hands on Barbarelli's shoulders and kissed his left cheek, then his right, in the traditional family greeting. "We need to talk, Joseph," he whispered. Then he motioned for him to get into the limousine.

A moment later, they were both in the car, but the car did not move. Don Catalano looked at Barbarelli and said, "Listen, Joe, what is going on with you and Gravano? I can't have two of my Capos going to war. It reflects badly on the organization."

Barbarelli shifted in his seat and swallowed hard. "Don Catalano, I hope you realize I would never purposely do something that reflected badly on you. Gravano has been falling behind on his payments for my services for years, and refused to catch up. He owed me a hundred grand, and I knew he had it. I couldn't stand the disrespect anymore, so I had Vincent and some boys take it... plus a small collection fee."

"How small?" He leaned back in his seat and pulled out a tin containing cigars from one of the limo's small compartments. They looked like Cubans, and he lit one without offering any to Barbarelli.

"Five percent."

"That's actually not too bad. You showed more restraint than most of my guys would have." He sighed as if he knew things would not be worked out without his intervention. "Joseph, when I told the two of you to work out your disagreements, this was not what I had in mind." He opened the window a crack, and then took a puff of the cigar and blew the smoke out the window. Barbarelli could smell the savory flavor of the cigar and he had to concentrate to keep his mouth from watering.

"I thought we had, but he continued to disrespect your wishes by refusing to pay me what he owed. He's reckless, defiant, and he's gonna wind up bringing unnecessary heat on your organization. Mark my words!"

Don Catalano just laughed and then said, "He says you're too old and that I should give your organization to him."

"Oh he did, did he? We'll see about that."

"Joseph, you are to do nothing." The steel hung in his voice as he leaned in close. The conversation had lost its friendly tone. "He has already been warned about retaliation and it looks like I'm going to need to have the two of you in for another discussion. I'll have Milano get in touch with you soon." With that, the back door opened from the outside and he motioned Barbarelli out of the car. After he exited, the bodyguard that had opened the door took his place inside the limo and closed the door. Barbarelli began walking towards his own car, wondering when the call from Don Catalano's consigliore would come. When he reached his car, his bodyguard Michael was waiting for him there. He was so lost in thought that he almost didn't notice Don Catalano's limo drive away.

*****

Friday night had finally arrived and Danielle was excited. Peter was coming to church with her and she knew he would love it. "Hurry up, Peter! I don't wanna be late," she called through the bathroom door. She heard the shower running, so she was speaking louder than she usually would.

"I thought you said they just hang out for like an hour before they start. How can you be late to that?" His muffled reply came back through the door along with the sound of the water hitting the tub.

"I'm meeting Laura and I have a surprise for her."

"You just saw her like two hours ago."

"I know." She smiled as she heard the shower turn off. She knew he'd be ready in time. "We'll have to walk to Victory and then take a bus to Clove Road. If we miss the six thirty buses, we'll be late."

"I know. I'll be ready in a few." He opened the door and the steam from the shower billowed out hitting her with a blast of heat. He laughed at his sister's impatience, rustled her hair, and disappeared into his room. Five minutes later he reappeared to a frown from his sister. "What, we've got plenty of time to catch the bus, what's wrong?"

She shifted uncomfortably, and then replied, "I was hoping you would dress a little nicer for church."

"This is who I am, Dani. If these people are as nice as you say, they won't care."

"I guess you're right, Peter. It's just that this place is important to me and so are you, so I want you to love it and them to love you."

"Dani," he said a little more seriously. "I hope you don't think I'm gonna become some kind of Christian or something. I'm only going to make sure this isn't some weird cult. I'm happy you love it, but I just want to make sure it's a safe place for you."

"It's not a cult, Peter. You know Laura; she's been going there her whole life. Does she seem like she's in a cult?"

"Well, she's not exactly normal," he replied, and then ducked as his sweatshirt flew at him. He plucked it out of the air and continued, "I'm just kidding. I just want to be sure, and you wanted me to come anyway, so it's a win-win, right?"

"I guess so. Let's continue this conversation at the bus stop." She picked up her Bible and her purse, and walked out the door. He put on his sweatshirt, grabbed his iPod, and followed his sister, making sure to lock up behind them. He was pretty sure his dad had lost his key again, and he relished the thought of him sitting outside the apartment waiting for them to return.

22

They lived in building four of the six-story red brick buildings that made up the Todt Hill housing projects. There were seven nearly identical buildings in all. There were over five hundred apartments and over a thousand people that lived in the projects. Danielle always thought they were lucky to have one of the three-bedroom apartments. The buildings soon disappeared behind them as they walked under the highway and made their way towards the bus stop on the corner of Manor and Victory.

They arrived at the bus stop with three minutes to spare and took the S66 bus to the corner of Clove and Victory. Then they took a second bus past the park, past an old cemetery, past the zoo, and finally to Clove Road Bible Church. The other reason Peter had wanted to come was that it was November now and he didn't like the idea of his sister waiting on the corner near the park alone in the dark. It was a nice park during the day with a playground, ball fields, basketball courts, and hiking trails through the trees. As nice a place as it was during the day, the park seemed more menacing once the sun went down and, sometimes, bad stuff happened there.

They walked towards the side door of the church, and Danielle was greeted by a big hug from Laura. She looked up at Peter and smiled. "I knew she'd get you to come. The guys are throwing a football around the gym if you want to play."

"No thanks, I'm gonna wait here for Austin," he replied as he dug his hands into his pockets to fight off the cold.

"You didn't tell me you invited Austin," Danielle said as she looked at her big brother.

"Of course I invited Austin. You didn't think I'd come to a cult alone, did you?"

"I told you, it's not a cult, Peter," she replied with a tad of impatience.

"What if it is and we need to fight our way out?" He began shadow boxing and dancing around as if he were fighting. "That's why I told Austin to come." He was having fun teasing his sister and the look of shock on Laura's face made it even better.

"Don't worry, that almost never happens," A deep but good-natured voice said from behind. Peter turned around to see an average sized, bearded man smiling. "I'm Nate, and you must be Peter." He held out his hand and Peter looked at him suspiciously.

"That's weird, Dani, how does this dude know my name?"

23

"Because I told him I've been inviting you. It's not weird. Stop it." She hit his arm and disappeared through the door with Laura.

"It's true, she always brags about her big brother, Peter," Nate said.

Peter shifted uncomfortably. "I was just kidding about that cult stuff and fighting our way out. I was just teasing Dani. You weren't supposed to hear that."

"No problem, man, teasing your little sister is pretty standard. But seriously, if you do have any questions or reservations about us, I'd love to put your mind at ease. I'm going back inside to make sure everything's all right. Come on in when you're ready." He turned and disappeared through the door, too. Peter heard the music and watched the kids going in as he waited and it all seemed normal enough. It wasn't his idea of a good time, but it didn't seem weird or dangerous. Austin finally showed up and they stood outside the church together.

"So, what's this place all about?" Austin asked. "It's a far cry from your day job with the Barbarellis."

Peter shot him a glare and replied, "Dude, no one can know about that, and I have no idea what this place is about. I'm just making sure it's safe for Dani."

"Pete," he began with an air of seriousness he rarely showed his friend. "She's old enough to make her own choices, bro. If she thinks church can fix her life then what's the problem?"

"Because it's my fault her life needs to be fixed and if church makes her happy, then that's great. I just need to make sure it's legit."

"Fine, let's go to church then. It shouldn't be too bad. I think I saw a kid with a football, and they have a gym."

"No beating these kids up, Austin. I don't want Dani to be mad at me."

"Fine, but you know how to take the fun out of everything." He laughed as he moved towards the door.

About an hour later, Peter and Austin had to admit they were having fun throwing the football around with perfect strangers. It wasn't serious like football practice, but it was still fun. Nate walked in, threw the ball with them for a few minutes, and then called for everyone to find a seat in the auditorium.

Peter and Austin walked in to the auditorium to the warming up sounds of a band already on the stage. Peter looked around the room and saw about eighty metal folding chairs set out in two sections with an aisle down the middle. There was a door in each corner of the room. One was the door they used to enter the church, one was the door to the gym they had just come through, and he didn't know where the two doors on the other side of the meeting room led. The ceiling looked to be twelve feet high and the stage in the front of the room stood about a foot above the floor. There were lamps turned on in the corners and stage lights highlighting the band, but the overhead lights were out. Two projectors were shining song lyrics to either side of the stage and Peter heard Austin subconsciously reading the lyrics in a low voice.

"Jesus, I'm living for your name, I'll never be ashamed of you. Our praise and all we are today, take, take, take it all." He paused as he looked at Peter and added, "What is this?"

"I think it's talking about God."

"Why?"

"I don't know. It's weird." As the words left his mouth, he felt another slap on his arm.

"It's not weird, Peter, these people just love God and so do I. Come on, sit with me and Laura." Danielle started pulling his arm towards the seats and he followed her.

"Fine, but only if we sit in the back."

"Yeah, we want to watch the whole freak show," Austin added with a laugh.

"Shut up, Austin," Danielle playfully responded.

"Hey, there's Hailey, what's she doing here?" Austin asked, suddenly feeling the need to stop mocking these people.

"I told you it's all regular kids. She's Laura's cousin and she's not the only cheerleader that goes here either. Toni Ann does, too," Danielle replied.

"Maybe this place isn't gonna be so bad," Austin quietly added to Peter as he watched Hailey sit down with her friends.

"I hope not," Nate interjected with a smile as he patted Austin's back.

"Where'd he come from?" Austin whispered.

"I don't know how he does that, bro, just don't say anything bad," Peter answered as Nate walked to the stage and they found their seats. It looked like there were almost seventy kids in the room and Wagner wasn't the only school represented. The group was fairly diverse, too. Ethnically, economically, athletes, preps, skaters, all different kinds of kids, and he was amazed they all seemed to be getting along. He leaned over to Danielle and asked, "Isn't it weird that all these kids hang out with each other? You never see this in school."

"It's not weird, they're all friends. Some of them have been coming here their whole lives and even though they're into different stuff now, they're still friends," she whispered.

"That's cool," Peter whispered back. He was really out of his element here. This was not what he had expected at all. He turned around as he felt a hand pat his back.

"Hey Peter, what are you doing here? Nice catch last week, man. That was a great game."

He looked and recognized Ted from the basketball team. *Finally, someone I know*, he thought. "Thanks, Ted, I'm just here to keep an eye on my sister. When does basketball season start up?"

"In about three weeks, we're gonna have a good squad this year, bro."

"That's what I hear. I'm looking forward to seeing Wagner dominate both football and basketball."

"Me, too, but 'dominate' might be a strong word," Ted replied and then paused. "Hey, thanks for sticking up for my brother the other day. He told me some guys were gonna beat him up, but you stopped them. Thanks, man."

"No problem, but to be honest, I didn't know he was your brother. I just hate to see people being bullied. He tried to thank me, but I just yelled at him to get to class. Sorry, I would have been nicer if I knew he was your brother."

"Don't worry about it; I'm not even nice to him," he said and then paused before continuing, "But that doesn't mean I want him getting jumped either."

"All right, everyone," Nate began from the stage. "Let's settle down and get ourselves ready for a time of worship."

"What's worship?" Peter whispered to his sister.

"It's where we sing songs to God because we love him," she replied with a smile and then quickly added, "Don't say it."

"That's not normal," Austin replied for him to a snicker from Ted behind them.

"Don't encourage them, Ted," Danielle whispered. Just then the music began and most of the kids started singing the lyrics that Austin had read earlier. Peter looked around the room as one song led into the next. Some kids were whispering to their friends, but most were singing, and some even had their eyes closed or hands raised. He wondered what that meant. *Who closes their eyes when they sing?*

He continued to watch what was going on around him. He studied his sister and she was really into it. She had the biggest smile on her face while she was singing and he took note of how happy she was. He really couldn't figure out what was going on and, with each song, he had more questions for his sister. He even caught Ted singing with his eyes closed. *I thought Ted was pretty normal, I guess not,* he thought as the music started winding down.

Nate walked back on stage and, without preamble, said, "Let's pray." The music was still playing softly in the background as he began. "Lord, we come before you tonight, thankful for another opportunity to meet with you! Thank you for another week of life that you have given us, Lord. We are thankful for the freedom to meet in your name. I ask that you bless this time..."

Peter lost track of what he was saying as he looked around at all the closed eyes and bowed heads. He looked at Dani and her eyes were shut tight. He looked over to Austin and saw the same look of confusion on his face. "What's going on here?" he mouthed, and Austin just shrugged. Then the prayer was over and a video immediately began to play on both screens. It chronicled human trafficking in Asia. When it ended, he noticed his hands were balled into fists he didn't remember making. The short video ended with a plea for monetary help for an organization that rescued some of these people.

"I know what you just saw may have been upsetting," Nate said as the lights came back on. "But this happens every day all over the world and we need to be aware of it. I'm going to pass the offering basket around and, if anyone would like to donate to help save some of these people, that would be great." The basket began to make its way around and Peter felt himself reaching for his wallet. He took out a twenty and noticed both Austin and Danielle's eyebrows raised at the gesture.

"Dude, I'm not giving any money," Austin leaned over and whispered.

"No one asked you to, bro, it's not a big deal." He put the money in the basket and noticed Danielle put some in, too. After the basket had gone around, Nate got back up on stage and sat down on a stool with a music stand in front of him. He looked like a professor about to give a lecture.

"Tonight we're going to talk about taming the tongue. Please turn to the book of James, chapter three."

Danielle opened her Bible to the table of contents and found James. She noticed Peter and Austin looking around a bit confused and asked, "What's wrong?"

"I never heard of the book of James, I thought you guys read the Bible here or something."

She smiled and showed him her Bible. "The book of James is in the Bible, I found out that there are sixty-six books in the Bible. I know it's confusing at first, but James is part of the Bible."

Nate began to read and just then Peter's phone went off. Thankful he had left it on vibrate, he stood and walked out of the room to take the call. It was from Barbarelli and he knew better than to miss a call from him.

*****

Peter made sure he was alone in the parking lot and answered, "Yeah boss, what's up?" He noticed the temperature had dropped while they were inside.

"Donovan," the angry voice screamed through the phone. "You better have a good explanation for this."

Uh oh, that doesn't sound promising, he thought as he replied, "For what, sir?"

"Gravano's five hundred short on his payment, kid. He says he gave you the right amount. Says you may have taken some."

"No way, sir. I would never steal from you. You've been very generous to me."

"You're my best delivery guy, Donovan. I'd hate to have to part company with you."

"I swear to you, sir, I didn't take anything. I'm not stupid and I need this job too much to jeopardize it doing something stupid."

"Well, what do you propose we do about this, then? I'm out five hundred, and that money's gotta come from somewhere."

"What if I catch him in the act?" Peter's heart was pumping and his mind was racing; he wasn't even sure what he was suggesting.

"What are you saying, Donovan?"

"I don't know. Maybe mention to Gravano that you don't trust me anymore. Next time I pick up his payment, we'll see if he takes the bait. I'll mention that it seems a little light and hope he says something to incriminate himself. I'll have my phone recording in my pocket."

"All right, I'll play your game, but if he doesn't bite I'm gonna have to assume you owe me the five hundred and then you're not getting paid this week. You better hope this works, kid. You know how upset I get when I'm disappointed."

"I'll do my best, sir." He replied. The cool fall air was beginning to seep into his bones.

"Where are you right now? I want to see how you're gonna make this work."

"I'm at Clove Road Bible Church with my sister." He knew how that was going to sound to his boss before he even finished speaking.

"Church!" Barbarelli yelled. "You're not finding religion on me, are ya?"

"No, sir, I'm only here because my sister loves this place, so I figured I better check it out and make sure it wasn't a crazy cult or something. Also, I don't like her waiting at the bus stop by the park alone in the dark. It's not safe and she's all I got."

"That's good. Remember that; if you're not around, she's got nothing." Peter immediately understood the implication as his boss continued. "I'll check your phone thing tomorrow before you go back to Gravano's. He's gonna be at a meeting I have to go to. I'm gonna lay down some hints that I'm losing faith in you. What time is your game over?"

"Four."

"Good, I'll see you at six and, if he's clean, I'm gonna be very disappointed in you." He let the threat hang heavy in the air before hanging up. Peter slumped against a Ford pickup and his mind raced. At least Gravano's antics seemed to make more sense now. He was so lost in thought he didn't even notice when kids started pouring out into the parking lot to throw the football around under the lights.

"Peter, what happened? What's wrong?" Danielle looked worried. "You missed the whole message, and it was really good." She seemed disappointed and he felt bad.

"I'm sorry, Dani, I got a call from my boss. There's a situation at work that he needs my help with." He noticed the look on Austin's face and knew he'd be explaining things to his friend later.

29

"Well, come inside and have some pizza. They also have cake."

"Okay. And I'll make this up to you. I'll come back next week and I'll ask my boss ahead of time to hold all calls from eight til..." he glanced at his watch and finished. "Nine fifteen, so I don't miss the church stuff again." He noticed she seemed happy with that and was thankful she hadn't detected the worry on his face. They went back inside and each grabbed a slice of pizza. Peter saw Hailey walking towards them and he noticed Austin straighten up slightly. She was wearing blue jeans with a maroon, American Eagle sweatshirt.

"Danielle," she called out. "Laura just showed me the birthday card you made for her. It's beautiful. I had no idea you were so good." She turned to Peter and said, "You have a very talented sister, Peter." She looked back to Danielle and continued, "Do you think you could make a card for my parent's twentieth wedding anniversary? I'll pay you for it."

"Sure, and you don't have to pay me, just tell me what you want it to say."

"I'll write it out for you, and I'm gonna pay you. I know your supplies cost money. You do good work and should be paid for it. I'll give you five bucks. Do you think you can make it by Tuesday?"

"Sure, Hailey, I'll give it to you in school on Monday."

"Thanks, I can't wait." She turned back to Peter and said, "I'm glad you and Austin came out tonight. I'll see you at the game tomorrow. Go Falcons." She threw her arm in the air in cheerleader fashion and then turned and walked away.

"Austin, you can pick your jaw up off the floor now," Peter said with a laugh.

"You heard that, right? She said she was glad both of us were here. Dude, I'm coming back next week. I don't care how weird this place is." He was clearly excited.

"It's not weird, Austin. It's just that God is important to us and sometimes it's hard to understand why, if you're not a Christian," Danielle said.

"I'm Catholic; my parents go to mass every Sunday. My mom even teaches catechism, but I still think this is different. I'm not making fun, I'm just sayin."

"It's fine. I have to go give Nate a card. I'll be right back." She started to walk over to the youth pastor.

"What's the card for?" Peter asked.

"His wife is pregnant and she's not feeling well, so I made her a get well card. She's super nice and I miss seeing her."

"Wow, that's pretty cool of you." He knew she thought of Nate's wife as sort of a mom or big sister-type, and he knew it was because their mom died when they were both very young. She never had that motherly influence, and Nate's wife seemed to be filling that role. He watched Nate light up as she gave him the card for his wife and then give her a one-armed side-hug while he held the card as if it were a treasure. Peter had to admit, his sister was happy in this place and he decided that, while it was a bit weird, it wasn't dangerous. He would come with her a couple more times, just to be sure, but he knew his sister had found a good place.

*****

They stayed and hung out until Laura's mom arrived to pick her up. She offered a ride and Dani accepted, while Peter and Austin decided to take the bus. They all said goodbye to Nate, and he thanked them for coming. Then Ted shot them a wave as they made their way to the bus stop.

"Bro, did you really stop some kids from jumping Ted's brother?" Austin asked. He knew what Peter wanted to talk about, but figured he would ease his way into it with another topic.

"Yeah, it was no big deal."

"But that kid is such a tool. He's a little nerd."

"So, that doesn't mean he should get beat up. If he had started it, and it was one on one, I would have watched like everyone else, and let him take his beating. It wasn't like that, though; they were picking on him for no reason, and then they started hitting him. I couldn't let Harris and his friends get away with that. Fight one on one like a man, it's not like he would have lost."

"So are you guys like friends now?" Austin smiled and Peter glared at him. "Ease up, I'm just kidding. What did Barbarelli want?"

"A guy named Gravano shorted him five hundred and pointed the finger at me," Peter replied with his hands in his pockets and his head down against the cold. He was beginning to wish he had taken the ride Laura's mom had offered.

"Dude," Austin replied in an almost reverent whisper. "What are you gonna do? You can't get on Barbarelli's bad side. Not if you want to be healthy enough to keep playing football."

"I know, he'll break my arms or my legs, or both if he thinks I'm stealing from him. I asked him to drop a hint to Gravano that he doesn't trust me anymore and then I'm gonna make another pick-up and hope he shorts me again. I'm gonna confront him and record Gravano's response on my phone."

"What if he doesn't take the bait?" Austin asked aware that it wouldn't be good.

"Then I'm in a lot of trouble." They walked in silence after that and gratefully stepped out of the cold when the bus arrived.

Danielle whistled while she walked into her apartment building. Most people thought it was a dangerous place to live, but she knew most of the people and they knew her. It wasn't that bad. She thought back to youth group earlier that evening. Peter had promised he would come again and she decided she would continue praying for him to become a Christian. Laura and Nate had loved their cards and Hailey was going to pay her to make one for her parents. While she was thinking about how much she loved youth group, she turned onto her hallway and her heart sank. Lying against the door of her apartment was her father and he was drunk again. There were several empty bottles of beer scattered around the floor and he looked at her through the dim light with an accusatory stare.

"Where have you been all night?" he slurred in a loud voice.

"Daddy, today is Friday. You know I go to church on Friday," she replied as she helped him to his feet.

"Well, I've been waiting here for hours for someone to let me in. Maybe you should have thought of that before you left all night." He swayed and his breath reeked. She hated having to come home to this. She wished Peter were here to help her although in this state, it might be better if her father didn't see Peter. She didn't understand why he hated his son so much. Peter was a little bit disrespectful, but he got okay grades, he was the best wide receiver on the Island, and he had a job. What more could her father want?

"Did you lose your key again, dad?" she asked.

After he nodded and slurred something unintelligible, so she said, "I'll go down to Bob's tomorrow and have another one made up for you, all right?" She slid her key in the lock and heard the tumbler click, and then she opened the door.

She helped her father into the apartment, and then to his room. She took off his shoes, turned him on his side and covered him with a blanket, then left

32

the room to his instant snores. She went back to the hallway and collected her dad's empty bottles as one of her neighbors looked on in disdain. It was all she could do to manage a smile as she picked up the last bottle and closed the door.

She placed the bottles in the recycle bin, looked up to the ceiling, and whispered in a voice that cracked, "God, why can't my dad just stop drinking?"

Peter walked in an hour later. He took one look at the recycle bin, looked at his sister, asleep on the couch and felt terrible. He knew her night had been ruined and it was just one more reason he hated his father. *She was so happy just a couple hours ago, and that monster just had to ruin it.* He was so angry, but he put it aside and put a blanket over his sister. She always slept in the living room when their dad was drunk, to make sure he didn't wander out and hurt himself. She looked up at him and smiled. "Thanks Peter."

He smiled back. *She's so resilient.* He kissed her cheek and said, "Goodnight, Dani. I'll see you in the morning." He hated to see his sister in pain. They weren't like typical brothers and sisters. They didn't fight very much and they both went out of their way for the other if the situation deemed it necessary. They still fought on occasion, but he had resigned himself to taking care of her a long time ago because it was his fault she had no one else.

He could never tell her what happened to their mom because he couldn't stand the thought of her hating him. *How can I tell her it's my fault mom died? If only I would have listened, why didn't I listen? I don't blame dad for hating me, but I do blame him for not taking care of Dani. What am I gonna do if Barbarelli doesn't believe me?* His thoughts kept him awake half the night, but eventually he drifted off to sleep.

He awoke to the smell of Belgian waffles and hot maple syrup. He walked into the kitchen to see his sister concentrating on making breakfast.

"I made game day waffles," she exclaimed. This had been her tradition since she learned how to cook in sixth grade. She always made him waffles on game day and he never turned them down.

"Thanks, Dani. You're lucky waffles are the reason we're seven and one right now."

"Well, you'll be eight and one after today; then it's on to the playoffs. We're definitely winning the Island this year. We're the best team and we have the best player and he get's waffles on game day." Her smile was infectious and he once again found himself amazed at how strong a person she was.

"Thanks, sis. Do you think you can do some shopping before the game today?" He pulled out an envelope with food money that he was sure his dad didn't know about. He gave her some money and was quick to hide the envelope away. They both knew why he did it that way. He let his sister believe it was their father's money, but it was his. He paid the utilities, he bought the food, and he kept his sister clothed. His father could barely pay the rent and he usually drank the rest of his check. He occasionally bought Dani a big gift to try and buy her love, or apologize for something, but that was it. He hated to imagine the debt his dad had racked up, but he didn't care. As long as the rent was paid, Dani would have a roof over her head.

"I was planning on it after the game. Laura's mom offered to give me a ride because they have to go shopping, too. So this week, I'll be able to get lots of stuff." She smiled again and he couldn't believe how content she seemed. Even small things made her happy.

"You're my hero, Dani. I'll look for you in the stands at the game. Love ya, sis." He downed the last bite of his waffle and gave her a hug. He picked up his bag with his uniform and pads, and hurried out the door when he heard his father stirring in his room. It was never a good idea to talk to his father before a game.

Just then, her father came out into the kitchen.

"Hi, daddy, I made waffles, do you want some?"

"Where's your lowlife brother?" he grunted.

"Dad, you know he's got a big game today, are you coming?"

"You know I'm not, Danielle, why keep asking?" His reply was dripping sarcasm.

She lost her smile and replied with an air of disappointment, "Maybe because I want us to be a family, did you ever think of that? Maybe I'm tired of how much you hate him. He's not a lowlife. He gets good grades, he's one of the best football players in the city and he has a delivery job, on his bike. Maybe he just needs to hear good job or something from you once in a while. Is that too much to ask?"

"Yes, Danielle, yes it is. It's never gonna happen. He's lucky I even let him live here. He's gone at eighteen, that's for sure; then I never want to see his face again. That's never gonna change, so grow up and get over it."

"Why do you hate him so much?" She yelled just trying to understand.

"Because he killed your mother!" he yelled back before he could stop himself.

"What?" she squeaked, not believing what she had just heard. She stuttered trying to find the words, "H... How?"

He sighed. The one thing he had ever done for his son was never telling his sister what had happened, and it was really more for her than for him, but now he had ruined that too. *I really am the worst father ever,* he thought. "When you were two and Peter was four, he ran out into the street after your mom had warned him not to, and a car was coming fast. The little idiot froze up and your mom dove into the street and pushed him out of the way just in time. Unfortunately, he lived and she didn't. That day ruined our lives and I'll never stopped blaming him for it. Now do you understand why I don't like your brother? Every time I see him it reminds me of what I lost because of him."

"Daddy, that's not fair. He was just a little kid. He didn't do it on purpose," she replied. She felt herself beginning to tear up. This was the first she had ever heard of this. She couldn't imagine the weight her brother had been carrying all these years. With his father always blaming him, he had to be blaming himself.

"Don't you take his side," he yelled. "You're all I have left of your mother. Don't you take his side!" She flinched as he drew close, expecting to be hit, but instead he walked back into his room and slammed the door.

She stared in disbelief at what she had just learned. She picked up her phone and her key and ran out of the house as her tears continued to fall. She cried all the way to Laura's house

Laura answered the door and immediately saw the tears. "Danielle, what happened?" She put her arm around her and guided her into the house where she just sobbed in her arms. They sat down on the couch and Laura held her. "It's okay, Danielle, just tell me what happened." She looked up at her best friend and just cried some more. She didn't even see Laura's mom come in the room before she felt her hand on her back.

"What's wrong, dear? Did something happen?"

Between sobs, she managed to tell Laura and her mom what had just happened with her dad. By the time she was finished, Laura was in tears with her and her mom was consoling two fifteen-year-old girls.

"Danielle, I'm so sorry. What happened is not your brother's fault. I'm so sorry you had to find out about your mom that way."

35

"Ever since I became a Christian, I've been praying that my Dad and my brother would like each other or at least get along. Now I know that it can never happen." She looked up at Laura's mom and continued, "And Peter, how has he carried this around his whole life? Now I know why he always looks out for me, because he really thinks it's his fault I don't have a mom."

"Maybe. But maybe he's just a good brother," Laura replied.

"What should I do?" She looked up at Laura's mom imploring her to have an answer.

"I don't know, sweetie." She looked down in sympathy and rubbed her back again.

"Your brother probably never told you because he's scared how you'll react." Laura said.

"Should I let him know that I know; let him know that it wasn't his fault?"

"I'm sure it would help him to know that you don't blame him," Laura's mom said.

"Can I hang out here until the game? I really don't want to go home right now."

"Of course, sweetheart. I'll make some hot cocoa and snacks." She disappeared into the kitchen.

"I know I don't know that much about God yet, but shouldn't he be trying to help my family or something?" Danielle asked.

"It's hard for us to understand how God works sometimes, but I know he put you in that family, and even though it's hard, you're the light for your brother and your dad. I don't really know what else to say." She put her head on Danielle's shoulder and they sat in silence until her mom came back in with the snacks.

Chapter 3

It was beautiful day for football, forty-two degrees and sunny. The blue sky provided the backdrop as Peter and the team had just finished their pre-game routines. All of the strategy, all of the warming up, and all of the preparation had them ready to go. They were all pumped up because they knew that if they won this game, they would be Staten Island champs. They ran out onto the field and Peter looked up in the stands for Dani. It was a ritual. In seven years, she had only missed one game and that was when she was sick. She was his good luck charm and when he didn't see her, his concern was instant. *I know she's not sick, why isn't she here? What if something happened? Where can she be?* It was time to take the field and he was freaking out. *How can I play when I don't know why she's not here? I bet dad did something; if he hurt her...* Austin interrupted his near panic attack.

"Check it out. Hailey is hugging your sister and Laura. I need to hang out with them more."

As the relief washed over him, he coolly replied, "You're such a tool, Austin. I'm not letting you use my sister to get close to Hailey." He jabbed his arm, laughed, and took off for the field as the visiting Port Richmond Red Raiders returned the opening kickoff to the thirty-seven yard line. Peter was happy to be playing both offense and defense today. He didn't mind pulling double-duty; in fact he relished the new challenge. He gave a quick wave to his sister and ran to his position.

The coach had them starting out in a zone because they were fielding a backup corner and starting wide receiver at the two corner slots and he wanted to ease them in. The Red Raiders' coach didn't see it that way. The first play from scrimmage was a lazy spiral in Peter's direction. As he ran stride for stride with the Port Richmond receiver, he timed his jump perfectly and came down with the ball at Port Richmond's forty-yard line. He took off back towards the line of scrimmage and quickly crossed the fifty-yard line before he evaded his first tackle. He crossed the forty and made it to the thirty-five before he was hit hard by the three players who finally managed to bring him down at the twenty-nine yard line. He quickly popped up and ran off the field.

"Great play, Donovan, take a minute," the coach called as he sent the offense out onto the field. He signaled for a running play so his star receiver could catch his breath, and the run got them a first down at the seventeen-yard line. "Are you good, Donovan?"

"Yes, coach," he replied.

"Good, get out there then!" he yelled.

Peter ran out to the huddle and his number was called. He knew the coach was rewarding him for the interception. The quarterback lined up in the shotgun formation and took the snap. He threw the ball as the Red Raiders linebacker hit him and drove him hard into the ground. He never saw the one handed grab in the corner of the end zone, or the little dance Peter did to keep both feet in bounds, but he heard the roar of the home fans and jumped up with arms raised. As the offense left the field, Peter flipped the ball to the official and shot a quick glance into the stands to see his sister cheering and waving.

"Nice catch, Donovan! You ready to get back out there on D after kickoff?"

"Yeah, coach," he yelled as his teammates swarmed him.

By the time the game was over, Danielle was feeling much better. She knew she would have to talk to Peter soon; hopefully when he got back from work that night. For now, she just planned to give him a big hug. The Falcons had won the game twenty-one to fourteen and Peter had two touchdowns. She knew he would be happy and didn't want to spoil his mood. She smiled as he made his way through the celebrating crowd and picked her up in a bear hug. At six foot two, he usually had her about a foot off the ground when he did that, and she always felt like a kid. After that, he disappeared into the locker room. She waited for him to come out in front of the school with the rest of the students that were still milling about. She was pleasantly surprised when Hailey stopped and stood next to her.

"My cousin told me you had a really rough morning. Do you want to talk about it?" She asked with a look of concern on her face.

"I do, Hailey, but if I do, I'm gonna start crying again and I don't want Peter to see me crying when he comes out. Maybe we could talk later?"

"All right, how about after church tomorrow?"

"Okay, if I can get there. Maybe Peter will ride the bus with me."

"You guys are pretty close, huh."

"He's really all I've got. He doesn't think I know, but I know that he buys all of our food. I know he gives me money and says it's allowance from dad. He even gets me clothes if I ask. Now I know why." She started to tear up and Hailey put her arm around her.

"It's all right, Danielle. Hey, he's coming out, we'll talk tomorrow." Danielle nodded and dabbed her eyes with a tissue.

"Hey, Dani, heads up," Peter yelled as he tossed the football in her direction. She smiled and caught the ball. Hailey looked impressed at the display. She was even more impressed when Danielle threw a perfect spiral back.

"Wow, I didn't know you could do that, Danielle," Hailey said with a hint of surprise in her voice.

"How do you think I got so good?" Peter replied. "It's all the practice with mini-Manning here." He flipped the ball to his smiling sister.

"You did so good today, Peter." She interlocked her arm with his as they started to walk. "Where's Austin?"

"He's getting yelled at by coach, I'll meet up with him after work. Do you want us to walk you home, Hailey?"

"That's really sweet of you, but I'm waiting for Toni Ann. We'll be all right." She waved and they were on their way.

"So, Hailey's really nice, right?" Danielle started with a sly smile.

"Not interested."

"What? How did you—"

"Because you're predictable, Dani. I promise if I start dating someone, I'll introduce you to them, but it's probably not gonna be a nice church girl like Hailey, even if she does look really good in her cheerleader uniform." He smiled as she hit his arm and they kept walking. When they reached home, Peter dropped his equipment in his room and began walking his bike to the door. "I've gotta go to work, I'll be back in a few hours. Do you want to get dinner? I get paid today."

"All right, I wanted to talk to you anyway. I should be back from the store by the time you get home."

"Cool, you got enough money?" He asked while reaching for his wallet.

"I'm fine, now get out of here or you'll be late." He turned to leave and she called after him, "Great game today, Petey."

*****

When Peter reached Barbarelli's restaurant, he went over the plan with his boss and showed him how he would record Gravano's response. He took out his phone and showed him the record app. "I'll just put this in my jacket pocket and hit record when I get to his block. I know this is gonna work because he's already been messing with me."

"What? How has he been messing with you?"

"He threatened me last Saturday night before he shorted me on the payment. I'm not sure what he wants from me, but he's gonna get a whole lot more than he bargained for." Peter put his phone in his pocket and grabbed his bike.

Barbarelli admired Peter's courage and resilience, and added, "I dropped the hints that I was gonna let you go if anything else went wrong and Gravano seemed to think I should do more than fire you." Just to be sure he added, "This is your last chance to come clean if you did it, Peter. I'd hate for your all-star season to be cut tragically short."

"I swear I didn't steal from you, Mr. Barbarelli. I would never do that."

"All right, kid, here's this week's pick-up list. You better hope he's as greedy as you think he is." He knew Gravano was lying, but he hoped Peter could get him on record saying he was purposely cheating. Then he could bring it to Don Catalano and then Gravano would have some explaining to do. "Before you get to the pick-ups, you've got one delivery this week." Barbarelli handed him a brown package about a foot and a half long, a foot wide and eight inches high. The packages were always different sizes, and he always wondered what he was delivering, but never looked. He took the package, put it in his backpack, and hopped up on his bike.

"He's lying to you, sir, I never took anything, you'll see." With that, he rode out into the darkness of the cool November evening. After making his delivery, he began pedaling towards the one place he didn't want to go. He knew he could get Gravano to say something, but the man was also just as likely to snap and come after him. Still, he had to clear his name or he was done. There was nowhere he could go and nothing he could do if Barbarelli thought he was stealing from him.

Peter had a long ride to think and he couldn't stop thinking about what would happen to Dani if something happened to him. Before he knew it, he was back up by the big houses and he stopped about a block short of Gravano's. He noticed the garage was already opened casting light out into the darkness and Gravano was working on a car. He hit the record app on his phone and put it in his jacket's chest pocket and buttoned it closed. He rode around the corner like he did every week and stopped his bike in the driveway in front of the open garage. Gravano looked at him with disdain. He was wiping grease from his hand with a rag; he was drenched in sweat.

"This week's pick-up; right on time," he said in mock greeting. He took out a sealed envelope and handed it to Peter and Peter secured it in his jacket pocket. Gravano tossed a nickel at him and said with an amused smile, "Here's your tip, kid."

Peter didn't even make an attempt to catch the coin. He was really nervous and he hoped it didn't show, but it was now or never and he had to clear his name. He looked at the big man with a cool smile and said, "Feels a little light, Gravano."

Gravano's amused look was quickly replaced by anger. "What did you say?" he asked loudly. "What did you just say to me, you piece of garbage?" He reached out and grabbed Peter by the neck.

Peter couldn't believe how quick his hands were, but he stood his ground. "I said it feels light. I know you shorted Mr. Barbarelli last week and blamed it on me."

"You lookin' to get buried, kid? Keep talking and see what happens."

"Fine, then you won't mind if I count it right now and tell Mr. Barbarelli how much is in this envelope while you're standing right next to me." He made like he was going to pull out his phone, but Gravano hit his arm.

"Of course I shorted him, and I'm shorting him again. He disrespected me. What was I supposed to do?"

"Not my problem," Peter interjected.

"Oh yes, it is," he said and then began to laugh. "It is most definitely your problem, it's always gonna be your problem." He laughed. "Do you know why?" he asked in theatrical fashion. "Cause he don't trust you, kid, that's why. That means I can pay whatever I want and blame the shortage on you. Now take what I gave you and get out of here while I still let you, you piece of trash."

"He's gonna find out, Gravano."

"Who's gonna tell him, kid, you?" Without warning, he hit Peter with a hard right cross in the left eye, knocking him off his bike. Gravano's large gold

41

ring had opened up a gash above his eye. He was momentarily thankful his jacket pocket was buttoned or his phone might have fallen out, but he forgot about that when Gravano's foot connected with his gut. When the second kick connected, he heard something crack and knew he had to get out of there fast. He was in pain, but he dodged the next kick, rolled away, and got on his feet. He grabbed his bike and took off, thankful that he would be travelling downhill, at least to start.

Gravano stalked into the street and shouted after him as his anger grew. "I know where you live, kid, and I know you got a sister. Think about that before you open your big mouth. You work for me now."

Peter yelled over his shoulder, "We'll see about that." Every word hurt as it came out. He was gasping for breath and he hadn't even started pedaling. Blood was flowing down his face from the shot he had taken to the eye. *I can't go home and lead him to Dani and I can't go to Austin's. If he chases me, I won't be able to make it back to Barbarelli's before he catches up with me. What am I gonna do?* He just pedaled as hard as he could. He ignored the fire in his side and the shortness of breath, and rode.

At that moment, Gravano realized he had just made a big mistake. He had just attacked Barbarelli's delivery guy. How was he gonna explain that away?

"Paulie, Matthew, get out here and get after that kid." His only chance would be to bring Peter back to the house and then take him somewhere and kill him. *I could make it look like the kid was trying to stick me up. Hopefully, Barbarelli will be none the wiser*; the frantic thought crossed his mind. As his two sons came out into the driveway he looked at them and said, "You bring that kid back here, do you understand? We can't let him make it back to Barbarelli." They nodded their understanding, hoped into their black Mustang and took off after Peter.

*****

Danielle had just gotten the last of the groceries into the apartment with Laura's help. She was so thankful that Laura's mom had offered to take her to the store. Her mom was an expert shopper. She showed her how to use coupons, find sales, and replace non-essentials with the generic brands. She had gotten a lot more than she thought she could and still had a few dollars left over. She wouldn't need to go shopping again, except for things like bread and milk, for another three weeks. She hugged Laura goodbye, said she would see her in church tomorrow, and started putting the groceries away. When she finished, she let out a content sigh; proud of herself for getting it all taken care of. Peter was going to be so proud of her when he got home.

She sat down at the kitchen table and then turned on the lamp she used when she drew. She arranged her art supplies and began making the card for Hailey's parents so she could give it to her in church in the morning instead of waiting until school on Monday. She drew each line and wrote each word with the care of a surgeon. After an hour, the artwork was practically finished. It only needed to be shaded and colored. *This is some of my best work. I really hope Hailey's parents like it.* She smiled and continued drawing.

She was half-finished with the coloring when the doorknob slowly began to turn. She hoped it was Peter because she was really hungry and she still wanted to talk to him about what her dad had said. She heard a mumbled curse as a bottle hit the floor and she immediately knew who it was. A moment later, his figure was standing in the open door, backlit by the dim hall lights. Her hand began to tremble when she tried to go back to working on her card. Her dad walked in and she hoped he hadn't noticed her dread.

Without looking up, she called in the most soothing voice she could manage, "Hi, Daddy, how was your day?"

"How do you think?" he slurred. He had already been drinking, but he wasn't really drunk, just angry. Now she was going to be stuck with him in a mood all night.

"I don't know; that's why I asked," she replied trying to sound as if everything was fine.

"Terrible, is that what you want to hear? I ran out of money before I was finished at the bar."

"I see you found your key, so that's good," she added, trying to change the subject. She was grateful that they didn't have to change the locks again.

"Of course I have my key," he yelled. "You can stop treating me like a child, Danielle!"

He was more aggravated than usual and she wanted to ask him if anything was wrong, but she didn't know how without upsetting him more. "I'm sorry, I didn't mean anything—" She noticed his anger was growing, and she stopped herself mid-sentence.

"Of course you did, just stop it!" he yelled. He shot her a menacing scowl and continued, "I don't need you treating me like I can't do anything, and I don't need you pretending everything is all right between us when I know you spent the day with your no-good brother."

"I didn't spend the day with him. I only went to his game. It was a big game today, dad, not just for Peter, but for the whole school. I wasn't going to miss it, and Peter did really well. He had an interception and two touchdowns. Then he walked me home and went to work. After that, Laura's mom took me food shopping."

"Oh great, you have other people buying us food now?" His arm motions were exaggerated and erratic. "What are we charity cases now, Danielle?" His tone was accusatory and his anger seemed to be building; she knew she had to watch her step.

She replied in a soft voice, "I bought the food, dad, with the money from our food account. Laura's mom just gave me a ride so I wouldn't have to carry it all home by myself."

"What food account?" Now he was angry and confused. *I don't remember setting up a food account.* "Where is this food account?"

"I don't know, dad, Peter usually takes care of it." She tried to play it off like it was no big deal, but she knew as soon as the words left her lips that mentioning her brother's name was a mistake.

Peter's name set her father off. He was instantly more animated than he had been. "I would never give that kid money for anything!" he screamed. "Give it to me! Give it to me right now!" Everything she said seemed to get him more agitated and she didn't know what to do. He had never gotten this angry this quickly with her before.

"There's no way I would leave any money out for him. He must have somehow stolen it, and that's why I ran out of money tonight. Give me the money he took!" He didn't remember setting aside any food money, but all he could think about was getting enough money together to get back to the bar.

He was still yelling and he wasn't going to be happy with what she had to say next. "I don't have it. I just spent it on our food, Dad."

"You what?" His angry scream echoed off the walls of the small kitchen. "There has to be more, give it to me." He was standing right over her yelling and she could feel the heat of his anger. His breath reeked of cheap liquor and his hand looked like it was trembling.

44

"Dad, stop, you're scaring me! Stop yelling, I didn't do anything wrong."

"Don't you tell me what to do! I'm the parent here; you got that? Now give me the money!" He needed the money to keep drinking. Running out before he was finished had been embarrassing and left him in a foul mood.

"Dad, I already told you, I spent it on food, I only have like eight dollars left."

"Eight dollars! Eight dollars!" he yelled. "How could you spend all of our money?" His anger was escalating faster than his daughter could deal with. At this point, another beating was a foregone conclusion.

As scared as she was, she had just about reached her boiling point. She already knew she was going to be getting hit, so she might as well say what she had to say. He was being really unfair, and drunk or not, she wasn't going to stand here and take it. "All of our money?" She raised her voice for the first time. "I didn't spend all of our money. You don't even know how much I spent, dad, and I used coupons and bought stuff on sale. Laura's mom helped me find the best deals. It's not like I wasted it!" She turned in anger, and stomped away.

"What's that supposed to mean?" he asked as he closed the distance between them faster than she thought possible. He grabbed her shoulders and roughly spun her around. "I said, what's that supposed to mean?" he yelled in her face.

Now she was really scared. She saw an almost feral look in his eye as she wondered, *what's gotten into him?* She meekly replied, "Nothing, I was just saying, it's not like I bought clothes or music; I bought food."

"No, you were saying that I waste all of our money. That's what you were saying. Let me ask you this, you ungrateful little brat. Who keeps this roof over your head, huh? It's not your precious Peter; it's me. Me! Don't you forget it!" He shoved her hard and she tripped over the leg of a chair and fell awkwardly to the floor. That was her breaking point and she began to cry. Her tears just seemed to anger him more. "Now give me the rest of the money your brother stole from me for food or so help me, I'll beat it out of you!" He gestured to take in the entire kitchen. "We obviously have more than enough food now." She was slow to stand, so he roughly hoisted her up and slapped her. "I said now!"

Tears continued to roll down her bright pink cheek as she dug her hand into the pocket of her jeans and pulled out her remaining eight dollars. "That's all of it," she said. Her tears had dried and were now replaced with anger. She abruptly turned away and walked towards her room.

"Don't you walk away from me! We're not done until I say we're done!" He turned her around and backhanded her, opening up the corner of her lip. She stood there in shock as the blood began to trickle slowly down to her chin. "What other money is your brother keeping from me?" He wasn't ready to let his tirade end, not until he had enough money to continue drinking.

Danielle was in a state of shock. Her father had never hit her in the face like that before. Hitting the body made it easier to hide the bruises, but bruising the face caused too many questions. She looked up at her father with defiance in her eyes; holding back the tears she knew would soon flow freely, she answered, "That's all of it. Sorry feeding your kids is such a burden for you!"

He could see the light from the kitchen gleaming in her angry, defiant eyes and it drove him over the edge. Before he could stop himself he punched her hard across the face. She fell to the ground and began sobbing, while holding her cheek as blood continued to drip from the corner of her lip. She tried to crawl away, but he followed her. She cried out in pain when he pulled her off the floor by her hair. He punched her once more in the stomach for good measure, and made sure she could see his smile as she was doubled over on the floor. She watched in tears as her dad took her purse and emptied it out onto the floor.

He got really close to her face and held up some more money. "So, you were holding back on me, you little liar. I should hit you again!" He raised his hand, causing her to flinch, which brought a satisfied smirk to his face. Then he took the thirty-five dollars her brother had given her for allowance.

"No I wasn't lying. Peter gave me that money, from his job!" she squeaked between sobs, still lying on the floor.

"Well then, this will just be a down payment on the money the two of you stole from me to buy the food." He stuffed the money in his pocket and walked to the door. He looked down at his daughter and still burned with anger. He stood by the door and said, "I told you not to take his side."

"Well, at least he never hit me," she replied. She cringed as her father came back in and slapped her across the face one more time before storming out. She should have told him it was Peter's money that had bought the food. She knew her brother wanted her to think it was their dad's money, and that he actually cared, but she knew better. Just like Peter had his big secret from her, this was her burden to carry. She could never let him find out their dad beat her. He would go crazy, and she didn't think she would be able to stop him from attacking their dad if he knew. This time it was different though, this time her dad had left marks on her face. How was she going to cover this up? She just sat on the floor crying, wondering what she had ever done to deserve this.

Chapter 4

Peter was riding for his life and he wondered; *what went wrong?* Every pedal, every turn and every jump was another jolt of pain emanating from his side. Every street he went down, Gravano's sons seemed to be there. Not only that, they called a couple of their friends. He was riding through alleys, over grass, jumping curbs and parking lot chains, but still, they kept coming. He wound up over by Reiman's Hardware and they were closing fast. Luckily, they didn't know the neighborhood as well as he did. Raymond Avenue, right next to the hardware store, was a dead end street with a small foot path going through to the next street. They'd never be able to follow him through and they would have to back out of the street and go around. He should have some pretty good distance on them by the time they made it around.

His breath was now coming in short, painful gasps. *I'm not sure how much longer I can keep this up,* he thought. He was thankful that his short cut had worked; at least he had some breathing room. He turned down Chandler Avenue and saw headlights. He thought it might be Gravano's people, so he turned and crossed Manor Road as fast as he could. He heard the distinctive roar of the Mustang that had been chasing him and pedaled faster. He turned onto Potter Avenue and rode past the old clapboard houses, when the thought hit him; *if I could just make it up to Royal Oak, then I can cruise down to Clove Lakes Park from there. I have to find a minute to send the conversation I had with Gravano to Barbarelli.*

He held his side as he rode; the pain was searing and he thought he might lose consciousness if he kept going. Without thinking, his legs kept pumping and his bike kept moving; he knew it was a matter of survival. He made it to Royal Oak and, as he was crossing the street, he was faced with a silver sedan that accelerated, gunning- towards him. Time seemed to slow down as he jumped his bike onto a parked car under a street-light to narrowly avoid being hit.

He heard the thud of the bike landing on the green hood of the station wagon. He heard the screech of the brakes as the Sedan stopped to back up and have another run at him and he heard two men get out of the backseat of the sedan and yell at him as they began to chase him on foot. Their faces were shadowy and vague until they ran underneath the street light. The smell of scorched tire filled the air. He jumped his bike off the station wagon and landed on the sidewalk with a pained yell. The guys on foot were catching up, so he pedaled harder. He crossed the ball field and rode up a grassy hill and looked back in disbelief as one of the cars chasing him followed. Infield dust filled the air as the men on foot gave up the chase and began running from the billowing dust cloud.

The ante was upped even further when he heard two gunshots ring out cutting through the night like thunder. He had no idea how close the bullets had come, but for the first time, the reality hit him that he might not survive this encounter.

By this point, sweat was pouring down his face, mixed with the blood from his cut and stung his eye, further clouding his vision. His shirt was now damp with sweat and clung to his back, while his trembling hands were slipping on the grips. His eye was almost swollen shut and his ribs cried out to him with every stray movement. Through the pain, a thought struck him. *I wonder if I'm gonna be able to play next week?* He thought it was odd that in the middle of a life or death chase, this is what popped into his head. Another jolt of pain ended that thought quick enough, and as his mind refocused. He knew if he could make it back to Barbarelli's, he'd be safe.

He saw his chance to escape, as he rode into the trees where he knew the cars could not follow. He came out of the trees riding downhill on Victory Boulevard towards Clove Lakes Park. He knew they would follow, but he also knew he could lose them in the park and maybe rest a bit. He was nowhere near the restaurant now; in fact, he was traveling in the opposite direction, but at least he could give Barbarelli a call.

*****

Peter rode out of the trees, onto the sidewalk, and cruised down the hill at nearly thirty-five miles an hour. The wind in his face was keeping the blood and sweat out of his eye, at least for the moment. He heard the screech of the sedan and the roar of the Mustang following him. *Thank God there's always traffic on Victory Boulevard. They can't get close to this side of the street and I should have a head start when I get to the park.* He passed the ice skating rink and turned left into the park. He rode past the basketball courts and began to ride around the lake. He heard car horns blaring and looked back to see the Mustang crossing Victory Boulevard. The car hopped the curb and began to tear through the park.

Peter was thankful there was no one around to see the fear in his eyes. He was now riding past the playground, and the Mustang was coming on fast. He just made it past the barricade and onto a grey stone bridge as the mustang screeched and fishtailed to a halt. Gravano's two sons popped out of their car and fired off a couple more shots. *This is crazy! I can't believe they're shooting at me,* he thought. He was riding past the ritzy Lake Club Restaurant when the Sedan turned into the parking lot, hopped the curb, and followed him over the bridge. He had to get off the walkways because they were all wide enough for maintenance vehicles. He turned right and, when he made it to the trees, he began up a steep incline through the woods. The driver of the sedan must not have seen him go into the trees because he flew past the entrance to the trail.

When Peter was sure he could no longer be seen, he dismounted his bike and collapsed to the ground, holding his side. *What am I gonna do? I can't bring this home to Dani.* He wanted to cry; he was so worried that something might happen to his sister because of this, but he just focused on trying to breathe. After a couple minutes, he began limping back towards Victory Boulevard, desperately trying to catch his breath.

Wiping some of the blood off his face with his sleeve as he walked, Peter looked for a safe spot in the bushes. He now had a minute to make what he prayed would be a life-saving phone call. He took as deep a breath as his ribs would allow and noticed his hands were shaking as he took out his phone and dialed Barbarelli's number. After the third ring his boss picked up the phone. "Donovan, where are you, you should have been back here almost an hour ago. You still got another two pick-ups."

He tried again to catch his breath as he prepared to answer. He looked in every direction just to make sure none of his pursuers were nearby. "Sorry, boss," he began, trying not to cry out in agony. "Gravano beat me up pretty good," he gasped. "I think he broke some of my ribs. Then he sent his sons and another car after me when I rode off. I've been dodging them all night and I can't get back to the restaurant. He knows I got him and he's trying to get me before I get to you, here, listen." He played the recording and his boss heard it all, including the beating Peter had taken.

"He thinks what?" His boss's fury came through loud and clear. "Gravano's gonna answer for this! All of it! Don't you worry, we're gonna make this right. Where are you right now?"

"I'm just past the ice skating rink, hiding in the park. Sorry, boss, I don't think I can make it back to the restaurant. He kicked me in the ribs and I'm breathing really hard right now. It might take me a while because I have to stay off the streets, but I'll try and work my way back to you as soon as I can."

"No, stay where you are, I'm sending Michael and some of the boys to you. Gravano won't try anything once he sees you with my guys. They'll be there in ten minutes, just stay where you are. You got my money?"

"Yeah, but he shorted you again, said it's because you disrespected him or something."

"Yeah, I heard. You're off the hook kid. I'll make sure Gravano leaves you alone. That's a promise, you'll be fine."

"He threatened me and my sister, sir. I might need to lay low for a couple weeks and make sure she's all right while my ribs heal."

"That might be a good idea, kid. We'll talk when you get here."

"They shot at me a bunch of times, too. They also tried to run me down in a silver sedan; I think it was a Civic." Just recalling the harrowing ordeal made him start to shake again and he wondered if he sounded as scared as he felt.

"Don't worry about any of that, Kid, you're okay now." He tried to keep it out of his voice but he was angry. Barbarelli wasn't yet sure how Gravano would pay, but Gravano was going to pay.

The conversation was over and all that was left was the waiting. Peter lay on the ground behind some bushes, holding his side and looking around. Eventually, he calmed down and his breathing almost returned to normal. It was a beautiful night for November. It wasn't very cold and there was a light breeze rustling the trees and bushes. From his hiding spot he could see the moon reflecting off the lake and he could actually make out some stars. It must have been a very clear night.

Normally, ten minutes wasn't a very long time, but after what he had just been though, it felt like an eternity. Every sound had him on alert. He heard more than saw Gravano's sons pass by in their mustang twice more as they continued their search. He didn't know how much time had passed as he lay on the ground hidden in the bushes. He decided to get up and sit on his bike. He needed to be ready to fly at the first hint of trouble. Suddenly, he heard the crunch of a stick under foot. He tensed and gripped the handlebar tight until he heard a voice. "Hey, Peter, where are you?" It was Michael, and Peter knew he wouldn't have to run anymore tonight.

"I'm coming out, Mike," Peter replied as his muscles loosened. He slowly walked his bike out to see a large Italian man waiting for him; there were two smaller men standing behind him making sure the area was safe. None of them looked happy to be out in the park looking for him. The three of them were so stereotypical for what you would think of a mobster that, in any other situation, it might have been funny. Michael stood almost six foot five, and unlike Barbarelli, there wasn't an ounce of fat on his body. He was a huge guy, with jet-black hair and dark eyes. He was usually a nice enough guy, but he could get mean if he needed to. At six two, Peter was a pretty big kid and he was in good shape from football, but he felt like a child standing next to Michael. He also felt safe, and tonight, that's what mattered. One thing that he was certain of was no one in their right mind would mess with Michael unless they had an arsenal with them; he was thankful they came for him.

He didn't know the names of the other two guys, although he had seen one of them a couple times. He could see the bulge under their suit jackets that indicated they were packing, which normally would have him on edge, but tonight he welcomed it. The man on Michael's left was stocky and his head was shaved bald; his dark suit and angry demeanor made him an imposing figure. The man to Michael's right was average in size and build with dark hair that was graying at the temples. The hard set of his eyes told Peter that this would be the wrong man to mess with. His grey suit was expertly tailored and, at the base of his sleeve, a gold watch peeked out. Peter had never felt as safe as he did right now; still, he wanted to go home, hug Dani, and go to sleep. Austin would also be expecting him, but he would be skipping Austin's house tonight.

Michael picked up Peter's bike with ease and put it in the back of the Escalade. The four of them piled in the SUV and took off for the cafe. Michael looked at the bloody bruise on his face and the tear in his jeans by his knee and said, "Don't bleed in my car." He handed him a white cloth and Peter winced as he pressed it against his face. When Michael pointed at his knee, he looked down.

He hadn't even realized he had cut his knee. "Sorry, Mike, I'll try not to." They rode the rest of the way in silence and, when they arrived at the cafe, there were eight men standing out in front.

Peter stiffened when he saw two of the men that had been chasing him in the silver sedan. Michael put his hand on Peter's shoulder and said, "It's all right, they won't try to hurt you again." He handed Peter his bike and walked over to Mr. Barbarelli. Peter followed, and it wasn't until he was close that he saw how scared the two men looked; he heard the driver's voice cracking as he pleaded his case.

"I'm sorry, Mr. Barbarelli. Gravano's son Paulie told me that you were after the kid. I swear, I would never think of hurting one of your guys." He was all but on his knees begging to be believed. "He told me the kid was stealing from you and that you put a hit on him, please, you gotta believe me."

"I don't 'gotta' believe anything. Use your head, Joey." He smacked him in the side of the head to illustrate his point before continuing. "When have I ever sent any orders through Gravano? Everyone knows who is authorized to convey my requests to people outside my organization."

Peter almost laughed when Barbarelli used the word request. Calling his orders a request was like saying that paying taxes was optional. He was glad that he was hurting too much to smile because he would hate for his boss to think that he thought any of this was funny.

Barbarelli looked away from the pleading thugs and smiled as Peter limped towards him. "Hey, kid, come here."

"Sure, boss," he replied as he produced Gravano's envelope and handed it to his boss, wincing when he held his hand out.

He took the envelope without looking and pointed at the thugs. "Were these guys at Gravano's when you were there?"

"No, sir, just Paulie and Matthew. He must have called them after I left." The thugs almost looked thankful, as if what he had just said supported their story until he added, "They did shoot at me and try to run me over, though." Michael looked at them when Peter said that last line and the men seemed to shrink further as if Michael scared them more than Mr. Barbarelli.

"All right, that fit's their story. We'll have to come up with some way to let them know they're not off the hook. I'm gonna let them squirm for a while, but I'm not sure I want to do any more yet." The reality was that he couldn't do anything to them without incurring the wrath of the Don. He looked at his bleeding, limping delivery boy and added, "You're done for the night, kid. Tony here is gonna make your last two pick-ups, but don't worry, you're still getting paid for it." He took out a hefty wad of cash and counted off eight one hundred dollar bills. He handed them to Peter and said, "I threw in an extra three hundred, you earned it, kid, now get out of here."

"Thank you, sir. Do you mind if I wash up before I go? I don't want Dani to see me like this."

"Yeah, just don't make a mess. Wipe all the blood out of the sink when you're done and bring the bag with the bloody tissues out to the dumpster before you leave." He smiled and added, "Can't have blood in the restaurant bathrooms now, can we?"

"No, I guess not. Thanks, Boss," he replied. He started to head for the back of the restaurant but then stopped and added. "I sent a copy of the recording to your phone in case you want to play it for Gravano when you see him later." He nodded and his boss nodded back, then he went inside the restaurant without another word.

"Now there's a loyal kid, Mike. After I get permission from Don Catalano, I want you to do to Gravano what he did to the kid."

"With pleasure," Michael replied.

"I only hope the kid still has the stomach for this when he gets better, it would be a shame to lose someone I know I can trust."

"If you don't mind my asking, Mr. Barbarelli, why do you take such good care of that kid? Sure, he's a good kid, but kids like him are a dime a dozen."

A remorseful look crossed Barbarelli's face and he put his hand on Mike's shoulder. "Ask me again sometime, Mike, for now let's get back to Gravano's buffoons."

Peter turned the light on in the bathroom and dabbed a wet paper towel on his eye. It was still bleeding and it looked terrible. *I'm think I'm gonna need stitches*, he thought. He looked down and lifted his shirt in a slow, painful motion to get a look at his injured side. There was a deep purple and blue colored bruise where Gravano had kicked him. This was the first opportunity he had to see it and he knew he was going to be sidelined for at least the first game of the playoffs. Thankfully, there was a week off before the playoffs started and their first opponent shouldn't be too hard, because it was probable that he was not going to be playing.

When he finished cleaning up, he did as Barbarelli asked and took the plastic bag with his bloody paper towels out to the dumpster. With a painful lift of the leg, he got back on his bike and began the slow journey home. He took out his phone and called Austin.

"What's up, bro?" he answered in greeting. "You done with work yet?"

"I just finished, I'm on my way home now."

"Dude, you gotta come to Mark's house. This party is off the chain, and you're the hero."

"I would love to, but I'm not feeling great, bro." He looked down at his side and imagined the ugly bruise he had seen there a few minutes ago. "Maybe after the next game."

"Yeah, right, like you'll ever skip a workday," he said with a laugh.

"I will be next week, and maybe the week after that, too," Peter replied, and for the first time, Austin could hear the pain in his voice.

Austin went out into the backyard where there were less people and asked, "Dude, what happened? You don't sound so good."

Peter debated whether or not to tell his friend what had happened and decided he would figure it out as soon as he saw him. He tried to take a deep breath, but was cut off by the pain as. "Gravano beat me up, pretty bad."

"He what? Are you okay? What did Barbarelli do?" He couldn't believe what he had just heard.

"I'll live, but I'm probably not gonna be able to play for a couple weeks." He heard his friend inhale sharply and he continued. "I think he broke a couple of my ribs and I'm probably gonna need stitches over my eye."

"Coach is gonna be mad, he hates that you even have that job. What are you gonna tell him?"

"I know he's gonna be mad, but he knows I need this job to support me and Dani. He knows my family situation. I'm just gonna tell him that I was mugged while I was making one of my deliveries." He went on to describe the whole chase in harrowing detail and could tell by his friend's reactions that he was scared for him. By the time he finished the story he was back on Manor road but he had to get off the bike. Everything was starting to ache and each step took a lot out of him. He was only a few blocks from home, and he felt like he was going to pass out; he just hoped he could make it.

"Are you going to the hospital, Pete?"

"I don't know. If I do, they'll make sure coach knows I'm not cleared to play. If I don't, there's still a chance. We do have a bye next week."

"I wouldn't mess with it, bro. You should get it checked out. Hey, if your dad hassles you when you get home, just come to my house for the night, my parents aren't even home."

"Thanks, dude, I just might." A few minutes later, Peter wanted to cry for joy when he saw his building. "I'm home, man, I'm gonna let you get back to the party. Later"

"Later, Pete." Austin hung up the phone and discovered he no longer felt like partying.

Peter put his phone away and made his way into his building. All he wanted to do now was make sure Dani was all right and then go to sleep.

Chapter 5

Peter walked his bike up the stairs to his third floor apartment because the elevator was out of service. His side hurt with each step and his mind drifted towards thoughts of football. He only hoped his team didn't lose without him. He turned onto his hallway and, as he looked at the narrow corridor, he suddenly remembered he had promised to take Dani out to dinner; now he felt even worse. He heard her crying softly as he opened the door. He wondered what she could be crying about. The turn of the knob must have startled her because he heard her jump. He wanted to kick himself for not keeping his word.

"Dani, I'm so sorry I'm late, things got crazy at work. We can still go eat if you're hungry." He looked over and she was sitting on the floor with her back against the wall and her arms wrapped around her knees; she was still crying. She was the last person in the world he ever wanted to see cry. She looked like she was in a daze and he wondered what was going on. "Hey, Dani, are you all right? I'm sorry I was late. There's no need to cry, we can still go if you want."

Her eyes focused a little as she realized what he had just said. "What? No, Peter. I'm not crying because of you." She looked up at him and saw the gash and bruise on his eye and concern replaced her despair. She cautiously got to her feet and touched his face. His eye was completely swollen shut now. "Peter, what happened to you?"

"I was mugged during one of my deliveries, no big deal. What happened to you?" Her eyes were red and her cheeks were puffy and he couldn't tell if it was because she was crying or something else. He gently touched his sister's cheek, causing her to flinch. "What happened, Dani? Did someone hit you?" His pain and tiredness were replaced by anger so fast it scared him. She looked away, shame evident in her eyes, and he knew instantly. "Did dad hit you?"

She could barely squeak out the word, knowing how angry her brother would get. "Yes." She began to cry again and slumped back down onto the floor. He sat down next to her on the floor and held her. He could feel every muscle in his body tense in anger, which caused him even more pain, but he knew that blowing up would do his sister no good right now.

After a while, he pulled her to her feet, wincing the whole way. Then he looked her in the eyes and said, "Get some things together, you're not staying

57

here tonight." He looked at her purse, carelessly emptied on the floor and knew exactly what had happened. "He took your money to go get drunk, didn't he?" She nodded, still on the verge of breaking down, and began to put her things back in her purse. Peter put his arm around her and kissed her head. He noticed the half-finished drawing and imagined how happy she was before Jim came home.

He hated himself for not being there to defend her and he hated his father even more for hurting her. "I'm so sorry, Dani. I'm so sorry. I should've been here." For a brief moment, as he looked at her, he had forgotten all about his problems. He noticed the cut on her lip and wanted to scream. For the first time, hating his father wasn't enough; he wanted to hurt him, too. The old man didn't deserve the love Dani so freely gave him.

"It's not your fault, Peter. You were working. You should go put some ice on your eye. You probably need stitches" She noticed him wince when he walked over to the freezer. "What else hurts?"

"I cut my knee and I took a couple good shots to the ribs. No big deal." He tried to downplay his injuries for her sake, but knew that would not be possible once he took off his tee shirt. He heard Dani gasp before he was even able to get to a mirror. He looked at the dark purple and reddened bruise that had developed where Gravano had kicked him and thought that it looked even worse than it did at the restaurant. He put on a smile for his sister and said, "Not as bad as I thought, I'll be fine."

"No you won't, Peter! You need to get that checked out." She poked at it, causing him to inhale sharply.

"Dani, stop it!"

"See, I barely touched it. You won't be fine."

"Just get your stuff together and call Laura. If you can't stay there tonight, then we'll both just sleep at Austin's. His parents are out of town and I already planned on going over there. I'm gonna take a quick shower, clean up my knee and eye, and get some clean clothes on. Then we're leaving."

"What about dad?" she asked, filling a backpack with clothes.

"I don't care about dad. He gave up his right to have you tuck him in when he beat you up for beer money. It's not safe for you here tonight, Dani." He closed the door and turned on the water. The heat felt so good on his tired muscles, but stung the cuts near his eye and his knee. He stepped out of the shower a few minutes later, toweled dry and put a Band-Aid on his knee and a

58

large bandage just above his eye. He got dressed and opened the door to his sister holding out a backpack for him.

"Laura's mom said I could stay over since I was already planning on going to church with them. She's also a nurse and she said she'll look at your side and see if you need to go to the hospital."

"Dani, why'd you do that?" Nurses and hospitals were the last thing he wanted to deal with, but he couldn't fault his sister for worrying. Even after everything she'd been through, she still looked out for him and he couldn't be mad at her. He had been indecisive, but now the decision had been made for him. "If the doctors say there's something wrong, I won't be able to play in two weeks, Dani."

"But if you're already hurt and you play, you could really hurt yourself bad. Please, Peter, just do it." She handed him his backpack and waited for him to take his wallet out of his ripped jeans before throwing them with the rest of his dirty clothes near the laundry basket in his room.

"So what happened, Dani? Why did dad hit you?" He tried to sound casual, but he was boiling inside.

"He came in mad, I think because he had run out of money to get drunk and then he saw all of the groceries he was convinced that you had stolen the money from him. He started yelling at me asking where the food money was and I told him I spent it all except eight dollars. Then he hit me and took the money I still had and the allowance money you gave me, and told me I shouldn't have sided with you."

"Sided with me? What was he talking about?"

"We had an argument this morning and I asked him why he hated you so much." She started to tear up again and Peter's whole body tightened. The moment he feared had finally happened and suddenly the pain in his ribs seemed insignificant. "He told me he blames you for mom getting hit by a car because she was saving you, but I told him it wasn't your fault, you were only four and you got scared. Then he yelled at me and told me not to take your side. I cried all the way to Laura's and told her mom everything. I'm sorry, Peter. I know you don't want people knowing our business, but I had to talk to someone"

"No, Dani, it's fine. I'm so sorry; it is my fault mom died and I never wanted you to know. I thought if you knew, you would hate me."

"It's not your fault, Peter; no matter what you think or what dad says. You can't blame yourself; you were just a little kid. And I could never hate you."

"But I do blame myself. Every time I see you look at Laura's mom, every time I see you sleeping on the couch because you're taking care of dad, I blame myself. She told me not to go in the street and I didn't listen. Then the car was coming and I froze. I was so scared. All I had to do was step out of the way and we'd still have a mom. Why couldn't I just step out of the way?" He had never talked about this out loud before and it was killing him.

"No, Peter, you were four and you got scared. It's not your fault, and dad shouldn't blame you. He should know better. You shouldn't blame yourself. You also shouldn't have to pay the electric bill, and buy all of our food and clothes, and give me money every week."

"How did you know I was paying for all of that?" He couldn't believe she knew everything and didn't hate him. Maybe today wasn't such a bad day after all.

"How did I know? You mentioned some of it when you and dad were arguing, but I already knew. The envelope system? Really, Peter? Like I would believe dad had the discipline to put money into envelopes for us. I know it's been you taking care of me the last few years. You don't have to, you know. You could go out and have some fun with your friends. I know you miss all the parties because you're working, and it's not fair to you."

"Yes it is. I do have to work, because it's my fault that you don't have the things other people have. So I'll work as much as I need to so that you can have what you need. Plus, I would do it anyway because you're my little sister." As he spoke, she loved him even more. He had been taking care of her this whole time and never once brought it up. Not when they were arguing, not when she yelled at him. Never. She really had been blessed with a great brother and she thanked God for him.

"Speaking of the envelope system, now that dad knows about it, we should get the money out of them, no sense in letting him take it," Peter said. He went over to the hiding place for the money and pulled it all out, but left the envelopes. He hoped his father would find the empty envelopes and get angry again.

"What else do you pay for, Peter? I know it's not just the power, the food, and our clothes."

"I pay the heat bill and our cell phones. Dad has the rent automatically deducted from his pay, it's the only reason we have a place to live, and then he drinks the rest. He won't even pay his own phone bill and I don't care because I don't want him calling me anyway."

"What about his credit cards and medical stuff? We might need that if you have to go to the doctor."

"Somewhere in that stack of unopened mail, I imagine. I don't care about any of that. I only pay for what takes care of you and me."

"Thank you, Peter. I'm gonna get a job, too, so I can help out around here." She never knew how much he was doing for her without ever asking anything in return. And he did it all because he felt responsible for their situation. "Peter, none of this is your fault; it's dad's! From now on, we take care of each other. You don't have to carry this alone."

"Thanks, Dani." *What did I ever do to deserve such a forgiving sister?*

"For what?" She smiled up at him.

"For not hating me, even though I've been hating myself all these years."

"As if I could ever," she leaned into his chest and then felt terrible as he winced. "Oh, I'm sorry, I forgot."

"Maybe you could just hug my left side for a while," he joked. He may have been angry at his father and in pain from his injuries, but a huge weight had been lifted from his shoulders and he felt it. He wondered if her willingness to forgive and to see the best in people was somehow related to her new faith. Just then, there was a knock on the door. Danielle answered it and Laura was standing there with her mom.

"Thanks for coming, Mrs. Jenkins. I know I've been a huge pain today already."

"Now you know that's not true at all, dear," Mrs. Jenkins replied as she took in the surroundings. Peter imagined she didn't approve, but could find no look of judgment in her eyes. "All right, young man, let's have a look at those ribs." Peter winced when lifted his tee shirt and he heard Laura gasp. Mrs. Jenkins poked and prodded around the injury before telling him to let his shirt down. "Peter, it looks like you have broken a couple ribs. We need to get you to the hospital to make sure they're not in a position to puncture your lung."

"But if I go to the hospital, I definitely won't be able to play in the next game. Isn't there something else I could do?" He felt like he had let the entire school down by getting injured.

"I'm sorry, no. I know football is very important to you, but your health has to come first. We should also get your eye looked at, it's going to need stitches." She could see how dejected he looked, so she added, "I know you're disappointed, but this is the right thing to do. If you take a hit to those ribs before they're healed it could puncture a lung, maybe even kill you."

"Fine, I should call my boss and my coach to let them know what's going on."

"Call them after, so you will have some facts for them. We need to get in touch with your dad."

"You can probably find him in the nearest bar." His comment drew an inquisitive look from Mrs. Jenkins, so he continued. "That's why Danielle has to stay with you tonight; maybe even a couple days, if it's not too much trouble."

"What do you mean?" She asked the question, hoping she wouldn't get the answer she suspected; that's when she noticed the cut on Danielle's lip and the developing bruise on her face. Danielle flinched away and Peter felt terrible.

"You didn't tell her about you, did you?" He spoke in a soft voice so she wouldn't think he was mad. "I'm sorry, Dani, I thought you told them."

"He hit you, didn't he?" she asked, already knowing the answer. "Is it always like this?" she asked, wondering if the city should be called.

"Is he always drunk? Yes, but it's usually way worse around this time of year."

"Because of the holidays?"

"No, because tomorrow is the anniversary of my mom's death," Danielle added, sheepishly. "He blames Peter, and he's mad at me for sticking up for him."

"Dani, that's too much information," Peter said.

"I'm sorry, Peter, they already know from before and they also know it's not your fault." She paused and then added, "But this is the first time he's ever hit me before." She saw the dubious looks on Laura and her mom's faces and added, "Honestly, I promise." She hated to lie, but she couldn't bear to think of how Peter would feel if he knew this happened whenever he was out. She hoped God would forgive her for the lie, even as she hoped the conversation would go no further.

Mrs. Jenkins seemed to see through her charade, but didn't call her out on it. "Okay, let's get going. Danielle is welcome to stay with us for a couple days. It's not safe here."

"Thanks, mom," Laura added as she put her arm around Danielle. They all left the apartment and Peter made sure he had every dime of his money either with him or locked up where his father wouldn't find it. *I hope dad has to sleep out in the hall tonight. It's no less than he deserves.*

When they were in the car on the way to the hospital, Mrs. Jenkins carefully brought back up the subject of Danielle's safety. "Danielle, are you sure this is the first time your father has ever hit you? He's never gotten physical with you before?" She was probing, she hated that this sweet girl had to live with the constant fear of being beaten by her own father. She silently prayed that her situation wouldn't deter her from her faith.

Peter answered for her. "Mrs. J, this is the first time I've ever heard that he hit her. He did it so he could take her money because he ran out of drinking money." She could hear the bitterness in his voice and felt so bad for these two kids, having to live with that behavior, that fear.

"And did he hit you tonight, too?" Mrs. Jenkins continued.

"No, I really did get hurt at work, Mrs. J. If he ever raised his hand to me, I'd break his arm. And if I ever saw him hit Dani, I'd break both his arms."

"Peter," Danielle chastised. "That's a terrible thing to say."

"I'm sorry, Dani, I'm just saying what I would do. No one will ever hit you in front of me."

"Well let's hope that never happens, then," Mrs. Jenkins said in a diplomatic tone.

"Mrs. Jenkins, please don't tell anyone. If you tell anyone, they're gonna split us up and I don't think I could handle that," Peter said. "I'll make sure he never does it again, trust me."

"I don't want to be taken away from my brother either," Danielle added. "Peter is all that I have."

"I'm sorry, I truly am, but I may have to tell. I will do everything in my power to see if you can stay at home, and more importantly, together as long as possible. I'm a certified foster parent, so you can stay at my house until this gets sorted. Do you understand, Danielle?"

"Yes, ma'am. Thank you." The disappointment in her voice was evident as she replied.

"Thanks, Mrs. J," Peter added. "I can probably crash at Austin's for a while."

*****

Ten minutes later, they arrived at the hospital and parked in the staff parking lot. Peter grimaced when he slowly stepped out of the minivan. Being stationary had caused the injury to become stiff. He lumbered to the emergency room and Mrs. Jenkins used her connections to get him right in. He had given the nurse at the desk the information on his father's insurance plan and they brought him to a semi-private curtain enclosure where they had him sit on the bed. Peter perked up a little when he saw the long blonde hair of the nurse who somehow made her gray scrubs look good.

She smiled at him as she said, "Hi, I'm Anna and I'm just going to run a few tests on you before the doctor comes in. How are you feeling?"

"I've had better days," he replied trying to sound casual. She smiled at him and her deep blue eyes had him captivated.

"Who is this with you?"

"My sister, Dani and her friend, Laura," he replied, unsure of where Laura's mother went.

"I need to take your blood pressure," she began as she took his arm and wrapped the cuff around it. She stuck a thermometer in his mouth almost as an afterthought, as the machine began to inflate the cuff. When the cuff began to deflate, she placed her stethoscope just under the wrap and started to keep time. A few moments later, she took the cuff off, checked his temperature, and wrote something down in a little folder that had his name on it. "So, Peter, what brings you to the ER tonight?"

He was pretty sure Mrs. Jenkins already told her exactly what was wrong, but she was still required to ask. "I got mugged, my eye really hurts and my ribs feel like they're on fire."

"Do you mind if I have a look?" she asked as she took the bandage off of his eye and frowned. "That's going to need stitches," she said in a matter-of-fact tone. Then she gently lifted his shirt to look at the ribs, lowered his shirt and added, "The doctor will be with you shortly, Peter." She wrote something else in the folder and walked away.

"Where's your mom, Laura?" Peter asked. He had a feeling she was off trying to find a police officer and that her errand would end with him and Dani no longer living in the same home.

"I'm not sure. She just told me to stay with you guys until she came back."

A few minutes later, Laura's mom was back and to Peter's dismay she had a police officer with her. He looked at Peter dubiously and then went right over to Danielle. "I'm Officer Fitzgerald," he said as he looked closely at Danielle's face. "It would seem you kids have had quite a busy night." He pointed to Mrs. Jenkins and said, "Kari Jenkins here tells me your father was drunk tonight and he hit you, is that correct?"

Danielle was really scared and she didn't know what to say. She looked first to Peter and then to Laura, then finally to Laura's mom.

"It's all right, dear, you can tell him what happened," Mrs. Jenkins said as she put her arm around her.

"My dad was really mad tonight because he ran out of drinking money." She paused and began to tear up as she recalled how brutal her father had been. "He saw that I had been food shopping with money my brother gave me and was convinced we stole it from him and then demanded that I give him whatever was left. Then when it was only eight dollars, he hit me." She was shaking as she spoke and Mrs. Jenkins held her tight.

The officer looked to Peter and asked, "Did you steal the money from your dad to give to your sister?"

"No, sir," he replied. "I work a delivery job and gave it to her from my pay." He hated to talk about this in front of his sister because he could see how upset she was.

The officer looked back to Danielle and said, "I'm sorry, Danielle, I know this is difficult for you, but do you mind if I ask you just a couple more questions?"

"O… Okay," she said, her voice almost inaudible while Mrs. Jenkins was still comforting her.

"Are you certain that this is the first time he has ever hit you?"

"Yes, sir." She wondered what Nate or Pastor John would think if they knew she was lying, but she just couldn't face the alternative.

"Would you be okay with Nurse Jenkins and Nurse Anna taking a look at you just so I can be sure?" He noticed she was almost about to break down and was quick to add, "In private of course."

Danielle looked to Peter who nodded that it was okay. She hung her head and a look of shame played across her face because she knew they were about to find out her deep dark secret. She went into the next semi-private area

65

and let her best friend's mom have a look. As soon as Mrs. Jenkins and Nurse Anna took off her shirt and saw the bruises she began to cry.

"Oh, Danielle, you poor thing," Mrs. Jenkins began, holding back tears of her own. "How long has this been going on?" She looked at nearly a dozen bruises that were in varying degrees of healing.

"A long time, almost every time Peter's at work," she sobbed. "But it's my fault, I'm not a good enough daughter and sometimes I talk back." She began sobbing uncontrollably now; her breath catching and her nose running. Everyone knew her secret now and her life would never be the same.

Mrs. Jenkins looked directly into her eyes and said, "Danielle, this is not your fault. You are a great girl, and even if you weren't, no one deserves this. This is all on your dad."

Nurse Anna noticed the fresh bruise on her stomach and asked, "Did he punch you in the stomach?"

"He usually hits my stomach or back, so no one will notice the bruises," came her timid reply.

Peter sat on the examination table getting more and more angry. He remembered his conversation on Austin's porch and it left a bitter taste in his mouth. *How did I miss all of that? What kind of brother am I?*

Mrs. Jenkins just held her as they opened the curtain; she knew Peter had heard everything and she could see the rage in his eyes and the hard set of his jaw.

"Danielle, none of this is your fault, but we are going to have to issue a warrant for your father's arrest." The officer turned to Peter and added, "I know you are angry, Peter, but you need to let us handle this. It would do your sister no good if you wound up in jail with your father now, would it? Do you understand?" Peter nodded, but none of the fire had left his eyes. The matter seemed closed, and then the officer looked back at Peter and asked, "Now, what happened to you?"

"I was mugged on my way back from one of my deliveries." His reply came out a bit more curt than he intended, because he was trying hard not to fly into a rage. Every glance at his still crying sister reminded him of what an utter failure he was for not protecting her.

"Where do you work?" The officer had his book out, prepared to take notes.

"I deliver for Barbarelli's restaurant." Peter blanched when he adjusted his position on the bed and he could see the look of concern in his sister's eye. He shot her a reassuring look.

The officer let out a low whistle. "Barbarelli's, huh, do you know what goes on there?"

"People eat lots of really good Italian food, occasionally there's a block party." Peter knew what the officer was really asking and, while he knew his boss was a bit shady and had guys working for him that did shady things, he really didn't have much information on what those things were.

"Food, that's it? You never see anything strange going on there?"

"Well, the other day, a guy proposed to his girlfriend and she threw wine in his face and then stood up and left." Peter laughed at the recollection. "That was strange."

"That's not what I was asking and you know it." The officer suddenly seemed less friendly.

"No, I've never seen anything that would make me think maybe I shouldn't be working there. If that's what you're asking?"

"What are some of the things you see there?"

"What does this have to do with me getting mugged?" Peter didn't like the fact that this officer was spending more time fishing for dirt on his boss than he was finding out what had happened to him.

"Humor me."

"Look, if you're asking if I see Italian men in expensive suits going in and out of the restaurant, the answer is yes. If you're asking if I know what they talk about or what else might be going on, I'm sorry, I don't. I'm just a delivery guy."

"He's not a good guy, kid."

"He's good to me. He pays me well and treats me well, and I need every cent of it because I have to pay most of our bills. I couldn't do that as a stock boy at the local deli." He paused and then added, "I've never seen anything illegal going on there." That statement was technically true.

"Fair enough, let's move on to tonight. Were you anywhere near the shots fired at Clove Lakes Park?"

Peter kept his poker face and hoped he hadn't given anything away. "No, Clove Lakes is way too far to deliver by bike. What happened?"

The officer knew he wasn't being entirely truthful, but couldn't exactly call him on it. After all, someone had beaten this kid up. "Witnesses said there was a black Mustang and a Silver Civic causing all kinds of problems at the park. Driving crazy through the grass and on the walkway around the lake, you didn't hear anything about that?"

"No, sorry, sir. I was pretty busy with my own problems." Peter knew there was no way he could tell the officer what really happened and after another five minutes of questions, Officer Fitzgerald was on his way. As soon as he was gone, Dr. Hernandez entered the room. He took one look at the bruised ribcage and shook his head.

"Peter, looks like you've got a nasty injury to your ribs. I'm going to send you to radiology for some X-rays, and a CT scan. Your injury looks bad and I want to make sure you don't have any internal bleeding. I'm also going to have the technician take a couple of X-rays and a CT scan of your eye, as well, just to make sure there's no damage to the eye socket or swelling on the brain. Then we'll stitch you up and move you upstairs. I'm going to keep you overnight for observation because I don't like the look of that bruise." He closed his file and looked at Peter before he added, "Any questions?"

Peter looked over to Mrs. Jenkins before asking, "What time can I get out of here tomorrow?"

"Any time after noon, provided you have a ride home."

"We'll make sure he does, Doctor Hernandez, thank you," Mrs. Jenkins replied.

The pretty nurse came back in and made sure she had his information correct and the next thing he knew, he was about to get his ribs and eye X-rayed and scanned. He had been given a hospital gowns to wear over his pants. During the entire process, he couldn't take his mind off his sister. *I can't believe she has been hiding the abuse for so long. How did I miss all of that?* Within a couple minutes, the technician was slipping the rectangle shaped cartridge into the machine for his third X-ray. Then he was off to get scanned and soon after he was finished. The nurse led him back to the curtained off area where the Doctor was waiting to stitch him up. Danielle and Laura were watching and Danielle said, "Don't forget to tell him about your knee, Peter."

Doctor Hernandez raised his eyebrow in a look that said he should have already had this information. "It's just a scratch, Doc, nothing to worry about," Peter said.

68

"Well, we may as well be sure. Why don't you roll up your sweats and let me have a look." Peter complied with the doctor's request. After removing the hastily applied Band-Aid, Dr. Hernandez took a look at the wound and smiled at Danielle. "Your brother's right, it's just a scratch. I'm going to have the nurse clean it a little bit better, but his knee is fine."

"Thank you, Doctor Hernandez," Danielle replied with a sheepish look on her face.

*****

Barbarelli waited outside the hospital in a black Escalade. "So, how'd the kid do?"

Officer Fitzgerald approached the passenger side of the vehicle and replied, "He did fine. He said the strangest thing he's ever seen at your restaurant was a guy propose only to have his girlfriend throw wine in his face and walk away."

"Yeah, I remember that," Barbarelli said with a laugh as Michael cracked a smile in the driver's seat. "It caused quite a scene."

"He said he was mugged by a couple of college kids he's never seen before while he was delivering a Chicken Parm to eighty-seven Mountainview Avenue. Said he had no idea what was going on in the park, he was pretty convincing, too. One thing is for sure; he knows you treat him well. I couldn't let him and his sister stay at the apartment like you asked because the nurses saw the proof of their father's abuse all over the poor girl's body, there was nothing I could do." He looked around to make sure his conversation wasn't drawing any unwarranted attention and added, "But Peter? He's about as loyal as they come, Mr. Barbarelli, though I think he might be spooked now."

"Spooked enough to quit?"

"I don't know, maybe." He nodded and then returned to his squad car. He couldn't be seen talking to Barbarelli for too long or people might get suspicious.

When Officer Fitzgerald had departed, Barbarelli turned to Michael and said, "I hope we don't lose the kid over this. Loyalty is hard to find." Michael nodded and they pulled away from the curb.

69

Chapter 6

The phone was on its third ring by the time Coach Bailey picked it up. It was unusual for him to receive a call this late and he was immediately on edge. "Bailey Residence," he said in greeting.

"Coach, it's Peter Donovan," he paused not wanting to continue. He really liked his coach and hated to disappoint him.

"Donovan, is everything all right? It's pretty late."

"I'm sorry about that, sir, I got mugged while I was delivering tonight and I'm in the hospital. I'm not sure what to ask the doctor as far as what to do and when I can play. I was hoping you could come down and help me. The hospital already tried to get in touch with my father, but they couldn't reach him."

He knew that meant he was out drinking. He sighed and replied, "I'll be there as soon as I can."

"Thanks, Coach." Peter ended the call and handed his phone back to Danielle.

Coach Bailey sat in his car for a moment. He briefly wondered how this was going to affect his shot at another city championship before cursing his selfishness. He put the key in the ignition and started the car. This was the worst way to spend a Saturday night.

*****

"Doctor Hernandez?" Peter asked while the doctor was wrapping his ribs. "My football coach is on his way down here. Do you think he could ask you some questions about when I'll be ready to play again?"

"He can ask," the doctor said. "He's probably not going to like the answer, but he can ask." When the doctor finished wrapping Peter's ribs, he opened the curtain to find Coach Bailey had already arrived. Danielle was filling him in on what had happened and Peter could see the sympathy in his coach's eyes. He knew it was Peter that provided for her, and being hurt meant he might not be able to.

"So what's the scoop, Donovan? Couldn't you wait a few more weeks to get mugged?" he joked in his gruff coaching voice. "All kidding aside, how are you feeling, son?"

"The painkillers finally kicked in, so not too bad, Coach. It's still a bit hard to take deep breaths and my eye really hurts."

"Yeah, that's some shot you took, Donovan." He paused and looked at the doctor. "So, Doc, what's the prognosis?" The doctor gave him a dubious look until he produced a piece of paper with Peter's father's signature giving him the right to be given any of Peter's medical information related to his ability to play football. "It's okay, Doc, I'm allowed to know."

"He has three fractured ribs. We're keeping him overnight for observation. He needed eleven stitches above his eye, but there was no damage to the eye or the orbital bone. I'm recommending no physical activity, that means bike riding or football for a minimum of three to six weeks."

"Three to six weeks? Doc, we've got the playoffs in two weeks," Peter protested.

"Not you, Peter."

"You said three to six," Coach Bailey said. "Does that mean there's a chance he could be able to play in three?" He kept his fingers crossed hoping to get an answer he liked. He knew he could win the first game without Peter; it would be close, but it was possible. He also knew they would really need him to win the next game or the championship.

"Coach, we have to make sure he's okay before we worry about football," Danielle protested.

"It's okay, Dani, I asked him to ask these questions. That's why he's here," Peter replied.

"I wouldn't recommend playing in three weeks, but if you want to bring him in the day before the game, we can check his progress and maybe clear him to play. I can't promise anything, it just depends on how seriously he takes his recovery and how quickly he heals."

"I'll make sure he takes this seriously, Doctor Hernandez," Danielle said. "Football or not, I want my brother feeling better." Doctor Hernandez smiled at the girl.

"I'll make sure, too, Danielle, and not just for football. Peter's health is more important to me than his ability to catch a ball," Coach added.

"I'm confident Peter will have the right people helping him recover. Now, if you'll excuse me, I'm going to have a nurse escort him upstairs and you will all have to come back in the morning."

"Even me?" Danielle asked in her sweetest voice.

"Yes, even you. He needs to rest. Don't worry, our nurses will take great care of him and you can come back in the morning."

"I hope Nurse Anna is the one taking care of me," Peter quipped and then Laura burst out laughing.

"I'll be taking you upstairs and then I'm going home," the pretty nurse replied when she walked around the edge of the curtain pushing a wheelchair. Now Danielle and Coach Bailey were also laughing.

"There's no chance you didn't hear that is there?" Peter asked while fighting off death from embarrassment.

"Hear what?" Anna graciously replied.

"I'll see you tomorrow, Dani. Bye, Coach, bye, Laura. Thank your mom for everything for me."

"I will, Peter. Feel better."

"Yeah, feel better, Donovan, and don't you worry. The Falcons will be ready to play come playoffs. You got us there, now some of the other guys will have to shoulder the load."

"And I'll still make you some lucky game day waffles."

"Thanks, Dani. Thanks everyone." His sister stood there and waved as the nurse wheeled him away and he could see Laura put her arm around her.

*****

Gravano looked at his sons in disbelief. "Shots fired? Driving like mad men through the park? Have you two completely lost your minds? And you didn't even get him. He made it back to Barbarelli and now we're all in trouble." He knew things were going to get very interesting. He had openly defied Don Catalano's wishes and knew the old man wouldn't take it well.

"What were we supposed to do? We almost had him." Matthew fidgeted as he spoke while Paulie seemed to know better than to say anything.

"What were you supposed to do?" Gravano yelled. "What were you supposed to do?" he yelled even louder and began shaking. "He was on a bike! And not even a motorized one and he had broken ribs! And you mean to tell me that you and your idiot brother couldn't catch up to him in your supped up Mustang?" Gravano was pacing and gesticulating wildly. He took out a handkerchief and dabbed at the sweat forming on his brow as he prepared to continue. "And to make matters worse, you called other guys in on it. Two cars full of idiots and you still couldn't catch an injured kid on a bike." Matthew thought his father might actually go over the edge and kill him as he continued. "And none of you could hit a guy on a bike with your guns? Seriously? Why did I even give you guys guns, you obviously don't know how to use them."

"Dad, you weren't there, he was a really good rider, jumping cars and finding short cuts. Maybe if it was light out—"

"Yeah, and maybe if he was riding a tricycle!" he yelled over his son's objection.

"Well, we know where he lives," Paulie said. "Let's just go get him now. We'll pop him right in his bed."

That might not have been a bad idea if Barbarelli didn't already know we tried to hurt him, he thought. "No, now we have to leave him alone, he's got nothing on us anyway. Forget about the kid, what are we gonna do to make this right with Barbarelli? We can't go to war with him yet, not until I convince the Don that it's in his best interests."

*****

The minivan was silent as they rode home. Mrs. Jenkins thought the girls might even be asleep. She looked up when she heard Danielle's voice.

"Mrs. J." She knew Danielle only called her that because Peter did and, that made her smile.

"Yes, Danielle, is everything all right?"

"Yeah, I just wanted to say thank you for everything today. Today was really hard for me and I don't think I could have gotten through it if not for you and Laura."

"Oh, sweetie, it's no problem at all. You can come to us any time. You may even be staying with us for a while." Her heart was breaking for this poor girl and everything she'd been through.

"I know I don't know a lot about God yet, but I think you and Mr. J and Laura are what Christians are supposed to look like."

She smiled in the rearview mirror and replied, "That might be the nicest thing anyone has ever said about us, Danielle, but we are far from perfect. We fight, we have bad days, and we get mad sometimes, just like everyone else."

"I know, but you used up almost your whole day off helping me when you could have been doing what you wanted to do and I think that's what Pastor John meant when he talked about putting others before yourself."

"Well, that's what you did today. You had a horrible day and it would have been very easy to focus on yourself and no one would blame you, but you put it all aside for your brother."

"Mrs. J?" she asked again, and this time Mrs. Jenkins could hear the apprehension in her voice. "Why do you think God lets my father get drunk and beat me? Why do you think He let Peter get beat up? I've really been trying to be a good Christian, when is all of this bad stuff gonna stop happening to us?"

What a heartbreaking question, what could she possibly tell this girl that didn't seem trite and formulaic? Suddenly, Laura began to answer. "I know this might not be what you want to hear, but God allows everything to happen for a reason. Sometimes we never get to know what that reason is, but we have to trust that there is one. I do know that when we go through bad stuff, God uses it to make us stronger and, sometimes, He uses it to build up something inside us that we might not have ever had if we didn't have those problems."

Mrs. Jenkins was so proud of her daughter; she couldn't have answered the question any better. "That's right, Laura. And, Danielle, you can read James chapter one if you would like. It might give you a better understanding of what Laura just said. Would you like to sit down with Pastor John after church tomorrow and talk to him?"

"Only if it doesn't take too long; I don't want Peter waiting too long. It's bad enough he has to be there alone tonight."

"He's not alone," Laura replied.

"Laura, he doesn't believe in God."

"I know, but he's got Nurse Anna." They both started to crack up and Mrs. Jenkins was thankful for their resilience. Danielle had taken all that life threw at her and she was still able to smile and laugh, although, she suspected more tears would come when she was finally alone with her thoughts.

"Mrs. J," Danielle said again. "I'm sorry I lied to you." She paused and then in a quiet voice added, "I was just so ashamed."

"It's okay. Just remember, you have absolutely nothing to be ashamed about. Do you understand? None of this is your fault." Danielle nodded her head and Mrs. Jenkins kept driving.

*****

Danielle awoke to the warmth of the sun shining on her face. Looking through the window, she wondered if yesterday had just been one long nightmare. She tried to stifle a yawn as she stretched and swung her feet over the side of the mattress. She walked to the bathroom and heard the shower running. She would have to wait for Laura to finish up before she could get ready to go to church. She wandered down the stairs and into the kitchen, when her stomach reminded her that she hadn't eaten since lunch yesterday. She put two Pop Tarts in the toaster and sat down. She noticed that the sink was overflowing with dishes and mused that it was because they had spent their day helping her. She stood up and began rinsing dishes before placing them in the dish-washer. By the time her Pop Tarts were ready, she was halfway done.

"You don't have to do that, Danielle, you're our guest," Mr. Jenkins said from the doorway, and then he sipped his coffee.

"It's all right, I know they are only here because of me, and I was waiting for my Pop Tarts." She took them out of the toaster and took a bite, savoring the sweet strawberry flavor and she took a sip of water to wash it down.

"Would you like some coffee or something?" Mr. Jenkins offered.

"No thank you, Mr. J," Danielle replied as she put another dish in the dish-washer.

"Mr. J, huh?" he repeated with an amused look. "Too bad I'm not a doctor." He smiled waiting for Danielle to get the intended joke.

She just stared at him blankly and asked, "Why?" Then she took another bite of her breakfast.

"Because, then I'd be Doctor J, how cool would that be?" He could tell she still didn't get the joke, so he just mumbled, "Never mind, it's before your time."

Just then, Laura yelled down, "Danielle, I'm done, bathroom is all yours."

"I'll be right up," she yelled back as she pushed the last bite of her Pop Tart into her mouth and started up the stairs.

*****

As Mr. Jenkins pulled into the parking lot of Clove Road Bible Church, the sight of the old brick building lifted Danielle's spirit. She was falling in love with this place because this was where she had fallen in love with Jesus. As they entered the building, a kind elderly couple greeted the girls before they went looking for Nate. Danielle didn't really want to let him know what was going on, but Laura had talked her into it. They ran into Hailey who greeted them both with a big hug.

"Still can't get your brother to come with you on Sunday, huh?" Hailey said with a chuckle.

"Actually, Peter's in the hospital."

"Oh no, I'm so sorry. What happened?" Danielle could tell her concern was genuine as she stood there waiting to hear what happened.

"He was mugged last night while he was making his deliveries. He's got a couple broken ribs and a bad cut over his eye."

"Eleven stitches," Laura added.

"They kept him for observation and we're going back to pick him up after church."

"Danielle, I'm so sorry, is there anything I can do? Maybe I'll bake some get well cookies for him."

"He'd like that," Danielle said. "If you do, he's probably going to be staying at Austin's for a couple days. We're having some problems with our dad and it wouldn't be a good time for Peter to be alone in the house with him."

Hailey nodded, not quite understanding what Danielle had meant as she turned to go into the sanctuary. "Church is about to start, I'll talk to you guys later." As she walked away, it suddenly hit her exactly what Danielle had meant about problems with their dad and she shook her head.

The church service seemed like most of the other services Danielle had been to, but her mind was stuck on Peter and her dad. She was having trouble following because her mind kept drifting. She silently prayed that God would help her to focus, but that focus still eluded her. Pastor John was really pouring it on today and the congregation seemed really into it. Some people were clapping; others lifted a hand and still more shouted "alleluia" or "amen." That's when Danielle finally began to focus.

"We often wonder what God's will is. We say we want to follow His will and do His will, but as soon as things get hard we pull back. I'm here to tell you today that life isn't easy.

Listen to the words of Jesus in John sixteen verses thirty-two and thirty-three. 'A time is coming and in fact has come when you will be scattered, each to your own home. You will leave me all alone. Yet I am not alone, for my father is with me." Pastor John looked up and interjected, "Jesus is talking here about his crucifixion and how his followers will abandon him." He looked back down at his Bible and continued reading. "I have told you these things, so that in me you may have peace. In this world you will have trouble. But take heart! I have overcome the world."

He looked out at the congregation and repeated. "In this world you will have trouble." He paused for effect. "Jesus tells us straight up, He doesn't say 'you might have trouble' He says 'you will have trouble.' When trouble rears its ugly head, it shouldn't come as a surprise to us because we already know it's coming. We live in a sinful world, a fallen world. Bad things are going to happen to good people. It doesn't mean God's not in control, or that God has failed us. No! It means we should rely on Jesus all the more because he tells us to take heart. He has overcome the world. And just as he wasn't alone on the cross, we're not alone in our troubles. Jesus is right there with us, we're not alone."

He paused and someone shouted, "Come on, brother, preach it!"

He smiled at the congregation and continued. Danielle was fully engaged now; she felt like he was speaking right to her. She wondered if Laura's mom had told him what had happened to her. "Church, let me tell you, if you came to Jesus Christ to make your life easier, you are going to be sorely disappointed. You will have trouble; it's unavoidable. Bad things will happen. But, if you came to Jesus Christ because you are tired and weary of trying to figure out those problems on your own, if you came to Jesus because you know you can't do it on your own, then get ready to experience the peace that passes all human understanding. Because our Savior lives to help his children overcome their troubles. He lives to see us through those trials.

Now, before you mistake that for me saying that he's going to do it for us, I need you to understand, giving us the strength to get through and doing it for us are two different things. And remember, God doesn't always help us in the ways we expect. In fact, it seems he prefers the unexpected. If you do have troubles in your life, take heart, Jesus wants to see us through it." He paused again and looked out at the congregation. Danielle could swear his eyes stopped on her as he continued.

"Some of us have problems at work, or school, or with our health, or with our families. Take heart, none of those problems are too big for God. There may not be an easy solution to your problems, but if you are looking for easy, you're in the wrong place. However, if you're looking for the type of help that only God can provide, then you are right where you belong." Pastor John put his Bible back on the stand and looked out over the congregation before adding, "Let's pray!"

As Pastor John was praying, Danielle continued to think of everything she had been through and wondered if God really did want to help her. She wondered if there really was any way to have peace in her situation. *Could God really help me in any situation? Could God save Peter and help dad stop drinking?* So many questions, so few answers. In the meantime she was in the middle of it and knew she needed God to help her through.

When Pastor John had finished praying and dismissed the service, Mrs. Jenkins approached her.

"Danielle, would you like to go speak to Pastor John now?"

She looked up at Laura's mom and wanted to say no, but she knew that was just nerves. This felt so official and that made her a little nervous. "Um, would it be okay if you sat in with us, and if Nate was there, too? I don't think I can get through it all twice."

"Of course, sweetheart," She turned to Laura and asked, "Could you go find Nate and ask him to come up to the Pastor's office?"

"Sure, Mom," she replied and then disappeared down the stairs.

Danielle and Mrs. Jenkins walked up to the front of the church and when they reached the pastor, he excused himself from the conversation he had been having and gave them his full attention. "Hello Danielle," he greeted. Then he took her hand and shook it. "Before we sit down and talk, let me just tell you what a pleasure it has been having you in our church. I know you've only been here a few months, but we consider you part of the family." As he guided them into his office, Danielle thought about what it would be like to have a real family. She didn't think she'd trade a real family like the Jenkins for her brother.

78

"Nate just texted me, he's on his way up. Why don't you tell me about yesterday; start with the morning," Pastor John said.

"Did the Jenkins tell you what happened?"

"Brian, um, Mr. Jenkins only told me you had a really rough morning and the day sort of went downhill from there. He did say it was some serious stuff." He looked concerned and Danielle wondered why he would care about someone he barely knew. Just then, Nate came in the office and sat down. While he was getting settled, Danielle looked around the room. It was a small office consisting of a desk with two chairs in front of it and an entire wall dominated by a bookcase. *Pastor John certainly has a lot of books*, she thought. There was a small couch along the other wall and that's where she and Mrs. Jenkins were sitting. Pastor John and Nate sat in the two chairs that were in front of his desk, but now faced the couch.

"Hey, Dani," Nate greeted with a solemn expression. He knew she had a rough family life, but it must have gotten bad for her to be here.

"Ok, Danielle, we're all here. Let's pray for God to give us wisdom and then you can tell us what's going on," Pastor John said.

After they prayed, Danielle looked nervously up at them and Mrs. Jenkins took her hand and encouraged her. "I suppose it started Friday night after youth group. I came home to see my dad passed out in the hallway with beer bottles strewn around him. He had forgotten his key and he was mad at me for coming home late and making him wait. After I put him to sleep, I went back out to the hallway to clean up his mess and the looks my neighbor gave me made me want to cry. I fell asleep on the couch because that's where I stay when my dad is drunk in case he wanders out or something." Nate shook his head as she paused. "Then, yesterday morning, he got really mad at me for making Peter waffles and going to his football game, because he hates Peter."

"Why do you think your dad hates your brother, Danielle?" Pastor John asked while sitting with his hands folded under his chin.

"I never knew why until yesterday. While we were fighting I asked him and he said it was because Peter was responsible for my mom's death." She went on to relay the rest of what happened as Pastor John and Nate listened attentively.

"What happened after that, Dani?" Nate asked with the same solemn look on his face.

"After the game, Mrs. Jenkins took me food shopping so that I wouldn't have to carry everything home by myself. I used money that Peter gave me from his delivery job. When my dad got home, he was already drunk and he was angry that he ran out of money. He saw the food I bought and went crazy. He was convinced that we stole the money from him to get the food and that's why he ran out of drinking money." Danielle started shaking again and Mrs. Jenkins put her arm around her.

"It's okay, dear, I can tell them the rest if you'd like," Mrs. Jenkins said in encouraging tone.

"No, it should come from me," she replied, her speech halting and nose running. Mrs. Jenkins handed her a tissue. Danielle took a deep breath and continued to tell them all of the harrowing details of her evening.

"I'm so sorry you had to go through all of that, Danielle. I hear the Jenkins have opened their home to you until this gets sorted. So, we'll all begin praying for your dad's salvation. God can change him, Danielle; never doubt that. God can change him, but your father needs to let him. Sometimes people resist God for a long time." He looked right into her eyes and she could see how much he cared as he added, "Hopefully, he sobers up sooner rather than later and realizes what an incredible young lady he has." Pastor John said with a kind smile. "And, in the meantime, you'll be safe with the Jenkins."

Pastor John hated meetings like these. As much as he loved helping people, meetings like these represented some of the worst things mankind had to offer. *How could a man beat his own daughter?* One thing a meeting like this did do, was it always reminded him that men are sinful and in desperate need of a Savior.

"Shortly after her father beat her, Peter came home beat up really bad," Mrs. Jenkins said. "He said he was mugged while doing his delivery job. The police officer didn't seem convinced, told him his boss wasn't a good guy. He had three fractured ribs and his eye was swollen shut. He needed eleven stitches to close the gash above his eye. They kept him for observation."

"Where does Peter work?" Pastor John asked.

"Barbarelli's restaurant," Danielle replied. "But he didn't do this; he likes Peter and treats him really well. He knows we're poor and pays Peter enough to pay all of our bills." Even as she said it, she still couldn't believe everything Peter had sacrificed for her.

"No one thinks he did it, sweetheart," Mrs. Jenkins comforted.

"But, maybe someone did it to send a message. We've got to get your brother out of that situation. He's not safe there," Nate added with an air of seriousness Danielle seldom saw from him.

"Well, it seems like we have a lot to pray about," Pastor John began. "Danielle, please keep us posted on what's going on. We'd like to help in any way we can."

"Thank you, Pastor. I think we need to go pick him up from the hospital now." Once again, she was overwhelmed that these people she barely knew were so willing to help her.

"I'd like to come with you, if you don't mind, Dani," Nate asked as his smile returned.

"Okay, I think Peter would like that," she replied. After they prayed, Danielle actually felt optimistic as they left to pick up Peter.

Chapter 7

The next two weeks flew by for Peter without incident. All of the questions about his injuries had been asked and answered.

Peter and Austin had gone back to Peter's apartment and packed up all of Danielle's belongings. Mr. Jenkins picked them up in his minivan because social services had approved Danielle to live with them until her father had gone to trial. Peter and Austin then packed up his possessions and Nate helped them bring his stuff to Austin's house. Danielle had gone back to her usual happy, loving self. It seemed being around the Jenkins was good for her. Hailey and Toni Ann were spending a lot of time with Laura and Danielle. Nate called it discipleship. Peter didn't mind; Hailey and Toni Ann were nice to his sister and Laura, and that's all that mattered to him.

Austin was taking practice with the first team for their playoff game. He was good enough to start for almost any team in the city, but on Wagner's team he was second string until the injury bug hit. He was so excited about starting at linebacker that Peter thought he was going to start tackling random people just for practice. His own injuries were healing nicely and he hoped that meant he could play in the team's second playoff game. He wouldn't know about that until the afternoon before the game.

Peter was sitting in the library with his earphones in and his math book open. Being injured had allowed him to catch up on some work, but he was still struggling with math. He was focused on the math problem in front of him as Pandora piped some classic rock through his headphones. He didn't see her enter and was surprised when, out of nowhere, his sister was hugging him.

"Peter, you're still coming tonight, right?"

"I don't know, Dani, I need to drop by the restaurant tonight, Mr. Barbarelli asked me to come by. It depends on what time."

"Petey, come on. You promised you'd go back. Austin is coming; he came last week, too."

"That's because he's in love with Hailey. I'll tell you what, I'll see if I can meet him later and then maybe hang out with you guys for a while at your youth group, okay. I'll try, I just can't promise anything."

"All right," she replied with a little less enthusiasm. "What are you working on?"

"Math, it's kicking my butt, I just can't seem to get it."

"You know who's really smart at math?"

"Don't say it."

"Hailey is. She noticed your last test score and has offered her services. You should let her help you." She smiled, waiting for his response.

"Dani, I'm really not interested. Plus, Austin really likes her and you don't break the bro code."

"The bro code is the stupidest thing I've ever heard of. Doesn't it matter what the girl wants?"

"It's not like that, Dani, of course it matters. No one is saying she has to date Austin. All I'm saying is, while he likes her, I'm not trying to go behind his back and date her. Plus, like I already said, I'm not interested."

"Fine, then it shouldn't matter if she tutors you." Dani folded her arms and frowned suggesting she knew she was right about this.

"You know what? You're right," Peter relented. "I'll ask Austin if he's okay with it and, if he is, I'll see if she can tutor me."

"All right, fine. Oh, Laura's mom is going to be here in about a half hour. She doesn't want you to have to walk all the way to Austin's from the bus stop."

"Dani, I'm fine, really."

"Do you want to play next week or not? Don't be a tough guy, just take the ride; please."

He hated to admit it, but she was right again. He smiled at his protective little sister and agreed. "Okay, I'll take the ride. But afterward, I really do have to go to Barbarelli's. Nothing I can do about that."

"Fine," she replied, satisfied with her brother's compromise and thankful he was coming back to youth group.

*****

Austin arrived at the church early and waited for Peter and Danielle outside; he didn't want to go in alone. He greeted them when they showed up.

"What's up, brother," Austin called out, as Peter unfolded his six two frame out of the minivan, careful not to strain his ribs.

83

"What's up, Austin," he replied, walking over and joining his friend. He gave him a subdued high five and then leaned against a parked car. "Is Hailey here yet?"

"No, why do you think I'm waiting outside?" Austin scanned the street for her parent's car.

"I have to ask you a question, bro, you might not like it," Peter said, a bit unsure.

"Sure, what?" Austin replied with an apprehensive look in his eye.

"I'm not doing well in math, and Hailey has offered to tutor me. You know I'm not interested, but I didn't want to go behind your back with it."

Austin thought about it hard. He knew his buddy would never purposely break the bro code, but tutoring was a tricky situation. "I don't know man, tutoring is tough. I know you're not interested now, but you'll be alone in a room, she'll be all hot and she'll hug you when she's happy you got the answer right and next thing you know, you're making out and I'm out looking in." Peter started laughing and Austin was confused, "What? What's so funny?"

"Dude, you just described like a dozen eighties movies. She's not gonna be teaching me Salsa dancing. We would be in the library with Miss Finch watching. And you know that if Miss Finch even sniffs someone having fun, she has to squash it. This isn't like some movie that winds up with me getting the girl; it's math. But I won't do it if you're not cool with it."

Austin was thankful his friend was being so respectful. Saying no would be like saying he didn't trust him. "Nah, it's cool, it's only math," and deep down, he hoped he was right.

Nate saw them talking and walked over. "Hey, Peter. How are you feeling, man?"

"A lot better than the last time you saw me, thanks for coming with Dani and Laura to pick me up from the hospital and for helping me bring my stuff to Austin's." He may not have wanted anything to do with being a Christian, but he had to admit, Dani's Christian friends had really impressed him over the last couple weeks.

"Any time, Peter. And I mean that. We're getting ready to start, if you guys want to come inside."

"We'll be in soon. We're just waiting for Hailey. I need to talk to her about tutoring me in math."

"Oh, she's already inside, she's been here since four o'clock helping out watching some kids while their moms decorate the church for Christmas."

"But it's not even Thanksgiving yet," Austin protested.

"True, but we really like Christmas around here." He laughed and then added, "Anyway, she's already inside." He turned and began walking towards the side entrance of the church with Peter and Austin following him inside.

*****

The group started similarly to the last time Peter had come, only this time there was no charity video or offering. Instead, there was a rock video from a musician he had never heard of before. The song was talking about God, but the music wasn't bad. The group actually had some talent. After the music video, Hailey walked on stage and he noticed that Austin was immediately focused.

"Hey, guys," Hailey greeted with an infectious smile. Nate asked me to come up tonight to talk about something Toni Ann and I are doing. The night before Thanksgiving, we're going into the city to the Bowery Mission to give some homeless people an early Thanksgiving dinner. I was wondering if any of you wanted to come out with us and help. You'd have to ask your parents, but it's not a church event, so you won't need to get anything signed. Just let one of us know after youth group if you think you'd like to come. Thanks, guys." She handed the microphone to Nate and sat back down next to Toni Ann.

"Thanks, Hailey," Nate said, while he dragged his stool and music stand into position. "I love that you guys want to help people in our community less fortunate than you are. We'll be doing it officially as a group the night before Christmas Eve, so be thinking ahead to that as well."

He took a breath and then said, "Tonight I'd like to talk briefly about forgiveness. How do you react when someone wrongs you? I'll go for about fifteen or twenty minutes and then we'll break into groups with our adult volunteers to discuss what I'm talking about." He launched into his talk about how forgiveness was essential to the Christian life and the whole time all Peter could think about was Gravano punching and kicking him and his father punching his sister. It was a good talk, but this was one of the main reasons why He didn't think he could ever become a Christian. He didn't even want to forgive them. He wanted to hurt them. He felt like forgiving them would be a copout. He knew his sister was going to take this talk to heart and start trying to forgive

85

her dad and, if it made her happy, he was all for it. But he was not about to let go of everything his father had put them through.

The discussion time came and, as predicted, Danielle mentioned that there was someone in her life she needed to forgive. Thankfully, she didn't mention names because he didn't want these people knowing their business. Enough people already knew and he didn't want to be pitied. The meeting ended, and Dani smiled at him and took his arm. "You stayed for the whole thing tonight, Petey."

"I told you I would."

"Petey, huh?" Hailey said as she hugged Danielle. "Nate told me you were looking for me."

"I was," he said. "My sister mentioned that you offered to tutor me and I was wondering—"

"Of course, Petey, you didn't even need to ask," She interrupted.

"Thanks, Hailey, but only my sister gets to call me Petey."

She looked over at Danielle and smiled. "All right, Peter," she exaggerated the pronunciation of his name. "Just tell me when."

"How's Tuesday after practice, in the library?"

"Tuesday it is then, Peter," she exaggerated his name again and then laughed as she walked away arm-in-arm with Danielle.

He smiled at her flirting, even as he remembered his promise to his best friend.

"So, is she gonna do it?" Austin's question almost startled him.

"Hmm, what?"

"Is she gonna tutor you in math?"

"Yeah, she is. Thanks for being cool with it, man. I really need to pass math."

"No problem, brother." His comment seemed carefree, but Peter could sense his apprehension and vowed not to let his friend down.

"I gotta say goodnight to Dani and make sure Mrs. J is picking her up, then I need to get out of here. Barbarelli is waiting on me, and it's not a good idea to keep the boss waiting."

"My mom is picking me and Danielle up in about ten minutes," Laura said as she walked past him.

"Thanks, Laura, let me just say goodbye and then get out of here." He found his sister and she was talking with Nate, Ted, and some kid he didn't know. He stepped into their conversation and said, "Sorry to interrupt, but I have to get going and just wanted to say goodbye to my sister."

"No problem," Nate replied and continued talking to Ted.

Peter hugged his sister and as he was letting go of the embrace he couldn't resist and whispered, "Remember, don't drink the Kool-Aid." Nate started laughing behind him as Dani smacked his arm.

"Stop it, Peter, that's not funny," she replied.

"Sorry," he said and then chuckled. He kissed her forehead and waved goodbye to Nate and Ted. He told Austin he'd catch him back at his house and then he was gone. He caught the bus back up to Victory Boulevard. When he approached Clove Road, he noticed three buses waiting. All three would pass the street he needed to go to before turning off in different directions, so he hurried aboard the first bus. Fifteen minutes later he was at the corner of Victory Boulevard and Jewett Avenue, heading into the back of the fine Italian restaurant.

"Hey, Donovan, how are you feeling, kid?" Barbarelli greeted the young man and then shook his hand.

"Still hurts when I turn or stretch, but not too bad, Mr. Barbarelli."

"I bet you're wondering why I called you here today."

"I figured you just wanted me to check in, maybe get a report of my progress."

"Well yeah, there's that, but I also wanted to give you something. Come on and sit down at the table with me and Michael." He motioned to a table in the corner. Michael was already seated and it looked like there was enough food for ten people on the table. "I hope you're hungry, kid." Barbarelli added.

"I could eat," he replied, and then he spied some ravioli and meatballs. He smelled the Marinara sauce before he even sat down. "Hey, Mike," he greeted, and the big man returned a nod.

After twenty minutes, Mr. Barbarelli put his fork down, wiped his mouth with the cloth napkin to his left and looked at him. "Peter, I don't usually do this, so don't let it get around. I felt really bad about not believing you, and you getting all beat up. I want you to know, Gravano's going to pay the price for laying his hands on you." He paused and withdrew an envelope, "I wanted to give you a bonus for what you went through, and I want your assurances that you won't mention to anyone what actually happened. It would reflect poorly on me and the business we do here if the authorities thought there was a reason to look into the relationship between me and Gravano. You understand that, right?"

"Yes, sir, and I promise I won't say anything. I already told the cop in the ER that I was mugged by some college kids I didn't know. Mr. Barbarelli, you've always treated me really well," he stopped and his boss could see the apprehension in his eyes.

"It's all right, Peter, you can say it."

"I don't want to seem ungrateful, but is there any way I can, um, not have to go to Gravano's anymore?"

"I'll see what I can do. You're a loyal kid, even after I accused you of stealing. You took a beating to prove yourself to me and I want to reward that loyalty. I know you haven't worked in a couple weeks now, and you won't be working at least this week, but I wanted to pay you anyway. Actually, the money is from Gravano, his payments just went up another hundred a week." He smiled and slid the envelope over to Peter. He took it and put it in his jacket pocket without looking inside. It felt a little heavy, so he knew it was good. Besides he didn't want to disrespect his boss by looking at it in front of him.

"Thank you, Mr. Barbarelli, you didn't have to do that."

"I know, but I know you also got bills, and I know you don't want to have to dip into the college fund you started for your sister to have to pay those bills."

The look of shock that crossed his face made his boss smile. "How did you know I was saving for my sister's college?"

"Peter, I know everything that's going on with my guys. I pay you five hundred a week. I know your food, clothes and utilities are not running you two thousand a month, probably not even half that. But you never come in here flashing expensive jewelry or anything else that says you got a grand a month to spare, so I looked into it. You've been pretty disciplined. You've got over fifteen grand already saved for when she goes to college, that's impressive dedication to your sister. That's why I also got you this," he slid a small rectangular box over to him and said, "This one you can look at, kid"

He opened the box and inside was a beautiful silver necklace with a diamond pendant hanging from it. It looked very expensive. "Sir, this is too much, I can't accept this."

"You can, and you will. Give it to her on her birthday; say it was from you. I know how much you love it when she's happy."

"I will, and thank you, but I'm not even sure I can still do this. I know you may not want to hear this, and I hate to say it because you've always been so great to me and my sister. I feel disloyal just thinking it, but every time I close my eyes, I see Gravano kicking me, or his sons shooting at me and I'm scared. I still want to do this, but I can't guarantee that I can. I will guarantee that I never breathe a word about my time here to anyone. You mean a lot to me and I would never want to let you down." He lowered his head and continued, "If you want the bonus back, I understand completely."

A look of disappointment passed over Barbarelli's face, but he quickly pushed it aside. "No, that bonus is yours, you earned it. And we'll talk about your future employment in a couple weeks when your ribs are fully healed. We don't gotta make any decisions now."

"Really, you're not mad?" Peter let some hope seep into his voice.

"How could I be mad? You went above and beyond for me and you didn't have to. I should have tried harder to protect you. We'll talk more in a couple weeks. Hopefully, your team will win tomorrow and you can play next week. I'd hate for you to miss the end of your season." He and Michael stood up and he continued, "It's getting late and I have places to be. I'll call you in a couple weeks."

"Thank you, Mr. Barbarelli, for everything. Dani is gonna love this necklace. Thank you."

He exited the restaurant with a wave. He had the necklace and the envelope stored safely in his jacket pocket. He knew it was a payment for his silence, hush money, and he didn't care. It wasn't like he was keeping quiet about a dead body. He was keeping quiet about the guy that beat him up, which he was planning to do anyway.

He pulled his hood up against the cold and walked to the bus stop. He didn't want to make the fifteen-minute walk with all the money and the necklace in his pocket, and he also wanted to save his ribs from acting up on a long walk. He looked around to make sure no one was watching and opened the corner of the envelope. He counted off ten one-hundred dollar bills and twenty fifty-dollar bills. Mr. Barbarelli had been very generous. He paid him for the entire month his injuries would have had kept him out of work. He had two thousand dollars in his pocket plus a diamond necklace and, for the first time in his life, he was worried about actually getting mugged. He was thankful the bus was mostly empty when it pulled over to let him on. He swiped his metro card and found a seat in the middle where he could keep an eye on the whole bus and still be seen by the driver. He couldn't wait to get home and get this money into the bank.

After Peter had left, Barbarelli could see the question in Michael's eyes as they walked to the car. "I'm gonna tell you something that can never be spoken of again. Do you understand, Michael?"

"Yes, sir."

"When I first got promoted to this position thirteen years ago, I went out with all the guys and celebrated. We went all night and into the next morning. When I was driving home, I was still drunk from the night before. A little kid wandered out into the road and I accidentally hit the gas instead of the brake. By the time I hit the brakes it was going to be too late." He paused for a moment. He had never mentioned this to anyone, and it was difficult. "The kid's mother ran into the street and threw her son out of the way just in time to bounce off the hood of my car."

"It was Peter's mom, wasn't it?"

"Yeah, I just kept going and sold the car to a junkyard in Delaware the next day. I later learned that the young mother had died. I was never caught, but it always weighed on me. This wasn't an enemy, this wasn't someone I wished dead, this was just a normal family and they didn't deserve what happened. Of course, I could never turn myself in, but when Peter turned fourteen and began looking for work to help support his sister, I did a little digging and found out that because of me their father had gone on to become an alcoholic. So, I hired Peter and I've always treated him really well. I know it could never make up for what I did, but at least it's something."

"Now it makes sense. I knew there had to be something about this kid to make it worth going to war with Gravano over a delivery boy," Michael replied as he opened the car door for his boss.

"Remember, no one on Earth knows about this except you and me, and I need to keep it that way."

"I'll take this secret to the grave, Mr. Barbarelli."

"I think I'm gonna let the kid go. I've messed up his life enough. Maybe I'll just put some money away for his sister for college and send her a fake college scholarship notice or something. I'll get my lawyers to do it when the time comes."

"I think that's a great idea, boss." He had to admit, even though he dodged the jail time, his boss was, at least on some level, taking responsibility

90

for his actions. He also knew that this conversation firmly cemented him as Barbarelli's most trusted lieutenant.

Chapter 8

Peter woke up late the next morning and his ribs were still sore. He took a quick shower and saw Austin's mom on his way out.

"Are you going to eat anything before you leave, Peter?"

"No thanks, my sister is making me waffles at the Jenkins."

"That sounds nice. Have fun, and make sure you look out for Austin. He's really excited to be starting."

"I know, he already left for the school; he's so pumped up." He turned to leave, but then turned back and added. "Thanks so much for letting me stay here until things with my father get worked out."

"It's no problem. Since you've been here, Austin's been on his best behavior, so we both win." She smiled and waved as he walked out the door. He wouldn't have time to deposit the money that Barbarelli gave him last night if he still wanted to have some waffles. *I'll just do it Monday. It should be safe here.*

Peter arrived at the Jenkins house and was surprised to see that Danielle had made waffles for everyone. As soon as he walked in the kitchen, Dani put the spatula down and greeted her brother with a big hug. "Peter, I missed you. You're late, by the way," she said with a frown.

"Sorry. I didn't sleep well, but I'm here now."

"Yes, you are. Go sit in the dining room and I'll be out with your waffles in a minute."

After a half hour and two waffles, Peter stood up and hugged his sister's neck. "Perfect as always, sis, I gotta go. I'm late and coach isn't gonna be happy."

"Okay, I love you, Peter. I'll be in the stands and I'll see you after the game."

He kissed her forehead and replied, "Love you, too, sis. I'll look for you." He waved to the Jenkins and thanked them for their hospitality as he headed for the door. His phone rang and he answered; the gruff voice of his coach asked, "Donovan, where are you?"

"I'm on my way, Coach. I'm sorry; I had a lot of errands this morning and in the craziness of it all I forgot to call." As the call ended, the coach readied himself for the pre-game pep talk. Peter arrived at the school twenty minutes later.

He walked towards the sideline, where his teammates were warming up, and he could see the stands were already packed. He was focused on making it over to his teammates when he heard a voice that chilled him to the bone.

"Ay, kid, I gotta talk to you." Gravano's voice boomed through the crowd. Peter thought about ignoring it and continuing to walk past the cement bleachers, until he saw Matthew and Paulie walking towards him.

He turned abruptly and answered, "What do you want, Gravano?" He was pouring as much ice into his voice as he could. He was still angry enough about the things going on in his life that it wasn't very hard to sound ticked.

"You should know better than to talk to me like that, kid. Remember last time?" He smiled a vile smile and began laughing.

"Barbarelli isn't gonna like you hassling me."

"Who's gonna tell him? You? What are you a full time rat now?"

"I ain't a rat."

"You had no problem ratting me out?" he looked angry and Matthew and Paulie were getting closer.

"Well you had no problem cheating Mr. Barbarelli and trying to set me up for it. You're just mad your plan didn't work. Don't try and blame your situation on me, you got no one to blame but yourself for what happened between you and Mr. Barbarelli."

"We'll see about that, Kid." He said and then he took a long sip from his bottle of water.

Peter turned to see Matthew and Paulie in front of him, but he was still running on anger and hatred towards both his father and Gravano. He yelled, "Get out of my way," and plowed through the two of them. They turned to follow, but Peter's display had drawn a bit more attention than they were comfortable with.

Nate assessed the situation and approached as Matthew and Paulie were following him and said, "Hey Peter, the coach wants you down at the field, pronto." He glanced at Peter's two shadows and added, "Team only, guys, sorry." He feigned a sympathetic look and then took off after Peter. When he caught up he asked, "So, were those the guys that mugged you?"

Peter stopped and looked at the youth pastor with as much seriousness as he could muster. "Leave it alone, Nate. You don't want to know those guys.

It's better for you and your family if you don't know those guys. I don't mean any disrespect; you've been great to me and especially Dani and that's why I'd hate to see anything happen to you. And when you know those guys, bad things can happen."

Before Nate could answer, they had reached the field and Peter was swept up into the pre-game excitement of his teammates. It was all an act though; football didn't even make the top ten list of things weighing on his mind right now.

Just before halftime, he finally started to get into the game. He noticed one of the offensive linemen for the Lincoln Railsplitters chop-blocking Austin on almost every play. He alerted the coach and the coach complained to the officials. It paid off two plays later, when the Lincoln quarterback connected on a twenty-seven yard completion that had them in striking distance of a touchdown, but the play was called back and they were given a ten-yard penalty because of the illegal block. The following play, Austin made it to the quarterback, almost unimpeded, for an eight-yard loss. That really energized the crowd and, following an incompletion, they were forced to punt. Wagner's return man ran it all the way back for a touchdown to give the Falcons a fourteen to zero halftime lead.

When the team was heading into the locker room, the coach put his arm around Peter and said, "Great call on the illegal block, Peter. If you hadn't noticed that, it could just as easily be seven all instead of fourteen nil. I know you've got a lot on your mind right now, and I appreciate you hanging in there with us even though you can't play yet."

"Happy to help, coach," he replied, hoping he sounded sincere and wishing he could be out there with his teammates.

While the coach was congratulating Austin on his sack, Peter's phone rang. He didn't recognize the number, but he picked it up anyway in case it was Mr. Barbarelli. He was shocked when he heard his father's voice. "Peter, it's dad. I'm in lock up right now, and I need you to come down and bail me out."

The shock at his father's gall hit him like a wave, and his anger boiled over instantly. He replied, "Are you kidding me? You've got a lot of nerve calling me." His coach turned to look at him when he heard that line.

"Peter, listen, I know we've had our differences, but I really need your help today. I'm stuck in jail and they're gonna make me stay all weekend until I can see a judge Monday. Please!"

He heard the fear in his father's voice and it actually made him smile. "I've already moved out, isn't that enough? It's what you've always wanted. Besides, I hope they keep you in jail a lot longer than that."

"You don't mean that, son."

Being called "son" pushed him over the edge. "I don't mean that?" he was yelling now. "You've told me you hate me for years. You beat my sister for years and then you punched her in the face for beer money; your own daughter! I hope you rot in jail for the rest of your miserable life. You'll never see me or Dani again." He ended the call by throwing the phone into the wall. He just let it fly. The entire locker room stopped to look at him and he didn't care. Both Coach Bailey and Austin were at a loss for what to do. After several seconds, he finally stopped and looked at them. "That was my dad," he explained with an angry look on his face.

"Got that," Coach Bailey replied.

"I can't believe he thought I'd bail him out of jail."

"Peter," Coach Bailey began with a serious but cautious tone. "I know you don't want to hear this right now, but you gotta let go of that hate, man. It'll eat you up if you don't. You'll never be able to be happy with that much hate in your life."

"You're probably right, Coach, but it's gonna take some time." He left it at that, and was grateful that his coach didn't pursue it any further. Instead, he launched into his halftime speech.

Almost an hour and a half later, Mark knelt down with the ball and ran the last seventeen seconds off the clock. Wagner was advancing to the city championship semifinals on the strength of their twenty-eight to fourteen victory over Lincoln. Peter looked through the stands and Gravano and his boys were nowhere to be seen, his presence may have just been another intimidation attempt, which meant he was likely planning something. He didn't even want to think about what that might be. He spotted Nate and made his way over to him. When he caught up with him he said, "Look, Nate, I'm sorry if I seemed scary earlier, it's just that those guys are mobbed up and really bad news. They already don't like me; I would hate myself if you wound up on their radar."

"It's already forgotten, Peter, but if your job is bringing you into frequent contact with those types of people, you need to quit before you or Danielle really get hurt."

"You're right, I've already told my boss I was unsure I could continue and he seemed okay with it. Maybe I'll tell him I'm done for good next time we speak. Now that Dani is with the Jenkins, I won't need as much money. Again, I'm sorry."

"It's no problem, really."

Peter left Nate to go find Dani. He knew she would want to go out to eat and he had no work restrictions this time, so he was looking forward to spending time with his sister. He still needed to go back to the apartment and get his metal lock box filled with his valuables out of its hiding place. He figured he better get to it before his father found it and, since his dad was in jail, that time would be today. After getting some pizza, Peter and Danielle walked across Manor Road and back into their building. It was the first time Danielle had been back since the Jenkins had taken her in.

"I need to get something from my room, Dani. Why don't you look through the rest of the apartment and make sure I didn't leave anything of yours behind."

He walked into his former room without waiting for a reply. A moment later he heard his sister's happy voice call out, "I found my spare charger. I've been looking all over for it. Oh and here are my gloves."

Meanwhile Peter was standing on his bed and had his head and arms up in the ceiling. He reached on top of the heating duct and felt around for his metal box. The box contained his emergency fund of three thousand dollars as well as a couple old baseball cards and coins. He also had his banking information along with his and his sister's passports, birth certificates, and social security cards. His father didn't even know they had passports, but Peter had gotten them in case they ever needed to run away from him. The last item in his little box was an old picture of his mom holding him and Dani at the beach. He emerged from his room with his box to see Dani standing there with a small pile of things Peter had missed when he hastily packed up her stuff.

On top of her charger and gloves, she had four books, a scarf, and some miscellaneous art supplies. She was looking at her belongings as she spoke. "Not bad, Peter, this is all you missed. Can we put it in your backpack? Where are we going next? Do you want to drop this stuff off at the Jenkins?" She suddenly looked up and saw his box. "What's that, Peter?" She had now seemingly lost interest in her own belongings.

"Just a few important things," he replied.

"Like?" She held her hands out in an expectant gesture.

He sighed, knowing there was no dodging this without an argument, so he opened the box. "I've saved up some money and it's in here. I have a couple old baseball cards and silver dollars and our passports..."

"You actually got us passports— how?"

"I forged dad's signature on the documents."

"Peter!"

"What? The whole point of us having these was so we could get away if we needed to. If dad knew about it that would have defeated the whole purpose."

"You're right, I'm sorry. What else is in there?"

"Just my bank info, our birth certificates, and an old picture of mom holding us when we were little."

"Can I see it?" Her eyes lit up as she held out her hand. He handed it to her and she smiled. She looked at it in wonder and then she took out her phone and snapped a picture of it. "Peter, this is amazing. It must have been one of the last pictures she ever took."

"It was," he replied. She could see the guilt in his eyes.

"I remember mom coming home from the one-hour photo and showing me the pictures of our family trip to the beach. They always used to give two of every picture, and for some reason I really liked this one. I asked her if I could have it. She said yes, and she put it in a frame next to my bed. She died a few weeks after that and when dad went through the house getting rid of everything that reminded him of her, I hid the picture. Ever since, I've only looked at it in secret. I was afraid that if you knew about it, you might accidentally tell dad and he would take it away from me. Eventually, I stopped looking at it and just kept it hidden because it was a constant reminder to me that she was dead because of me."

"Peter, you know that's not true."

"Yes it is, Dani, maybe I'm starting to realize that it wasn't my fault—"

"It wasn't," she interrupted.

"But the fact is that she still died saving my life. Dani, why didn't I listen? Why did I have to run out in the street?" His emotions had crept up on him and he was on the verge of tears.

She just hugged him and replied, "I don't know, Peter, but it's not your fault."

"We better get out of here, in case dad found someone else to get him out of jail."

"Okay, but first I want to show you something." She opened one of her books and there was money stashed in between several of the pages. "You aren't the only one with an emergency fund. I saved up two hundred and fifty dollars." She smiled up at him and he could see how proud of herself she was.

"Looks like we both had the same idea. I guess great minds do think alike. I need to stop at the store and pick up a new phone; mine is kind of broken." She looked at him but didn't say anything. He took her pile and his box, and packed everything into his backpack before they left. They walked to Austin's first, so he wouldn't be carrying that much cash and those important documents around the neighborhood. He now had five thousand dollars hidden in Austin's house and decided he might skip first period to make sure he got it all into the bank on Monday morning.

A little while later, Danielle received a call from Mrs. Jenkins letting her know dinner would be ready in a half hour, so she and Peter began walking back towards Laura's house. "Peter, you don't have to walk me the whole way, you should take it easy on those ribs."

"I know, but I just want to make sure you're safe."

After they arrived at Laura's, Peter was saying goodbye when Mrs. Jenkins opened the door and said, "Peter, why don't you stay for dinner."

"Thanks, Mrs. J, but I don't want to impose."

"Oh please, we have more than enough, come on." She waved him in and Dani looked up at him with pleading eyes.

"Come on, Petey, please stay."

"All right, I'll stay. Thanks, Mrs. J." They walked into the house and Peter was surprised to see Hailey there as well. Now he was happy he stayed, even as he chastised himself for the thought. *I'm not gonna do anything to hurt my best friend,* he reminded himself.

"Hey Peter, glad you could join us for dinner. My parents are finally having their anniversary dinner, so I got dumped off with the cousins," Hailey said as she greeted Peter with a hug. "Are you going to the victory party tonight at Mark's?"

"I'm not sure, Hailey. I haven't been to one all year because of my job. Maybe I'll check it out tonight."

"I've only been to a couple, and I don't usually stay late because of church. Do you want to walk over together after dinner?" She looked at him with hopeful eyes and he wondered if there was more to this than just showing up at a party together.

"Yea, sure, that would be cool. What do you say, Dani, do you want to go to the party with us?" He looked to see if there was any disappointment on Hailey's face when he invited his sister and there wasn't, so he felt a little better. Now, he just had to get Austin here somehow.

"No thanks," she replied. "I'm going to show Laura and Mrs. J how to make origami with the artwork already on it."

"Sounds fun," he replied, while making a face that said it was anything but. He turned back to Hailey and added, "Looks like it's just us, is Toni Ann coming?"

"No, she's going with Austin."

He doubted he did a very good job at hiding his shock as he replied, "Really?"

"Yeah, he asked her out today and she said yes. He's been going to youth group and that's her parents' rule. If she's going to date, she has to date someone in youth group. She's had a big crush on him for a long time, so I guess I'm happy for her."

Peter could see some apprehension there, so he replied, "I'll make sure he doesn't hurt her, but now I have to go call him." The news had blindsided him and he wondered why his friend hadn't told him of his sudden change of heart. He walked out onto the porch and waited for Austin to pick up the phone. When he finally answered, Peter began without preamble, "Dude, when did you start liking Toni Ann?"

"How do you know about that, it just happened?"

"I walked my sister to back to Laura's house and they invited me to stay for dinner—"

"Right, and Hailey is there today," he finished his friend's sentence. "I was talking to Ted and he told me Hailey has a big crush on someone else, and that Toni Ann has always had a crush on me."

"Yeah, but you've liked Hailey for a long time, bro. You can get over it that easy?"

"Yeah, we both know I was never going to ask her out and Toni Ann is super-hot, too, so…"

Peter started laughing into the phone, "You amaze me sometimes."

"Plus, I'm really starting to get into this youth-group-God stuff; I actually like it."

"That's cool, I guess," he replied, afraid he might be losing his friend. "As long as you don't expect the same from me. Don't get me wrong, these are some really nice people, and they've stepped up and helped me and Dani a lot, but I'm not ready to join the club."

"We all make our own choices, man. Are you coming to the party tonight? I know you're not working."

"Yeah, that's actually why I called. Hailey wants me to walk her to the party and I was calling to get you up here to walk with us, but I guess there's no need now."

"Nope, have fun, but I don't think she'll date someone that's not a Christian. Ted said that, too."

"Well, I guess it's a good thing I'm not planning on dating her then. And when did you get so tight with Ted and the other church kids?"

"They're pretty cool and, come on, it's not like football players hanging out with basketball players and cheerleaders is some big social taboo."

"You got me there. Dinner is about ready, so I gotta go. I'll see you at the party." He hung up and stepped back inside. He walked into the dining room expecting to see en empty seat next to his sister, but instead, the empty seat was next to Hailey. He looked over to see Dani and Laura smiling and knew he'd been set up. He took his seat without a word and after a moment everyone bowed heads.

Peter wasn't sure what was happening, but Hailey nudged his arm and motioned for him to bow his head. Mr. Jenkins said grace and, when he was done, Mrs. Jenkins began placing servings of chicken and rice on each plate.

The confusion must have been evident on his face because Mr. Jenkins looked at him and said, "We like to say a prayer to thank God for the food He's provided before we eat,"

Peter tried to play it off like it was no big deal, and replied, "That's cool."

When dinner was over, he thanked the Jenkins family before leaving with Hailey to go to the team's latest celebration. While they were walking Hailey looked at him and said, "I heard you got into a big fight with your dad on the phone during halftime."

He wasn't surprised; it was very public and the whole team heard it. "Yeah, I guess now I know why coach doesn't allow phones in the locker room," he joked.

She wasn't fooled by the bluster. "Peter, is everything all right?"

He knew she knew more than he would like, so he figured she might be the one person besides Dani and Austin he could tell. "I don't know how much of our story you know, but my dad and I do not get along. We pretty much hate each other. And since I found out he's been hitting Dani all this time, I really hate him. He called and actually had the nerve to think I'd bail him out of jail, and it just set me off. I couldn't stop myself. I blew up at him in front of the whole team." They continued walking down the tree-lined street, the November wind had picked up and a chill swept through him.

Hailey stopped and took his hand. He wasn't sure why she did, but he liked it. "Peter, I know you don't want to hear this, but you have to forgive him. I know Dani is trying, but it might be easier for her if you did, too."

"Why, Hailey? Why should I waste a second trying to forgive that man? He's done nothing but tell me he hates me for what happened to my mom my whole life. He's made me feel worthless and, worst of all, he's been hitting Dani! Not just once or twice either. I heard the nurse tell the cop it's been going on for years. To me, that's more unforgivable than anything he's ever done to me. How do you do that to your own daughter? How could anyone hit Dani? She's the one truly good person I know"

"Your sister is an amazing person. She's the reason Laura is even still in school. If Danielle hadn't stood up for her to those other girls and befriended her, my aunt and uncle were going to home school her because she came home in tears every day." She looked up at him and sighed, "Believe me, my whole family knows what a good person Danielle is. I can't even begin to imagine how someone could beat her up, especially her own father."

"So how do I forgive that? And please don't say, 'God', because you know I don't believe in that stuff."

"What do you believe in, Peter?" Hailey asked as they continued walking. They turned left onto a street lined with one-story houses and almost no trees.

"I don't really know. There might be a god or something out there that made us, or it could have happened like they say in science class, but I don't believe there's any cosmic big guy looking out for me 'cause, if there is, he dropped the ball."

Hailey understood why he felt that way, but it was still hard for her to hear. She liked him, but she didn't want to date someone who didn't believe in God. She pushed those thoughts aside and she tried to encourage him. "I'm not going to try and talk you into becoming a Christian, Peter, but you can still forgive your dad."

"I'm sorry, Hailey, I just don't think I can."

"Peter, forgiveness isn't just for the other person; it's for you, too. If you let that much hatred fill your heart it's eventually going to turn into bitterness and it poisons your life. It poisons your relationships; it ruins everything. Just look at your dad - do you want to end up like that, completely unable to love?"

"No way, I'll never be like that."

"You never think you will, but that's what hatred does. Your sister is really struggling with it right now. She puts on a brave face and a smile for you, but she's struggling. I just think it would be easier for her if she knew you were trying, too." They turned onto Mark's tree-lined street, so she knew the conversation was coming to a close.

"I'll think about it... and thanks, Hailey."

"For what?" They climbed the steps of the large brick house; the music was blaring and it sounded like there were a hundred kids inside.

"For looking out for my sister and not being too preachy to me."

She pulled open the screen door to Mark's house and replied, "You're welcome. Now let's have some fun." She smiled and then they entered the raucous house.

Chapter 9

The next morning, Austin went into the basement to wake Peter up. He was surprised to find that Peter was already awake.

"What's up, man?" Peter asked

"I was coming to check and see if you wanted to come to church? I didn't think you'd be awake so early after such a crazy party last night."

"I didn't stay that long. Hailey wanted to leave when things started getting crazy and asked me to walk her home. Then I came back here and fell asleep early." He shrugged and picked up his iPod.

"So are you two—"

"Still not interested," Peter replied before Austin could even finish the question. "I mean, she's obviously beautiful, and she's really nice—"

"But?" This time it was Austin's turn to interrupt.

"But she's really into this God stuff and I'm not. I get the feeling it's a big deal to her, so I'm gonna respect that."

"That's cool," Austin replied. "So, are you coming to church or not?"

"You know what? I think I will. I know it will make Dani happy and I haven't had any of the Sunday Kool-Aid yet. I guess it's time to try a different flavor." They both laughed, but Austin was relieved he didn't have to show up there alone.

*****

Peter and Austin walked up the front steps of Clove Lakes Bible Church for the first time. Up until this point, they had only come in through the side door. Peter had never even seen the sanctuary. A kind, older woman with a big smile greeted them at the top of the stairs. She handed them a flyer with the church name on it just before Peter was almost tackled by his sister.

"Dani, ribs," he grunted. Her eyes grew wide when she realized her mistake.

"I'm sorry, Petey, I was just so excited that you were here. Why didn't you tell me you were coming?" Her smile was infectious and she intertwined her arm with his.

"I didn't know I was until Austin asked me this morning." Austin smiled and Danielle nodded her thanks.

"Well, there's that Dani Donovan smile we all love so much," Nate said, as he shook Peter's hand and gave Danielle his standard side hug.

"Hi, Nate," Danielle returned the greeting. "I'm smiling because I didn't know Peter was coming and I'm happy he's here." She turned back to Peter and said, "Let's go get seats with our friends." She led him to a row near the back of the church where Laura, Ted, Toni Ann, and Hailey were already seated. Austin slid in next to Toni Ann and Danielle sat down next to Hailey, leaving the end for Peter, in case he needed to take a phone call.

Hailey hugged Danielle and then leaned over to whisper in Peter's ear. "Hey, thanks for walking me home last night. I know that you almost never get to go to the parties and I hated asking you to leave early."

"It was no problem. It was getting a bit too loud for me anyway. Plus, I really should be resting these ribs. I really want to play next week."

"We all want you to play next week," Danielle added with a smile.

"I'm still getting waffles, right?" Peter asked with a grin.

"Of course you are," she replied, and then went on to explain the waffle tradition to Hailey. Just then the music started and people began singing.

Peter and Austin felt as lost as they had during that first Friday night. There was so much they didn't know about how things were done at church. Peter felt like everyone was looking at him when he didn't stand at the right time or sit at the right time. Finally, the up-and-down seemed to stop when Pastor John climbed the three steps onto the stage and started to preach. Peter decided he was going to try to listen more closely to see what was so special about what these people believed. Pastor John stood next to his wooden podium and spoke to the congregation.

"Today we're going to talk about Jesus calling the first disciples. Turn with me in your Bibles to Luke chapter five; we'll begin with verse one." Peter noticed a lot of people turning pages in their Bible and then Pastor John began to read.

"One day as Jesus was standing by the Lake of Gennesaret, with the people crowding around him and listening to the word of God, he saw at the water's edge two boats, left there by the fishermen, who were washing their nets. He got into one of the boats, the one belonging to Simon, and asked him to put out a little from shore. Then he sat down and taught the people from the boat.

When he had finished speaking, he said to Simon, "'Put out into deep water, and let down the nets for a catch.'"

Simon answered, "'Master, we've worked hard all night and haven't caught anything. But because you say so, I will let down the nets.'" When they had done so, they caught such a large number of fish that their nets began to break. So they signaled their partners in the other boat to come and help them, and they came and filled both boats so full that they began to sink."

Pastor John continued, "When Simon Peter saw this, he fell at Jesus' knees and said, "'Go away from me, Lord; I am a sinful man!'" For he and all his companions were astonished at the catch of fish they had taken, and so were James and John, the sons of Zebedee, Simon's partners. Then Jesus said to Simon, "'Don't be afraid; from now on you will catch men.'" So they pulled their boats up on shore, left everything and followed him."

The pastor closed his Bible and paused before speaking again.

"Let me give you a little context here. At this point, Jesus is an unknown. He's teaching the people, and whatever he's saying is drawing a crowd. Peter, James, and John notice this crowd when they are bringing their boats ashore after working all night. They are probably even wondering what's going on and then suddenly, Peter is a part of it. Jesus asks him to cast off with him aboard so he could teach the people, and he does. Remember, no one even really knows who Jesus is at this point.

He finishes teaching the people and then gives Peter some fishing advice. I'm surprised Peter even listened to him, but he did and he was rewarded when he caught more fish than he could carry. James and John came out to help him. They get back to shore and then they leave it all behind to follow Jesus. These are regular guys with jobs, who just made the catch of their lives. Those boatloads of fish represented a lot of money for them, and they just left it, all of it. Why? Why would grown men leave a fat paycheck, not to mention all of their other responsibilities, to follow a man they barely knew? I think it's because there is something attractive about Jesus. People wanted to be around him, people followed him to be close. There was something about Jesus that attracted a crowd—"

Peter's phone went off and he was thankful he had set it to silent. He stood and walked out of the church and then answered his phone. He felt bad leaving, but he knew better than to miss a call from Mr. Barbarelli. He took a deep breath and said, "Hey, Boss. What's up?"

"Peter, I need you to come to the restaurant tonight, we gotta talk," Barbarelli replied.

"Sure, Mr. Barbarelli, what time do you want me to come by?"

"Come down at eight o'clock, and Donovan— don't be late."

Peter didn't like the sound of that, but still he replied, "Yes, sir." The call ended and Peter sat on the church steps wondering what the meeting would hold for him. He was so lost in thought he didn't even notice Nate sit down next to him.

"Is everything all right, Peter?" Nate asked

"I just got a call from my boss and it seemed a bit weird. I'm not sure what to make of it."

"Have you given any thought to quitting?"

"I have. It's pretty much all I think about since the um... mugging. I'm just not sure how. I know Mr. Barbarelli is not exactly an upstanding citizen, but he's always been good to me. He remembers my birthday, he buys me things to give as gifts to Dani and he pays me well. I know he expects a lot in return, but it's always been a fair deal, you know?"

"Not really, Peter. I never had to provide for my family when I was in high school, I didn't have a dad like yours. I can't imagine the pressure you've been under and the things you've had to go through while taking care of your sister. But the thing is, if you stay at this job, you're not only putting your own life at risk, you're putting your sister's life at risk, too. I know you don't want that."

"You're right, Nate, I'm just not sure Barbarelli is gonna let me go. Still, I have to talk to him."

"I know this isn't easy, but you're making the right choice. Do you want me to come with you?"

Peter's eyes grew wide and he looked right at Nate. "No way! I honestly don't know what he would do to either of us if he thought I was talking about his business with you. I'll handle it. Thanks, though." They sat out on the steps until the service was over. As the people were making their way to their cars, Danielle and Austin came out the front of the church looking for Peter. They were relieved to see him talking to Nate.

"Peter, what happened? Are you okay?" Danielle asked, worry evident in her voice.

"I'm fine, Dani. I just got a call from my boss. He wants me to come in at eight o'clock tonight."

"Do you want some company?"

"What? No way, Dani; promise me you won't come near the restaurant. I'm quitting tonight and that'll be the end of it, but I need to know you'll be safe." Peter thought he felt his heart skip a beat when his sister mentioned coming with him. He would never forgive himself if anything happened to Danielle as a result of his association with Barbarelli and his people.

"Fine, okay, I won't come. Just promise you won't be long. I don't want them to rope you back in."

"I'll keep it as short as I can," Peter promised.

"All right, I'm going to go out for a girls day with Hailey, Toni Ann, and Laura, but come see me after you finish at work. I just want to make sure you're okay before I go to sleep."

Peter tried to hide his smile because he didn't want Dani to think he was laughing at her, he just thought it was funny that she would be the one trying to protect him. "Do you want me to tuck you in, too?" he joked. He noticed her frown and added, "I'm just kidding. Of course I'll come see you after work."

"And don't worry about him today," Austin began. "He'll be hanging with me, Ted, and Nate."

"I will?" Peter asked more than said.

"Yep, Ted found a new burger joint we gotta try. Nate's driving and you're coming with us." Peter looked around at his sister and their friends. He never would have thought a kid like him would be hanging out with religious people. At least they were nice, and with Austin coming he wasn't expecting it to be too bad.

"All right, but I gotta be at work by eight," he replied. Danielle gave him a hug, careful not to squeeze his ribs, and then she took off with the girls.

*****

Gravano knew it was now or never. He was driving into New Jersey to see Don Catalano. He was going to have to explain his actions regarding the Donovan kid. If he made it through that conversation unscathed, that would mean there was an opening. He knew his plan for Barbarelli's part of the business would get the Don excited. He only needed to get Barbarelli out of the way first.

He pulled up to the gate of Don Catalano's home in his candy apple red 1941 Buick Fastback Coup. He knew the Don loved the old classic cars of the forties and fifties, and the Coup was one of his favorites. Gravano had found out about the Don's love of forties Coups almost fifteen years earlier, and immediately began searching for one to restore. This one still had the original body, tires, interior, and leather seats. He had given it a paint job, matching the original color exactly, and he had updated or restored all of the chrome. This car was a work of art, and he hoped that seeing it would put the Don in a good mood. He would even give it to him if he needed to, as long as he got what he wanted.

One of the armed guards opened the gate, allowing Gravano to drive through. By the time he had navigated the winding, tree-lined driveway, the Don was out on the front steps of his palatial estate. One of his men must have mentioned the car. *So far, so good,* Gravano thought. He put the car in park and stepped out to greet the Don. "Good afternoon, Don Catalano."

"Salvatore," Catalano replied. He smiled widely and embraced him, kissing each cheek and then unwinding from the embrace. "This is some car— a 1941 Buick Fastback Coup. I've never seen one this pristine. Is it all original?"

"For the most part; I've updated some of the chrome, and gave her a paint job, but other than that, she's entirely 1941."

"How did you come about such a beauty? I've been looking for one for years." He bent low and ran his hand along the curve of the protruding fender.

"One of my hobbies is restoring classic cars. I bought this from an estate sale almost seven years ago and have been fixing her up since. Finding original parts for a forty-one is not easy, but some things are worth the wait."

"I agree, Salvatore." He leaned into the open window and admired the craftsmanship of the interior. "My parents had one of these when I was a boy. My father loved it and kept it throughout my childhood and into my twenties before he finally bought something newer." He paused and straightened up. "This really brings back the memories. Now, enough about an old man's childhood, let's go inside and talk business."

A few short moments later, they were seated in the living room and a maid was bringing them coffee. Gravano looked around the room. The walls were a light peach framed by white crown molding on three walls. The fourth wall was red brick, and dominated by a fireplace. Each of the peach walls held an expensive work of art. The Don's art collection was legendary and was rumored to contain a Rembrandt and a Monet. They were both sitting on the deep red couch facing the fireplace and it seemed as though the Don was waiting for him to begin.

He knew why he had been called there, so he decided he should address it first. "So you heard about Barbarelli's delivery boy."

"Salvatore, what were you thinking? If Barbarelli hadn't had the good sense to keep his boy quiet, you could have been brought up on charges,"

"Third degree battery at best, Don. I wouldn't have even seen the inside of a cell."

"Or attempted murder, if your sons and their clown friends' antics were connected to you, but that's not the point." He took a deep breath before continuing. "The point is it gives the cops license to come into your home, look through your life, and shine a light on our organization that I don't want shining. We are under enough scrutiny as it is. I don't want my top guys under the microscope for a stupid feud they cannot resolve."

"I gotta tell you, Don, Barbarelli needs to go. He's going soft and he's unreasonable. He's ready to go to war over an Irish delivery kid. He needs to be taken out." An angry look crossed Don Catalano's face and Gravano wondered if he had pushed too far, too fast.

"You're suggesting I let you take out a man I've been working with for over forty years because of his affinity for those in his employ?"

"No, Don, I'm just—"

"I know what you were suggesting. I may be old, but I'm not stupid. He told me he thinks you're reckless, and I can see some truth in those words, but he never suggested taking you out." He fixed Gravano with a glare that could melt ice and Gravano lowered his head under his boss's gaze. He thought he had just made the biggest mistake of his career until he heard Catalano's next words. "Still, you may not be wrong." He took a sip of his coffee and appeared to be lost in thought,

Gravano saw an opening and decided to take a chance. "I'm sorry, Boss, but what do you mean, I may not be wrong?"

"You're not the first to mention that Barbarelli is going soft, you're not even the second." He took another sip of his coffee and continued. "I do worry that if the authorities get any dirt on him it might hurt us all. Still, taking him out would bring too much unwanted attention."

"Not if we make it look like the DeAngelo family did it."

"I assume you already have a plan."

"Yes, sir, I do." Gravano spent the next ten minutes outlining his plan.

When Gravano finished speaking, Don Catalano fixed him with another intense gaze and asked. "What is your plan for Barbarelli's segment of our family business?"

Without hesitation, Gravano detailed his vision for Barbarelli's holdings. He had practiced this speech a hundred times, never thinking he would be in a position to give it. "Under my leadership, I would take Barbarelli's import and distribution network and expand it to an import / export business. Sure import is thriving, but there are many useful resources we've got here that could net us quite a gain elsewhere. We would double our profits within the first year."

Catalano was intrigued and motioned for him to continue. Gravano then spent the next twenty minutes going over every detail of how he would make Barbarelli's business thrive, and just when he was feeling really good about the whole situation, the Don interrupted him.

"I know I don't need to tell you this, but I think I'm going to anyway." He leaned forward and said in almost a whisper, "I will not tell you that you cannot carry out your plan. But you need to know, if you decide to proceed, it has to be by your hand. I need to know you can do it. Then, if something goes wrong, you have only yourself to blame. Just remember, if you are implicated in any way, you are on your own. And if I even get a hint that you will make a deal that hurts this organization, I will see to it that you and your entire family are wiped out. Do you understand me?"

Gravano let his boss's words sit for a moment, sinking in as he suppressed a shudder. "I understand, Don Catalano. This will not come back on you in any way."

"Remember, you may have permission, but I am not complicit in this in any way! Got it?"

"Yes, sir." They both stood and the maid showed him out. While he sauntered to his classic car he decided it would be a gift to the Don after he had taken over all of Barbarelli's operations. Then he would find another oldie and begin the restoration process again. He found himself whistling as he opened the door of his Coup and sat on the seventy-three year old leather. He started the car and drove back through the winding driveway. He made a note that the boss was looking at the car through the window as he left.

*****

Later as the girls were on their way home, they were about to pass the restaurant Peter worked at when Danielle got an idea. "Hey, Hailey, drop me off here, would ya? I want to walk home with Peter when he's finished quitting."

"Are you sure, Danielle? What if it takes him longer than he thought?"

"Then I'll eat a couple slices of pizza and wait. I just miss him. I'm used to seeing him every night before bed and walking to school with him in the morning, but now I don't see him as much."

"He said he didn't want you to come down. Are you sure he won't mind?"

"Of course, he won't mind. It'll be no trouble, trust me." By the time Hailey pulled over, they were about a block past the restaurant. Danielle got out of the car, leaned in the window, and said, "I'll see you guys in school tomorrow."

She waved and then began walking towards the restaurant as Hailey drove away. She zipped her jacket up against the chill of the late November air; she wished she had a hat with her. As the cars passed by one after another in the endless stream of traffic that Victory Boulevard produced, she noticed Peter walking from the other direction. "Hey, Peter," she called out, waving when he looked at her. She jogged over to hug him.

"Dani, what are you doing here? You can't be here," He said as he looked into the restaurant.

"Peter, what are you talking about? I came to walk home with you, I miss you. I'll just get a slice and wait for you while you talk to your boss."

"Dani, you need to go, it isn't safe. There are some bad guys here, and I'm quitting tonight, so they might be upset. How did you even get here?"

"Um, Hailey dropped me off. Peter, you're scaring me— what bad guys? What are you talking about?"

"I can't talk about it now. I promise, I'm not one of the bad guys, and I promise I'll explain the rest later, but you have to go. Please, call Hailey back here." Just then, Peter stiffened when he saw Gravano and his two sons enter through the back of the restaurant with several other men. He was pretty sure they hadn't seen him, but now he really needed to get Dani out of there. "Please, Dani, call Hailey back right now. This is gonna be bad."

Chapter 10

Gravano strode with confidence into Barbarelli's restaurant where, the smell of marinara sauce filled the air. The cook looked a little startled to see someone entering the restaurant through the kitchen, but Paulie and Matthew's guns kept him from asking any questions. He did wonder what happened to the two men Barbarelli usually had standing guard at the back door.

It's time to settle things once and for all, Gravano thought with a wicked smile. Paulie and Matthew stood in the back with the other men waiting for their father's signal to come, which they knew would come soon enough.

Gravano sauntered into the dining area where Barbarelli and Michael had sat down to eat some linguini and meatballs. *A fitting last meal,* he thought as Michael stood up. Gravano's draw was fast. He put two in Michael's chest, spraying the meal with blood and sending him through the decorative plate glass window. Paulie and Matthew were quickly inside firing and taking down Barbarelli's other three men. Even the cooks had been killed. Barbarelli hadn't even had the opportunity to stand up and draw his weapon, and now he was seated with six armed men standing in front of him intent on killing him.

"So, it's come to this, has it, Gravano?"

"Yes, it has, old man. Your time is up. You don't have what it takes to lead your part of the organization anymore. It's time we went in a new direction."

"Oh, and you think you do have what it takes to lead this organization?" Barbarelli replied. "You're never gonna get away with this. My people will hunt you down like the dog you are. Then they're gonna make you watch while they kill your two boys before they kill you. You've got one chance to live, Gravano, leave now and my people won't kill you." He poured every ounce of bluster and intimidation he had into that comment. He was playing for more time hoping his people or even the police would show up. He wasn't ready to die and he sadly mused that everyone he was close with wasn't going to be far behind. All he could see was his bodyguard and friend bleeding on the pavement and his beloved restaurant covered in blood.

"You think I don't have what it takes? I beat you, didn't I? And don't worry about your people, they'll fall in line or they'll get thrown in the river."

113

Gravano raised his gun again and emptied the magazine into Barbarelli's chest. Blood sprayed the wall behind Barbarelli as his lifeless body fell off the chair to the ground. Gravano stepped forward and spit on Barbarelli when he heard a scream from outside the restaurant.

*****

Danielle pulled out her phone to call Hailey to come back, but she was so upset she could barely dial. She had just found out that her brother was working with some bad guys and she didn't know why, but it bothered her— a lot. "It went straight to voicemail, Peter."

"Try again, or call Laura, she was in the car, right?" He could see how frazzled she was, so he added. "It's gonna be all right, Dani. I'm not a bad guy, I promise. I just delivered packages."

"When you got mugged, was that because of these bad guys?" she asked, but he suspected she already knew the answer.

"Yeah, it was, that's when my eyes were really opened and that's why I was coming here to quit tonight. You can even ask Nate, I told him this morning. But I really need you to go, because the guy that beat me up just went in to the restaurant with his sons."

Before Danielle could reply, they heard several gunshots coming from inside the restaurant. Bright flashes flared through the restaurant windows and, a moment later, Michael came flying through the decorative window with a bleeding hole in his chest. Peter took out his phone to dial 911, but then froze when he saw who was holding the gun. Peter and Danielle looked into the restaurant in time to see Gravano standing in front of a seated Barbarelli. Peter started filming with his phone when, all of a sudden, Gravano pulled the trigger and killed Peter's boss. He went on to empty the entire magazine into Barbarelli, and Danielle screamed. Gravano looked out the window when he heard the scream and yelled, "Paulie, Matthew, someone's outside."

Peter turned white at the sound of Gravano's voice. He looked at Danielle, and she looked like she was having a panic attack. He didn't have time to be gentle, so he put his phone away, grabbed both her shoulders, shook her, and he said, "Dani, we have to run!" She didn't move and he thought he saw a tear running down her face, so he shook her a little harder and yelled, "Dani, run!"

He took off, grabbing her hand and pulling her with him, snapping her out of her momentary shock.. They rounded the corner and ran across the street. They cut through someone's yard and onto the next street. They hid in some bushes and watched as Paulie and Matthew stalked around in search of them. Then they heard sirens and Gravano pulled around the corner and yelled for his sons to jump in the car.

Peter's heart dropped when he heard Matthew say, "It was that delivery kid you beat up, and he had some girl with him." They sped off in Gravano's charcoal Jaguar, leaving the bloody chaos behind.

Peter let his breath out; at least they were safe for now. He knew they had to get out of town fast, so he looked at his terrified sister and said, in as kind a voice as he could muster, "We've gotta go right now, Dani. They saw us and they know we saw them." They started walking as the first police cars were entering the parking lot of Barbarelli's Restaurant.

Just then, Danielle's phone chimed. The unexpected noise almost made her jump out of her skin. She hit the receive button and in a shaky voice answered, "Hello?"

"Hey Danielle, It's Hailey, I saw I missed a couple calls from you, is everything all right?"

"Um, not really," she started to break down, so Peter took the phone from her.

"Hey, Hailey, we ran into a bit of trouble, do you think you can pick us up at Austin's? I have to stop there and then we have to stop at Laura's for a minute. After that, I'm gonna need a big favor."

"Peter, what's going on? Are you guys in some sort of trouble?"

"Yeah, but we can't talk about it. Trust me; it's safer for you if you don't know. Please, hurry though, we don't have much time." They continued walking towards Austin's house, and Danielle was still really shaken up.

"What have you gotten Danielle into, Peter?" Hailey asked.

"I didn't get her into anything, we just witnessed a crime, and that's really all I want to tell you. You're safer if you don't know, trust me." A few minutes later, Hailey pulled up to Austin's. Peter was thorough in checking both directions before he and Danielle emerged from the bushes. She took off for the car and he went inside Austin's house. "Thanks so much for this, Hailey. I think we're in big trouble."

Hailey kept the car running in front of Austin's house while Peter was inside. He was thankful no one was home. He ran into the basement where he had been staying, packed a backpack with some clothes, toiletries, their important documents, and the picture of their mom. He changed his clothes putting on jeans with a navy blue zip up hoodie, navy blue sneakers, and his brown leather jacket. It was as nondescript an outfit as he could think of. He was thankful he hadn't had the chance to deposit his money in the bank, because he knew they would need it if they had to go on the run. He grabbed his money and the necklace Barbarelli had given to him for Dani, and put them in his jacket pocket with his iPod. Then he went into Austin's room and put his expensive baseball cards and silver dollars on his friend's bed along with a note thanking him for letting him crash there and then he was out the door. The whole stop took about five minutes. He knew it would take longer at Laura's house because he would have to explain what happened to Laura's parents.

When he rushed to the car, Hailey's face was white and he knew that she knew. "You saw those men get murdered, didn't you?" He looked to Danielle who was still in tears, but Hailey continued. "She didn't tell me, it was just on the radio. Peter, what are you going to do?"

"I don't know, we gotta get Danielle's stuff and then we're gonna go to the police."

"The police? Why don't you just go to them now? Go right back to the restaurant."

"Yeah, but we need to be ready to run in case the mob owns them, that's why we need our stuff, and we'll go down to the 120 precinct, because the guys that killed my boss will probably be expecting us to show up at the restaurant or at the 121. Plus, if things don't look good, we can always just jump on the Ferry and get lost in the city."

They pulled up in front of Laura's house and all three of them went inside. "Dani, just pack a couple outfits, some toiletries, whatever money you have, and your iPad. We might not be back for a while. And, Dani, don't wear anything too noticeable." While Danielle did as Peter asked, he told Mr. and Mrs. Jenkins what they had seen. Laura ran up the stairs in tears, hoping everything would be all right with her best friend, while Peter and Hailey sat with the Jenkins.

116

"Dani and I just witnessed a murder at my restaurant and we're gonna have to be ready to run. I don't want her here because then you guys will be in danger."

"I think you're jumping the gun a bit here, Peter," Mr. Jenkins replied. "Why don't we all just go down to the police station and see how it plays out?"

"We can't, Mr. J, Barbarelli was a mobster and not only can I identify the guy that killed him. I know he's in the mob, too. If you guys or Hailey are anywhere near this, you'll be in a lot of danger." Peter was shaking slightly and Hailey grabbed his hand. He barely noticed as he looked across the table at the kind people that had taken his sister in, no questions asked.

"Peter, it's never as bad as we think it is. We just have to trust—"

"It's worse, Mrs. J," Peter hated to interrupt and wasn't even sure he should finish the comment. These people were nice and they didn't deserve what he had brought down on them, neither did Dani. He started to tear up as he continued. "It's worse because the guy that murdered Mr. Barbarelli is the guy that beat me up a couple weeks ago. He already hates me and now he knows me and Dani saw him pull the trigger. He probably would have tried to kill me anyway, but there's nothing he won't do to kill me now." He started crying and added, "Now Dani's in danger, too, and it's all my fault."

"Peter, did you know these men were criminals while you were working for them?" Mr. Jenkins asked. He was starting to understand how much danger his own family could be in and he was getting scared.

"I knew they were shady, but I needed the money to support Dani. I didn't really know they were bad, bad until I got beat up and my boss paid me two grand to keep it quiet. I talked to Nate about it, and I was going there to quit tonight. I just don't understand why Dani followed me. I wish she wouldn't have followed me." He was trying to hold it together, but he realized that his decision to work for someone he knew was shady had just ruined his sister's life.

"It's my fault she was there," Hailey admitted. "She wanted to surprise you and walk home with you. She asked me to drop her off and I didn't want to at first, but she talked me into it. I didn't know you worked at a bad place, Peter. I'm sorry." Now it was Hailey that was in tears.

"I wish you wouldn't have dropped her off, Hailey, but it's not your fault, it's mine. That's why we need to go. I can't have any of you getting hurt because of me. If you could just give us a ride to the ferry, I think we'll go into Manhattan and talk to the police there."

"What about the station down by the ferry?" Hailey asked, wondering about the change.

"No, it's a small Island, I'm not sure even that precinct will be safe."

"Peter's right. They need to go and they need to go now. Our family will be in danger if these criminals think we know anything." Mr. Jenkins stood up and added, "Hailey, go get Laura and Danielle. We're going to pray and then I'm going to take Peter and Danielle into Manhattan." Peter looked like he was going to object, but Mr. Jenkins waved him off. "It's much safer than the ferry, and you know it."

Danielle was crying while she packed her backpack. She didn't want to put too much in because she knew she was going to have to carry it around for a while. She couldn't believe what she had just witnessed. She continued to cry, and Laura continued to try to console her.

"Why does all of this stuff keep happening to me, Laura?" Danielle managed to say in between sobs. She was carefully putting her clothes in her backpack, making sure she had everything she needed.

"I don't know, Danielle, just don't lose faith. God has a plan I promise." She knew it sounded hollow even as she said it, but it was all she could come up with and it was true. She was on the verge of tears herself at the thought of losing her best friend.

"I was finally in a place where I knew I could be happy. My dad couldn't beat me anymore. Peter didn't have to provide for me anymore." Thinking about her brother almost caused her to break down again. "He's gonna miss the rest of the playoffs, Laura. And this is all my fault. If I hadn't shown up unannounced, they would have never even known he was there. If I didn't scream, they wouldn't have known either of us were there," she began crying again as she put her iPad in the backpack and zipped it up.

"This is not your fault, Danielle, and Peter knows it." She hugged her best friend and, just then, looked over to see Hailey stand at the door.

"Danielle, you guys have to get going. Peter doesn't think it's safe for you guys to be here and my aunt and uncle agree."

"Mom and dad said that?" Laura asked in disbelief.

"Yeah, Laura, this is very serious. The guys after Peter and Dani just killed nine people in cold blood," Hailey replied.

Danielle checked her backpack one more time and then they all went downstairs. When they reached the living room, Mr. Jenkins began to pray.

"Father, we come before you right now and ask that you protect our friends Danielle and Peter from these evil men. Lord we pray you would give the police wisdom, and that our friends would be safe. Please thwart any attempts these men make to get to Peter and Danielle, and keep our family safe as well. I pray that through this situation, that Danielle and Peter would begin to see you in a new light and understand you in a deeper way. We pray these things in Jesus name, Amen." He opened his eyes and looked at Peter, "Okay, let's go," He grabbed his car keys and made his way to the door. Laura and Mrs. Jenkins both hugged Danielle tight, while all three of them cried.

"You come back to us safe, Danielle. Do you understand?" Mrs. Jenkins said as she continued to hug her and Laura tight. Peter could see some tears escaping Mrs. Jenkins's eyes and it killed him to think about what could happen to them because of him.

"I will. And thank you so much for everything."

Hailey went and hugged Peter. "Looks like I won't be tutoring you anymore," she tried to joke, but the tears were in her eyes, too. She held him tight and then looked up at him and kissed him. It was short, but unexpected and he questioned her with his eyes.

"What was that for?"

"I just always wanted to do that," she said, "and I knew I might not get another chance."

Peter started to say something, but then Mr. Jenkins rushed them out the door.

"Bye, Hailey, and tell Austin bye for me." Peter managed to call out as he and Danielle got into the car. When they drove off, they could see Mrs. Jenkins, Laura, and Hailey standing in the doorway until their car turned the corner.

Chapter 11

Gravano sent two of his men to the Donovan's apartment, while he and his sons got rid of their guns and clothes. Joey picked the lock and Anthony pulled his gun out, prepared to go in first. Joey heard the last tumbler give way and opened the door. Anthony didn't waste a second as he entered hoping to take the Donovans by surprise. It turned out the surprise was on him, because no one was home. Joey pulled out his phone and called Gravano.

"Are they there?" Gravano asked.

"No, Boss, it looks like they both moved out. Recently, too."

"What makes you say that, Joey?"

"All of the kids stuff is gone, but the pantry is stocked with stuff they would eat." He replied, as he went through the kitchen cabinets. He put the phone on speaker so Anthony could hear, too.

"Good catch, Joey, you're not completely useless after all."

"Thanks, Boss," he deadpanned while Anthony grinned at him.

"So where is their father? He'll know where they are."

"No Idea, Boss. He must be out," Anthony answered the rhetorical question.

Joey just looked at Anthony and frowned. "Yeah, we got that, genius, but out where? He'll be able to point us in the kids' direction."

"Actually, he won't," a voice called out from the hallway. Joey and Anthony put their guns away and the voice revealed itself to be a man in his early twenties. He looked like a stoner and they waited for him to continue.

"He was arrested Friday for drunk and disorderly, and he couldn't make bail, so he's in 'til Monday. Plus, he was arrested a couple weeks ago for beating his cute daughter and both the kids were put into foster care, no one knows where because the cops didn't want the father to be able to find them." He finished his explanation and walked into the kitchen. He began eating some cookies from the cupboard and Anthony had to stifle a laugh. Finally, as if the thought just hit him he asked, "Are you guys cops? Because any evidence of prior beatings is long gone, but for the right price I can be an informant and tell you about all the times I heard him beating her. The walls are pretty thin here."

Joey smiled and replied, "Yeah, we are cops, and your testimony might prove useful. The detective here is gonna give you his number," he said, pointing to Anthony. "Then, you're gonna give us a call if you see either of the kids, because we need to get their eyewitness testimony. We have to make sure they are safe from their father." He handed the stoned neighbor a fifty dollar bill and added," How does that sound?"

"I can do that, Detective," he replied, while shooting off a sloppy salute that almost had Anthony in tears.

"The NYPD thanks you, citizen," Joey added. "Please, lock up our crime scene when you're done eating our suspect's cookies." With that Gravano's men left and when they had exited the building, Anthony finally broke down in a fit of laughter.

"Lock up when you're done eating our suspect's cookies?" he said with a laugh. "That dude was so stoned, he's gonna eat everything in that apartment, ha-ha." By this time Joey had already begun walking towards the car. "Hey wait up," Anthony called and ran after him.

"That was a good idea paying him to call us if the kids show, Joey," Anthony said, as they got into their Jaguar. "It may turn out to be useful, especially since that moron thinks we're cops."

"It's a long shot, Anthony, but we gotta do everything we can to find these kids. They're the only ones that can point a finger at the boss, so we gotta put them in the ground."

"None of our sources in the 120 or 121 precincts have seen them yet. They might just be running away, Mr. Gravano." Joey said into the phone as Anthony put the car in drive and pulled away from the projects.

"I hope so, but I doubt it. That Peter kid already hates us, and he doesn't seem like the type to pass up some revenge. They'll turn up. I just gotta hope I got guys in place when they do. We've gotta get them before they get to some cops I can't control. Get everyone on this."

"Everyone, Boss?" Joey thought it was too much manpower to put into finding two kids who were probably too frightened to say anything.

"Yes, everyone! Trust me, we need them found! Now!" Gravano ended the call and returned to disposing of the incriminating evidence.

*****

As Mr. Jenkins drove over the Verrazano Bridge, Peter's phone rang. He saw it was Nate so he picked it up. "Hey, Nate, did you hear the news?"

He paused as Nate was slow to reply. "Yeah, I heard, what happened?"

"I was on my way in to quit, but then Dani showed up." He could see his sister's face and knew she blamed herself, so he added, "She surprised me because she wanted to walk me home and it's a good thing, too. She saved my life. If she didn't show up, I would have been in the restaurant and everyone in the restaurant was killed." He saw her face brighten a little as if she hadn't thought of that.

"What are you going to do? Are you heading down to the police station?"

"No, we're on our way out of town. I can't give you any more details than that for your own safety, and Dani and I are gonna have to turn our phones off, just in case." Danielle was already turning her phone off and he motioned for her to take out the battery as well. "Thanks for everything, Nate. Yeah, Dani would definitely like it if you prayed for us. Okay, I gotta go." He sent a quick text to Austin and then turned his phone off as well. He took the battery out of the phone and looked out the window. When they reached the Brooklyn Queens Expressway, Mr. Jenkins finally broke his silence.

"I'm really sorry this happened to you guys, and I hope you didn't think I was rushing you guys out of the house," he paused and added, "Okay, I kinda was, but only for my family's safety and yours. You understand that, right?"

"Yes, sir, I felt terrible even going to your house, but we needed to get some stuff for Dani. I understand, and I'm sorry I brought this trouble on you after you've been so great to my sister." He paused and looked over at Laura's dad as he drove. "Can I ask you a question?"

"Yeah, of course, Peter. What's on your mind?"

"When you prayed before, do you really think it worked? Do you really think God is gonna keep us safe?"

"Well, think about it." Mr. Jenkins replied, switching lanes to get around a slow-moving SUV. "We were in a situation where every second counted and we stopped to pray, so that should tell you something. Now, do I believe God is going to protect you just because we prayed for it? Yes, but also because He loves you. Now His protection might not wind up being what we imagine it might be, because God doesn't usually answer our prayers the way we think He will, and sometimes the answer is no. Sometimes we ask for something and it's not in his plan for us to have it, so he flat out tells us no. In those times, it's important for me to remember that God's plan is going to be far better than my plan even if I can't see or understand it. That's why it's called faith."

"What if I don't believe any of that stuff? Will God still care about Dani?"

"He cares for both of you, Peter, even if you don't believe." They were now crossing the Brooklyn Bridge, which would let them off at City Hall, and that would be the end of the line. When they arrived, he pulled the car over to let the passengers out.

"Thank you for driving us, Mr. J, and for... everything," Danielle said, as she got out of the car.

"Yeah, thank you, sir," Peter echoed. They shot him a quick wave as he drove off before descending into the subway where they would take the R train to Times Square.

Peter put his battery back in his phone when a thought hit him. *I'd better back up this recording just in case the cops erase it.* He hated to think the worst of everyone, but with the exception of Dani's church friends, he usually saw the worst from everyone. He emailed the video to his school email account and his personal email account, just in case. He took the battery back out as soon as he was finished and then looked at his sister.

"Are you ready for this?"

She nodded and he took her hand. They walked over to the turnstiles and they each swiped their metro cards. Moments later, they were through the turnstiles and Danielle held her brother's arm tight as they waited for the R train. "It's gonna be all right, Dani," he said.

"Are you sure?" she asked with brown, pleading eyes, eyes that were puffy from crying.

"I'm not gonna let anything happen to you." He leaned over and kissed her forehead and she clung to him even tighter.

"I'm sorry I screamed, I was just really scared, it's all my fault that we can't go back to Staten Island. It's my fault you're gonna miss the rest of the playoffs, and it's my fault I can't go back to church." She started to tear up again and Peter put his arm around her.

"Dani, none of that is your fault, it's mine. If I wasn't involved with shady people, this wouldn't be happening to us. It was my actions, not yours, that led us here. Plus, I didn't lie to Nate. You being there saved my life, even if you did scream; I would have already been dead if you weren't there."

"Really? You're not mad?"

"Mad? Dani, this is now twice I've ruined your life, I'm just praying you're not mad at me." Just then, the high-pitched whine of the R train brakes and the accompanying rush of wind let them know their train had arrived. They entered the train and found seats. They put their backpacks on the floor in front of their seats in between their legs, and Peter leaned back as if he could finally rest for a moment.

"Maybe we're both to blame on this one, Peter," Dani said, her head leaning on his shoulders. "This way we can't be mad at each other."

"I was never mad at you, Dani, I only shook you because you were in shock and we needed to run. I was terrified that something would happen to you, but I was never mad."

They sat in silence until their train reached the Times Square station. They exited the train and began walking through the underground maze of passages that made up the busy station. Eventually, they found their way to the surface and stepped out into the semi-organized chaos that New Yorkers called Times Square. It was almost midnight and the area was still bustling with activity. Peter spotted their destination across the street, nearly a block away; the Times Square police precinct. He hoped this precinct was far enough away that it wasn't within Gravano's reach.

Peter and Danielle crossed the street and approached the police station with a great deal of apprehension. "I don't know if I can do this Dani," he said, backing away from the door. The bright lights of the enormous video screens at either end of Times Square, combined with hundreds of other lights and advertisements, almost made it feel like the middle of the day. There were certainly enough people out and about. The only indications that it was night were the dark alleys in between buildings and the black sky above the lights.

"Well, what should we do then, Peter?" Danielle asked. She was clinging tight to her brother, clearly not willing to trust any of the passersby. Peter was glad he had separated his money into several pockets, his bag, and his shoes. He didn't want to chance losing it all to a single pick-pocket.

"No, we need to do this," he said, as his determination returned. "Or we'll be running for the rest of our lives." He took a deep breath and walked into the police station. The scene that greeted them was so chaotic, Peter thought

124

they might have entered a movie set. There were some prostitutes being processed for practicing their trade, a drunk handcuffed to a bench, four police officers separating two inebriated combatants, and a nearly naked woman screaming at a man dressed like a seventies pimp. Police were hustling in several different directions at once— some carrying papers, and some escorting law-breakers. There was a certain flow to the station, almost rhythmic, as if this were just a well-choreographed ballet that their presence was about to disturb.

Peter approached the reception desk with Danielle still clinging to his side and said, "I'd like to report—"

"Have a seat and I'll be with you shortly," the man interrupted in a no-nonsense tone without looking up.

"But this is impor—"

"I said, have a seat," the man replied in an even less friendly manner than the first time.

"Let's get out of here, Dani," Peter said, as he was walking away from the desk.

"No, Peter, we should stay, we have to tell someone what we saw."

"Well, these guys don't seem real interested. Let's go," Peter abruptly turned to leave and walked right into an officer entering the building.

"Whoa, where's the fire, son? You almost spilled my coffee," he said with a chuckle. "Now add a couple doughnut crumbs and that would be a bad stereotype." Danielle laughed and the officer smiled at her. "Is there something I can help you kids with?"

"We came here to report a crime, sir, but no one would listen to us," Danielle started.

"What type of crime, young lady?"

"A murder, Officer, it was awful." She gripped Peter's arm tighter as the memory of what she had seen came rushing back. She felt like she was about to cry, but she tried to hold it in.

"A murder? You both witnessed this?"

"Nine murders, actually. And yeah, we both witnessed Sal Gravano commit them on Staten Island a couple hours ago," Peter replied.

The officer's eyes went wide when he realized what they were talking about. He looked at their backpacks and knew they fled the island for their own safety. His smile was now gone and he looked around the station. "Come with me," he said. "We'll need to get you hooked up with some detectives immediately. I'm Officer Pulaski, by the way."

He led them to a small room and then left to get his captain. The room looked like one of the rooms they might use to interrogate a suspect, but instead of two, there were four chairs around the metal table. The walls were a dirty white and there was a large mirror dominating one wall of the room. Peter knew from watching television that the mirror was a window they could be watched from on the other side. The light from the two florescent light fixtures was harsh and he wasn't sure about these accommodations.

They had been allowed to keep their backpacks, which meant that Officer Pulaski did believe them. The room was probably the only available space in the busy station. Officer Pulaski was gone almost two minutes before he came back in with another man. This man was tall with dark, graying hair and a gray mustache. He carried himself in a way that told Peter this was an important man. His suspicions were confirmed when Officer Pulaski introduced him.

"This is Captain Sanchez, I need you to tell him what you're doing here." the officer said.

Danielle looked at Peter and they were both silent for a moment. Captain Sanchez looked at them and said, "It's okay, Officer Pulaski told me what you told him. I just need some more details," he paused and then added, "Whenever you're ready." He could tell these kids were already wary and he didn't want to spook them, but even as the young lady began to speak, he wondered if they knew how important their testimony would be. He thought of the impact it would have on all of the organized crime in the city with Joseph Barbarelli dead and Sal Gravano going down for the crime.

Danielle took a deep breath and then began, "I went to Barbarelli's restaurant to meet my brother after work so we could walk home together. I don't get to see him as much as I like because I'm in foster care now and he's at another house."

"Dani, he doesn't need to know all of that," Peter said.

"No, it's okay, anything you want to tell us will help us put everything in context. Please, Danielle, is it?" She nodded and he added, "Continue. Why were you put in foster care?"

She felt ashamed as she sought the words. Peter gave her a look of encouragement and said, "It's okay, Dani, tell them everything."

126

"I was in Foster care because my dad was arrested a couple weeks ago for beating me. He would get drunk and beat me up, but I never said anything because I didn't want Peter to feel bad, but then two weeks ago, he beat me up worse than usual and I couldn't hide it. Then Peter got mugged during his delivery job and we had to go to the hospital." She continued with the story and the Captain sat there patiently listening and taking notes.

Finally, she finished the back-story and got to the more relevant information. "So I saw Peter going into work and called out to him. Then I ran over to him and we were right in front of the restaurant." She started trembling, as the memory of what happened came rushing back. She tried to compose herself and Peter took her hand as she continued. "He told me it was dangerous, and that I needed to leave because he was quitting and he didn't know how they would take it. Before I could go, we heard a lot of gun shots and a man came crashing through the front window of the restaurant. I could tell he was dead. And then we saw a big man with black hair and a light grey suit shoot Mr. Barbarelli a whole bunch of times." She was talking faster now. "I screamed and then he saw us. I know I shouldn't have, but I was scared. It was so terrible. Then, two other men came chasing after us, but we got away. We went back to the places we were staying at, packed our backpacks, and then came here." She began to tear up as she finished her account of the murder.

"That was very good, Danielle, thank you," Captain Sanchez said. "It'll be okay. We won't let anything happen to you." He looked over to Peter and added, "Now, let's hear your story."

"My story starts two weeks ago as well. I wasn't actually mugged that night. I lied on the police report because I didn't want my boss to get in trouble."

"Your boss was Mr. Barbarelli?"

"Yeah."

"What did you do for him?" The captain asked hoping he had someone here that could shed light on that whole operation.

"I was just a bike delivery guy. I delivered what he called 'hard to acquire items.' I would also pick up payments from certain people once a week."

"What kind of items were you delivering?"

"I was never told, and the items were wrapped, but I did see a couple of the packages after they were opened. I delivered an antique wooden shelf to an elderly woman. I delivered a Bob Marley vinyl record to another man and the only other item I ever saw was a gold pocket watch that the recipient said was from the civil war. Those are the only things I know for sure I ever delivered."

"Did anything ever seem off to you? Did you feel like you were doing anything wrong?" Officer Pulaski asked.

"Actually, no. Nothing I ever delivered felt like drugs or guns or anything like that." He noticed the dubious look on the Captain's face and added, "Look, I know my boss was shady, but he never had me do anything illegal that I know of, and he was good to me. He paid me well, and I needed the money because my dad wouldn't support us. Without my job, we wouldn't have had food, clothes, cell phones, heat or electricity. I couldn't just walk away from that kind of money."

"So, why were you quitting then?" Captain Sanchez asked. He saw an impatient look cross Peter's face and added, "Just bear with us, Peter. The DA is going to want all of this information. You're not in any trouble."

"I was quitting because two weeks ago, when I said I got mugged, I didn't. I was actually beat up by Sal Gravano who had been shorting Mr. Barbarelli on the money he owed. After he beat me, his sons chased me all over in their mustang. They even called in another car. They shot at me, tried to run me down, and chased me all through Clove Lakes Park.

After the beating, Mr. Barbarelli asked me not to tell anyone what really happened, which is why I lied on the police report. I do have a voice recording of the confrontation with Gravano." He took out his phone and played it for them and they seemed eager to get that recording into evidence, but Peter indicated there was more.

He squeezed Dani's hand for reassurance as he continued. "That's why I was quitting tonight. I guess I knew it was all shady, but it never seemed wrong or dangerous until I got beat up. After Michael got shot through the front window of the restaurant, I started filming on my phone and I got Gravano shooting Mr. Barbarelli several times at close range." He played the video for them and they were shocked. Even on the small screen they could see who it was doing the shooting. Sal Gravano was going down as long as they could keep these kids protected.

"That was good work, Peter. This video is going to put a vicious criminal behind bars for a very long time," Captain Sanchez said, as he took out his phone and called the Attorney General's office. After a brief conversation, he hung up the phone, satisfied that the FBI would be on their way to the station along with a federal prosecutor to interview the witnesses and get them to a safe house.

Chapter 12

Gravano and his sons had dumped all the evidence and returned home. They were eating dinner and waiting for Joey to call them back with more information, when all of a sudden a dozen police cars were outside their house. Gravano stood up and peered out the window. "That Donovan kid must have made it to the cops." He knew that, even with the police he had on his payroll, he wasn't going to avoid this arrest. So he sent a text to his lawyer to meet him at the police station. After sending the message, he put his phone away. His sons were still eating at the table when the police busted through the front, side, and rear doors simultaneously.

"Police! Don't move!" the lead officer shouted.

"On the ground, hands behind your head," an older officer yelled. Gravano and his sons did as instructed and after they were cuffed, the same officer told them what they were being charged with and began reading them their Miranda Rights. "Salvatore Gravano, you are under arrest for the murder of Joseph Barbarelli. You have the right to remain silent. Anything you say can and will be used against you in a court of law. You have the right to an attorney..."

When the officer finished reading him and his son's their rights, the police stood him up and began walking him to the squad car. Gravano looked at the cop and said, "I want a lawyer. Get my lawyer down to the station house now!" He poured menace into his voice hoping to intimidate the young officer. He knew his lawyer was already on the way, but wanted to see how far the officer would let him push.

The officer just looked at him and replied, "You will be able to call whomever you'd like after you've been processed at the police station."

"Do you know who I am, kid?" He yelled at the cop, hoping his growing agitation would cause the officer to lose his resolve.

"I know exactly who you are, and you're out of your mind if you think I'm giving you any special treatment. You get a phone call from jail, like everyone else. That's it!" The officer replied.

"You're denying my rights," he yelled as the people on his block had all come out of their houses to watch the spectacle.

"I would never dream of denying your rights. You'll get to make your call after you've been processed. That's what you're entitled to and that's what you'll get."

"At least let me know why I'm being arrested, Officer."

"You've already heard the charges."

"Who said it was me? I was here all night with my sons. Whoever said it was me is a liar. Who is it?"

"You'll have the opportunity to confront your accuser in court. Now shut up and get in the car." He placed his hand on Gravano's head and guided him into the squad car with a shove that was a little bit less than gentle. Gravano glared at him the whole time. Once in the car, he started back up.

"I demand to know who is accusing me. I want to talk to him right now. Where is he?" By this point, the officer was ignoring him. He knew Gravano was just trying to get any detail he could to give to his lawyer. He didn't have any of the information, but Gravano wouldn't have gotten it from him anyway. Still, the man carried on and, from the look of it, his sons were doing the same thing to the officers taking them in. The young officer wished he could tase Gravano, just to get some quiet, as he drove off towards the 121 precinct followed by the cars containing Gravano's sons.

*****

"Are we safe here, Captain?" Danielle asked.

"Of course you are. The FBI is on their way, and you'll have an armed escort with you everywhere you go until the trial," Captain Sanchez replied with a reassuring smile.

"We do have to warn you though; Gravano is going to do everything in his power to get to you before the trial. We're going to have to keep you in an undisclosed location until the trial is over with, and you'll probably have to go into Witsec afterward," Officer Pulaski said.

"Precautions will be taken for your safety. Your well being is our biggest concern," Captain Sanchez added.

"Peter had us take out our cell phone batteries as a precaution," Danielle said.

"That was great thinking, Danielle. Good idea making sure no one could follow your phones," Officer Pulaski said. "You probably won't be allowed phones again until after the trial." He then looked at them as if a thought has just struck him. "So, why come all the way out here to report this, why not stay on Staten Island?"

"We thought he might have guys watching the precincts on Staten Island and I'm pretty sure he's got a couple cops on his payroll. I figured he wouldn't expect me to come out here," Peter replied.

"That was smart, Peter, and we have some men picking up Sal Gravano and his two sons as we speak. As soon as Mr. Stevens from the Attorney General's office gets here, we can go over your options, but I have to warn you, whether you testify or not, your lives as you knew them are pretty much over," Captain Sanchez said with a frown.

"Does that mean I won't be able to go back to church? Even after the trial?" Danielle asked, hoping she didn't break down in tears again.

"I'm sorry, kiddo, that's not likely, but there are churches pretty much everywhere, so you will probably find another good one." Officer Pulaski tried to encourage her, but it didn't seem to be working. He could see her countenance fall.

"Will my testimony be enough? I'd like it if Dani didn't have to testify," Peter asked.

"That's a question for the federal prosecutor, Peter. Although, it's probable he'll want both," Officer Pulaski replied. "No offense, but even if you weren't doing anything wrong, you were working for Mr. Barbarelli. Your sister on the other hand is a sweet, church-going girl, and the jury will eat her testimony up." Peter hated that the officer was right.

It was nearly three in the morning by the time Mr. Stevens and the FBI officers arrived, and Dani was sound asleep at the table. Peter had been wide-awake, unable to stop blaming himself for once again ruining his sister's life. Even if he had taken Nate's advice and quit earlier, he still would have had to go when Mr. Barbarelli called. Employed or not, there would have been no way for him to avoid being there. The one silver-lining was that he and Dani would be together. He could keep an eye on her and make sure she was protected. A few minutes later, the door opened and a tired man wearing a navy blue business suit that looked like it was thrown on in haste stepped into the room.

"Hi, Peter, I'm Mr. Stevens. I'm a federal prosecutor from the Attorney General's office. It would seem that you and your sister have had a rough go of it lately. If it's not too much trouble, I'd like to go through your statements with you and Danielle just to make sure we have everything relevant and that there will be no surprises. Hopefully by then, your safe house will be ready and then you and Danielle can get some real sleep. How does that sound?"

"Sounds fine, I guess," Peter replied. He then tapped his sister's shoulder and said in a quiet voice, "Hey, Dani, wake up. They're almost done with us and then we can go rest."

After another hour of recounting everything he had ever seen that was suspicious and every encounter he ever had with the Gravanos, from the first time he picked up until the intimidation at the football game, they were finally finished. Dani's testimony was a lot shorter because it focused on the actual murder and why she was there. He hated that she had to tell strangers about their father's abusive behavior, but she was getting through it fairly well.

"And where is your father right now?" Mr. Stevens asked. "Does he know you're here?"

"No, he's still in lock-up for a drunk and disorderly charge on Staten Island. Unless he found someone to bail him out, he's there until he sees a judge tomorrow," Peter replied.

"We may need his permission to put you in the program," he added. "He may even demand to come with you."

"No, absolutely not!" Peter replied. "He's not even allowed to have contact with Dani, there's no way we're going on the run with him. He's a drunk, he'll blow our cover and if he touches my sister again, I will break his arm."

"I think there are enough mitigating circumstances to get around him accompanying you. I'll see about it tomorrow," Mr. Stevens said.

"Peter, it's okay, if it takes us meeting with him to get him to sign, I'm willing," Danielle said.

"No! No way, Dani! Mr. Stevens, make sure we don't need to be there when he signs the permission. If he won't, offer him beer money or something. Just get his signature and walk away. I don't want to see him or talk to him, and I don't want Dani to, either. Look, I don't want to be a jerk or anything, but this is my condition. If I have to let Gravano walk in order to protect my sister from our dad, I will. If he winds up anywhere near us during this process, I won't testify."

Mr. Stevens could see how much this meant to Peter and he even agreed with him. His sister should not have to be anywhere near the man that habitually beat her for the last few years; he only hoped he could convince a judge of that, because if Peter walked away, he was as good as dead.

"Peter, I will do my best to make sure you and Danielle are protected, but I want you to understand something. If you choose to walk away, you'll be getting yourself killed, and probably your sister, too. I'm not trying to scare you. You should already be scared. I'm just trying to tell you how it is. In fact, for your own protection, I cannot legally let you go. Now, let's get you guys to our safe house so you can get some rest."

"Thanks," Danielle said, with a weary look in her eye. "I'm really tired."

"We'll get to sleep soon, Dani," Peter replied as he helped her out of the police station and into the waiting car. The prosecutor was coming with them to make sure everything was ready for them and he would be leaving a four-man detail with them at the house. He knew these were the two highest priority witnesses he would have in his career and he didn't want anything to happen to them.

When Danielle finally put her backpack down in her temporary room, she looked up towards the ceiling and began to pray. "Lord, I don't know what to do. You know that there are some pretty bad guys out there that want to hurt me and Peter. Please keep us safe from them. Could you help us to stay safe? I don't even know if it works that way. God, I wish I knew more about you, then I wouldn't waste your time asking these questions. In the meantime, help me to keep learning more about you and please keep us safe. Maybe I should have more faith, but I'm really scared. I hope that doesn't disappoint you. I'm very tired right now, so I'll talk to you tomorrow. Amen" When she finished praying, she closed her eyes and sleep wasn't far behind.

Peter could hear Dani talking in the room next to his and he wondered whom she was talking to. He heard her mention God and then knew she was praying. He wondered what this situation was going to do to her faith. *I hope she doesn't stop believing,* he thought. Soon after, he found himself praying for the first time in his life. "God, it's Peter, I don't really think you're real, at least not in the way Dani and her friends believe. But if you are up there, do me a favor and protect my sister. She's a good kid and doesn't deserve to pay for my mistakes. Thanks, umm, that's it." He thought for a minute then added, "Right, I'm supposed to say amen at the end, sorry."

Peter was still wide-awake and the realization that his life was over was beginning to sink in. The ironic thing about it was this was the first time he was ever really thinking about what he wanted out of life. He had always thought about getting Danielle through college as the end-all, be-all of his existence. Now, however, he thought it would have been nice to play college football, or date Hailey. It would have been nice to apply to the fire department and fight fires. He wondered if he could still do any of that. *Not as Peter Donovan, that's for sure. I wonder what my new name will be.* After hours of sleeplessness, his eyes became heavy and he drifted off to sleep.

****

Sal Gravano sat on the metal chair with his hands cuffed to the table of the interrogation room. He looked at the police officer sitting across from him and said, "I demand to see my lawyer. I'm not gonna tell you again!"

"And as I've already told you, he's on his way. I just want to hear your version of what happened," the Officer replied.

"Listen, we both know I'm not gonna say anything, so why don't you do me a favor. Shut your mouth, uncuff me, and get me some coffee." He poured intimidation into his request, but the cop just laughed at him.

"I'll tell you what, Gravano, because you're such a nice guy, I'll grant your first request." He stood and left the room. As the door was closing, Gravano actually thought he heard the man laughing at him. He made a mental note to get the officer's name and find out if he had any family. A moment later, two FBI agents walked into the room.

"I'm agent Davis and this is agent Parker of the FBI. This is quite a predicament you find yourself in, Gravano."

"Where's my lawyer?"

"I have no idea, did you call one?" Agent Parker said.

"You know I did, and I ain't saying a word until I see him."

"That's what guilty men always say, Agent Parker, isn't it?"

"That's what I would say if I just murdered nine people," Agent Parker replied.

"Enough of the witty banter! Get my lawyer in here, now!"

"We'll see what's keeping him," Agent Davis said. He flashed Gravano an unnerving smile and then he left the room followed by Agent Parker.

Almost two hours later, a short, well-dressed man carrying a brief case entered the holding cell. He was in his late fifties, and his dark hair was immaculate. He had a small crook in his nose from a battle he lost with a taxi-cab door, and he was accompanied by the scent of strong cologne. He looked at Gravano with piercing brown eyes and said, "It's not good, Sal. I haven't been able to get a copy of the evidence, but my guy tells me the kid was recording, and you are crystal clear in HD."

"It took you over two hours to come up with that, Rosenberg?" Gravano slammed his palm down on the metal table for effect, but since his hands were cuffed to the table his palm only had about two inches of play. Still, the lawyer received the message.

"No, sir, it took me a half hour to find that out and get to the station. Then the process to get in here to see you took another hour and a half." He opened up his brief case and took out a pen and pad. Is there anything I need to do from the outside to help?

"Was it Donovan that filmed the incident? And who else was with him?"

"Yeah, it was Donovan. My guy in the DA's office confirmed it. His sister Danielle was the girl that was with him. My source also told me the feds swooped in and took them away."

"Okay, that wasn't unexpected. Let me ask you this, if they're gone, how much does the video evidence still hurt me?"

"It depends on how much they got? We could argue context, or attack the authenticity, but I won't know until we see it. Even so, if the kid testifies, the video will bury you."

"Well, hire my usual contractors to make sure Donovan and his sister never talk to anyone again, and then we'll work on the video. And go talk to the father to see if he knows anything."

"That's unlikely, seeing as how he was recently arrested for beating the daughter and lost custody of her. I'll check the foster home the girl was in. To my knowledge, Peter was just floating around. He didn't have a foster home." Rosenberg continued writing in his notepad. His sole purpose in life was now to make sure that Sal Gravano would once again be a free man.

"I don't care how you do it, who you talk to, who you have to hurt, or who you have to pay. Just make sure that those kids are found and taken care of. And start working on bail. I hate it in here."

"Yes, sir, Mr. Gravano. I'm already on it, but it doesn't look like it's gonna happen." He stood and nodded at his client. Then he knocked on the door and when the guard opened it, he hurried out. The door closed, and Sal was alone with his thoughts.

*****

Danielle woke up at noon. She looked around the unfamiliar room and realized that yesterday had not been a bad dream. The room was painted white and had white shades covering the windows. Her bed and a lamp on a small wooden night-stand were the only furnishings, and the only splash of color came from the cozy pink comforter she had wrapped around herself. She wandered out of the room and noticed a bathroom on the right. She saw some soap and shampoo and a few towels folded up on the counter next to the sink. She decided that a nice hot shower might help her to feel a little better.

After her shower, she dressed and walked out into the living area. She again saw only the bare minimum of furnishings, and two men with guns were watching college football with Peter. They were different men than the ones that had brought them here.

"Hey, Dani," Peter said with a wave from across the room. "I let you sleep in because we were up so late, I hope you don't mind. How are you doing today?"

"I don't know. Part of me thinks this isn't really happening. Part of me is really sad that I might not ever see my friends again. Part of me is still so mad at myself for screaming and getting us seen. I also feel numb, like I just don't know what to feel. Plus, I'm missing my algebra test right now." She looked like she was about to tear up. She started to tremble just a little, and then she added, "I'm just really scared, I guess."

"Well, that's why we're here," one of the cops said. He was tall and bald, he looked to be in good shape and he had intense blue eyes. "I'm Marshal Lancer, but you can call me Tom. Scarvelli and I will be here twenty-four, seven until the trial, and there will always be another two Marshals outside, patrolling the area. You're perfectly safe here." Just then, Scarvelli let out a cheer accompanied by a fist pump as one of the teams they were watching scored a touchdown. "Scarvelli's a huge Florida fan. Do you watch any football, Danielle?"

"Just my brother's games. He plays wide receiver for the Wagner Falcons."

Scarvelli looked over at Peter, apparently impressed. "Wow, you're that Peter Donovan?"

"I guess," Peter replied a little sheepishly. "Probably not for much longer."

"I'm really sorry you're gonna miss the rest of the playoffs because of this. You guys have a good chance to win the city this year," Scarvelli added while still looking at the television.

"They had a good shot— Peter's their best player; that's gonna hurt," Tom added.

"We still have a shot. I have faith in my teammates," Peter said defensively.

"Me, too," Danielle said. "Our guys are really good this year. Even without Peter."

"Well, I hope your school does okay," Tom said. "Unfortunately, you're going to be stuck with us for a while." He turned back to the Television to see the Gators kick off to Alabama. Danielle noticed the score was tied at fourteen just before the half.

"I'm really sorry you have to be away from your families because of us," Danielle said, changing the subject from football.

"I needed some time away from the wife anyway," Scarvelli said with a chuckle. His dark eyes lit up, adding. "Don't feel bad, this is the job, and we knew that when we applied." He stood to go into the kitchen and she saw that he was about average height. *With his dark hair and last name, I bet he would fit in perfectly on Staten Island,* and even as that thought hit her, she wondered where they were.

"Jackson is stopping by the deli," Tom said. "Are you two hungry?"

"Very! I haven't eaten since yesterday afternoon," Dani replied. She hadn't even realized how hungry she was until the officer mentioned it. "Can I have a chicken parm hero?"

"Sure," Tom replied, and then looked at Peter.

"I'll have a turkey, ham and Swiss, with lettuce, tomato, oil and vinegar. Can we get a bag of chips, too?"

"Sure, I don't see why not." He relayed the order to Jackson and then hung up the phone. "Should be about twenty minutes or so."

"Thank you, Marshal," Danielle replied while she turned to leave the room.

"Where are you going?" Peter called after her.

"I just want to explore the house. Then maybe I'm going to read until lunch gets here."

"Read. Really? At a time like this?"

"Why not? I don't want to watch the game, and we can't go outside. What else is there to do?" She thought for a moment and then added, "I might draw a bit. I did bring some of my supplies."

"Whatever," Peter replied. Then he turned his attention back to the game.

Danielle walked into the kitchen and opened the refrigerator. It was well stocked with water and soda, but little else. She opened the cupboard and saw a fair assortment of snacks and easy to cook items like soup or mac and cheese. There was a small metal table with two folding chairs near the back of the kitchen, and the walls were covered with flowered wallpaper. *I bet this hasn't been updated since the seventies,* she thought. She looked past the table and out the back window to a small yard. The lawn, if you could call it that, was patchy and not well kept, but there was a large chestnut tree with branches that extended towards the house. She couldn't see the end of the branches and just assumed they hung over the roof. Chestnuts dotted the ground falling indiscriminately on the grass and dirt patches. *I think I'm going to sketch that tree after lunch.*

She poked her head into the barren dining room. Mint green walls surrounded an orange carpet. There was a folding plastic table and six folding chairs strewn in a hap-hazardous manner around it. *This room has no soul,* she mused. She turned and walked a few steps across the kitchen and began to turn the knob to the basement door when Scarvelli came into the room.

"Where you going, Danielle? Not trying to run out on us, are you?"

"No, I just wanted to see what's in the basement. Why would I run away?"

"Just making sure. There's a side door on the basement landing and if you go down, I have to stand here and make sure you don't exit the premises."

"I didn't know about the side door, I'm sorry." Danielle opened the door and looked down the stairs, and there it was, right where Marshal Scarvelli said it would be, a brown door leading outside.

"You know the basement is haunted, right?" His laugh lightened her mood a little.

"I don't scare that easily," she replied, accepting his implied challenge. She descended the stairs and when she reached the bottom, a musty smell hit her and she took a step back. She placed her hand over her mouth and nose trying to escape the assault on her olfactory senses. She had to stay down there for a reasonable amount of time or face the possibility of Marshal Scarvelli teasing her about the ghosts. She had to squint until her eyes adjusted to the darkness.

She looked around and there was junk everywhere. She almost found it funny how much stuff was down there as opposed to the rest of the house. Leaning piles of rusted metal objects almost met to form a giant pile. Old Christmas decorations were laid near some chicken wire, tools, siding, and an ancient washer machine. Around the edges of the room there were piles of news papers, wooden beams and some old bicycles. There was no rhyme or reason to the way it was set up. She touched the top of one of the piles and it toppled over with a series of clangs, gongs and thuds. A dust cloud kicked up and she started to cough.

"How ya doing down there? Are you all right?" Scarvelli's question almost startled her.

"I'm fine. Not scared if that's what you mean. I just knocked over some stuff. What's with all this junk anyway?"

"No idea, I've never even been down there," she could hear him begin to walk down the stairs. When he reached the bottom he said, "It stinks down here." Then a moment later he added, "Wow, there is a lot of junk down here. Maybe they were hoarders. Have you explored enough, Dora?"

"I suppose, and I used to love that show." She turned and started back up the stairs with Scarvelli behind her. She looked back at him and added, "I used to carry my backpack everywhere and pretend to explore. My friends thought I was so weird."

"My girls love that show, too, and they do the same thing."

"How old are they?"

"Four and six, and they're all I can handle," he replied with a hint of pride in his voice.

"That's a fun age. Sometimes my friend Laura and I volunteer with the kids that age at our church on Sundays. They're so cute."

"Where do you go to church?" Scarvelli asked. He turned and closed the basement door behind him and locked it. They walked back into the living room where Peter and Tom were still watching the game.

140

"I go to Clove Road Bible Church. It's by the park."

"I know where that is. I used to go to Mass at Saint Teresa on Victory and Slosson. I grew up right down the street from Clove Lakes."

"We live in the Todt Hill projects. I pass that church all the time. Did you go to school there?"

"I did, actually. Then I went to Saint Peter's for high school."

"Wow, we were practically neighbors. Hey Peter, Marshal Scarvelli grew up right near Saint Teresa's."

"That's cool, Dani," Peter replied absently as he watched the Crimson Tide run the ball to the Gator's seventeen yard line.

"Did you even hear what I said?"

"Yes, I did and, no offense, but it's nowhere near as interesting as the game." Both Marshals began to chuckle, while Danielle frowned at her brother. She began to climb the stairs to get her sketch pad when the doorbell rang.

She started to walk towards the door when Tom called out, "Danielle, let me get that. You two have to stay hidden."

"Right, sorry." She noticed that Scarvelli had put his hand on his gun when the bell rang.

"Don't worry about it," he replied as he crossed the living room to the front door. He looked out the window and saw that it was Jackson with lunch and opened the door just enough to accept the bags. Scarvelli took his hand off his gun and Tom handed him one of the bags. "Thanks, Jackson," Tom said and then closed the door. Scarvelli brought the food into the dining room and began to lay the sandwiches out on the table. Danielle's mouth began to water when she smelled the marinara sauce from her chicken parm.

Peter picked his sandwich up and hurried back into the living room. Tom and Scarvelli followed behind with their food, leaving Danielle alone in the soulless, minty dining room. She decided to take her food into the living room as well. "Why are you so interested in this game Peter?" she asked.

"I have a bet going with Tom. I got the Tide and he's got the Gators. Loser has to clean the dishes tonight." He smiled and winked at his sister and then turned back to the television. She just rolled her eyes and took a bite of her sandwich. She savored the taste of the chicken, covered in mozzarella and smothered in marinara sauce with a hint of garlic. She knew they had to still be somewhere in or near the city or the sub wouldn't have been this good.

"Can you tell me where we are?" Danielle asked

"Unfortunately, for your protection we have to keep that information to ourselves. I wish we could tell you. Sorry," Scarvelli replied.

"I understand, I guess," she replied with a slight air of disappointment. She stood and walked into the kitchen and called back to the living room, "Do you guys want water or Coke?"

"Water," Scarvelli replied.

"Coke," Peter answered.

"I'll have a Coke, too," Tom replied. Danielle came back into the living room with two waters and two Cokes. She passed the drinks out and returned to her sandwich, while they all watched the game. Both Marshals were clearly rooting for the Gators and she knew that's why Peter was rooting for the Crimson Tide. She decided she would stick with her brother and began cheering for the Tide, too.

*****

The afternoon passed by pretty fast. It was the Monday before Thanksgiving and there were plenty of holiday shows and sports on television. Since the guys had the remote, Danielle had gone upstairs to read her Bible for a little while. She wanted to pray, but was unsure what to say. Eventually she had brought her sketch-pad into the kitchen and sat down at the metal table to draw.

Peter walked into the kitchen, opened up the refrigerator, and took out a bottle of water. "Do you want one, Dani?" he asked.

"Yes please," she replied and stood ready to catch his toss. He gave it an underhand toss and she caught it and put it on the table next to her pad.

He walked over to the table, took a swig of water and said, "That's coming out nice, Dani."

"Thanks. I think I'm going to leave this one black and white."

"That's cool." He turned to go, then turned back around and said in almost a whisper, "Remember, don't unpack too much of your stuff. We may need to leave in a hurry."

"Okay, I won't." He was just trying to be sure she was ready, but she had just started to lose herself in her art and forget their situation. Peter's reminder brought it all back to her. He walked back into the living room and she wanted to cry. *Will I ever see Laura again? Will I ever be able to go to church again? What's going to happen to us?*

Peter came back in a moment later and asked, "Do you think I should call off the bet with Tom? I mean, I don't think he knows the game is a replay from Saturday and I already know who the winner is. I'm pretty sure Scarvelli knows and just wants to make fun of Tom after he loses."

"Let him squirm. He should know better. I mean really, who doesn't know that college football is usually on Saturday," she replied and then they both started cracking up.

"What's so funny?" Tom asked as he walked into the kitchen to get another bottle of water.

"Nothing," Peter replied while Danielle just laughed harder. Tom just rolled his eyes and left the room.

After some Chinese food for dinner, and some Monday Night Football, Danielle went upstairs to go to sleep. She heard Tom complaining that he had to clean up the kitchen, since the Crimson Tide had won the game on a two-point conversion with six seconds to play. He complained even more when he found out it was a replay that Peter had already seen. She left the door to her room opened a little and then sat on her bed.

After a moment, she started to pray. "Lord, I just don't know what to do here? I don't know where I am, if everything's going to turn out all right or if I can ever go home again. I really want to see Laura and Hailey again. I want to go back to youth group this week like nothing ever happened. I don't know if that's even possible. Please keep all my friends and the Jenkins safe. Please keep me and Peter safe. Help me to find a good church if we get new identities. God, I'm just so scared. I want to believe you'll protect us, and I want to believe that everything is going to turn out okay, but I'm not sure. I'm sorry I don't have more faith. I'm just trying to learn more about you, so maybe I'll know what's going to happen. I just don't—"

"Who are you talking to, Danielle?" Scarvelli asked as he opened the door to her room.

"Oh, I'm just praying. I'm sorry if I was bothering you."

"No, it's no trouble. I just had to make sure that you weren't talking to anyone on a phone or Skype or something. I have to make sure you and Peter are safe. Can you say a prayer for my little girls, too?"

"I would love to, and don't worry about me trying to Skype or anything. I don't even think we have Wi-Fi here. Plus, the police took my phone."

"Just making sure. You have a good night and get some sleep." He closed the door most of the way and a moment later she heard his footsteps going down the stairs.

Peter passed him on his way up and Scarvelli asked him, "Does your sister always pray like that?"

"Like what?"

"You know, out loud, like she's actually talking to someone?"

"I don't really know, to be honest. I was usually working. She probably prayed when I was out. I do know she loves her church and she seems to love God."

"What about you? Do you believe the same thing she does?"

"No, not at all. I guess there might be a god out there somewhere, but he hasn't had any impact on my life. Still, it makes Dani happy to believe, so I hope he's real, for her sake." He continued up the stairs while Scarvelli checked all the doors and windows to make sure they were locked.

Peter walked into Dani's room and asked, "Is everything packed up?"

"Everything except my shoes and jacket."

"And you're wearing sweats to bed, right?"

"Yes, Peter. Is all this really necessary? The Marshals look like they have everything under control."

"I really hope they do, Dani, but Gravano has a long a reach. All it takes is one person looking for a little extra cash to sell us out. If they find out where we are, four Marshals are not going to be enough to save us. First sign of trouble, we gotta be ready to bolt. If these guys can't do the job, we'll have to do it on our own."

"Peter, it scares me when you talk like that."

"I'm sorry. I just have to make sure you're safe. All of this is my fault and I'd hate myself if anything happened to you. Just be ready."

"Okay and it's not all your fault. I was there, too, and I screamed. I'd already be dead if you didn't shake me and practically drag me to safety."

"That's kind of you to say, but we both know that's not the whole story."

"In my mind, the rest of the story is you providing for me for the last four years. You giving up all your fun to make sure I had what I needed. I blame dad for making you have to do it by not taking care of us."

"I blame him for a lot, Dani, but I made the decision to continue working for Barbarelli, even after I knew he was shady." He hung his head and turned to leave.

As he was closing the door, Danielle called out behind him. "None of that matters now. From now on, we look out for each other." Peter left the door open just a little, and she heard his door creak open. She didn't hear the creek close and she knew he was just trying to stay ready, just in case.

*****

Tom and Scarvelli were sitting in the living room, each holding a cup of coffee. "Why don't I take first watch tonight," Tom said. He stood and began to peer out the front windows. He saw their backup wave from the blue sedan across the street and then he moved on to the dining room windows.

Scarvelli stood, walked across the living room, and began to trudge up the stairs towards the unoccupied bedroom. "Okay, wake me in four hours."

"Will, do," Tom replied from the kitchen, where he continued to peer out the windows for anything amiss. After his round was finished, he went back to the living room and turned on Letterman. He repeated the process every half hour until it was time to wake Scarvelli.

Chapter 13

A week passed and they were still at the safe house. Thanksgiving dinner had been an interesting experience, eating turkey subs with strangers. Mr. Stevens had been by with paperwork signed by Mr. Donovan allowing his children to enter the witness protection program without him. Peter wondered how much or how little it took to get him to sign. Stevens also had them sign some affidavits concerning their testimony.

After Mr. Stevens left, lunch arrived and with it, a newspaper. Peter grabbed the paper before he even looked at the food, and rifled through the sports section.

"Did we win?" Danielle asked hands clasped in anticipation.

"I don't know yet," Peter replied, while he continued thumbing through the oversized pages of the newspaper. A moment later, he found the high school sports page. "Here it is," he said. "We won the game by a field goal and we're heading to the city championship game in two weeks! Yes!" It was the first time he had felt even a moment of happiness since the night Gravano killed Barbarelli.

"That's great, Peter!" Danielle yelled as she hugged him in celebration. "I'm so happy. I wish I could have seen it."

"Me, too," Peter whispered.

"Peter, I'm sorry you had to miss it," she said and hugged him tighter.

"I know, thanks, Dani. At least we won, right?" He put a smile back on his face and swung his sister around. He let out a soft grunt when he put her down. He grabbed his sandwich and sat down in the minty fresh dining room. Danielle walked into the kitchen and retrieved two bottles of water from the refrigerator for them to drink. She sat down opposite him and opened her bag of chips. The Marshals were eating by the front door while they talked to Jackson. She thought they might be giving him the dinner orders.

"Dani, I'm sorry," Peter said without preamble.

"For what?" she asked, while she unwrapped her chicken salad sandwich.

"For all of this. For making you miss school, and church, and the Jenkins." His shoulders slouched and he sighed. "You finally had a real family and I ruined it for you. I wish—"

She was up so fast it startled him. She pointed at him and said, "First of all, let's get something straight. You are my real family! The Jenkins are awesome and I love them, but they did not give up the last four years of their lives making sure I had everything I needed. You did!" Peter started to say something, but she just kept going. "And don't give me any of this, 'it's because it's your fault I didn't have a mom stuff,' because I'm not buying it. There is no place on Earth where a four-year-old has to take responsibility for his mom getting hit by a car." She was on a roll now and didn't want to stop. He had blamed himself for far too long and it needed to end.

"Dani, I—"

"I wasn't finished." She was now as animated as he had ever seen her. "Maybe I thought it was dad providing for me when I was in sixth and seventh grade, but by eighth grade I had figured some of it out, and by last summer I had figured most of it out. Every time I asked dad for something, you bought it for me, with your money. You let me thank him, and you never asked me for anything. You gave me money, bought my clothes, made sure no one picked on me and Laura. You are my family! No one else, just you!"

"But I brought all of this danger on you. I should have never worked for Barbarelli, and now you are on the run, maybe for the rest of your life. We'll never be truly safe again."

"Well, it's a good thing that I think God will keep me safe then. And yeah, maybe you should have quit Barbarelli's sooner, but it's not like you knew he was a criminal when you started working for him. You were only fourteen, and by the time you did think it might be shady, you had no other way to make enough to support us. I could never be mad at you for wanting to provide for me, so stop apologizing."

"The lady is making some sense, Peter, you should listen to her," Tom said as he walked into the room with a bottle of water.

"Look, I know you will keep blaming yourself, but you need to know that I don't blame you." Danielle sat back down and took a bite of her sandwich.

"Thanks, Dani, it really means a lot." Peter pushed his chair away from the table and stood up. He left the room and then Danielle heard the soft creaks of the third and fifth stairs a moment later.

"You're a good sister, Danielle," Tom said, "but he's going to need time to work through all of this, and he won't even begin to do that until after the trial. You understand that, right?"

"I do. I just hate seeing him like this."

"Give it time. He'll eventually figure it out," Tom said before walking back into the living room.

*****

Gravano shuffled through the drab holding facility in his orange jumpsuit with his hands and feet shackled. Grey wall after grey wall with little character or imagination passed as his slow trek continued. His lawyer had finally arrived to break the monotony of the long day. He had been arraigned the morning after he was arrested and then straight to the federal holding facility until Wednesday's hearing. He passed the bars of each small cell, and the thought that he didn't belong, that he was better than the people in those cells kept running through his mind. He had nothing but disdain for his incarcerated brethren. He approached the small room he would be meeting his lawyer in and hoped his long time counsel had some good news for him.

"Give me some good news, Rosenberg."

"I do have news, Mr. Gravano, but you'll have to be the judge of whether or not it's good," He replied. He put his briefcase down on the table and took out some papers.

"Where are we on finding the kids?"

"Close, I've been able to find out that Lance Stevens has been assigned to them. He's out of DC and we've got nothing on him to exploit."

Gravano glared at his lawyer. "How is that good news? It's been over a week and all you got is a name! What am I paying you for?" He started to jump up, but his shackles prevented him from being as animated as he would normally be.

"Having a name is better than not having a name, sir," Rosenberg replied. "And now that we have a name, we've been able to start working out a schedule. We know he's been in Yonkers, Schenectady, Danbury Connecticut and Fort Lee, New Jersey in the last week. I've also seen affidavits signed by the kids within the last week which means—"

"They are in or near one of those locations. That is good news. Why don't you lead with that next time?" He sat back down and looked at his lawyer. "How do we know where he's been?"

"I sent Joey and his hacker cousin to DC to gather intelligence. They posed as bike messengers to get in the building without raising any suspicions. Once they were in, the hacker kid was able to use the building's Wi-Fi to get into the Federal Prosecutors schedules and we figured out the rest from there."

"He hacked the Attorney General's office? Why didn't the kid get us more information?"

"The kid has concentration issues, and he lacks critical thinking skills. He only did exactly what we asked. When I asked him why he didn't get more info, he said something about the scheduling apps on the smart phones being the easiest thing to hack and that a bigger intrusion into their network would have been noticed." He sighed and pulled some more papers out of his briefcase.

"Do you think the kid was right? I don't know a whole lot about hacking computers or phones or anything like that."

"I don't know much about that sort of thing either, but I do know, we paid the kid to do a job, and he did it. Regardless of if he could have done more, he did what we asked, and we can't fault him for that." He shuffled the papers on the table and continued. "We already have guys searching all of those locations. If the kids or the Marshals make a mistake, we've got them."

"Good! Now, what about bail? When can I get out of here? Orange isn't exactly my color."

"Unfortunately, it doesn't look like the judge is going to grant bail. I'll put my argument together for the hearing tomorrow, but I've already been told that your prior record will make it nearly impossible. I'm sorry, Mr. Gravano."

Gravano could feel the anger rising in him, but he knew better than to take it out on his lawyer. He knew that Rosenberg had done his best, and that if there were a way to spring him, Rosenberg would have found it. He took a moment before replying. "That's unfortunate."

"Don't worry, sir, once we get those kids, you'll be in a much better position."

"What about my boys, how are they doing? Does it look like either of them are going to crack under the pressure?"

"No, they are both doing pretty well, and it does look like Matthew has a shot at bail, because he has no record and his face was not captured on the recording of the incident. I may be able to make a case that he wasn't even there."

"But the Donovan kid's testimony puts him there."

"True, Mr. Gravano, but the video doesn't, and if there is no Donovan kid, the case against Matthew and possibly even Paulie will get thrown out. In the meantime, I'll try every trick I know, and call in every favor I can to get Matthew bail."

"Good enough." Gravano took one of the papers and began writing out some instructions for his lawyer to deliver. He signed several other papers that Rosenberg had prepared. When he was finished, he handed the papers to Rosenberg and said, "Give this to Joey or Anthony, no one else."

"Yes, sir," he accepted the papers from his boss and put them in his briefcase. "Is there anything else you need?" Rosenberg asked.

"No, just for you to make sure my guys get rid of the Donovan kids," Gravano replied. Rosenberg nodded his understanding and turned to go.

*****

The following day, the Gravanos had their hearings. As expected, Sal and Paulie were denied bail, but surprisingly, Matthew's bail was set at three million dollars. Bail was paid by the afternoon and Matthew had his freedom. He couldn't leave the city, but at least he was on the outside to convey his father's wishes to the rest of the organization.

"Mr. Rosenberg, I need to go see Joey and Anthony, immediately," Matthew said to the lawyer as they walked down the steps of the courthouse. The sky was dark and rain had been forecast for the late November afternoon.

"I've got a car waiting for you around the corner. I've got to stay in Manhattan and take care of a couple more things for your father. Before you say anything to Joey or anyone concerning this case, make sure the area and any electronic devices you might be using are swept for bugs."

"No problem," he replied. He stopped and shook his lawyer's hand before turning to go.

"I'm serious, Matthew," Rosenberg called to him. "The feds are pulling out all the stops to put your whole family behind bars. You have to be very careful."

"I will," he called out as he continued walking towards the waiting car. He stopped short of the black Mercedes to purchase a hotdog from a street vendor before ducking into the back seat of the car. The sky opened up before they even reached the Brooklyn Bridge and traffic began to back up.

Matthew listened to the rain patter off the Mercedes, while his patience with the traffic started to wear thin. "Hey," he called to the driver. "Did Rosenberg give you an extra phone for me? I've got people to talk to and I don't want to wait for this traffic."

"Yes, sir, Mr. Gravano," the driver replied, and then he handed him a phone, never taking his eyes off the road.

Matthew took the phone and started dialing, his first call would be to Heather.

*****

Joey was on his way to meet with Matthew when his phone started buzzing. He answered the call and the voice on the other side of the call started to speak. "Joey, It's Vic. I'm in Danbury and I think I've spotted something."

"What do ya got for me, Vic? I'm on my way over to talk to Matthew. It would be better if I had something good to tell him." He tapped the gas pedal and his car moved forward almost twelve feet. He hated rush hour on the Staten Island Expressway.

"I'm sitting outside a mom and pop deli on Main Street and I see a guy go in by himself. He looks like a cop, so I wait for him to leave and then go in right after. I asked the old lady if he's a regular and she tells me that lately he is."

"Lately?"

"Yeah, as in five times in the last couple weeks, and she ain't never seen him before that."

"That's something. He could just be new in town, though, Vic." A car horn blared somewhere behind him followed by a loud crashing noise and he smiled to himself, knowing the people behind him were in for an even longer commute than he was.

"Maybe, but he always buys six sandwiches."

"Maybe he's married with four kids."

"Possibly, but I think it's a cop and he's got three buddies and two witnesses to buy for." He exited his car and hustled across the street. "I'm on my

151

way down the street to the Chinese place now. I want to see if the same guy has come in at all."

"Okay. Let me know when you find out." Joey hung up the phone and continued to concentrate on the stop-and-go traffic. *I really hate rush hour*, he thought.

Victor walked into the Chinese restaurant and was greeted at the door by a polite middle-aged woman. She picked up a menu and began to walk through the room decorated in red and gold. "I'm sorry, ma'am, I'm not here to eat. I was wondering if you've seen a buddy of mine recently." He pulled out his phone and showed the woman a picture of the man that he had taken at the deli.

"Yeah, I've seen him three or four times this week."

Vic took out a twenty and said, "How many meals does he usually order?" She palmed the twenty and it disappeared into her pocket.

"He was here last night and he ordered six."

"Fantastic, thank you." Vic left the restaurant and called Joey while he walked back to his car.

"What's the word, Vic?" Joey asked.

"Tell Matthew we've got a legitimate lead. He has been to the Chinese place several times in the last week as well. I'm gonna stake out the Deli and follow him next time he comes in. As soon as I know his destination and whether or not the kids are there, I'll let you know."

"Excellent, good work. I won't send anyone else until we know for sure. I wouldn't want to scare them off. We probably won't get a second chance with this." He hung up the phone and smiled. Rosenberg would indeed have some good news for Matthew's father.

*****

Dani was alone in her room. She had taped a few of her drawings to the walls to give the room a little more character. She sat on the floor, wrapped herself in her pink comforter, and drew. She was working on a picture of Peter catching a touchdown pass. She hoped it would be good enough that he would hang it in his room.

While she drew, she began to think of her friends at church. She really missed them, especially Laura and her family. She silently began to pray; "God do you think I'll ever see Laura and Hailey and the Jenkins again? Do you think

152

I'll ever be able to go back to church again? I've been reading James Chapter One like Laura's mom told me to, and I'm wondering, what purpose could you have for all of this? How does going through this make me a better Christian? I wish I had the answers, God." She stood up and moved over to the bed, it was getting late, and she was tired. She continued praying until she fell asleep.

The next morning, she woke up to the smell of bacon. She followed her nose to the source and it was Marshal Jackson delivering their breakfast. He delivered four bacon, egg, and cheese sandwiches with salt, pepper, and ketchup, along with four individual cartons of Tropicana orange juice. Danielle yawned and stretched as she walked over to the food Scarvelli was holding. He handed her a sandwich and a juice while he continued talking to Jackson and she sat down on the couch with her breakfast. She was halfway through when Peter began to make his way downstairs. He accepted his food and joined her.

"How'd you sleep, Dani?"

"Not bad. That comforter is really cozy."

"I think I have the same one in blue," he said, taking a big bite of his sandwich. His sister laughed at him as she wiped a streak of ketchup off of his cheek.

"Why don't you try to take a bigger bite next time, Peter?"

"Maybe I will." He smirked at her and took the biggest bite she had ever seen. She cracked up watching him try to chew and swallow it all. To his credit, he did, but not before almost spitting it all out when Scarvelli did the same thing. They both looked at him and watched him chew until he was finished.

"What? I thought it was a contest."

"No, it was just my brother being stupid and me laughing at him," Danielle replied.

Peter feigned annoyance and then began to chug his juice, finishing the whole container before coming up for air. "Let's see you do that, Scarvelli."

"Challenge accepted!" Scarvelli tore open his juice and guzzled it like Peter had. When he was finished, they both looked to Danielle. She raised her juice to her lips and took a single sip, knowing her brother and the Marshal would mock her.

"I see the youngest among you is the most intelligent," Tom said, pulling a chair towards the couch. Danielle smiled at him, but Peter just held up his container and squished it against his head, while he tried to keep a straight face.

153

"Let's see you do that with a can?" Scarvelli said.

"Challenge accepted!" Peter replied. He started towards the kitchen, but Tom stopped him.

"Sorry, Peter, we need your head to remain undamaged until you testify." He looked at Scarvelli and added a little bit louder, "Don't we, Scarvelli?"

Scarvelli shifted in his seat and said, "Yeah, I suppose slamming metal cans into your head should wait until after the trial."

"Or not at all," Danielle replied, not realizing they were joking. They all started to chuckle and she realized they hadn't been serious. She was really beginning to like these Marshals. It almost felt like a real family with them. She knew it wasn't, but she enjoyed the thought.

*****

"I got em, Joey. Tell the boss I found the Donovan kids," Victor said with a hint of pride in his voice.

"Really? How?" Joey was dumbfounded at how fast Victor had gotten results after identifying a man he thought to be a US Marshal.

"I staked out the Deli like I said I was gonna, and he was back this morning for egg sandwiches. I followed him to a house and the guy who answered the door only opened it halfway and his body was in position to block the opening. The guy gave him the sandwiches and kept one for himself and one for the other guy in the car."

"Sounds like four Marshals guarding two people. How can we be sure it's the right two people?"

"Joey, Joey, Joey, I can't believe you would think I would leave the job half done. You should know me better than that. I found a spot a few blocks away where I could get a clear view of the house and watched it with my camera. About an hour later, the girl sat down by the window in the kitchen to draw. One of the Marshals was doing a sweep of the neighborhood, so I left, but not before I got a picture." He sent the image to Joey and waited.

After a few moments, Joey said, "Great work, Vic! This is unbelievable! Stay out of sight. I'm gonna run this up to Matthew and wait for his instructions. I'm sure you'll be getting a crew tonight, just don't let these Marshals see you before then. Send me the address, too." He ended the call and Victor

154

immediately texted him the address. Joey's next call was to the only Gravano that had made bail.

"Matthew, we found them. Vic got eyes on the girl up in Danbury."

"I want eight guys up there tonight, Joey. No one leaves that house! Do you understand me?"

"I'll lead them up myself."

"Good, now I have to call Rosenberg, he's about to deliver some great news to my father." The call ended and Matthew called the Lawyer and relayed the information.

Rosenberg was excited to have some good news for the boss. He had dreaded going back to the holding facility with nothing new to report, but everything had worked out as planned. Joey's hacker cousin had been right, hacking the schedule was the best way to go and now the witnesses against his boss were about to be eliminated.

Chapter 14

The moonlight danced off the hood of the silver Mustang, while Jackson walked past, patrolling the area. It was a frigid night and he rubbed his hands together trying to keep them warm. It had gone from chilly to very cold fast and he was ill-prepared. He wished he had won the coin toss for the car, but it wasn't meant to be. "Tompkins, come in," Jackson called into his radio. He had already tried the cell phone, and they hadn't been given comms, so it was up to the old-school radio. His fingers ached as he pressed the cold button. He was beginning to worry that he hadn't heard from his partner when without warning, a bullet ripped through his leg. He cried out and fell to the ground, dropping the radio. He scooted behind the nearest car for cover, still unsure of where the shot had come from. He realized that he hadn't heard the shot, which meant silencers. That meant the mob had found them.

He fumbled for his gun forgetting the cold and the pain, but before he could squeeze off a shot to alert Tom and Scarvelli another bullet ripped through his shoulder. He dropped the gun and stared at it for a moment, dazed. Then he reached for it with his good arm, crying out with the pain every movement caused. In his agony he thought he could see three men walk up to him, then one of them pointed something at him and it all went dark.

Joey and Vic led the six men towards the house. Three would go in the front, two in the side door and three in the back. No one would be leaving alive.

Inside the house, Tom was getting worried. He hadn't been able to raise Tompkins or Jackson for a couple minutes, and they were late returning from their rounds. "Jackson, come in," he called into the radio. "Tompkins, are you there?"

Scarvelli walked over to him and asked, "Is everything all right?"

"I'm not sure. Jackson, are you there?"

Peter heard the conversation going on in the living room because he never closed his bedroom door. He slipped out of bed and put his shoes on. He put his hoodie on and checked to make sure his backpack was ready. He tip toed into his sister's room and gave her shoulder a gentle shake. Her eyes opened up and his hand covered her mouth. He put his finger to his mouth and she nodded her understanding.

"What's wrong, Peter?" she asked in her quietest whisper.

"Tom and Scarvelli can't reach Jackson on their walkie-talkies," he replied in a low voice. "It may be nothing, but it's not sitting well with me. Put your shoes and sweatshirt on." He looked over to see that her bag was mostly packed. He put her drawing pad and her pencils in the bag while she got ready.

"What now?" she asked and he could see the fear in her eyes.

"Now we wait. Get your jacket on, I'll be right back." He disappeared into the dark of his bedroom and she could hear the window being opened. It was slow going because he didn't want to make any noise. A moment later Peter returned. He had his brown leather jacket on. "If I don't like how things are going, we're going to go into my room and climb down the tree into the yard. Then we run through the yard to the next block, and keep running 'til we're safe."

"It's probably nothing. I bet the batteries just ran out because of the cold." Even as she said it, she had a hard time believing it.

Joey gave the signal and all three doors opened at once. Eight men poured into the dark house firing their weapons. The silencers kept the noise down until Scarvelli started firing back. Then the fight was no longer quiet.

"How'd they find us, Tom?" Scarvelli yelled drawing the fire of two of the thugs. He continued shooting in their direction until he hit one of them. His next shot emptied his gun.

"I don't know, but we gotta get these kids out of here," he replied while shooting one of the attackers in the leg. The man went down and Tom shot him again.

"I don't see that happening, Tom," Scarvelli said, as he dropped his empty magazine on the floor, retrieved a new one off his belt, and slapped it in without looking. Years of training paid off in that instant. He started firing again, hitting another intruder before he took two in the shoulder and one in the leg. He cried out in pain. He fell to the floor still firing until another shot silenced him.

"Scarvelli, No!" Tom yelled. He continued firing and managed to hit another of Gravano's men before he was cut down from three separate weapons.

When the firing finally stopped, Joey surveyed the scene. He pointed to one of his guys and said, "We gotta get those kids fast! Someone had to hear all that and the cops are probably already on the way."

Peter grabbed Dani's hand as soon as he heard the first shot and led her out of her room. When they crossed the hallway at the top of the stairs, Peter saw three men climbing the stairs. They had almost reached the top. Peter's presence surprised them and, before they could bring their guns to bear, Peter kicked the lead man as hard as he could in the chest sending him tumbling down the stairs and tripping up the other two.

"Run, Dani!" he yelled as he picked himself up off the floor. A bullet whizzed by his ear and he threw himself into his room, slamming the door behind him. *That was too close!* He jimmied a folding chair under the door handle, hoping it would hold off their attackers while they climbed down the tree. He saw Danielle waiting for him on the roof with frozen tears on her cheek, and he swept his backpack up off the floor and onto his back in one fluid motion. "Go!" he whispered. She climbed out onto the tree branch that had stretched out over the roof.

"I'm scared, Peter." Dani whispered while she lowered herself onto a different branch.

"It's okay, just don't look down." he replied.

"I'm not scared of the tree, how did these guys find us? Where are we gonna go?" Her voice was beginning to rise just above a whisper while she climbed. "How are we—?"

"Dani! Shhh!" Peter dropped from his branch landing in silence on the ground. He reached up and grabbed his sister's waist and helped her down. He took her hand and they ran through a small gap in the hedges and through the neighbor's yard.

"Did you get them?" Joey called up the stairs to Anthony.

"Not yet, they're barricaded in their room, we'll have them soon. What about the Marshals?" He asked, while continuing to fire into the hinges of the oak door.

"We got them. As long as there's not more than four, we should be all right."

"What about our guys?"

"We got one dead and three wounded."

"How serious?"

"One is pretty serious, the others not too bad. They've already left for a doctor we can trust." Just then he heard a crash, as the door was busted open.

"We're through, Joey. Oh no!"

"Oh no? What's oh no? I don't want to hear 'oh no', Anthony!"

Anthony and the remaining two men ran down the stairs and past him. Before they reached the back door, he called out to Joey, "The kids went out the window and down the tree. They're gone!"

"You guys give chase on foot. I'll search in the car. We've gotta get out of here, now!" Joey ran out the front door into the frigid night. He jumped into his car and drove away. He was driving pretty slow, looking for any sign of the two kids that were proving to be a lot more trouble than he had bargained for.

Anthony, Victor and Dom followed Peter and Danielle's path out of the yard, but when they came out on the next street they were faced with three options. Just a couple houses down, a side street intersected the block.

"Which way do you think they went, Vic?" Anthony asked while they stood in front of the old Victorian house.

"My gut says they went towards the park. There's a lot more places to hide in the park, but we need to check the other directions as well."

"Okay, we each take a direction. Keep your phones handy, and let's get these kids." They split up and jogged off in different directions to begin their search.

"Are they following us?" Danielle whispered while she continued to run. They had made it all the way to the park unnoticed. They continued running into a heavy patch of trees.

"I don't know, Dani," Peter replied. They came to the end of the trees and saw some flowing water. It was not quite a river, but it was too wide for them to cross. Peter stopped and looked around. "The trees are pretty thick here, let's go up and try to wait it out."

"Do you think Tom and Scarvelli will find us?" She asked in a hopeful voice.

Peter hated to answer, but he didn't want to lie. "Dani, I don't think they survived."

"You don't know that," she said and then started to cry. "They have to be okay. Scarvelli has two little girls. Who's going to take care of them?"

Peter put his arms around his sister and said, "You're right, Dani, I don't know. For now we have to hide, and we don't come out for anyone. Okay?" He held her shoulders and looked into her eyes.

She wiped her tears and her nose with her sleeve and said, "Okay."

"Good, now, let's start climbing, and we have to be quiet." He picked her up and she reached for the lowest branch. When she took hold of it, he put his hands under her feet and boosted her up into the tree. "Keep climbing as high as you can go."

"Peter, it's too cold, it's hurting my hands." She said as she continued her slow climb.

"I know, just keep going. We don't have a choice. We weren't prepared for this weather and we don't have warm enough clothes." He jumped up and grabbed the lowest branch. While he pulled himself up he grunted in pain.

"Are you okay?"

"Yeah, just keep climbing and no talking." They were two thirds of the way up the towering tree when they heard something and froze.

"Did you find them, Vic?" Joey called from the road. He got out of his car and jogged over to his associate. A steady breeze left a constant reminder that it was unseasonably cold out.

"Not yet, although I'm pretty sure they are still in the park somewhere." They both began to walk into the wooded area.

"We don't have very long to search, Vic. Cops are gonna be swarming this town soon."

"But we're not gonna get another shot at these kids if they make it back into custody." They looked out at the water and Joey threw his hands up. "Where did they go?"

"Why didn't Anthony have someone stay out back?" Vic asked. Then he began a slow turn to take in the entire area. He looked up, down, everywhere and couldn't see anything. There may have been some moonlight, but in the dense woods, not much of it was getting through.

"No one made it past him, Vic. How could we have possibly known about the tree outside the kid's window." The wind began to pick up and Joey shivered and thrust his hands in his pockets.

"This is why you don't plan a hit without thoroughly scouting out the area." He didn't think that now would be a good time to tell Joey that he had seen the tree when he took Danielle's picture, and didn't account for it as a possible means of escape.

"Gravano needed this done now, that's why we planned it on short notice. Don't forget we just killed four Marshals, so we can't get caught in this area, Vic." Sirens began to blare in the background and Joey knew that was his cue to go.

"Looks like we're done searching for the night. Let's hope these kids are too scared to go back to the cops. If they go on the run themselves we still have a shot." They turned to go and Victor heard a soft click like a breaking branch. "Did you hear that, Joey?"

"Hear what? With all this wind, I can barely hear you." His phone beeped and he picked it up. After a minute, he said, "Okay, we'll be right there." He started walking and noticed a branch under his foot. He looked back to see Victor still looking around and said, "Hey, Vic, I think you heard me stepping on this." He pointed to the branch and added, "Come on, we gotta go. The cops are starting to pour in and we have to go get Anthony and Dom." Victor was reluctant, but he finally nodded and then the two of them jogged through the park back to the car

"We should stake out the bus stop and the train stop. If the kids try to run, there's a good chance they end up there."

"Good idea, Vic."

Peter could see the men below them, but he was pretty sure that they were high enough up in the tree that they wouldn't be seen. If it had been daytime, that would not have been the case. He couldn't hear what they were saying because the wind was so strong. Dani was on the limb next to him, shivering, but otherwise quiet. He felt a knot developing in his stomach and he was frozen with fear. He prayed in silence they would remain hidden because he knew they had no more running left in them.

He almost jumped out of the tree when he felt a tap on his shoulder. "What is it Dani?" he asked in a whisper so soft even he had trouble hearing it.

"I think I'm slipping, Peter." Her voice was quiet enough but he could still hear the dread in it.

"Just hold on. I know it's cold and I know it hurts, but there's nowhere for us to go. Now might be a good time for you to pray or something." The wind had picked up and the trees were beginning to sway.

"I've been praying," she whispered. "But I'll keep going." She shifted her leg, and the branch she was using for balance cracked. Danielle started to slip and Peter reached out and grabbed her backpack. He managed to keep her from falling, but it seemed as if one of the thugs had heard. He grimaced as his ribs strained, but he was not going to let his sister fall.

161

"Hold on, Dani, I've got you," he whispered. He kept his eyes trained on the men below and one of them was looking around. Peter almost cried out in joy when he heard the faint sound of police sirens over the whistle of the wind. A few moments later, the two mobsters began jogging back to their car. When they reached the car and drove away Peter felt free to speak a little louder than a whisper.

"I think they're gone, Dani. Try to get resituated."

"Why, can't we get down now?"

"Because they may still have someone watching the park. We'll have to get comfortable; we're up here for a while. We can climb a little lower where it's more stable." When they had reached a safer branch to hide on, Peter took his backpack off and unzipped it. He pulled out the only other sweatshirt he had with him and handed it to his sister.

"What's this for?"

"Put it on under your jacket. It's really cold and you don't have a hat or a hood."

"What about you? Your jacket isn't any heavier than mine."

"But I have a hood."

"But you must be freezing."

"Don't worry about me, you need to cover your head or you'll get sick. Plus, when we do get down, it will help keep your face hidden."

"Thanks, Peter." She put the sweatshirt on over her other sweat shirt and then rushed to put her jacket back on. She zipped it up all the way and then put the hood on, drawing the strings as tight as they would go. Then she leaned over and put her arms around her big brother and he put his arms around her. "This should help with the cold," she said and leaned her head against his chest.

Peter had no idea how much time had passed, but Dani had fallen asleep leaning on him. He could hear his own teeth chattering, his legs had fallen asleep, and to make matters worse a light snow had just begun. "Dani. Dani, wake up. It's time to go."

She began to stir, "Peter, I'm so cold. Can we get down now?"

"Yeah, let's go. We'll stay side by side until we reach the bottom, then I'll jump down and help you. Okay?"

"Okay." Her lips looked blue and her teeth were chattering. He knew he needed to get her out of there fast. "Let's go, nice and easy." They climbed down to the bottom limb and Peter jumped down. He winced again, cursing his injured ribs. Danielle threw her backpack to him and hung down from the limb until she could feel her brother's hands clutch her legs. She let herself down a little further until her brother had her around the waist. He was careful not to twist his upper body as he put her down.

"Peter, are you okay? I didn't hurt your ribs, did I?"

"No, they're just a little stiff from the cold. Let's go. We don't want to leave tracks in the snow." They walked through the park as the snow continued to fall. When they were several blocks from the crime scene they exited the park.

They continued walking for hours. They didn't dare stop; they didn't dare trust anyone. Eventually they found themselves trudging along Route Seven. They came to a stop sign and they saw an eighteen-wheeler coming their way.

"Peter, I'm so cold and I can barely move. It's been snowing for hours and my feet are soaked. Please can we ask this guy for a ride?" As if to punctuate her point, she sneezed three times and looked up at him with weary, pleading eyes.

"Okay, Dani, let's try it." He was just as tired as she was, and he knew the best way to get more distance between them and Gravano's men would be in a vehicle. He stepped a couple feet out into the road and began waving. The truck pulled up to the stop sign and the driver rolled down the window. He was a large man wearing a red flannel coat and a wool hat. He had a black beard that was fairly well kept, kind eyes, and rosy cheeks.

"Can I help you, son?"

"Good morning, sir, my car broke down several miles back, and my sister and I have been walking all night. Do you think you could give us a lift?" He paused for a moment and then added, "We could give you some gas money."

He looked down at the two of them and they looked miserable. Just then Danielle sneezed again, and he decided he'd take a chance. "Sure, where are you heading?"

"We were trying to get to Niagara Falls, but anywhere warm will do for now?"

"Hop in. I've got a delivery to make near Albany, and then I'm heading west to Syracuse. From there you should be able to get a bus to Niagara. You can save your gas money for that."

163

"Thank you so much, sir," Danielle said while Peter helped her up into the rig. "I didn't think I'd ever be warm again." She put her hands right up to the vent that was pumping out the heat. She smiled when some feeling started coming back to her hands.

"Yeah, thank you," Peter echoed. He sat next to his sister in the truck and closed the door.

"No problem. Looks like the weather caught you two off guard. You're not dressed nearly warm enough. I'm Jake by the way." He put the rig into gear and their road trip began.

"Hi, Jake. I'm Danielle and my brother's name is Peter." Peter nodded his hello.

"Well, it's nice to meet you," Jake replied.

Almost three hours later, the trucker made his delivery to a small warehouse near Albany. He had complained that it was slow going because of the snow, but Peter and Danielle didn't mind because they were finally warm. Ten minutes later, they were stopped at a diner. It was a greasy spoon by the side of the road, but Peter and Danielle were so hungry they would have eaten anything. Peter had a burger and fries with a coke and Danielle had a bowl of chicken noodle soup, which came with a half a sandwich. She had chosen ham and Swiss, and she also ordered a hot chocolate. After they ate, Peter paid the bill, much to Jake's delight, and then they were back on the road to Syracuse.

*****

"They what?" Gravano yelled loud enough to be heard in the next room.

"They lost the kids, Mr. Gravano," Rosenberg replied.

"How is that possible? They killed all the Marshals, right?"

"As far as I know, they did. Joey went in with seven other guys and two were killed and two more were injured. All four Marshals were reported killed, but during the firefight, the kids barricaded themselves in an upstairs room and by the time Anthony got through, they were out the window, down a tree and out of the yard. Joey, Anthony, Vic and Dom searched the area until the police showed up to the safe house."

"Do we know if they're back in federal custody?"

"At this point, we have no idea," Rosenberg admitted.

"What a mess. We're never gonna get another shot at these kids." He pounded his fist on the desk. "What's our next move?"

"I'm not sure we have one. If the kids testify, we're buried. I can attack their credibility, I'll throw the whole bag of tricks at them, but the bottom line is if their testimony even remotely syncs up with the video, we're done."

"Not good enough. Get out of here and come up with something. I'll see you then." Gravano was disgusted with the incompetence his men had shown by letting the kids get away. He needed to be alone right now.

Rosenberg got his papers together and put them in his briefcase in an organized fashion. Gravano had written out some orders for him to have carried out. "I'll contact you as soon as I have something. In the meantime, I'll coordinate with Matthew to figure out if the feds have the kids."

"Good! I'll see you when you have some good news, then." He turned and rapped on the door. A moment later, a guard opened the door and escorted Gravano back to his cell. Rosenberg stayed behind for a moment wondering how his life had become about getting children killed.

A few minutes later, Rosenberg was outside the holding facility, on the phone with Matthew. He didn't like the kid very much. He had never done anything to earn the respect he demanded, and he enjoyed rubbing his position in people's faces. This didn't sit well with Rosenberg, being one of the usual targets of the boy's ire. The kid was treating him like it was his fault the witnesses were still alive when the fact was it was Matthews friends that botched the job.

"Just make sure we can find these kids again, Rosenberg. What do you think my father is paying you for?"

"Your father pays me to keep him and his sons out of jail. That's what he pays me for! My plan to find the Donovan kids worked, the problem was with the execution of the plan."

"What are you saying, Rosenberg?"

"I'm saying your friends screwed up, and if those kids are back in custody we're not gonna get another shot at them."

"You had better pray they are not back in custody then."

Rosenberg hated this back and forth so he decided to be the bigger man and let Matthew's stupidity slide. "Your father has some things he needs for you to do over the next couple days." He read off the list of chores, savoring each of Matthews's complaints, and suggesting that if he had problems with his

165

assignments, he take it up with his father. The conversation finally ended when he reached his car. He took his glasses off and squeezed the bridge of his nose before he started rubbing at his eyes. Then, he finally sat down in his car and let out a sigh.

Chapter 15

Dozens of police, FBI and crime scene techs poured over the safe house trying to figure out what exactly had happened in there. They moved about—back and forth. Some of them carrying evidence bags, others taking pictures, and still others searching for clues. To the casual observer it might have looked like chaos, but the work was actually fairly organized.

Bystanders stood in the cold snow. They were lined up just outside the yellow, caution tape perimeter the police had set up, wondering how a shootout of this magnitude could have happened in their quiet neighborhood. With the exception of the officers tasked with keeping the crowd back, the Police and FBI went about their business, ignoring the onlookers.

Lance Stevens stood alone in an upstairs bedroom looking over some of the drawings Danielle Donovan had left on the wall. He speculated about whether or not the Donovan kids were still alive. It would be a shame if they weren't; he thought they were nice kids. They were easy witnesses, as well. The only thing even resembling a demand either one of them had made was when Peter got passionate about his sister not seeing their father again; which was a completely reasonable request. He wondered how the safe house had been compromised. He was lost in thought, and didn't hear the crime scene tech and the Special Agent come into the room.

"The kid could draw, huh, Stevens," the tech said as he entered the room.

"Yeah, and she was a sweet kid, too," he replied.

"Probably still is," the tech replied.

"Wait, you have news?" Agent Davis asked

"I believe so; I wanted to give it to both of you together."

Stevens and Davis looked at each other and then motioned for the tech to continue. "So, what do you have?" Davis asked.

"We believe seven or eight men attacked the safe house. Marshals Jackson and Tompkins were killed before the attackers hit the house. We've found large amounts of blood from two different people, and smaller amounts of blood from two additional people. None of that blood matches Scarvelli's or Lancer's blood which means they hit at least four of Gravano's men before they went down. I wouldn't be surprised if one or two of them died from their wounds judging by the amount of blood they left at the scene. The Marshalls put up one heck of a fight."

"How does this help us know if the kids survived?" Stevens asked.

"It doesn't, it's the evidence in the other bedroom that suggests they might still be alive." They walked into the other room and the tech continued. "Several shots were fired into the hinges and knob of the door and when it finally came down it landed on top of a folding metal chair suggesting it was propped up keeping the attackers out. Also the open window suggests the kids made it onto the roof and down the tree."

"So the kids made it out alive?" Stevens asked, letting just a little hope build up.

"That's what the evidence suggests," the tech replied. He looked at the other two men and then looked out the window. "They likely went through that small gap in the hedges onto the next street." He pointed to the spot while he spoke. "The attackers may have followed them, but because of the extended fire fight and the need to remove the injured, they probably didn't have much time to search."

Before the tech had finished speaking, Davis was on his radio telling his men to go out the back and search for clues in every possible direction. He looked at the tech and asked, "Is there anything else?"

"If you don't find their bodies within a reasonable proximity, they are probably still alive," the tech replied.

"If they are alive, where are they? Why wouldn't they go right to the police?" Stevens asked.

"They're probably too scared. Their safe house didn't turn out to be very safe," Davis said. Before Stevens could reply, one of Davis' men was on his radio.

"Agent Davis, we've got something on the next block, you should come hear this."

"Copy that. I'm on my way." Before he left the room, a thought occurred to him. "Did you find any blood belonging to either of the kids?"

"Preliminary tests show all the blood to be male. I won't know any more than that until the rest of the tests come back."

"Thanks," Davis replied then he was out the door with Stevens in tow. When they reached the next block, two of his men were talking with one of the neighbors. A young agent and a Hispanic man walked towards them. "Agent Davis, this is Jorge Tejada. He witnessed part of what went down last night."

"Hello, Jorge. Can you tell me what you saw last night?" He could see his breath and wondered when this cold front would finish passing through.

"As I was telling your men, not a whole lot. My family and I were all sleeping when the gunshots woke us. My daughter came into the bedroom because she was scared. I was scared that a stray bullet would get one of us, so I put my little girl in the tub. Then I heard something in the yard. I looked out the front window and saw two teenagers running through my yard. When they reached the street, they turned and ran towards the park at the bottom of the block."

"A boy and a girl?" Stevens asked

"I think so, but it was dark. Then almost three minutes later, three men came through my yard. They stood out in front of my house for almost a minute before splitting up. One went up the street, one went down the side street, and one went towards the park. He was met by a dark SUV at the bottom of the street. I don't know what kind."

"Thank you, Jorge. That was very helpful. One of my men is going to stay and take your full statement." He walked back towards the safe house and called over the radio. "Parker, I need you to take some men to search the park."

The words "Yes, sir," echoed out of his radio, and then he turned to Stevens and said, "I think these kids made it."

"We need to get a BOLO out right away, then."

Davis looked like he didn't really like that idea. "I'm not sure."

"Agent Davis, if those kids are out there on their own, they are easy prey for Gravano's goons."

"Unless Gravano thinks we still have them, then he won't be looking for them. I say we keep it quiet and just have the Bureau search for them."

"That's taking an awfully big risk; I'm going to need my boss to sign off on that."

"It's just as big a risk plastering their faces all over the place. Then it's just a race between us and Gravano to see who can get to them first."

"It already is. I'm sure the guys that attacked the safe house know the kids got away, and I'm sure they are monitoring local police stations to see if the kids went back into custody."

"I guess we'll let our bosses decide then," Davis said.

169

"This is probably the most important case we'll have this year. We have to get those kids back or Gravano might walk."

"Even with the video?"

"It would be tough, but it's possible. Rosenberg is a good lawyer." He rubbed his hands together and added, "We just really need those kids."

*****

Danielle waved goodbye to Jake and watched as the big rig pulled away. The sputtering sound of an accelerating truck and the smell of burning diesel fuel filled the air. As promised, he had dropped them off at the bus terminal. The sign on the building read: Syracuse Regional Transit Center. Next to the building, Dani saw a lake. It was a pretty big lake and a cold breeze was coming off the water. On the far side of the water, she could see a tree-lined shore. As cold as it was, she could smell a difference in the air and she liked it.

"Look at how beautiful it is up here, Peter."

"Dani, it's freezing out here, let's get inside."

"Just give me a minute to look. I wish I had my camera." Peter waited patiently for her to finish looking across the lake. He had his back to the breeze with his hood up and his hands in his pockets. He turned back around and saw Danielle's cheeks practically glowing red.

"Come on, Dani. I don't want you to get sick." They walked to the building and Peter held the door for his sister. The building was warm and the first thing Peter spotted was some hats and scarves hanging on a rack in the station gift store. He nudged his sister and pointed at the items they desperately needed. Her eyes lit up and they walked over to the store.

"Oh look, they have everything we need, hats gloves, scarves. They even have sweatshirts with hoods in my size. Now I can give you back yours." Danielle began to look through the gift store. It was filled with trinkets and clothing emblazoned with the Syracuse University logo. There were a few things that were from the city itself, but it was mostly the type of souvenirs people would buy after visiting the university. It wasn't long before Danielle had picked out everything she needed.

When she reached the register, Peter was already waiting with his items and a smile. "Beat ya," he said. The woman at the register smiled at them and then began to ring up the items.

"Looks like you got caught unprepared for this weather. I've sold a ton of hats and gloves today. The storm just rolled in so quickly, didn't it? I heard the temperature dipped to negative six degrees with the wind chill this morning. I hope you weren't stuck out in that."

"Yeah, we got hit pretty hard, but we made it, and now we'll be prepared." Danielle replied.

The woman placed the merchandise in a shopping bag and after Peter paid her she handed him the bag over the counter. Once they were out of the store, they began to take the price tags off the merchandise and put them on.

"I never, ever, want to be that cold again," Danielle said, looking over her new sweatshirt. Peter had purchased a long sleeve tee shirt to put under his sweatshirt as an extra layer. After he put it on, he put his hoodie and jacket back on. He put his new hat and gloves in his pocket.

Danielle handed him back his extra sweatshirt after she put on her new one, and he put it in his backpack. She also put her hat and gloves in her jacket pockets and wrapped the scarf around her neck. They walked over to the counter and purchased two bus tickets to Niagara Falls. The bus would be leaving in an hour and fifteen minutes, so they decided to get some lunch.

After they purchased their food, they found a table overlooking the lake Danielle had been looking at. "It's much nicer to look at from in here when we're not freezing," Peter said.

"The lady in the store told me it's called Lake Onondaga," Danielle replied in a cheerful tone. "It sounds Native American. Isn't that cool?"

"You're amazing, Dani. After everything that happened, all it takes is some warm clothes, a little food, and a nice view and you're perfectly happy."

"I know we're in danger, but I believe God is going to protect us, Peter."

"I wish I had your faith, sis, but just because you believe God will take care of things doesn't mean we can relax. There are a lot of people that want us dead."

"I know, Peter, but that doesn't mean we shouldn't enjoy what we can. This is the first time we've ever been out of the city."

"Yeah, I guess it is pretty cool. Now hurry up and eat, we need to stay out of sight and off people's radar as much as possible."

"Why can't we just go back to the police?"

"They can't keep us safe, Dani. Obviously, someone leaked something, because they found us, and it didn't even take them very long to do it."

"Do you really think the Marshals are dead?"

"I'm sorry, Dani, but yeah I do."

"But how do you know?" She was starting to tear up at the thought that Tom and Scarvelli were no longer alive.

"Dani, there was a lot of shooting, and when the shooting stopped it was Gravano's guys that came looking for us. If Tom or Scarvelli were alive, it would have been them looking for us."

Danielle felt hot tears start to stream down her face. She looked at her brother and knew he was right. "Scarvelli will never see his little girls grow up now, because of us." She rubbed at her eyes and her breath started to catch.

"That's not true. They died doing their job, and we're alive because of it. It's Gravano's fault Scarvelli won't see his girls grow up, not ours. We didn't make any mistakes that led those guys to us. It was all on their end." They finished their meal in silence, and then they walked to the bus platform. Forty five minutes later, they were on their way to Niagara Falls.

*****

"Broken branch high in this tree suggests the kids hid up there last night," Agent Parker said to Agent Davis.

"Really, you get all of that from a broken branch?"

"No, I climbed up and wiped the snow off the branches and saw evidence of climbing on several limbs. On that big limb halfway up I saw evidence of two people. This is where they hid."

"And Gravano's people didn't have enough time to do a thorough search."

"It would have been very difficult for them to see the kids that high up in the tree in the dark. It was a pretty impressive climb for a couple kids with only a three minute head start."

"Ain't that the truth? Keep me updated on anything else you find. It looks like I'm gonna lose the BOLO battle, and pretty soon these kids faces are going to be plastered everywhere. I hope to have a lead on these guys when that happens."

"Yes, sir." Parker replied as Davis plodded through the snow towards Stevens.

"I need to get back to the field office in New York. I'm expecting some information from the Attorney General's office about how they found the kids. It's all hush, hush," Stevens said.

"I'll take you. My team can handle the rest of the clean up here. I've got everything I need," Davis replied. "Let's get out of the snow, shall we?"

"Best idea I've heard all day." Stevens rubbed his hands together again to try and ward off the persistent cold. They both entered the SUV and Davis was quick to turn on the heat. When they arrived back in the city, both Davis and Stevens were shocked to learn that the Attorney General's office had been hacked.

"How is that even possible?" Stevens yelled at the video screen. "I would think our office would be an almost impossible hack."

"A hacker figured out that if he hacked our phone's scheduling app, it would be less intrusive and less difficult to spot, and he was right. That's not the problem though. The problem is the hack only searched for one person's schedule."

Stevens had a sinking feeling when he heard that. "Let me guess, mine."

"What does that mean?" Davis asked.

"It means that whoever did this already had the information that Stevens was assigned to this case, which means—"

"We have a leak," Davis finished. "If we have a leak, we might as well go with the BOLO."

"Why the change of heart?" Stevens asked.

"Because there's no way to tell where the leak is or how big it is. If the leak is on our end, Gravano will find out soon enough that the kids are not in custody. We might as well have every available resource on this since we can't keep it quiet."

"I agree," Stevens said. "Let's get it out there, coast to coast, as quick as possible."

"I'll get my office on it right away."

*****

"The kids never went back to the Cops, Matthew." Rosenberg said, happy to have some good news. "I just found out the FBI is about to put out a nationwide alert for them. We may still have a crack at this."

"That's good news. Now all we gotta do is beat the feds to the kids. Have you told my father yet?"

"No, I'm on my way in to tell him now."

"Good. I'll get Joey and Anthony on this. They won't let us down again."

"That's refreshing, because our hacking trick won't work again. They found out that someone had hacked their phones so I'm sure they'll change their protocols."

"That only matters if the feds get the Donovans before we do." He ended the call and dialed Joey. "Hey, Joey, get some guys and head upstate."

"Why?"

"The feds never found the kids, and I'm guessing they went north."

"What makes you think north?"

"Because we're down here, and if I was a scared kid, I'd take off in the opposite direction of the people that want me dead."

"Sounds like a plan. If we catch up with these kids, they won't be getting away again." Joey stepped into his black Mercedes, while Victor got in the other side.

"They had better not." The call ended and Joey started his car.

"Come on, Vic, let's go round up the boys, we're going on a road trip."

"Seems like a good idea to head out. If they are up north, we'll have a head start on the feds if Rosenberg finds out where they are," Vic replied.

"I'm sure that's why Matthew has us doing it." His next call was to Anthony and Dom. he told them to get four more guys to replace the ones they lost in Danbury. "I can't wait to kill these kids, Vic."

"You do realize how messed up that sounds, right?" Victor looked at him and laughed.

"Oh, and you're Mother Teresa?"

Chapter 16

Danielle was asleep when the bus stopped at Niagara Falls. Peter took in the sight for a moment before he woke his sister. He had always heard about the falls, and had even seen a picture once, but pictures and words did not do it justice. They were still on the New York side of the falls, but he had a great vantage point for the Canadian side, the more famous horseshoe shaped falls. Blue-green water turned white as it rushed over the edge of the falls, dropping what seemed like a couple hundred feet. A steady mist rose almost halfway back up as the never-ending deluge struck the Niagara River. It was almost surreal, and then Peter heard someone comment that the water flowed over the falls at over four million gallons a minute. The beauty of the falls was accompanied by the loud rumbling of rushing water. Peter shook his sister knowing she would want to see this.

"Hey, Dani, check it out. Niagara Falls."

She opened her eyes, let out a yawn and then her eyes grew wide. She leaned across her brother to take in the sight. "Peter, this is the most amazing thing I've ever seen."

"Even better than that lake in Syracuse?" he asked with his eyebrow raised.

She elbowed him in the arm and said, "Don't tease me. Of course it's more beautiful than some random lake. It's one of the most famous places in the world."

"In that case I'm glad I woke you to see it."

"Thanks, Petey, I'm glad, too. When I see this, I really understand the whole; beauty of God's creation thing I always hear about at church. The more we see, the more it hits me. How can it not hit you here in one of the most beautiful places ever?"

"I'm sorry, Dani, I don't see God's hand of creation or whatever, I see a waterfall. I'm glad you see more, but I don't."

"I'm gonna keep praying for you, and one day you will." She didn't say anymore, she just put on her hat and stood up from her multi-colored bus seat. She took her backpack out of the overhead rack, yawned again, and trudged towards the front of the bus. Peter followed behind with his pack in hand.

When they exited the bus, the first thing they noticed was that the snow had been shoveled off the walkways and the observation platform. Huge snow mounds scattered around the attraction reminded them of their trek through the storm. Peter shivered, once again, wishing he had a warmer coat, and he walked across the street towards a small bus area. Danielle walked right up to the observation platform of the falls while Peter purchased two bus tickets to Toronto. He felt bad for his sister that their bus would be leaving in twenty minutes, because he knew she could stay and look at the falls all day. After purchasing the tickets, he bought some snacks for the rest of their journey, and then went out to find his sister.

"Dani," Peter called out when he reached the observation platform, but he couldn't see his sister. "Dani," he called a little louder. A knot colder than the freezing air began to well up in his gut when he still couldn't see her. "Dani!" he shouted again, with a frantic edge to his voice as he began to move a little faster through the crowds of people.

An older gentleman saw the look in his eye and asked, "Is everything all right, son?"

"I can't find my sister," he replied while continuing to scan the crowds. "Dani!" he yelled again.

"It'll be okay, son. What does she look like?"

"What?" he asked, still not meeting the older man's eyes.

A strong, steady breeze began to harass the observation area and the older man lifted his collar and thrust his hands in his pockets. "What does she look like?" he repeated.

"She's five three, she has long brown hair. She's wearing a cream colored coat and a blue Syracuse hat." He paused for a minute and then added, "And she's carrying a black backpack."

"I'll keep my eyes open. Why don't you go talk to one of the security officers?"

The mention of security snapped Peter out of his funk. He looked at the man for the first time and said, "It might be a little early for that. I think I'll look a little bit more first." He walked away from the man and yelled again, "Hey, Dani!"

"What?" a soft voice called back. A moment later, Danielle was emerging through the crowd and relief hit Peter like a wave.

"Oh, thank God. Where were you, Dani? I was yelling for you for like five minutes."

"I was up at the front. I couldn't hear you because of the noise of the falls. I'm sorry."

"It's okay, just don't wander off again." He took her by the hand and began to walk towards the bus station. "Our bus leaves in ten minutes. I'm sorry you didn't have much time to see the falls."

She let go of his hand and said, "I just need one more look." Then she ran into the breeze to the front of the observation deck to take it all in one more time. She took a deep breath through her nose to remember the smell, listened to the sound of the water, and drank deep with her eyes to imprint every last detail on the tablet of her mind. She wanted to remember this forever.

After a long couple minutes, Peter took her gloved hand and said, "I'm so sorry, but we really have to go," he started to lead her to the bus stop, and after a few steps, she finally turned around and walked by his side.

"That was the greatest thing I've ever seen, Peter."

"I wish you could have seen it longer."

"Me, too. I'm going to draw it as soon as we get on the bus. This is my favorite place I've ever been." She smiled up at him and he gave her a quick half hug and followed the gesture by pulling her hat down over her eyes.

"Hey," she said and then fixed her hat and gave his arm a good whack.

"What are brothers for?" Peter said, and then he laughed at her frown. They boarded the bus and waited for it to begin what he hoped would be the last leg of their journey.

"Austin came up to the Canadian side of the falls last summer," Peter whispered.

"So?" she asked while shuffling into a window seat so she could see better when the bus crossed the bridge. She put her pack on the floor and sat down.

"So, he said they didn't stamp his family's passports. They just looked at them and then hand them back. They ask you a couple questions like; what you are going to Toronto for? And then give you back your passport." He put his pack in the overhead rack and sat down next to her. He opened up his bag of snacks and offered her some.

"Why are you telling me this?" She asked while she pulled out a bag of barbeque chips and a bottle of water.

"They don't log it into any computers or anything, so there won't be a record of us going into Canada."

"Which means?"

"Which means, the FBI and Gravano will have no idea we went into Canada, so we should be safe for a while," he replied in a patient tone. "Now, when they ask, tell them we're going to Toronto for a long weekend." He opened up a coke and took a sip and then added, "Also, we packed our own bags and we don't have anything illegal... if they ask."

"Gawt it," she replied with a couple chips in her mouth. She covered her mouth and started laughing. Peter just shook his head and closed his eyes when the bus started moving.

A few minutes after the bus had started moving, they were stopped at the Canadian border. A border patrol agent boarded the bus and started asking to see passports. Peter could see that his sister was nervous and jabbed her and whispered, "Just play it cool and I'll do all the talking unless they ask you specifically. Okay?"

"Okay," she whispered back.

*****

Joey looked around the majesty of Niagara Falls and didn't see any of it. He was focused on finding out if the Donovan kids were there. He picked up his phone and called Matthew. "We don't see them up here. I got eight guys going through the crowd."

"Keep searching, you probably beat them there."

"Will do. What if they beat us there and they're already over the border?"

"That's unlikely. They would have had to have passports with them when they initially went on the run, not to mention they probably don't have much money. No, they're gonna have to beg, borrow and steal just to get there, then they'll probably try to sneak across."

Joey went into the snack area to get out of the cold and noticed the Donovans faces up on the television. "Looks like the cops finally put the kids faces out."

"Really?"

"Yeah, I'm staring at them in high def right now."

178

"Is anyone reacting to the photos?"

"Nah, most people aren't even paying attention."

On the other side of the room, an elderly gentleman was making a call. The operator answered, "Nine-one-one. What is the nature of your call?"

"Yeah, hi, I, umm, I think I just saw those kids up on the TV."

"What kids, sir?"

"The Donovan kids. At least I saw the boy." He paused and then coughed into his arm.

After a moment, the operator seemed a little more interested. "Are you sure, sir?"

"It was definitely the boy, and he was calling out his sister's name. He seemed like he was about to go into a panic. I asked him what his sister looked like and he described her to me. Then I suggested he ask security to help find her, and he got a little squirrelly on me and disappeared into the crowd."

"Where are you now, sir?"

"I'm at the observation platform on the American side of Niagara Falls."

*****

"And how about you? What is the reason you are coming to Canada, today?" The border agent asked while he held their passports.

"Just a long weekend of sightseeing, sir. My sister has always wanted to come to Canada."

"Is that true?" He looked at Danielle and she shifted in her seat.

"Well, not always, but I wanted to come ever since I read about the CN Tower."

He looked over the pair in front of him and asked, "Did you pack your own bags?"

"Yes, sir," they answered one after another.

"Are you carrying anything illegal with you today?"

"No, sir," Dani replied.

"No, sir," Peter said when the man's gaze shifted to him.

He smiled and handed them back their passports and said, "Welcome to Canada. Enjoy your stay." He then moved on to the row behind them, which was the final row on the bus. After another minute, he was exiting the bus and they were on their way to Toronto.

179

"Good job, Dani. I wasn't sure you had it in you," Peter whispered.

"I have wanted to come ever since I read about the CN tower, Peter. I wasn't lying," she replied.

"I know, I just didn't think you'd play it cool like that."

She looked at him feigning offense and replied. "Of course I can play it cool, I am cool." She smiled like she had just won the argument and Peter just shook his head at her.

"Just wake me up when we get to Toronto, would ya?"

After a few minutes, she leaned over and whispered, "Hey, Peter, can we really go to the CN Tower?"

"Dani, you do realize this isn't some grand road trip adventure we're on, right?"

"I know, but we'll already be there. Why not go in?"

"We'll see. I suppose we have at least a day or two before anyone figures out where we are. I guess we can go to one place."

"Thank you, Peter," she replied as she put her head on his shoulder.

"But we carry our backpacks everywhere in case we have to run, understand?" She nodded and he continued. "We also have to always keep our hats on, maybe even buy some sunglasses, too. Just in case." The bus pulled off at a currency exchange and everyone began to exit.

"Okay, I get it. People are looking for us."

"We'll probably have to leave after a day or two."

"And go where?"

"West I guess. All the way across Canada if need be. Why's everyone getting off the bus?"

"I think they're all exchanging their money for Canadian money," she said.

"We should do that, too." They waited for their turn to exchange their money. Peter went first, and he handed the clerk two thousand dollars. The clerk raised an eyebrow and looked at him. "I've been saving for this trip for four years," he said.

The clerk handed him his Canadian money and said, "Enjoy your trip."

After Danielle exchanged her money, they boarded the bus once again. "Look, Peter, Canadian money is so colorful. Ours is so boring compared to theirs. Ooh, and the lady said, 'eh,' to me, just like a real Canadian. She said, Enjoy your vacation, eh."

"Dani, I don't think they all say, eh, all the time. I think that's a stereotype."

"Well, if it is a stereotype, it's a fun one."

When they had taken their seats, Peter turned to his sister and said, "Now, let me sleep. I'm really tired." He pulled the little lever and his seat reclined almost three inches. He closed his eyes and waited for more questions that never came.

*****

"They went to Toronto!" Agent Parker cried out as he burst into Davis' office.

"Are you sure?"

"We have footage of Peter buying two bus tickets to Toronto from Niagara Falls, and then buying snacks for the trip."

"Any footage of the sister?" Davis asked while picking up his phone.

"None that we noticed yet, the tipster said Peter was looking for his sister. Maybe they got separated. Our techs are on the footage."

"How long ago?" Davis asked while pulling out his phone and beginning to dial.

"An hour and a half or so," Parker replied.

Davis held his finger up and spoke into his phone. "I need a plane to Toronto ASAP," he paused and then said, "I don't care what it takes, talk to the Canadians and let them know we're coming. Have them get CSIS and the Mounties on this. We need their eyes everywhere. Gravano probably already has people on their trail. I'm leaving the office now and that plane better be ready when I get there." He paused again while he put on his jacket. "Fine, I'm on my way." He ended the call and then looked back over to Parker. "Anything else?"

"Not at the moment, but shouldn't we go to Niagara?"

"No, we'll send someone else to handle that. We are going to Toronto. Get Agent Sandoval and Agent Lin ready. We leave in five."

"Yes, sir."

They arrived at the airport almost forty minutes later. Davis knew that by the time they arrived in Toronto, the kids would have a few hours head start on him, but he had to find them. Stevens promised them they would be safe and they weren't. He understood why they ran, but he had to get them back into custody.

*****

Danielle nudged Peter awake when the bus finally came to a stop on Yonge Street. They were in front of a long building with the words Toronto Eaton Centre emblazoned in white over the entrance. Right below it were the words Urban Eatery, written in white on a red sign.

Peter followed Danielle off the bus avoiding the accumulated slush and he took a moment to orient himself. He looked across the street and saw what looked like a mini Times Square. He was serenaded by the sounds of an outdoor concert mixed with the rhythm of the city. He was surprised the storm hadn't deterred the musicians or the audience. On one end of the square he saw a booth for sightseeing tickets, and on the other, a subway station that he heard several people call the underground. *I thought the underground was in London*, he mused. *Maybe they're tourists*. He glanced at a sign that read Dundas Square, and he thought he might enjoy sitting at one of the tables and listening to the concert if it weren't so cold. *Maybe next time.*

"This place is awesome," Danielle said, loud enough to be heard over the cacophony of noises around them. "It's like Times Square only smaller, and with more tables and chairs."

"I know, right." Peter looked back at the Eaton Centre and the eatery sign reminded him that he and Dani hadn't eaten anything but snacks since Syracuse, and it was just passing seven o'clock in the evening. "Let's get something to eat in here. I think it's a mall with a giant food court." He opened the door and as Danielle walked through added, "We should get new jackets and hats in case anyone is tracking us."

"Don't you think you're being paranoid, Peter." She replied while they walked through a wide, well-lit tunnel.

"No, I don't." He began to follow the signs towards the food court while his sister walked right next to him. "Dani, do you realize how many people are looking for us right now? The FBI, the police, the Marshals, Gravano's men, probably some bounty hunters, and maybe even the Canadian police are looking for us. We have to ditch our coats and buy new ones. Plus, ours aren't warm enough anyway."

182

"But I really like this coat."

"I know and I'm sorry, but we can't afford to be found."

"Why don't we just go to the Canadian police? I'm sure Gravano doesn't know any of them."

"Maybe, but they would have to turn us back over to the FBI." They emerged from the tunnel into an impressive food court. Peter didn't know how many options were available and he didn't care. He was hungry and there was a burger place off to the right.

"Ooh, Japanese," Danielle said while she drifted towards a date with some sushi.

"Dani," Peter called. "We'll meet at those tables right over there after we have our food." He pointed at the closest set of tables and then walked towards Big Smoke Burger for a burger and fries.

While they ate, Peter saw a sporting goods store next to the food court. When they were finished, they went in to buy some new winter apparel. "Okay, coat, hat, gloves and backpacks, Dani."

"Do you have enough money for all of that?" she asked.

"Yeah, but don't go crazy. Try to get something you wouldn't normally wear."

"Okay," she replied as she disappeared into the coat section.

They met back up at the register, each carrying an armful. "Good job, Dani, I've never seen you in lavender before."

"I know, and I got a purple hat, scarf and gloves to offset the light lavender of the coat." She held up a pair of thick-rimmed glasses and said, "Look, hipster glasses. There's no prescription in them, but they look real."

"Nice! And you got a purple backpack, too, I see."

"Yep, and I see that one hour in Toronto has converted you into a Blue Jays fan." An expression came over his face that made her laugh.

"Very funny! No one would ever think to look for me in this." They put their purchase on the counter and the cashier rang them up.

"Gearing up for the winter, eh?" The cashier asked.

"Something like that," Peter replied while Danielle stifled a grin.

After they paid for their new coats, they walked back towards the food court. "Gearing up for the winter, eh?" Danielle repeated with a laugh. "Canadian is so cool."

183

Peter smiled at his ever-optimistic sister and wondered if she really understood how much danger they were still in. Maybe she did, or maybe this was just a big adventure for her. "Okay, I have to admit, Canada is pretty cool so far."

He sat down at the closest table and began to remove the tags from their purchase. He took everything out of his old, black backpack and put it in his new, blue backpack while his sister did the same. Then he took off his jacket and Syracuse hat and stuffed them in his shopping bag with his old gloves and backpack. He cringed a little as he donned his Blue Jays coat and hat. He stuffed the scarf and gloves in his coat pockets and looked up to see that Dani had finished donning her apparel.

"What now?" she asked. Her light lavender ski jacket and purple hat made her look younger.

"Now you become a blonde."

"What?"

"They're looking for long brown hair, not short blonde hair."

"Peter, is that really necessary? I was saving my hair for Locks for Love."

"I think it is necessary. Come on, it'll be fun." They began to walk towards the stairs and a homeless man approached them.

"Can you spare a couple bucks for food?"

"Sure," Then a thought hit him. "How about some coats, too?" He handed the man the shopping bags containing their old jackets and accessories, and then he handed the man a five-dollar bill. The man lit up at the money and waved his thanks as they walked away.

Peter and Danielle continued on towards the closest Salon and forty-five minutes later, Danielle had gone from brown hair that reached halfway down her back to shoulder-length platinum blonde hair. Meanwhile, Peter had gone from his almost shaggy, tousled brown hair to not quite a military style buzz cut. Danielle exited the Salon with an apprehensive look on her face.

"Wow, Dani, that looks awesome."

Her face lit up and she replied, "Really? You like it?"

"Yeah, a lot. What do you think about mine?" He took off his hat and she gasped a little.

"Peter, wow. Are you joining the army after this?"

"Maybe." He put his arm around her neck and they left the Eaton Centre. "Now we have to find a place to stay. Tomorrow morning we'll go up to that tower you want to see, and then we have to move on, okay?"

"All right." They walked out onto the street and the concert was still going on. They began to walk in the other direction towards a Motel six they saw a sign for. "I just wish we could stay longer. Toronto is a lot of fun."

"I know, I kind of like this place. Maybe when this is all over we can come back and see the city the right way."

"Really?"

"Sure, but we have to make it through this alive first."

"We will."

"How do you know that?"

"Because God is going to protect us."

"Dani—"

"He will. Just wait and see!"

Chapter 17

"Toronto? You're sure? That's good news Matthew. We're already in Niagara. We can be there in an hour and a half." Joey ended the call with a smile. He looked at Anthony and said, "Matthew's contact puts the kids in Toronto."

"How did they get over the border?" Anthony asked.

"No idea, these kids are pretty resourceful, but the feds think they are in Toronto so get your passports out and let's go."

"Are eight guys gonna be enough/ Toronto's a big city."

"We've got some guys up there we can call, too," Joey said while he walked back to his car. Hopefully they would find the kids fast. He really hated the cold.

*****

"We're getting ready to land, Agent Davis," the pilot called over the plane's intercom. "Sorry for the delays."

"This weather is killing us," Davis said. He buckled his seatbelt for landing and returned the Donovan file to his briefcase.

"The kids have a seven hour lead on us now, they could be anywhere," Parker said.

"Have we heard anything from the Canadians?"

"No, sir. No sightings as of five minutes ago." Agent Parker could feel his stomach begin to protest the plane's descent. He gripped his armrest a little tighter and set his jaw to endure the landing. A moment later his ears popped and he could no longer hear very well. He noticed Davis was saying something to him and yelled, "What? My ears popped. I can't hear."

"I said are you okay?" Davis yelled back.

"I'll be fine when we're on the ground. I don't mind flying, but I hate the landings."

"You'd never know," Davis said.

"What?"

186

"Never mind!" A few moments later, the back wheels touched the ground. After a brief screech and a hop, they touched again followed by the front wheels. After the deceleration, the pilot was back on the speaker.

"Welcome to Toronto, Agent Davis." The plane taxied on the runway and came to a stop at a private gate. "Thank you for flying Air Fed."

"We always get the comedians," Davis said.

"What?" Parker yelled while he wiggled his finger inside his ear, hoping to get it to pop.

"Never mind." Davis and his team piled into a waiting sedan and left the airport. After a short drive to the local police department, They met up with one of the Mounties assigned to help them. He was dressed in plainclothes and he held a heavy black parka under his left arm.

"I'm Officer Grey," he said, while Parker silently wondered where his traditional red garb was.

"We don't wear the uni when we're under cover," he answered the unasked question. "I've got three guys each leading a team of Toronto's finest out searching for the kids, but it's a big city." He paused and looked over to Davis. "Agent Davis, you'll stay here with me and coordinate the search, and I thought it might be a good idea to put one of your agents on each of the three teams already searching. I have liaisons that can drive them over now if there's no objection."

"There's no time like the present," Davis replied. He turned to his team and said, "Okay guys, follow Officer Grey's men and get out there. Remember, we're also looking for anyone that works for Gravano. If he doesn't already have men here, he will soon." Parker, Sandoval and Lin all followed their liaisons while Davis followed Grey to a room where they could watch the officer's progress in real-time.

*****

Peter woke up and noticed from the light shining through the curtains that it was already morning. He would have liked to have slept longer, but he knew they needed to get going. He walked into the bathroom and turned on the shower. When the water had warmed up, he stepped in. The hot water felt really good on his sore muscles and he wished he could stay in that moment forever. Instead he took a minute to enjoy it, and then was quick to wash up and get out.

He toweled dry, dressed, and stepped out of the bathroom in time to see his sister's eyes open.

He sat on the corner of his bed to put on his socks and said, "Hey, Dani, I'm going to go find some food while you get ready, okay?"

She looked at him and yawned. "Okay," she said while she stretched her arms and swung her legs over the side of her bed. "Hurry back, I want to get to the CN tower before it's too crowded."

"Crowds are our friend's, Dani, but don't worry, I want to get there early, too. Then we can be on our way out of Toronto sooner." He slipped his sneakers on, stood and walked towards the door while he wondered if letting his sister see this tower was really a good idea. He closed the door behind him and walked across the street.

Fifteen minutes later, Peter opened the hotel room door to see Dani dressed and towel drying her hair. He noticed she was wearing the fake glasses she had bought the night before and took note that she did look a lot different with them on.

"It's so much quicker to shower now that I don't have as much hair."

"I got a couple egg sandwiches and donuts from Tim Horton's. I think that place is the Canadian version of Dunkin Donuts." He sat down next to her and handed her a small brown bag and a coffee.

Danielle's mouth began to water when she smelled the Columbian blend of the coffee. "It smells so good. Thanks, Petey, I'm starving." She took the bag from him and opened it up. Her eyes drifted to the donut first. Ten minutes later, they were checked out and on their way to Dundas Square to catch the subway to the tower.

They emerged from the Subway and it was a short walk to the CN Tower's entrance. Danielle craned her neck to try and see the top. "This is the tallest thing I've ever seen, Peter"

"It is pretty huge," he said. Then he looked around and whispered, "Hey, don't call me Peter anymore, call me Carl or something."

"I'm not calling you Carl," she replied with a laugh while they entered the building and followed the crowd to the cashier's station.

"Seriously, people are looking for Peter and Danielle, so we need to be something else. I'll be Vlad and you can be Olga," he said in a continued whisper

"I'm definitely not going to be Olga," she whispered back with an annoyed look on her face.

"Whatever pick a name, but we can't keep calling each other by our real names."

"Okay, call me Brittany. I've always wanted to be a Brittany."

"Fine, I'll be Eddie then," he paused and checked to make sure no one was paying attention and said, "So from now on we are Eddie and Brittany unless we need to show our id's. Okay?"

"Fine," she replied as they reached the cashier. Peter paid to go up to the top of the tower, and the Sky Pod, and then they followed the people in front of them to the elevator. Tower employees checked their backpacks and then they waited on a short line. The Elevator ride was almost a minute and a half long and Danielle heard the operator say that the Sky Pod was almost fifteen hundred feet in the air. Peter's ear popped from the pressure and a moment later, the door opened.

Danielle hurried to the window and gasped. "Look at this, Pet, umm I mean Eddie, we can see the whole city from up here. I wish I had a camera." She took out her sketchpad and began to draw the scene she was looking at. "I'm glad we got here early, Eddie."

"Me, too, Brittany." Calling his sister anything other than Dani just didn't feel right to him, but it was necessary. He could see Dani smile a little every time she called him Eddie. "I'm going to check out the other side."

"Okay, I'll be here drawing."

"Okay." Peter walked around the pod looking intently in each direction. He was astounded. The clear blue skies afforded him a view of the city that stretched for miles. He looked at all of the downtown buildings in one direction, he saw the Rogers Center where the Blue Jays play in another direction. In a third direction, he could see the Air Canada Center where the Raptors and Maple Leafs play, and finally he could see water. There was also a small string of islands. He wasn't sure what they were called, but he noticed a small plane airport on one of them. He briefly wondered before realizing it would be a bad idea.

"Eddie, this is amazing," Danielle said, bringing him back to the present. "I wish I had time to draw all of the views."

"Me, too, Brittany," he replied, still not feeling right about the name change. "Unfortunately, we have to get going soon. Let's check out the observation level. I hear they got a glass floor and we can go outside."

"That sounds fun. I bet it's windy and cold though."

"Probably, but I'm still gonna do it," Peter said.

"Might as well, we are in Canada, eh." She smiled at her brother and then they walked to the elevator. After another half hour of looking at the city, they were ready to leave the tower.

"Let's take the train back to Dundas Square and get some lunch in the Eaton Centre. Then we need to start finding a way to get out west."

"Why, what's out west?"

"Nothing, that's the point; we have to find a place where nobody will think to look for us. Eventually, we'll have to get back into the US, probably up near Seattle." They walked out into the cold air and made the short trip to the subway station. They merged with the crowds of people waiting for the next train.

*****

"Parker, I just received word from our people up at Niagara that the Donovans might be going to the CN Tower. One of the customs agents remembers a teenage boy and girl traveling with no adults and they were talking about going to the tower."

"Are they sure it was the Donovans?"

"She positively identified them. Your team is closest, so go check it out."

"Do you really think the kids are going to stop and sight see while they are running for their lives? That doesn't seem very smart."

"They probably think they have some time before anyone figures out they came up here. Plus, they're teenagers. When did that become synonymous with good decision making?"

"I see your point. Our Canadian friends tell me that we can be there in five minutes."

"Fine, let me know the moment you have eyes on them."

"Will, do," Parker replied before ending the call. Davis looked at the board showing the whereabouts of his three teams and wondered if they would find the kids before Gravano's people did.

"It's always tough when it's kids that are in danger, eh," Officer Grey said while he handed Davis a cup of coffee.

"They're pretty good kids, too, from what I understand. The boy is a fantastic athlete. The girl gets straight A's and is as sweet as they come, even during such a difficult time. I just really want to find them before Gravano hurts them." He took a sip of his coffee and continued watching the screens

"If they're such good kids, why are they running from you?" Grey asked while he warmed his hands around his ceramic coffee mug.

"We had them in protective custody, and Gravano's thugs found out where they were. They killed three of the Marshals protecting them, and the fourth is just barely hanging on. The kids escaped somehow, and they don't seem willing to trust their safety to us again. I can't really say I blame them, but it's making my job a lot harder."

*****

"Where are you right now, Anthony?"

"I'm at this place called Dundas Square. It looks like this is where the sightseeing tours take off. Also looks like there's a huge mall across the street. It's a pretty busy area. I'm just gonna have the boys walk around here for a while. This place seems to be in the middle of everything."

"Sounds good. I've got some guys down by the Air Canada Center and the CN Tower, and some more guys up by Casa Loma, just in case the kids try to go see the castle."

"Oooh, Joey, if we kill the kids at the Castle, can we do it with a sword?"

"What's the matter with you, Anthony?" He shook his head and ended the call. He dialed Matthew and waited for an answer.

"I hope you got some good news for me, Joey," Matthew answered in greeting.

"We know the kids are in Toronto, and we know they haven't been found by the FBI or the Mounties yet."

"Well, that's a start. How many guys do you have looking for them?"

"With the guys your uncle sent us, we have about twenty. Still, it's a pretty big city."

"I'm well aware of the size of Toronto. I don't want excuses, Joey. I want results! Find the Donovans and take care of them. Do you understand?"

"Yes, sir. We're all doing our best."

"You had better hope that's good enough. I don't have to tell you how bad it would be for everyone if those kids testify, do I?"

"No. I get it. I'll let you know as soon as there's something else to know."

*****

The crowd pressed against Peter and Danielle while they tried to exit the subway at Dundas Square. "This almost feels like New York, Huh, Brittany?"

"Is it always this crowded?"

"No, it's lunch time, so it's probably more crowded than usual." They emerged above ground and were greeted by an arctic blast of wind in their face.

"It's so cold, Eddie," she said, "Let's get across the street fast." Peter was happy that Dani was using their fake names more frequently, but he was still hearing a slight pause when she said it.

He took his sister by the hand and led her across the street. They passed two Italian guys when they walked into the Eaton Centre, and Peter felt the hair stand up on his neck. He wondered if they were Gravano's men. *Maybe I'm just being paranoid. He can't have guys everywhere.* Still, he kept a wary eye out as they walked through the tunnel to the Urban Eatery.

The Eaton Centre proved to be a fantastic place to get lost in. It contained several levels of shops topped off with high, arched ceilings. Wide staircases led to expansive walkways and at the edge of the walkways you could look over the railing and see several levels down. There were plenty of escalators, staircases and elevators, and the whole complex had an airy feel. The white and grey tile of the floors matched the white of the walls and grey of the elevator, and the whole place was very well kept. Danielle could see herself getting lost in this mall for days at a time under better circumstances.

They were almost halfway through their meal when Peter spotted someone he knew. His eyes widened a bit, and a hard lump developed in his throat. It was one of the men that had come out to pick him up at clove Lakes

Park the day that Gravano had attacked him. He was stalking around the food court. *What's he doing here? Did he join up with Gravano after Mr. Barbarelli was killed?* He looked over to his sister failing to keep the worry from his face and whispered, "I see someone that used to work for Mr. Barbarelli. He's probably working with Gravano now. He knows me, so we need to split up for a little while. I'll meet you at that big bookstore we saw. What was it called?"

"Indigo. P... Eddie, are you sure? I don't want to split up," she whispered back.

"Positive! Wait five minutes after I leave and then go straight there. These guys may have a picture of you, but you're a blonde now. Keep your hipster glasses on, too. You totally don't look like you right now. If I can't get to you at Indigo, we'll meet up tonight at the motel we stayed in." He stood and turned away from the man and began to walk away. He felt his hand shaking and put it in his pocket. Danielle tried to continue eating, but she had lost her appetite. She fiddled with the food on her plate for a couple more minutes, all while trying not to look at the man Peter had pointed out. Then, she stood and began to walk towards the escalator.

"Hey, mind if I join you?"

Danielle almost jumped out of her skin. She looked behind her and saw a teenage boy. After she had regained her composure, she said, "I'm going to Indigo if you want to come." He moved up one step and stood next to her. He was about her height with blonde hair. He was wearing skinny jeans and a thick brown coat with a skullcap on.

"I'm Trevor." He thrust his hand out and she shook it. "What are you up to today?"

"Hi, I'm Brittany, and I'm meeting my brother in a little while."

"At Indigo?"

"Yep."

"And you don't mind my tagging along?"

"No, why would I?" She smiled at him and he smiled back. She took the opportunity to glance back to the food court where she could still see the man looking around. He was graying at the temples, but had a cold look in his eyes that frightened her to her core. She began to lose herself in the thought of that man hunting her down and she trembled for a moment.

"You're heading in the wrong direction, you know."

"What?" Trevor's statement had jolted her back to reality.

"If you're going to Indigo, you're going the wrong way. We need to go in the opposite direction."

"Oh, I always get turned around in this mall."

"I'll lead the way, then." He put his hand on her back to guide her in the other direction and then she could see it, a little ways down and a couple levels up.

"Thanks, Trevor," she said.

"No problem." A short walk and a couple escalator rides later, they were approaching the bookstore.

Peter had his head down and his hands in his pockets. His Blue Jays hat was pulled down low and his sunglasses covered his eyes. He was walking with a purpose, but froze ever so slightly when he heard, "Hey, kid, come 'ere." He looked briefly to his left and saw a man dressed in mostly black talking into his cell phone. "It's him!" he exclaimed. "I got him on the lower level." He started walking towards Peter, but Peter took off running through the crowd. The man took off after him and yelled, "Did you think a Blue Jays jacket would fool us? I got guys all over the mall. You ain't going anywhere!"

Peter kept running. It was as if cold fear kept his legs pumping and his mind was removed from the equation.

Danielle stood outside the Indigo bookstore with her new friend Trevor when she heard a commotion begin to rise through the Eaton Centre. It was coming from the lower levels and her face became painted with worry.

"What is it?" Trevor asked. "What's wrong?"

"I think someone is chasing my brother." Her suspicions were confirmed when she looked over the railing and saw a Blue Jays jacket almost fly by a few levels below. A moment later, two men ran past and she knew Gravano's men had caught up to them.

"Why would someone be chasing your brother?"

"It's a long story, but he might be in some serious trouble."

"We should go help him," Trevor said.

"Thanks, but it's better if we're split up right now, but I would love it if you hung out with me for a little bit longer." Just then there was a crashing noise and she saw Peter sliding across the floor while two shoppers were picking themselves up off the floor.

The light of understanding hit Trevor's eyes. "Ah, they aren't expecting you to have a friend, are they, Brittany?"

"No they aren't," she replied. She winced when she saw three men after Peter. He had recovered nicely and was now taking the stairs three at a time. By this point, there were dozens of onlookers watching the drama unfold, and Danielle knew it was only a matter of time before the police arrived.

Peter ran across the circular patterns of the Eaton Centre floor and noticed a splash of pink color in a store window. He looked up and saw two more men heading in his direction. He turned around and saw the other three winded, but still coming after him. He turned and ran full speed towards the railing meant to keep people from falling.

"He's not gonna—"

"I think he is," Danielle replied. She half turned away, squinted and made a soft whine as she watched her brother trying to evade Gravano's men.

Peter jumped up on the rail and leapt for the elevator housing. A collective gasp rose up from the onlookers as he grabbed hold of a vertical pipe attached to the outside of the housing. Momentum caused the rest of his body to slam into the pipe, but he held on and he slid down to the lower level. The crowd reacted in disbelief and Danielle heard Trevor whisper, "That was so cool." Peter took off under the cover of the walkway before the men chasing him could react. They all ran for the staircase to follow him to the level below.

Danielle heard an exasperated mother saying, "Don't you ever do anything like that. Do you understand me?" to her small son who could not take his eyes off of the elevator housing.

"Do you think he's still going to meet you here?"

"Probably not, Trevor, but I want to stay here for a while anyway. You don't have to stay if you don't want to. This could get dangerous." She already regretted dragging someone else into this.

"Are you kidding me? This is the most excitement I've seen around here... ever!" His arms were working overtime as he spoke. "I'm not going anywhere!"

A few moments later, they saw Peter running towards them only one level below. He was no longer sporting the Blue Jays gear, but he still had his backpack. He disappeared under the walkway they were standing on, but a moment later they heard, "Stop, this is the police." Then they saw Peter running across the colonnade towards the escalator. Three Police officers were running after him, while three more police began chasing the men that were following him. The chaotic scene had most of the Eaton Centre on edge.

Peter reached the escalator before the police caught up to him and slid down the railing. Most of the people in the area were now glued to the drama unfolding. At the bottom of the escalator another policeman waited, but one of Gravano's men knocked him out with one punch. Peter lifted his legs and launched off the escalator rail right into the man waiting for him. He hit the thug with both feet right in the chest and sent him sprawling. He rolled to his feet and continued to run. Two of the police stopped to arrest the man that had hit their comrade and the third kept after Peter. "There's no need to run! We're here to help you, son," he shouted while continuing the chase.

"This is intense. It seems like everyone is after you guys. What did you do, Brittany?" Trevor asked while remaining glued to the various chases going on in the plaza below.

"I'm sorry, but I can't really talk about it."

*****

"Donovan is in the Eaton Centre, Agent Davis," Parker said into his phone while opening the door to the building. "And from what I understand, he's causing quite a scene."

"That's good news, is his sister with him?"

"Negative, none of the reports we've received mention a girl; just Peter being chased all over the place by Gravano's goons." He looked around while the rest of his team went ahead of him. "That doesn't mean she's not here, they may have split up."

"Officer Grey," Davis called out while he held his phone to his chest. "Can we get all available units to the Eaton Centre? It appears Gravano's men are making a mess there while chasing our boy."

"Most certainly," he replied, and then Davis heard him speaking into the radio.

"Backup is on the way, and so am I. Do not let that kid get out of this mall, Parker. We can't lose him again."

"I'll do my best, sir. He's proven quite elusive so far." Just then a commotion alerted him that the action was coming his way. "I'll call you back, sir, just get here quick." He ended the call and ran towards the noise.

He was disappointed when it wasn't Donovan. Three of the men that had been chasing Donovan were heading his way with police on their tail. He ran

196

towards them yelling, "Stop! FBI!" They didn't even slow down, moving as though they intended to run right through him and his team. Parker steadied himself and when the first thug reached him, he went low and upended the man with a loud yell. The thug went sailing head over heels in the air landing badly on a couple metal trash bins. His head hit the tile floor with a loud thud, and the man stayed down. Parker then grabbed the second thug and spun his body using the man's momentum to throw him to the floor hard. He sat on top of the man and began to cuff him when he saw his Canadian partner take down the third man.

A crowd had gathered, many filming with their phones and many relaying the events that had just unfolded to newcomers. Parker was thankful they had taken down the three thugs with no injuries, and he heard that a forth was already in custody, but there was still no sign of Donovan. By this time, the whole place had to be surrounded, but there were just so many ways in and out.

*****

Peter was starting to tire. He had been running for a while now, but he was in good shape from football, and adrenaline was keeping him going. He hoped his sister had had the good sense to leave the Eaton Centre, because he didn't want to have to worry about her while he was running for his life. There were now only two of Gravano's men pursuing him, but the police were on the scene. He had to find a place to hide, and get something to disguise himself with.

"Excuse me, ladies," he shouted as he ran in between them. He heard the gasps as he leapt up onto the rail of the up escalator and began sliding down. Halfway down, he took hold of a pole and slid to the floor below. He took advantage of the fact that his pursuers had lost sight of him to run down another corridor and duck into a clothing store. He rushed to the back of the store, put his backpack on the floor and tried on a black, North Face coat while keeping an eye out for Gravano's men.

"May I help you?" a store clerk asked.

"Yeah, I'd like to get a hat that matches this jacket. Oh, also could I try them on in the dressing room? I want to check it out in a mirror."

"No problem, right this way, please." She guided him to the dressing area and said, "I'll be right back with a hat for you." She left him in the dressing room and returned shortly with a few different hats.

"I like the one with Toronto written in the red trim," he said. She handed him the hat and returned to the front of the store. Peter peered past the edge of the curtain to see outside the store. He froze when he noticed Gravano's guys walking past the store. He let out a breath when they didn't enter and prepared to step out of the stall only to flatten himself against the back of the changing room when the men ran past the store at full speed. A moment later he realized why when he spotted several police officers on their trail.

"I wonder what that was all about?" Peter asked while he put the coat and hat on the counter.

"I don't know. There's been some huge chase going on in the mall. I've seen loads of police officers." She rang up the items and he handed her the money.

"I hope the police get their guy," he said. She handed him his change, and he put it in his pocket.

"Have a nice day?" she said with a wave as he left the store with his new coat. As soon as he passed the window, he ripped the price tag off and put the coat on. He zipped it up to the top which came just below his nose, and then he put on the black and red hat and pulled it low. He put his backpack in the store bag, put on his sunglasses, and set a casual pace towards the nearest exit.

Chapter 18

"We've lost most of the guys we sent into the Eaton Centre, Joey," Anthony said while trying to keep his voice calm.

"Do the cops have the kids?"

"I don't think so. No one even knows where the girl is. My guys chased Donovan all over that mall and not once did they report seeing the girl."

"How did he get away? You had seven guys on him."

"I don't know. He is a good athlete and the boys said he showed some serious parkour moves."

"Par what?" he said in exasperation. "What are you talking about?"

"Parkour, you know, when you're running all over the place doing crazy stunts and stuff."

"Well if you can't catch him, focus on the sister. If you get her, he'll come running."

"Will do."

"Don't miss him again, or Mathew will have both our heads. Do you understand?"

"Yeah. I got it."

"Good." He ended the call and prepared to dial Matthew. He wished he had better news, but at least the feds didn't have the kids. "I need to get better guys," he mumbled.

*****

"I think we should get out of here, Trevor."

"Okay, let me call my sisters and we'll all leave together. Whoever those guys are, they probably won't be looking for you in a group of kids."

"You're probably right, thanks," she said. Trevor made his call, and a few minutes later his sisters met them at the bookstore. The four of them walked out of the Eaton Centre onto Yonge Street with no hassles. Trevor was carrying Danielle's backpack while they walked.

"Hey, let's go to Johnny Rockets. No one will be looking for you there."

"Okay, I have a while before I'm supposed to meet my brother anyway." She hated to think that she was going to sit down to a meal with some nice kids while her brother was out who knows where getting chased by everyone, but she knew he wanted her to be safe and out of the way, and this seemed like a good plan. It seemed to her that Trevor liked her, and under different circumstances, she could see herself liking him back.

They walked into the fifties styled restaurant, and the hostess seated them against the far wall. Popular fifties music blared through speakers that weren't built for the loud volume almost distorting the music. The smell of burgers and fries filled the air, and Danielle watched the hostess return to her position at the end of a long red counter near the door. Danielle took a seat facing out into Dundas Square hoping to catch a glimpse of her brother if he was still in the area. After a few minutes, a waitress stopped at their table to take drink orders. After ordering Danielle got an idea. "Hey, Trevor, can I borrow your phone?"

"Sure, why?"

"I need to call a friend in the US and let her know that I'm all right. Please! I can pay you for the call if you want." She leaned back on the shiny, red leather bench and looked at the old vinyl records on the wall across the restaurant.

"No, no problem." He reached into his pocket and dug out his phone. He handed the phone to her and watched her dial the number.

"Hey, Laura, it's me."

"Danielle? Oh, my gosh. I can't believe this!" Laura wanted to cry. She didn't think she would ever speak to her best friend again. "Where are you? Why is your picture all over the television? What happened to the police guarding you? I'm so scared. We've been praying for you every night."

"Laura, I don't have much time. I just wanted to let you know that I'm okay. We're in Toronto, but I got separated from my brother, and I'm borrowing a boy's phone. His name is Trevor." Trevor looked over at the mention of his name, but his sisters were locked in conversation and paying no attention to the phone call.

"Trevor? Danielle, what are you talking about? Why don't you and Peter go back into police custody? Why are you running?" She heard fifties music coming through the phone and wondered where she was.

"Because he doesn't think the Police can protect us." Danielle noticed Trevor raise an eyebrow when she said that and hoped she hadn't disclosed too much, but she needed to talk to someone, and Peter was nowhere to be seen.

"Of course they will protect you, Danielle, what are you—?"

"You weren't there Laura. The bad guys found us and killed all four of the Marshals protecting us. Even Scarvelli and he had two little kids. Now they don't have a father anymore, and it's because of us." She had started to cry while she was talking, and now Trevor's sisters were also listening, but Danielle didn't seem to notice. She wiped her face with a napkin and continued. "We barely escaped with our lives, Laura. They were shooting at us. We had to climb out the window and down a tree to escape."

Laura let out a soft gasp and hoped Danielle hadn't heard it. "I didn't know. I'm so sorry."

"Now Gravano's men and the cops are chasing Peter all over the city and I don't know where he is. Laura, I don't know what to do."

"Danielle, where are you now? What's that music?"

"I'm safe for now, that's all I can say. I gotta go. Please keep praying for us, we really need it." She looked over at Trevor and motioned for one more minute.

"Of course we will. Will I ever see you again?"

"I don't know. I have to go now."

"Bye, Danielle."

"Bye, Laura." She ended the call and handed the phone back to Trevor. He was staring at her in disbelief along with his sisters.

"Your name's not really Brittany is it?" was all he could think to say.

"No, but I can't tell you what it really is." She put her head in her hands and looked at the black and white, checkered floor. After a moment, she looked back up. "I've already said too much."

*****

"What's the good news, Rosenberg?" Gravano asked as he walked into the room. The guard closed the door and Rosenberg waited a moment before speaking.

"Not good news, just news. We've spotted Peter Donovan in Toronto."

"Did they catch him? What about the girl?"

"No, they didn't catch him. According to Matthew, his guys said the kid pulled off some impressive acrobatics to get away. The Canadian police have also apprehended six of our Toronto associates and one of Joey's guys."

"How is this good news?" Gravano shouted and then pounded the table with his fist.

"I didn't say it was good news. No one has spotted the girl yet, and we do know that Donovan was also running from the police so it looks like he still doesn't trust them." Rosenberg sighed and then sat down at the table. "The FBI and the Canadians are all over Toronto looking for the Donovan kids. Maybe we should back off until they're in custody again. We already found them once. We've also been able to follow the Bureau's every move to this point. Why waste any more guys?"

"Are you crazy?" Gravano said while he was pacing the floor. The room was a little bigger than his cell, but still a terrible room for pacing. "We need them taken care of as soon as possible."

Rosenberg's phone chimed and he gave Gravano a look as if to ask for permission. Gravano nodded and he picked it up. "This had better be good," he growled.

"We just picked up a call from Danielle Donovan to her friend about ten minutes ago."

"What? How?" Rosenberg stammered.

"We hacked into the FBI tap on the kid's phone so they have this info, too. We traced the call to Dundas Square in Toronto. There was fifties music playing so I'm thinking Johnny Rockets."

"How do you know there's a Johnny Rockets there?" Rosenberg asked while Gravano looked on.

"I'm looking at a layout of the area on my laptop. Remember, the feds have this info, too, so it's probably best to act fast. The phone is still in the restaurant."

Rosenberg ended the call and looked at Gravano. "The girl is in a restaurant near where Joey is. I'm gonna give him the details." He dialed his phone while Gravano broke into a smile.

"If we get the girl, Donovan will never talk. Tell Joey not to come home until he has one or both of them."

*****

"I need to go buy a new phone. I saw a place a couple stores down. I'll be back in a few minutes," Danielle said to her new friends. Trevor started to stand, but she waved him down. "I'll be back, don't worry." She had to lose them now that they might know who she was.

"Brittany, you should stay here with us. At least eat something before you go," Trevor said with a plea evident in his eyes.

She sent him a reassuring look and exited the restaurant. The last thing she would ever want was to get them mixed up in her nightmare. The door closed and she stepped out into the cold. There were huge snow piles in each of the corners of Dundas Square, and plenty of slush. She pulled her purple hat down over her ears, but left enough room for her shorter blonde locks to still be seen. She zipped her coat up and began walking back towards the Eaton Centre. She was hungry and she could pick something up there.

She walked under the information pavilion, just past the entrance to the subway and heard the words, "Well, what do we have here?" She looked up to see an Italian man with an unfriendly look in his eye. She began to panic and her body froze. She tried to keep walking, but her legs were not obeying her mind's command. "And just where do you think you're going, Danielle?" A short gasp escaped her lips and she finally turned to run, but the man was too quick. He grabbed onto her jacket and yanked her towards him.

"Leave me alone!" she yelled while she tried to kick at the man. "Stop it! Leave me alone!" she yelled again, drawing the attention of several people on the street. She connected with her foot to his shin and he backhanded her to the ground. A welt instantly formed on her cheek but she refused to give him the satisfaction of seeing her cry. A clamor arose on the street, and someone stepped up to intervene, but Gravano's thug pulled out a gun. First he aimed it at the would-be hero, and then he aimed it at Danielle.

The man looked as though he was going to pull the trigger, but instead said, "We're getting out of here. Anyone gets in our way and I will shoot her." He pulled Danielle to her feet and started to walk towards the subway. Without warning someone in black came running out of the crowd and slide tackled him to the metal grating. The grating was slippery and the man lost his balance easily. When he fell, his gun went clattering away. The man in black popped up and kicked him in the ribs sending him even further away from his weapon.

The rescuer turned to Danielle and she instantly recognized her brother. He put out his hand and she took it, then they disappeared into the subway. The abductor tried to give chase, but the man he first pointed the gun at hit him and knocked him back down. Soon after, the police arrived on the scene.

*****

Peter and Danielle hopped the turnstile and boarded a waiting train. A moment later, the doors closed and the train left the station. They had no idea where the train was going, but they were just happy to be away from danger, even if it was only a momentary reprieve.

"Are you okay, Dani?" Peter asked, worry plastered all over his face.

"I am now." She leaned into her big brother and continued. "I was so scared. First I had to watch you get chased all over the place, and then that guy almost captured me. How did you know where I was?"

"Luck really." He put his backpack on the floor and continued. "After I got out of the Eaton center, I was about a block up when I saw you going into that restaurant with those three kids." He rustled her hat and continued. "Good thinking finding a group of kids by the way. After that, I just stayed in the area. Why did you leave?"

"You're gonna be mad when I tell you," she said then she leaned back onto her own seat. "I didn't know where you were and I was scared and I didn't know what to do so I called Laura."

"You what? Dani! We have to be smarter than that."

"I know, but I just really needed to hear her voice, and we only talked for like a minute. Both the police and Gravano's men already knew we were in Toronto, so I didn't think it would be a big deal. Then I thought maybe they could trace the call so I got out of there. I didn't think anyone would trace it that fast though. I'm sorry, Peter. It won't happen again."

"It's all right, we got away. Just be more careful. This is serious. Life and death serious, and sometimes I don't think you know that."

"I'll do better," she said. She leaned back on her brother's shoulder and asked, "Where are we going now?"

"I have no idea where this subway ends, but wherever it does, we're gonna either catch a cab or hitchhike right out of the city." The sound of the subway moving through the tunnel was present, but bearable. Peter found that it was almost rhythmic. The dim light of the subway car almost made it easy to get lost in thought. He suddenly found his eyes getting heavy.

"I think the police will have all the ways out of the city covered," Danielle said, bringing him back to the present.

"You're probably right. They may even have the stations covered at the end of the line. Let's get off at the next stop."

A short time later, an announcement alerted them that the next stop was King Street. The train began to decelerate and a moment later came to a stop. When the door opened, Peter noticed two police officers looking in the next car. He took Danielle by the hand and worked his way into a crowd of people exiting the subway. He kept his head down like everyone else and they made it past the other policeman at the exit without incident.

When they were almost half a block away from the subway Danielle leaned towards Peter and whispered, "They were looking for us. Did you see them looking in the subway cars?"

"Yeah, it's a good thing we got off the train." They walked in silence, trying whenever possible to stay in a crowd. Danielle saw a streetcar passing them and wished they had time to ride it, but thought better of it when she saw some police on board. When they reached Parliament Street, they saw several police officers on the other side of the street. Peter pulled Dani in closer to a couple other teens that were walking and turned down Parliament Street. Danielle sneezed and Peter whispered, "God bless you."

After a short walk they approached an area marked by several old, red-orange brick buildings. Even the pavement was red brick, and a large green iron girder stretched from one building all the way across the street to another. Most of the doorways and window trim were the same color green as the large girder. They walked down several alleyways and through a few streets and most of it looked the same. The crowds were beginning to thin out and Peter began to worry there was nowhere else to go. The light was starting to fade, it was getting colder, and they were still stuck in the city.

Danielle sneezed again, and Peter silently hoped she wasn't catching a cold. They weren't likely to be out of the freezing temperatures anytime soon. "Are you, okay, Dani?"

"I think so. I think my nose is just stuffed up. I am really tired though."

"Me, too. Hopefully we'll be off our feet soon."

"I really like this place. I wish I could sketch it. Do you know where we are?"

"I think this place is called the Distillery District. It's like a landmark or something."

Danielle shivered and said, "Well, it's really cool. It's got character."

"Character?" Peter repeated with his eyebrow raised. "This place has, character?"

"Yes it does! Don't make fun of me." She crossed her arms and shivered again.

"I'm not. I'm just wondering when you grew up?"

After wandering for a few more minutes, they stopped in front of a brick building called the *Mill Street Brew Pub*. It looked like all of the rest of the buildings with green doors and trim, but it had some outdoor seating. Peter saw what he was looking for at the end of the street. A man was in the process of unloading several kegs for the pub from a box truck. Peter watched for a minute before telling Danielle the plan. They leaned against the back of another brick building feigning indifference to the surroundings.

Peter's stomach knotted up when two police officers walked by. Either the police didn't notice them or they didn't recognize them, because they kept walking.

Peter leaned over to Danielle and whispered, "We need to get off the street. As soon as I move, you move. Got it?" She shook her head while her brother watched the officers round the next corner.

As soon as the delivery guy rolled the next keg down the truck's ramp, and disappeared into the pub, Peter and Danielle looked around to see if anyone was watching. When the coast was clear they jumped in the back of the truck. They went all the way in and hid behind some empty kegs.

A moment later they heard someone outside the truck ask in a deep voice, "Where are those kids that were just standing here?" Danielle felt a sneeze coming on and pinched her nose. Peter pleaded with his eyes for her to hold it in.

"I don't know. They must have gone back the other way," A less imposing voice replied.

"Have you seen any teenagers hanging around here?" Deep voice asked.

"No, sir. I've just been delivering some kegs." He rolled his hand truck up the ramp into the back of the truck, and fastened it to the wall while he glanced around. One of the police officers climbed in and was looking over his shoulder. Then they both turned and stepped down off the truck's back. The driver then pushed the ramp back into its housing under the truck.

"I guess they did round that corner," Deep voice boomed. "Let's go, I think it was those two everyone is so uptight over."

"What do you think they did? Eh?"

"Witnessed some crime or something. I just wish the Americans could keep their problems on their side of the border." Deep voice was beginning to sound further away as he spoke and Peter let out a sigh. A moment later Danielle let out a quiet sneeze and then she took a deep breath.

"I don't think I could have held it any longer."

"You did great. Let's just hope this guy leaves the city and doesn't catch us getting off his truck."

Chapter 19

"She actually called you, Laura?" Nate asked. "Where was she? What did she say?" Nate was walking towards the church Gym and Laura was walking fast to keep up. The halls, along with the rest of the church were decorated in the festive colors and lights of Christmas.

"She said the FBI couldn't protect them, that all the Marshals guarding them died and they barely escaped with their lives."

"That's unbelievable. Wait, how did she even get a phone to call you?"

"She said it was some boy, Trevor's phone. She only called because the FBI and the bad guys already knew where they were. She was separated from Peter and pretty scared. We really need to pray for them, Nate."

"Do your parents know she called?"

"Yes, and I told Hailey and Austin, but that's it. I didn't tell anyone else."

"Good, don't tell anyone else. I don't want it getting around. The wrong people might think you know more than you do." They both stopped walking and Nate watched the teens playing basketball and football for a moment.

Laura swallowed hard at the thought of the bad guys coming after her or her family. "But we'll pray for them, right, Nate?" Laura asked.

"Of course. We just won't go into specifics." He took a few steps into the gym and yelled, "Okay everyone, it's time to get started. Put the balls down, you can finish your games later." A collective groan went up from the kids on the basketball court, but they joined everyone else and filed into the youth room. Only the stage lights and the Christmas lights hanging from the ceiling were lit.

After everyone was seated, Nate stood up and said, "As most of you know, Danielle and Peter Donovan are in a good deal of danger. From what we've seen on the news they are still on the run. We need to pray that God will keep them safe. We should also pray for them to have the wisdom to find their way back to the people that want to protect them."

"Do you think we'll ever see them again?" Hailey asked. She put her arm around Laura and pulled her close. She knew this whole ordeal had been really hard on her younger cousin.

"I don't know. We can pray, and we can hope, but we just won't know until the whole situation is resolved. We do know that God is in control, and we have to believe and trust in that." He looked over the crowd of nearly eighty teens. He knew Laura, Austin and Hailey were hurting the most through all of this, but the rest of the group missed their friends, too. Everyone loved Danielle, and Peter, despite his initial reluctance, was becoming a part of the group as well.

Austin looked around the group. He didn't know much about God, but he thought it was odd that all these kids would want to pray for his best friend. He knew that Peter didn't even know half of them. Then he heard a noise behind him and several adults began filing in led by Pastor John.

"Hi everyone," Pastor John said with a smile, and then he walked to the front of the room. "I heard you guys might be praying for the Donovans tonight. Would it would be all right if we joined you?" Adults were still filing into the room and Austin looked up to Nate to see what would happen next.

By the time the adults were all in, the room had become crowded. Nate had given the microphone to Pastor John and waited for him to begin. Pastor John looked over the crowded room and said. "I know this isn't typical for a youth night, but you guys have some friends that are in great danger. When Nate told me you would be praying for the Donovans tonight I made some calls and asked some of our congregation to come down as well. You can never have too much prayer." He paused and looked at Nate. "I know this whole situation has been hard on you guys..."

Austin looked around again. Now he was at a complete loss for words. *How is it possible that all of these people who don't even know Peter and Danielle would want to take time out of their night to come and pray for them? Maybe prayer really does work.* He didn't know what to think anymore. He had started coming to church for a girl, and now he saw there was so much more.

*****

"What do you mean no one can find them, Parker? They're just a couple of kids! There's no way they should be able to evade a citywide dragnet. We have to get them back. Have the Bureau send more guys if you need to, but we need to find them!" Davis was beside himself. He just couldn't understand how

Peter had gotten out of the Eaton Centre. Then, right across the street, his sister had gotten into an altercation with another one of Gravano's men. Her brother was spotted there as well, yet still, they escaped.

"We'll get the kids back, Davis," Officer Grey said as he entered the room with two cups of steaming coffee in his hands. He offered one to the tired FBI agent and added. "It's not likely they've slipped the perimeter and left the city. We'll get them back to you, safe and sound."

"I appreciate that. I just can't shake this picture of one of Gravano's guys killing them before we can find them. I just wish they would trust us."

"It's hard to get that trust back once it's lost."

"I know." He took a sip of his coffee, licked his lips and added, "I would just hate to see anything happen to these kids, you know?"

"We have every available resource on it. We'll get them," Officer Grey replied.

"I hope you're right."

*****

"Peter, I'm so cold," Danielle said. They had been in the back of the truck for over an hour and the cold was threatening to overpower her. She shivered and then sneezed. Peter could just make out her form in the dim light of the truck.

"I'm sorry, Dani. Hopefully when this guy stops we'll be far enough away from the city to get another room. For now, just put on your extra sweatshirt."

"I already— ahchoo— did." She pulled a tissue out of her bag and began to wipe her sore nose.

"Here, take my extra." She blew her nose and then took the sweatshirt from him. She took her jacket off, put the extra layer on, pulled the hood up over her hat, and then put her coat back on and zipped it all the way up. "Are you feeling okay, Dani? You don't look so good."

"I think I'm getting a cold or something." She sneezed again and repeated the process of blowing her nose.

"As soon as this guy stops, we'll have to get you some medicine, and some hot soup or something to warm you up."

210

"Do you think he'll stop soon?" He could hear the congestion building up when she spoke.

"I don't know. Unfortunately, we are stuck here 'til he does."

"I'm not sure I can keep it together 'til he stops, Peter. I'm scared, I'm tired, I'm sick and I think we should go back to the police." She punctuated her statement with another sneeze.

"I wish we could, Dani. It's just that Gravano's guys found us so fast last time. I just think we can do better on our own." He put his arm around her and she leaned into him. She closed her eyes and tried to fall asleep, but the cold, bumpy ride refused to comply with her wishes.

An hour and a half later, the truck finally lumbered to a stop. Peter listened closely and heard the truck door open. He motioned for Danielle to be quiet and then the back of the truck opened. The driver pulled out the ramp from under the truck and locked it into place. Then he took hold of his hand truck and loaded a keg onto it. As soon as he was gone, Peter ran to the edge of the truck, looked both ways and said, "Dani, come on." He jumped down off the back of the truck and then helped his sister down. They scurried over to where another truck was parked, before taking in their surroundings.

"Look, Peter, a diner," Danielle said and then looked up at him with pleading eyes. "I think we're far enough away from Toronto, and I'm really hungry." She put her hands together and added, "Please."

"Okay, let's go." They trudged towards the Huntsville rest stop. Peter saw the driver returning to his truck from a bar across the parking lot.

"Are we still in Canada?" Danielle asked followed by a double sneeze.

"I think so, why?"

"Huntsville doesn't seem very Canadian, it seems more southern."

"Well I can tell you for sure that we're not in the south," he replied. He exaggerated pulling his leg out of the snow to keep walking. They reached the rest stop and Peter opened the door for his sister, and then followed her in. He took in his surroundings looking for any police that might have been there, and he noticed the establishment seemed to be half restaurant and half convenience store. He guided his sister towards the restaurant side and said, "Let's get something warm to eat and then we can look through the store for some medicine."

When they had finished eating and purchased some cold medicine, Peter and Danielle started to leave. Peter turned back to the clerk and asked, "Are there any hotels around here. We've been traveling a long time today and we need to sleep."

The clerk looked at him and then looked at his sister. She pointed a knobby finger toward the highway and said, "There's a bed and breakfast about a half mile down the road on the left. Can't miss it. It ain't the Ritz, but it's not bad."

"Thanks," Peter turned and followed his sister out of the rest stop. They began the half-mile hike through the snow and Peter silently hoped his sister could make it.

"I think I'm gonna sleep for two days," Danielle said. Her steps were slow and cautious. "I don't know how much further I can walk, Peter."

"Don't worry, Dani. It's not that far."

*****

"What do you mean no one's seen the kids for five days, Rosenberg? Where could they possibly be?" Gravano paced back and forth while Rosenberg sat at the table.

"I have no idea, Sal, they didn't just evade Joey, they slipped the FBI's manhunt as well. As far as we know, they're still in Canada, but Canada's huge and we've only got about a dozen guys searching." Rosenberg let out a long sigh. "We lost too many guys in Toronto, and your brother doesn't have anyone else to send at the moment."

"Why hasn't Matthew sent more guys up? What's he waiting for?"

"Don Catalano put a stop to it." Rosenberg replied.

"He what?" Gravano yelled. He hit the metal table hard with both hands and leaned over Rosenberg. He stopped breathing as if waiting for a satisfactory answer.

Rosenberg pulled himself together and replied. "He said there's already way too much publicity on this case and he doesn't want any further light being shed on the organization. He wanted me to remind you that you work for him and until you have actionable intelligence, the guys you have out there now are the only ones you get."

"He can't do that. I've always been allowed to handle my business before." He sat down across from his lawyer waiting for more information that he knew he wasn't going to like.

"He also asked me to remind you that he distinctly remembers telling you that in your handling of the Barbarelli situation you were not to draw any attention to the organization. Eight of our guys getting arrested in Toronto was the last straw for him."

"If those kids testify, it'll draw a whole lot of attention to the organization."

"No, it will draw a whole lot of attention to you, Paulie and Matthew, not to the organization." He stood and began readying himself to leave. "Look, I'll talk to him again, but I don't see him backing off this. Matthew has already been instructed not to send anyone else. We just have to hope that Joey, Anthony and the guys they have will be enough. If they want to hire any mercs out of pocket, they could probably do that, but no one else from the organization is to be involved."

"I'm not happy about this." Gravano said.

"No, I imagine you're not, but you can talk to Matthew if you'd like. Maybe sending him to Catalano might get you a more favorable decision, but he won't change his mind with me. I know that much for sure." Rosenberg knocked on the door, and the guard opened the door, he turned back to his boss and said, "I'll be back as soon as I have anything useful for you." He turned and walked through the door and the guard closed the door behind him.

Gravano sat at the table alone with his thoughts. It wasn't a good sign that Catalano had become involved. The last thing he needed was the Don distancing himself from the situation. If that happened, chances of a favorable outcome were decreased significantly. The guard opened the door again and entered the room with a pair of shackles. His partner followed him in, and after they had bound Gravano's hands, they marched him back to his cell.

*****

"We just received a tip that the Donovans were heading west on the Route Transcanadienne two days ago, Agent Davis."

"They're heading west on the what, Officer Grey?"

"Route Transcanadienne. You might know it better as the Trans-Canada Highway."

"Not really," Davis replied with a frown.

Officer Grey shrugged off his counterpart's ignorance of Canada's main thoroughfare and continued. "A truck driver just called in the tip. Said he gave the kids a ride a couple days ago and left them in Winnipeg. He didn't know we were looking for them until he got home."

"What's taking them so long?" Davis asked. Agent Parker queried a look and Officer Grey raised his eyebrow.

"What's taking them so long to what?" Grey asked.

"What's taking them so long to get away from here? It's been almost nine days since we've seen them, right?" He stood up and began to pace the office. "You would think after all the close calls they had here in Toronto, they would want to be as far away as possible as fast as possible. So, why did it take them a week to get to the next province?"

"Well, they are probably hitching rides like they did with the trucker. Maybe they haven't been very successful," Parker said while he looked at a map on his phone. "Winnipeg is still a pretty good ways from here."

"Twenty-two hundred kilometers," Officer Grey said.

"That's like what, almost fourteen hundred miles?" Parker asked. "That's about two hundred miles a day. That's not too shabby."

"No, it's something else," Davis replied while looking at the trucker's statement. "He picked them up just outside Huntsville, and took them all the way to Winnipeg." He pointed to the report and said, "It says here that only took two days. What were they doing for the other five days? I'll bet they made it to Huntsville the same day they escaped Toronto. Let's get up to Huntsville, and let's get that trucker back on the phone. Something made those kids spend five days in Huntsville and I want to know what."

"Where do you think they are heading?" Parker asked.

"Well they've got a ton of options from Winnipeg, haven't they?" Grey replied. "They can go north up into Nunavut, in which case it might be weeks before we even hear about it. They could be continuing west to Alberta or British Columbia, or they could go south and get back into the US either in Minnesota or North Dakota. Two days, they could be just about anywhere in America or Canada by now." He put on his coat and followed Davis out of the room with Parker right behind him.

"Let's find out what they were doing in Huntsville first. Then maybe we can figure out their destination." Davis opened the door and was greeted with a cold blast of air. He shivered and put his gloves on, and then he followed Grey to a waiting car.

Two and a half hours later they were at the Huntsville rest stop. "This would have been one of the first things they saw around here," Grey said.

"Let's go inside and see if anyone remembers seeing them," Davis replied.

A few minutes later, Agent Parker was talking to an elderly cashier and he called out, "Agent Davis, they were here. This woman remembers them."

Davis and Grey hurried over and Parker said, "Could you tell them what you just told me, Clarice?"

"I suppose," she replied. "They came in over a week ago. I was working the night shift and they came in late, maybe eleven o'clock. They were very hungry and tired. The girl had blonde hair and glasses, but she was definitely the girl in the picture."

"Do you remember anything else about them? Anything that might help us find them? It's very important," Davis asked with his fingers crossed.

"They asked about a hotel and I told them about Tessa's about a half mile down the road."

"That's very good, thank you," Grey said.

"Wait, I'm not finished. The girl looked sick and they bought some cold medicine. I didn't think she'd even make it to the hotel, but they left anyway. Is that helpful?"

"Very helpful. Thank you, ma'am," Davis said. He turned to Grey and said, "Let's go see that bed and breakfast." He purchased a cup of coffee and Parker bought a bottle of water and then they were on their way.

Officer Grey was the first to enter the bed and breakfast. It had the feel of an antique store. The furniture was very old, but in great condition. There were shelves on two walls filled with knickknacks and baubles. The living space was dressed in light and dark blue flowered patterns, and the smell of vanilla filled the air. At the far end of the room was an old wooden counter. He walked up to the counter and asked, "May I speak to Tessa?" Agents Davis and Parker were standing right behind him.

"Yes you may," the friendly woman replied. "I'm Tessa. What can I do for you?"

He showed her his badge, pulled out a picture, and asked, "Do you remember a couple teenagers staying here maybe a little over a week ago?" He held a picture of the Donovans up in front of her.

She took the picture and looked at it. "He was here, but the girl had short blonde hair and glasses. I suppose she could have been the same girl, but she was really sick while they were here."

"It was the same girl, we have information that suggests she cut and dyed her hair, and with everything we know about Peter, he would never leave his sister behind."

"It had to be them, then. She called him Peter and he treated her like a sister, not a girlfriend. I wouldn't have rented to them if I thought there was going to be any funny business."

"You said the girl was sick while they were here? Could you tell us how long they were here for?" Davis asked.

"Yeah, they were here for five days. The kid paid in cash and the girl almost never left the room. I brought soup up to her several times, but she didn't seem to be getting any better. In fact, she was getting worse. If she were my daughter, I'd have taken her to the hospital."

"Unfortunately, those kids don't have anyone to look out for them," Parker said with a shake of his head.

"What a shame, they seemed like such nice kids, too."

"They are, ma'am," Parker said.

"Then why are the police after them?" she asked.

"We're trying to protect them. It's a long story, but they haven't done anything wrong."

"Well I hope you find them, then, but they left here four days ago, they could be anywhere."

"We'll find them," Grey replied. "Thank you so much for your time." They walked back to the car and got in.

"Now we know what took them so long to get to Winnipeg. How does this help us?" Parker asked. Officer Grey started the car and pulled out onto the empty road.

"Danielle is sick. She probably has the flu or worse from being out in the cold for so long," Davis surmised. "So, if you're a couple kids and you can't go to the doctors, and you can't stay in one place too long, where do you go?"

"Someplace warm," Grey answered. He took the next left and began to merge onto the highway. "If I'm the Donovan kid, I want to get my sister someplace warm."

"Do you think a teenager thinks that way?" Parker asked.

"I think so," Davis replied. "We can at least rule out North. Let's try and get eyes on as many of the border crossings between Minnesota and Washington State as possible."

"What about us?" Parker asked.

"When we get back to Toronto, we're going to rendezvous with Agents Lin and Sandoval, and hop a plane to Vancouver."

Chapter 20

"Peter, I don't know if I can make it to the border," Danielle said. Speaking set off a coughing fit, and she was shivering almost non-stop. After a few moments of what sounded like hacking, she looked at her brother and said, "Please can we just stay somewhere tonight and start fresh in the morning? I don't think we can find our way through the woods and over the border in the dark anyway."

They stood outside the classical, grey brick building with the words Pacific Central standing upright in large white letters on top of the building. Buses moved freely in and out of the terminal, and Peter could hear the sound of train horns in the background. Vancouver was no warmer than Toronto had been and he knew his sister was sick. "I know you're tired, Dani. I just think it will be easier if we go at night. Are you sure you can't make it? I'll be here to help you."

"I just can't walk anymore," she protested in a congested voice. "I'm not trying to make it hard on you, Peter. It's just that I've been sick for so long now and I've never felt so drained before. I just don't seem to be getting any better. I'd have a hard time making it into that building over there, let alone several miles through the woods."

He knew she was right, he couldn't march her through the woods and then hitchhike all the way to Seattle. He needed to get her somewhere warm. He looked at the buses going in and out and decided to take a chance. "Okay, Dani, we'll catch a bus to Seattle and then we'll take another bus to San Diego. You can sleep the whole way, and by this time tomorrow night, you'll be somewhere warm. I'm sorry I was pushing you so hard when you're so sick."

"Really?" Hope began building inside her. "What about the border?"

"You sit in the back and I'll sit near the front and we'll just have to take our chances. You can sleep on the bus. We need to get you out of the cold once and for all."

"Thank you, Peter. I hope we don't get caught because of me." She gave him a weak hug and he held her tight. He wanted to kick himself for letting her get so sick.

"I'd rather get caught and go back into custody than lose you. Let's go." They walked into the busy hub and purchased two tickets to Seattle from Pacific

Coach Line. Danielle plodded to the departure area and boarded the bus first. Peter ambled along and boarded almost five minutes later. She was already asleep by the time he got on board. After checking on her, he sat down near the middle of the bus and waited for the departure.

Peter watched the scenery pass by in the form of dark shadows for nearly an hour. When the bus approached the border, Peter whispered a quick prayer. "God, if you're real, and if you can hear me, please help us not to get caught at the border, and please help Dani to feel better." He pulled his hat low, put his bag in his lap and pretended to sleep. A few minutes later, he felt a tap on his shoulder. He looked up and saw the customs agent holding his hand out. Peter produced his passport from his coat pocket and handed it to the man. The agent glanced at it and handed it back. Peter almost pumped his fist in triumph, but he still had to wait for his sister to be cleared.

Danielle was awakened from a sound sleep and she was confused. She looked around for a minute to get her bearings before she figured out where she was. She saw the customs agent standing there and, in a groggy voice, said, "Hi, I just need to get my passport out of my jacket." She rummaged through her pockets and after a minute she found what she was looking for. She handed the passport to the agent and then cringed when she heard a loud crash outside the bus.

The agent leaned past her and looked out the window to see that a car had rear-ended another car. There was broken glass and twisted metal sprayed across the ground. There appeared to be injuries and several agents were on their way out to assess the situation. The driver of the vehicle that had failed to stop, stumbled out of his car and fell to the ground. Blood was pouring out of his nose and down his face onto his jacket.

"Lousy drunk drivers! What a mess!" the customs agent said and started to rush off the bus.

"Um, sir," Danielle called in a hoarse voice. "Could I get my passport back, please?"

He glanced at the passport still in his hands and said, "Oh, sorry." He took two steps back towards her and handed it to her. He hadn't even looked at it. He hurried off the bus and the bus was waved on. "Thank you, Lord," Danielle whispered. She saw Peter get up from his seat and walk towards the back of the bus. He sat down next to her and she offered him a weak smile. He returned her smile, but she could see the worry in his eyes. He put his arm around her and she put her head on his shoulder and fell back asleep.

*****

"Agent Davis!" Agent Parker called from across the tactical room. "The Donovans were spotted in Seattle two days ago. Video surveillance of the bus terminal puts them there at roughly the same time as our tipster said they were. Techs are going through the footage to see if they can find a destination." He walked over to his boss and showed him a surveillance photo from the station two nights ago.

"That's good news, but we're still two days behind them. How in the world did those kids get back over the boarder? When this is all over, I just might recommend this kid for Quantico."

"If he lives through all of this, I'll second the recommendation," Parker replied. Vancouver police officers were hustling around the room where a dozen conversations about a dozen cases were taking place. Vancouver's busiest station was about to get a little less hectic.

Davis motioned for his team to pack up their gear and then walked over to Officer Grey and said, "Looks like we'll be leaving your great country. Thank you so much for all of your help." Their Canadian friend had been with them the whole time and they were grateful for it. Davis knew he had other cases that had been put on hold for this and not once did he complain or mention that he needed to get back to his life.

"I only wish we could have brought them back into the fold." Grey stood as Davis approached; he knew the kids would not be coming back to Canada and that this was goodbye.

"Me, too, but hopefully we'll know where they were going by the time we reach the airport and then we'll only be a day behind them. Thanks again, Officer Grey. If you're ever in New York, dinner's on me." He shook his counterpart's hand while his team turned to leave. He was anxious to bring this case to an end and get back to his city, his office, and his family.

"I may take you up on that, Davis," the Mountie replied. There's a car waiting to take you to your plane. Good luck.

"Thanks, again," Davis replied. He turned and left the room with his team in tow. The car was waiting for them just as Officer Grey had said, and the drive to the airport was quick. They loaded the plane and while they were waiting for clearance to take off, Parker received the news he was waiting for.

"Peter Donovan bought two tickets to San Diego from Seattle. It would have taken them almost a full day to get there by bus which puts us only about a day behind them."

"Tell the techs, great work. I'll get our flight plan changed and I'll get eyes in San Diego looking for them." Agent Davis had hope for the first time in over a week that they would find these kids alive and bring them back into protective custody. "Do we have any more information on who the leak could be?"

"Not that I'm aware of," Parker said with a frown. "Lin has a buddy in tech that's like a computer ninja and we've put him on it. That's his sole purpose in life until the leak is plugged. If he's half as good as his rep then whomever Gravano's guys are getting their info from will be caught."

"Let's hope they're caught soon, because as soon as this flight plan goes through, the mole will have access to that information and we'll be putting those kids in danger again." He stretched his neck and rubbed his eyes before leaning back in the seat. He hadn't had a good night sleep since this case began and it was starting to catch up to him.

"Maybe the Donovan kid is right not to trust us if that's the case," Parker said as he buckled his seat belt.

"Let's just plug the leak so we won't have to find out."

*****

"San Diego?"

"Yeah."

"You're sure?"

"Yeah."

"How are you getting this information, Matthew?" Joey asked.

"My girl's cousin works for the Bureau. She's a clerk or something. She can get in and out, get our info, and no one suspects a thing. She's actually one of the support staff for the team tasked with finding the Donovans."

"I didn't even know you were seeing anyone."

"No one does. That's the point. If people knew, they'd put two and two together, and the feds would find our girl. Now get out to San Diego and get this done once and for all."

"We'll get em," Joey replied.

"No excuses, Joey! My father's not gonna let you and Anthony back if you screw this up again." Matthew stepped out of his car and walked into the fine Italian restaurant for his meeting with Rosenberg. He knew the sauce here gave the lawyer heartburn, and so he always chose this location.

"We got this, Matthew," Joey said with all the bluster he could manage, but for the first time he began to think of what would happen to him if he failed.

"I gotta go, I'm meeting Rosenberg," Matthew ended the call and put his phone in his pocket. He approached an attractive hostess, and she took him to his seat. They walked past the cozy tables nestled into booths that offered privacy and arrived at his table. Rosenberg was already seated, and he had a smile on his face.

"What are you so happy about?" Matthew asked.

"I think we may get judge Reinhart for the trial. He's one of the more lenient judges on the bench." He spread his napkin out and placed it in his lap.

"So what does that mean if we're found guilty?" Matthew asked while he took his seat.

"It won't mean no jail time if that's what you're asking, but it could mean significantly less jail time. It could especially mean less jail time for you and Paulie."

"What about my father?"

"He's still looking at life without parole." He noticed Matthews frown and added, "But at least we're not talking the death penalty."

"Still, life without parole? What kind of life is that for my father?"

"It's better than death, Mathew. And, as long as he's alive, we can continue appealing the decision. Nothing is ever permanent in this system. Now, for you and Paulie we could be looking at as little as seven years before you get paroled."

"Seven years? How is this good news?"

"You guys are accused of killing nine people, Matthew. Nine!" Rosenberg said while trying to keep his rising voice low. "Seven years is less than a year per person. Best-case scenario we get you five and your brother seven before parole. The worst-case scenario is ten and twelve. Trust me, you won't find a better option."

"Unless the prosecution's two star witnesses are unable to testify," Matthew said.

A waitress approached the table and asked, "Would you like something to drink?"

"I'll just have a bottle of water," Matthew replied.

"I'll have the house wine," Rosenberg said. The waitress scurried off leaving them to their conversation.

"About those witnesses?" Rosenberg asked.

"In San Diego right now. Joey and Anthony know not to come back here at all unless the problem has been taken care of. The kids have about a day lead on us. Once it's done, what are our chances?"

"Well, the video is still pretty powerful, but without the kids' testimonies, it probably takes life off the table for your father, and further reduces your brother's sentence. I might even be able to get a not guilty verdict for you if we get a sympathetic jury."

The waitress returned and placed their drinks on the table. Matthew picked up his water and said, "Well here's to finding those kids then." Rosenberg raised his glass and touched it to Matthew's bottle. "So, when are you going to see my father again?"

"As soon as we know what's going on in San Diego."

*****

"Christmas is only nine days away, and all I want is Danielle and Peter to come back," Laura said to her mother as they drove to the Church.

"I know you miss Laura, sweetie. We all do. She's a special girl, and Peter has been a great brother to her," she replied and then put her blinker on to make the left turn onto Clove Road. She felt so bad for her daughter. Danielle had been the best friend she ever had, and now she was gone.

"Do you think they'll be able to come back after the trial, mom?"

"I don't think so, sweetie. I think they are going to have to go into witness protection for a long time. I don't know what that means for your chances of ever seeing her again." She stopped at a red light and turned to see the downcast look on her daughter's face. "I am sorry, sweetie."

223

"Do you think she'll stick with her faith, mom? I mean, they're on the run, she probably hasn't been able to get to church and she doesn't have any Christian influence in her life right now."

"I think so. She seemed very motivated to learn as much as she could and to be a good example for her brother. I don't think that's going to go away." The light turned green and her foot pressed the gas pedal. At the next block she turned into the parking lot of the old brick church. "I think you guys are going to pray for them again tonight."

"Is the whole church going to come again? That was pretty cool. I know Austin was really touched that so many people cared."

"I don't think everyone's coming down again, but rest assured, they are being prayed for constantly, as is Austin." She parked the car and they both stepped out into the parking lot. It wasn't as cold as it had been for the past two weeks, but she still watched her daughter shiver and jog for the door to the gym.

"I'll see you later, mom."

"Just text me when you're ready to leave, I'll be upstairs with the women's group." She watched her daughter nod an acknowledgment and then disappear into the gym. She could see the light from the gym pour out into the parking lot and she could hear the music playing. She walked into the church thankful for such a great place for her daughter.

"Hi Nate," Laura said with a wave and then made her way over to her cousin. Nate waved from across the room and then continued shooting hoops with some of the guys. Hailey was sitting with Toni Ann and they were watching the pickup game. She could hear the distinctive squeak of sneakers on the gym floor, over and over ,while she walked to the bleachers.

"Hi, Laura," Hailey said and greeted her with a hug. Toni Ann stood up and gave her a hug, too. Laura noticed that she was wearing Austin's City Champions tee shirt. She sat down right in between them and watched the game with them.

"Have you heard anything else from Danielle?" Hailey asked. Laura knew that as much as she liked Danielle, she was really asking about Peter.

"No, sorry. Nothing since that one time she borrowed that kid's phone. My mom doesn't think we'll hear from them or see them again."

"Well we can hope, right?" Toni Ann said in encouragement to her two friends.

"That's almost all I pray about these days. I pray for their safety, and that we'll see them again." She looked at her cousin and continued. "I know that's probably a little selfish, but I just miss them so much. I know Peter wasn't technically my friend, but he always treated me good because of Danielle. He was almost like a big brother to me, you know?"

"Yeah I do," Hailey replied. "And I know we never dated, but I was really hoping we would. I know he would have kept coming to church because Austin likes it so much and his sister was always here. Maybe something would have eventually sunk in. I really miss him, too."

"Poor Austin, it's almost like he lost a part of himself," Toni Ann said. "They were best friends since kindergarten." She paused and swallowed. "Sometimes he doesn't know what to do. I've seen him pick up his phone and start to dial Peter a bunch of times."

"That's so sad," Hailey said with a frown.

"I think Nate is really helping him through it, and Ted has been hanging out with him a lot. I know he'll eventually get over it, but I don't think he wants to," Toni Ann said.

"I don't want to either," Laura replied. The three of them sat there in silence after that, just watching the games going on in the gym and missing their friends.

*****

San Diego was unseasonably warm for December and Peter was thankful for every extra degree. It was close to eighty degrees and he had ditched all of his and Dani's winter gear and sweatshirts to lighten their load. He purchased two San Diego State sweatshirts, a pullover hoodie for Dani and a zip up hoodie for himself. He was hoping to blend in with the college crowd. Right now, his sweatshirt was in his backpack, but Dani was wearing hers over a tee shirt and a long sleeve tee shirt. She still couldn't get warm and he was really getting worried about her.

They ambled along the Pacific Beach Boardwalk and they were almost to the famous Crystal Pier Hotel. The smell of the ocean was in the air, and the sun was out. The rhythmic sound of the waves crashing along the shore provided a good soundtrack for walking. The boardwalk was crowded and that suited

Peter fine. They had nowhere to go so they had decided to stay in heavily trafficked areas.

Peter had ditched the military cut and was now sporting a full on crew cut as close to the scalp as he could get it. He hoped that his lack of hair, and his sunglasses would be a good enough disguise. Dani was still sporting the blonde locks, but she had lost the glasses somewhere along the way. She had her hair in a ponytail coming out the back of her Padres hat. With the exception of the sweatshirt, she looked the part for a warm day at the beach.

"Can we stop at that bench and rest, Peter? I'm really tired." She slowed down and pointed to a bench ten feet away.

"Sure. You rest and I'll go buy us some lunch, okay?"

"Okay. I am a little hungry."

"Good, you need to keep up your strength. Maybe now that it's warm, you can start feeling better. I'll be right back." Peter handed her his backpack and then disappeared into the crowd. Danielle sat down on the bench and put both hers and Peter's backpack on the ground right in front of her. Her mind flashed back to the last time they split up and she got a terrible feeling that something bad was about to happen.

Peter walked along the boardwalk looking for something to eat. He saw a cluster of stores right on the boardwalk and headed in that direction. Each building was a bright gold color with the brown Spanish-tile roofing. He liked the feel of the area and wished he could stick around and enjoy it a little more. In fact, he and his sister had been to a lot of places he wished he could see more of. He slowed his pace to take in more of the local flavor and then spotted a burger joint.

He walked into the restaurant and stepped up to the counter. The restaurant was crowded with people sitting at each of the oak tables. The walls were adorned with pictures of people enjoying the beach. The ceiling was cluttered with beach themed objects hanging above customers' heads, and in the middle of the room stood a wooden counter with a surf board sign above it directing customers to: Order Here! He stepped up to the counter and a cute girl in jean shorts and a red tank top smiled at him. A quick glance around the establishment confirmed her outfit to be a uniform.

"Welcome to Beach Burgers. May I take your order?"

Peter returned her friendly smile and said, "I'll have two burgers, an order of fries, and two waters to go."

"How would you like your burgers cooked?"

"Medium is fine."

She tapped a few keys on a register that looked more like a computer and then said, "Your total is: Twenty-one oh one." He handed her Twenty-two dollars and put the change she handed him in the jar by the register. "That should be ready in about five minutes," she said.

"Thank you," Peter replied. He walked over to the window and stared out at the Pacific Ocean while he waited. He felt antsy being away from his sister, but she needed to eat. He wondered if he would ever be able to come back to a place like this. After a few minutes, the girl who had taken his order handed him his food.

"You have a nice day," she said.

"Thanks. You, too." Peter hurried back to the bench where he had left his sister. He was almost to the Crystal Pier when he heard, "Hey Donovan!" He thought his ever so slight pause was missed, but learned he was wrong when he heard, "Gotcha."

Chapter 21

Agent Davis waited to speak to the Captain of the Northern Division of the San Diego Police Department. He was sure that Peter and Danielle Donovan were somewhere nearby, but he was having trouble getting every available officer tasked with finding them. The receptionist finally called his name and led him into the Captain's office. He was a tall, thin man with a hooked nose and a stern look in his eye. One glimpse of the man told Davis this department was a tight ship.

"Hello, I'm captain Hendershodt. What can I do for you, Agent Davis?" he said. He stood behind his desk and thrust his hand out. Davis leaned forward and shook it. The desk was just large enough to make it awkward. Davis didn't address the awkward handshake or the fact that he had been kept waiting for no good reason. Both of those offenses were meant to make him think the good Captain was in control. Instead, he sat down before he was invited to do so. He knew he had the authority to co-opt the Captain's men, but it would be a lot easier if Hendershodt volunteered them.

"As you know, there's been a nationwide manhunt for two very important federal witnesses. Peter and Danielle Donovan have managed to evade both the criminals tracking them and us for almost two weeks now. They have proven extremely resourceful. They even managed to cross the border into Canada and then back into the United States. We know they have been in Niagara Falls, Toronto, Winnipeg, Vancouver, Seattle, and now we believe they are in San Diego."

"Sounds like you've got your finger on the pulse, Davis. What do you need from us?" The Captain leaned back in his chair and rested his head on his hand.

"We need your help finding them before Gravano's men do. San Diego is a big city and, like I said, Peter Donovan has proven himself quite skillful at evasion."

"Come on, the kid's what? Seventeen? And you're trying to tell me that no one can catch him. How hard can it be?" Captain Hendershodt stood and walked over to his personal water cooler. He poured himself a cup of water and motioned to his FBI guest to see if he wanted some. Davis shook his head no, and the Captain returned to his seat.

"Donovan was spotted at a mall in Toronto being chased by almost a dozen of Gravano's men. The police surrounded the mall while dozens of them entered the mall. Several of them had eyes on Donovan at one point or another, and while we apprehended eight of the men chasing him, he still managed to escape the mall. Then, the Police practically put the city on lockdown, and he still made it out. All of this while taking care of his sick little sister. I wish I could tell you how he did either of those things." Davis leaned back in his own chair and paused. "All of this to say, we could use all the help we could get."

Hendershodt considered what Agent Davis had just said. It was impressive that the kid had been able to evade them for this long, and he certainly had no desire to see a notorious criminal like Sal Gravano get away with murder. "I've got sixteen officers you can have for the next two days, and I'll put the rest on alert to keep their eyes open for the kids. If they are spotted by my guys, they won't be slipping any perimeters."

"That would be wonderful. Thank you, Captain." Davis stood and the Captain came out from behind his desk and shook his hand again, this time man to man. He guided the Agent out of the office and called the duty Sergeant in to assign men to Davis' team. Now Davis had seven agents and sixteen officers. They broke up into twelve pairs. He and each of his men would be paired up with an officer from the San Diego Police Department and the remaining eight officers would provide backup.

They had been given a small room to work out of and while Sandoval set up the equipment they needed, Parker took a phone call. A moment later he ended the call and said to Davis. "Peter was spotted on the Pacific Beach Boardwalk. The tip seems credible, but they're saying he has a really close-cropped, crew cut now. Surveillance photo is en route." A moment later his email beeped and he downloaded the photo into their facial recognition software. Even with the sunglasses on they got a match.

"Match is good, sir," Parker said.

"Let me see that picture, Parker," Davis said. Parker turned the screen towards Davis and he stared at it for a long moment.

"Is everything all right, boss?" Sandoval asked.

"I'm not sure. Who's this guy?" He pointed to a man three people behind Peter. "Can we ID this guy?" he asked and then handed the photo to Sandoval.

Sandoval ran the face through the software and it was a match for Joey Delancy. "Boss, we got a problem. Delancy has Peter in his sights as of..." He looked at his watch and did the math. "Ten minutes ago. We may already be too late!"

"Okay everyone. Let's get down to the beach. Standard search grid, and alert any officers working the boardwalk to keep their eyes open. We need to get eyes on the sister, too. Let's go, move!" They created quite a commotion as they left the station. Twelve police cars with sirens blaring proved to be an intimidating sight and they made it to the beach in just under seven minutes. They turned the sirens off on their approach, and they broke up into eight groups of three and began searching different parts of the Boardwalk.

*****

"Joey has the Donovan kid in his sights, Matthew," Anthony reported. "We've got guys closing in on him from four directions. Once we have him, his sister should be an easy grab. This is almost over."

"You had better be right, Anthony. We cannot afford to let those brats testify."

"I know what's at stake, Matthew. We'll get them. I gotta go; they're heading this way." He ended the call and put the phone in his pocket. He signaled a heads up to his guy across the street and they readied themselves to get rid of Peter Donovan for good.

Matthew Called Rosenberg and waited for the lawyer to pick up his phone. "Did they get the kids?" Rosenberg said after he picked up the call.

"Anthony said they are closing in on him from four directions and he has nowhere to run."

"What about the girl?"

"Once they get him, she'll be easy pickings."

"Let's not get too ahead of ourselves here. We need them both. It's all or nothing on this and it's probable that her testimony will carry more weight than his. Remember, she's the sweet, straight A, church girl."

"They know what's at stake. I couldn't have made it any clearer. I should have news for you to bring my father within the hour. I want you to be ready to go as soon as I call with the good news."

"Of course. Is there anything else?"

230

"Not at the moment. I'll talk to you soon." He ended the call and waited for Anthony or Joey to get back to him and let him know it was done. He hated waiting, but he had no choice.

*****

Peter was tired of running. He had been running his whole life. First from his father, then from his own guilt about his mother's death, and lately he had been running, literally. He and Dani had been chased across two countries and he didn't know how much longer he could last.

"There's nowhere to run, kid," the large man behind him bellowed. Every direction he looked, he could see more of Gravano's goons trying to box him in. Worst of all, Dani was nearby and she was in no condition to move, let alone run. He had to do something to get the attention of the police. He wasn't thrilled about going back into custody, but at least they weren't trying to kill him. Plus, they would get Dani some medical attention. He mused that this revelation may have come too late for both of them.

Peter saw something that he might be able to use to draw attention to himself, so he made a sharp right across the boardwalk. He started yelling, "Out of the way! Move!" while he ran.

"Hey, watch where you're going!" an angry man yelled.

"Are you crazy?" another man shouted.

"Lookout, Honey!" a woman shrieked while pulling a man out of his path.

Peter continued running full speed. The desperation on his face drove most people out of his way. He clipped the front of a bike with his leg. The force of the collision spun him around, but barely slowed him. The bicycle went flying and the rider sprawled into two young ladies. As if that commotion wasn't enough, one of Gravano's guys tried to tackle him head on. He met his would-be attacker with a stiff arm to the face and knocked the man to the floor. By this time, the chase had drawn a crowd.

Peter ran full speed towards the Crystal Pier Hotel. The gate was closed and the security guard started shouting for him to stop, but Peter leapt for the gate anyway. He was able to grab the top of the gate and pull his body over in one fluid motion. The guard tried to grab him, but was knocked out of the way when Gravano's men forced the gate open. The Crystal Pier Hotel turned out to be a collection of white cottages with blue trim that stretched out almost halfway down the pier. Each cottage had a table with an umbrella and some chairs on its deck, all beach themed, blue and white.

Peter made a sharp left past the first building and jumped up on the deck railing near the closest cottage. He then leapt from the railing to the cottage and pulled himself up on the roof. Gravano's men stopped for a moment while Peter ran across the roof of the cottage. He reached the end, and jumped to the next roof. He landed on the next roof and that was when he heard the first gun shot.

His mind was taken back to that night in the park when Gravano's sons had been shooting at him. The next shot brought him back to the present as he leapt to the next cottage. He could smell barbeque chicken being cooked on the deck below him, and he saw the vacationing family cowered behind their cottage. Another shot, then another, each one sounding like a cannon fired through the ocean air. He began zigzagging as he ran before leaping to another roof. He glanced back at the boardwalk and people were scurrying for cover, their beautiful day ruined by violence. For a moment, Peter felt bad, but then he saw what he was looking for. The police had arrived.

*****

"He's at the Crystal Pier and he's being shot at. All units to the pier!" Davis shouted into the radio while he ran towards the pier.

"Two bike officers are already on the scene. Should they engage?" Agent Lin asked.

"How many assailants?" Davis asked to no one in particular.

"They count at least eight so far," Parker replied.

"And where's Donovan?" Davis asked while his car came to a stop. He and his police partner exited the vehicle and began running towards the Crystal Pier Hotel.

"He's jumping from rooftop to rooftop of the hotel," Agent Sandoval replied. "And Gravano's thugs are shooting at him from the ground."

"Tell the officers to wait for backup. I don't like the odds. We'll be there in under a minute." Davis could see a figure jumping from Cottage to cottage, but the gunshots had stopped. "That kid is crazy," he mumbled while he ran. He could see most of his men converging on the entrance of the hotel along with three bicycle officers. "Go, go, go!" he shouted and they all began to run onto the pier. With each cottage they passed, vacationing families would run out past them onto the boardwalk.

Peter leapt onto the last cottage, ran across the roof, and jumped down onto the pier. He landed with a roll and kept running across the sea battered wood of the pier. When Gravano's guys saw him, more gunshots rang out, but Peter was running an unpredictable pattern from side to side and the shots missed. Peter reached the end of the pier and a deep voice boomed, "You're out of room! There's nowhere to go, kid!" The threat was followed by laughter.

Peter yelled back, "There's nowhere for you to go either, stupid!" Then he turned and ran the last few feet to the railing. He leapt for the railing and more gunfire rang out. A bullet hit him in the back while he was in the air and he fell nearly twenty feet into the water below. The freezing water was like a slap in the face, and he swallowed a mouthful of the seawater when he fell in. The waves were pounding him and he couldn't tell which way was up. His back felt like it was on fire and he wondered if there were any sharks nearby that would smell his blood. It hurt too much to move his left arm, so he swam using only his right.

He was still under water when a wave pushed him hard into one of the pylons holding up the pier. He was in a lot of pain and he started to panic when his ribs hit the pylon again. The waves felt like they were crushing him, and he didn't know how much longer he could hold his breath. His panic was almost his undoing, but his will to survive kept his wits about him. The only thing he could think about was Dani, and he decided that he wasn't going to leave her alone.

*****

"This is the FBI! Drop your weapons and put your hands in the air. This is your only warning," Parker yelled. There were close to twenty officers on the pier, most in good cover. Gravano's eight men didn't stand a chance if they engaged. One by one, the men dropped their guns. When the last thug had put down his weapon, the police moved in fast. They cleared the weapons and then cuffed the gunmen. Seven of them were led away while officers read them their rights, and the last one was brought over to Agent Davis.

"Anthony Costanza," Davis said. "Where's Donovan?"

"How should I know?" he replied with defiance in his eyes.

"What did you do to the kid, Costanza?" Davis asked. His question was only met with laughter.

"Sir, we've got traces of blood on the railing." Agent Lin said to more laughter from Anthony.

"Good luck finding the kid, Agent Davis."

"Get some units down to the water right now!" Davis said into his Radio. "I believe Donovan is in the water and he may be hurt." Davis rounded on Costanza, put his finger in the criminal's chest and said, "You're going to jail for a long time, Costanza. And I'm not talking about some minimum-security cakewalk, or a prison where Gravano can protect you. You shot a kid in California." He saw that what he had just said was beginning to sink in and relished the fear in Costanza's eyes. "You'll be incarcerated out here, three thousand miles from all of your buddies. Think about that while you're laughing." He started to walk away and then turned back. "Where's Joey Delancy?"

"Who?" Anthony replied, and the smile was back.

Davis motioned to two of the officers and said, "Get him out of here! He makes me sick."

Peter's head finally broke through the water and he was gasping for air before he went back under. He popped back up, took a deep breath, and then pushed off the Pylon towards the next one. He swam from pylon to pylon until the water only reached his waist. Then he stood and began walking. His wet clothes clung to his body, blood still flowed from his shoulder, and he was coughing up the salty seawater. Only a few steps from the shore when a large wave hit him in the back, he surged forward with the water and collapsed in the sand.

He braced for the worst when he heard someone shout, "He's over here." A moment later he opened his eyes to see a police officer kneeling above him. There was compassion in her dark eyes, and a gentle touch kept him in place. He was too tired from the run and the swim to move yet anyway.

"A lot of people have been looking for you, Peter. I'm Officer Sanchez."

"The Marshals were killed so we ran," He said in between coughs. "Did you find—?" A coughing fit kept him from finishing his question.

"Don't try and talk, Peter. Just lie still." Two other police officers had almost reached him.

"Dani! I have to find Dani."

"We will. Don't worry," one of the new officers on the scene said. He was tall and well built and Peter wished the man were guarding his sister instead of him.

"You don't understand. She's sick. Really sick." He started to stand and the two new officers helped him up. When one of them took hold of his left arm he cried out in pain.

"Peter, are you all right?" Officer Sanchez asked.

"My shoulder!"

"He's been shot," the officer said after looking at his back.

"Don't worry; an ambulance will be here shortly."

"Dani needs it more than me." He was starting to think more clearly now, and he continued walking towards the boardwalk. "She was on a bench near the pier. Come on!" They walked with him, but he was aware that the tall officer had not let go of him yet. He was thankful for the assistance, but his strength was returning.

"Everything is going to be all right, Peter," Officer Sanchez said while they were walking towards the boardwalk. He could already hear the wail of the ambulance in the distance. When they reached the boardwalk, Peter caught a glimpse of his sister. She was still on the bench where he had left her. His gut tightened when he saw one of the men that had been chasing him standing over his sister. Then he noticed that she was awake, and she was terrified.

He broke free of the tall officer's grasp and ran for his sister. The police thought he was trying to run again and were immediately on their radios.

"Agent Davis," Agent Sandoval called. "The police say the kid is trying to run."

"Where is he gonna go?" He was walking back towards the boardwalk when he saw it. He saw Peter running, the girl on the bench, and Joey Delancy. "He's not running!" he shouted into his radio while he took off at a run. "He's trying to save his sister. I got eyes on Joey Delancy."

Peter was running as fast as his battered body would carry him. His shoulder still felt like it was on fire, the battering his ribs had just taken in the ocean left them protesting his every move, and he was coughing up seawater, but he was still moving pretty fast. He was going to save his sister, or die trying. He noticed an FBI agent running towards him, and he couldn't figure out if the agent was trying to help him or stop him, so he continued on. By the time

Delancy noticed him, it was already too late. He launched himself at the man threatening his sister and tackled him over the bench.

They both landed on the ground hard. Peter rolled a few feet away and he saw Gravano's man bring a gun to bear. Peter's eyes widened and he tried to push himself away from the man, but the last thing he heard was the sound of the gun.

"Peter! No!" Danielle yelled. She saw her brother lying on the ground, blood pouring from his chest and she slumped back on the bench and began to cry. While she cried she also began to pray.

Joey knew he had no choice now, he was caught and his boss wasn't gonna help him out in prison unless both kids were dead, so he stood. He saw an army of police and FBI running towards him, but he knew he had time to pull the trigger once more. He brought his arm up and then two gunshots took him off his feet. He lay on the ground, still conscious, and knew it was all over. The bike officer that had shot him cleared the gun and stood over him. Joey hated the fact that of all the FBI agents, SWAT team members, and police on the scene, he had to get shot by a bike officer.

Officer Sanchez reached Peter and put her hands on his wound to slow the bleeding. "We need to get him to the hospital now!" she shouted.

The tall officer reached Danielle and knelt down next to her. She barely had the strength to sob and he put his arm around her. "Hey, Danielle, it's all going to be all right."

"Peter. Peter!" she cried out in between sobs and coughs.

"It's okay; he's going to have the best doctors. We just have to remember that God is in control. Even in the midst of all this craziness, God is in control. I know you believe that."

"D... do you believe that?"

"Sure do, kiddo."

Danielle couldn't keep her eyes opened any longer. Consciousness began to slip from her and her last thought was for her brother before she passed out.

The tall officer looked over to Officer Sanchez and said, "Donovan wasn't lying; his sister is in bad shape. We need to get her to the hospital fast."

*****

Agent Davis surveyed the scene, or more precisely, the chaos. This whole assignment had been a debacle. The whole area had been cordoned off, and hundreds of people had returned to watch the clean up. His two star witnesses were both in bad shape and at this point, it was unclear if either of them would make it. He had nine of Gravano's men in custody and there was a fair amount of damage to the Crystal Pier Hotel. This was the last field op he was likely to lead if those kids didn't survive. He watched the two ambulances carrying the Donovans rush from the scene with several police cars providing escort. He would wait for Delancy's ambulance to cart him off before he joined Agent Parker at the hospital.

Officer Sanchez approached him and said, "Donovan told me that he ran because all the Marshals protecting him and Danielle were killed. It was the first thing he said when we found him collapsed on the beach."

"Did he say anything else?"

"Only that his sister was really sick and he needed to get back to her."

"How did he break free from you guys to go after Delancy?"

"He was shot in the back of his left shoulder, so only one of the men was holding onto him. He was injured and he appeared completely drained, but as soon as he saw his sister and Delancy, it was like the adrenaline kicked him into overdrive." She shifted a little and added, "I'm sorry, sir, we still should have been able to restrain him. If he dies, that's on us."

Davis looked at the young woman standing before him, ready to take the blame, but he wouldn't let her. "No, Officer Sanchez. None of this is your fault. We lost him in NY, we lost him in Toronto, and you got to him first here. You did a good job."

"Thank you, sir."

He started towards the ambulance when his radio chirped, "Agent Davis, we're ready to go."

"On my way."

Chapter 22

Danielle woke up to the antiseptic smell of a hospital room. She noticed the tubes going into her arm and the machine that beeped off to the side of her bed. She looked at her hospital gown and the clean sheets and blankets she was wrapped in. She looked across the room and saw a police officer sitting in a chair. The police officer noticed her looking around and smiled.

"Welcome back," she said. She stood and opened the door. She leaned her head out and called out, "She's awake." She left the door open and walked across the room to the bed. "I'm Officer Sanchez. How are you feeling?"

Danielle started to speak but her voice was hoarse. Officer Sanchez offered her some water and she took a small sip. "Where's Peter?" she asked. Before the officer could answer, the doctor walked into the room.

"Good afternoon, Miss Donovan. I'm Doctor Albright and I've been looking after you. You gave us quite a scare, young lady. You have bilateral pneumonia, which means you have it in both lungs. Your fever left you severely dehydrated as well. You waited far too long to get treatment and it was almost too late." Seeing the look of worry cross her face, he added, "Don't worry. We did get to it in time and you will make a full recovery." He looked down at her chart and continued. "We are going to keep you here for a few days for observation, and then you'll be on bed rest for another three weeks. I want you to take it easy. You're only job is to get better. Do you have any questions for me?"

"Where's Peter?"

"Peter has not awakened from surgery yet. He was shot twice, once in the back of the shoulder and once in the chest. The second shot punctured his lung. Both bullets were taken out, but he's hooked up to a chest drainage tube until his lung fully heals. Your brother is very strong, Danielle. We almost lost him, but it looks as though he'll make a full recovery as well. He will also need to take it easy for quite a while."

"Can I see him?"

"Danielle, you're too weak to walk right now." He saw the tears begin to stream down her cheeks and added, "I'll tell you what. When he wakes up, I'll see if we can get a nurse to wheel you in to see him. Okay."

"Thank you, Doctor. I'm sorry. It's just that I was so scared and then the man shot him right in front of me and I thought he was dead. Then I woke up here and I haven't had time to work through any of it yet. I promise I'm not trying to cry to get my way." She rubbed at her eyes and took a deep breath.

"That's okay, Danielle. No one would blame you for being scared after everything you've been through, but you're safe now, so you just get your rest. You have one more visitor and then I need you to try and get some more sleep."

For an instant she thought it would be Laura before realizing that would not be possible. "Who is it?"

"I'm Special Agent Davis. I'm the one that has been following you and your brother all over North America. I just wanted to let you know that I'll be handling your security personally until you recover and we hand you back over to the Marshals."

"It's nice to meet you."

"Likewise. I also have a message for you from Marshal Scarvelli." He saw her eyes brighten when he said the name. "He says hello and that he bets he'll be out of the hospital before you and Peter will."

Tears started running down her cheeks again, but this time she was happy. "Scarvelli made it?"

"Yes he did, and he's proud of you for escaping the ambush."

"So he'll be able to have Christmas with his little girls?"

"Yep. It might have to be in the hospital, but they will be together."

"Thank you, Agent Davis. You don't know how much that means to me. What about Marshal Tom?"

"I'm sorry, he didn't make it. None of the others did."

"Did he have a family?"

"I don't know." Davis' phone beeped and he said, "I'm sorry, but I have to take this." With that everyone left the room and Danielle was alone with Officer Sanchez.

"Officer Sanchez. Do you think you could get my Bible out of my backpack?"

"No problem, Danielle." She picked up the girl's bag and dug through it for the Bible. By the time she put it on the table next to her bed, her charge was already asleep.

"Agent Davis, Sandoval's tech found the leak. A member of our support staff named Linda Anderson was passing info to her cousin Heather who has been seeing Matthew Gravano on the sly," Parker said.

"And she confessed?" Davis asked while still standing in the hospital hallway.

"Yeah, before the door was even closed in the interrogation room she was squirting big crocodile tears and apologizing. Like she didn't know what she was doing. We're about to go pick up Heather, now."

"Wait, before you do, how was Linda getting the info to Heather?"

"By text."

"And you still have the phone?"

"Yeah we do, and I think I see where you're going with this."

"Tell Linda that we'll give her some leniency in her sentence if she waves her right to a lawyer and voluntarily enters our custody for the next few weeks. After that she can contact whatever lawyer she wants. In the meantime we send some misinformation to the Gravano's about the kid's whereabouts." He paused and added, "If she balks, remind her that she's as much a liability to Gravano at this point as the kids are."

"Hold on, I'll see if she's inclined to see things our way." A minute or so passed and then Parker was back. "She's agreed, where do we want to send Gravano's men?"

"How cold is it in Minnesota right now?" They both laughed and then he continued. "Text her that Peter and Danielle will be holed up near Saint Paul, Minnesota while they recover." Davis ended the call and walked down the hospital corridor thinking, *At least the kids will be safe for a little while.*

*****

Gravano sat at the metal table with his head cradled in both of his palms while his hands covered his face. "Joey and Anthony both arrested, and the kids are still alive?"

"Sorry to say, but yes." Rosenberg replied. "Most of their men were arrested, too. Of all the men we sent after the Donovans, only three made it back. I expect our associates up in Toronto to be back before too long, but right now we're a little low on manpower. "

240

"And the kids are recovering in Minnesota?" He shifted in his seat while Rosenberg pulled out some papers.

"That's what Matthew's contact believes and she hasn't been wrong yet. Peter was shot twice; once by Anthony off a twenty or thirty foot pier into the ocean, and once by Joey in the chest from only a few feet away. I don't know how the kid is still breathing"

"How many guards do they have on them?" Gravano was starting to think he was finished.

"We don't know, but supposedly a lot until they recover and can be moved again. We're not going to get another shot at them until they are back with the Marshals."

"When will that be? Because the trial starts in another month."

"I'm sorry, Sal, I don't have any more information for you. At least for now we should start concentrating on our defense." He pulled out some more papers and looked up at his employer.

"What defense? They got the video and they got the kids. What do we got?"

"Matthew is still on the outside. He may still figure out a way to help you out."

"I wouldn't count on it." Gravano replied bitterly. "They're probably gonna be charging him with witness tampering. He'll be back in here with us soon enough."

*****

Peter woke up and the white room immediately led him to the conclusion that he was in the hospital. He noticed the police officer in his room out of the corner of his eye and didn't care that he was back in police custody. He just felt lucky to be alive. His entire upper body hurt, but he didn't mind. He did, however, want to throw on some sweat pants or shorts as soon as possible. The tall officer noticed him fidgeting and said, "Hey, welcome back to the land of the living." He stood and opened the door. He said something to someone outside and a moment later a doctor walked in the room along with a man in a suit and a nurse.

The Doctor said, "Thank you, Officer Tillman." He turned and then looked at Peter. "Hello Peter, I'm Doctor Jackson. How are you feeling today?"

Peter cleared his throat, took a sip of water, and replied, "Where's Dani?" He tried to sit up straighter, but the stab of pain that shot through his upper body made him think better of it. He looked down and saw a tube of some sort sticking out of his chest.

"Peter, you need to lie still, you were shot twice and the second bullet did a lot of damage. You were in surgery for several hours and we almost lost you. It's very important that you stay as still as possible so your lung can heal. You're gonna be our guest for a while."

"What about Dani? Where is she?"

Davis was touched by Peter's devotion to his sister. He replied, "Danielle is going to be fine. She had a very bad case of pneumonia, but the doctors got to her in time. She's resting comfortably right now."

"Is she warm enough? She couldn't get warm enough."

"She's fine," the doctor said. "And she can't wait to see you. She's asleep right now, but as soon as she wakes up we're going to bring her in."

"Thanks." Peter's eyes were starting to feel heavy, and the nurse walked over and stuck a thermometer in his mouth. He didn't notice the cuff around his arm until it automatically began inflating.

"That's the blood pressure machine, it's going to do that every so often," she said while she typed his temperature into another machine and then left the room.

"I'll be back to talk to you a little bit more tomorrow, Peter," the Doctor said and then followed the nurse out of the room.

"Peter, I'm Agent Davis. The FBI assigned me to your case as soon as your safe house was compromised. I chased you all the way across Canada and then down here."

"Sorry about that." Peter coughed and then winced. He took another sip of water and swallowed hard.

"No, don't worry about it. You were scared. I get it." Davis paused and continued. "I do have a few questions for you if you feel up for it?" He took out a pen and pad and prepared to write down what they talked about.

"Yeah, no problem, but if I fall asleep, don't take it personally."

Davis chuckled, "Don't worry. I won't." He took a deep breath and asked, "How did you escape the ambush at the safe house?"

"As soon as we got there, I started planning our escape in case anything went wrong. I made Dani sleep in her sweats and we never unpacked our stuff in case we needed to run. There was a tree in the yard and the branches had grown over the roof of the house. As soon as I heard a noise I didn't like, I woke Dani up. Then we started hearing all the shooting and yelling. We rushed across the hall, ducking bullets, and I knocked a guy down the stairs while he was still firing. I barricaded my door and then we went down the tree and ran. We hid up in a tree in the park until everyone had cleared out and then we hitched a ride north."

"Wow. That sounds like it was intense."

"I know we should have gone to the police, but I was scared and Gravano's guys had found us so fast— I didn't know who to trust. The only adult I've ever trusted is Coach Bailey. I thought I could protect us better than you guys could. I guess I was wrong."

"No, you did a good job keeping your sister safe. How did you get across the border?" He looked up from his pad and waited for Peter to get comfortable enough to answer.

He squinted and took a breath. "The first time was easy. I think we crossed before you started looking for us. The second time we just got lucky. I sat near the front of the bus and Dani sat in the back. We crossed in the middle of the night."

"Because people pay less attention when they're tired. That was smart, Peter."

"Yeah, and I figured anyone looking would be looking for both of us together. There was an accident in the next lane before the guy could look at Dani's passport. He had it in his hands, but he never opened it. He just gave it back and ran off the bus."

"That was pretty lucky for you." He wrote some notes down and then asked, "Where did you get the money for all of those bus rides and motels, and coats and food?"

"I had five thousand dollars with me split up into a bunch of different pockets and my shoes. I also had our passports with me when we went to the police. Earlier that weekend, Barbarelli had given me two thousand dollars to pay me for the weeks I couldn't work after Gravano beat me up." He shifted again in an effort to get comfortable, but only winced at the results.

"You know what that money was really for, right?"

"I knew it was hush money, but it's not like I could have refused it. I was staying with my friend Austin, so I put the money in his house until I could get to the bank. Then I went back to my apartment when my dad was in lockup and got the rest of my stuff. I had hidden a box in the ceiling with three thousand dollars that I had saved for an emergency. I put it with the money Barbarelli gave me, and when everything went down and we needed to run fast, I figured some travel money would come in handy."

"Wow, you are a very well prepared teenager."

"You should see how much I saved for Dani's college. Barbarelli paid me a lot and I saved a lot of it for her."

"You're a good brother, Peter." He jotted down a couple things in his book and continued, "Why did you go up on the roof of the cottages on the pier?"

"I wanted to get the police' attention because I knew I couldn't get away from Gravano that time, and I thought if I got them all out on the pier, it would be easier for you to capture them. Plus, I was leading them away from Dani. I always planned to jump into the ocean. I just didn't plan on getting shot on the way in."

"That was some good thinking." He shook his head amazed at the kid sitting in front of him. "Okay, last question, and this is the one that's really been baffling me. How did you get out of the mall? And how did you get out of Toronto?" He smiled and added, "I guess that was actually two questions."

"I just kept running and jumping off things until I could sneak into a store at the mall. Then I bought a new coat and hat, zipped it up all the way and walked right out a crowded exit. Then later, we hid in the back of a truck filled with kegs that some dude was delivering and we stayed in his truck until we reached Huntsville. That's when Dani first started getting sick."

"Peter, when this is all over, you would make an excellent FBI agent."

Peter started to laugh but then clutched at his chest. "Don't make me laugh, it hurts too much."

Davis stood up and said, "All right. Thanks for talking with me. I'm gonna let you get some rest now. Don't worry. You and your sister are safe." He stood and walked out of the room and then Peter drifted off to sleep.

*****

The next time Peter woke up, the first thing he saw was his sister's smiling face. She leaned over and kissed his cheek and then sat back down. "I'm so happy you're okay." She started to tear up and Peter wiped one of the tears off her cheek with his finger.

"I'm happy that you're gonna get better, too. You had me really scared you know?"

"Me? You got shot right in front of me saving my life. I thought you were dead. I can't get that image out of my mind. The only thing that helps at all is when I read my Bible." She wiped her eyes and then held her brother's hand. "Thank you for saving my life."

"You're my sister. It's my job" He yawned and started to close his eyes. The steady beeping of the hospital equipment was almost rhythmic. "I'm sorry I'm so tired, Dani."

"I'm tired, too. I just had to see you to make sure you were okay. I'll come back later. I love you, Peter."

"I love you, too, Dani. Now get some sleep, I hate being all mushy." He smiled and she chuckled while she wiped her tears.

"Okay. I'll see you later." The nurse turned her wheelchair and wheeled her out of the room. She looked back the whole way.

"Bye, Dani," he said when she reached the door. Her visit had really lifted his spirits.

"Your sister believes God protected the two of you during this whole ordeal, Peter?" Officer Tillman said when the door had closed.

"Yeah, but I don't call getting shot twice and almost dying very good protection," he replied.

"I could see how it might seem that way, but the truth is, only a couple millimeters were the difference between life and death for you. Some people might think that was God's hand of protection."

"I don't know, sounds like a coincidence to me. Do you believe all of this God stuff, Officer Tillman?"

"I do, and I'm convinced that God protected you and Danielle. I've already told Danielle as much."

"Oh great, now she'll be going on about it forever," Peter said with a sigh. His eyes lids were continuing to grow heavy. "To be honest, I don't really know what I believe, but I'm happy for her that she has her faith."

"You look pretty tired. We can pick this up later if you want to," Officer Tillman said and then stood.

"That would be great, thanks." Peter's eyes began to close and the tall officer left the room and closed the door behind him. Peter knew he was right on the other side of that door, and somehow that thought comforted him.

*****

A week later, Danielle walked into Peter's room shadowed by Officer Sanchez. "Petey, Officer Sanchez bought us some playing cards for Christmas. We have a regular deck and we have Uno. Do you want to play?" Her smile was infectious.

"Sure, as long as you don't mind watching the football game while we play."

"Of course not," she said. Peter could notice all of the color had returned to her face. She was walking in and out of the room now and eating like she used to. "Oh, guess what?"

"What?"

"The doctor said I could be released today."

"Really? Where are they going to take you?"

"No where yet. I have to stay here until you are released."

"So what's the difference then?"

"I don't know, I guess I'm just happy I'm better." She began to shuffle the Uno cards and looked over to her shadow. "Officer Sanchez, do you want to play with us? It's way more fun with three people."

"I'd love to, sweetie, but I'm on duty." Danielle looked over to Officer Tillman and Officer Sanchez added, "He's on duty, too."

"Okay, it'll still be fun. I always win Uno." She dealt the cards and they began to play.

After her fourth straight win Peter looked at her and said, "I'm sorry we missed Christmas and your birthday."

"Don't worry about it. We're together and we're both going to be all right."

"I have a present for you. I got it a couple days before this whole thing started and I brought it with me. I meant to give it to you sooner, but I was so tired and kept forgetting."

Danielle frowned and said, "Petey, I didn't get you anything."

"That's okay. Just seeing you here is enough Christmas for me." He reached into his backpack and pulled out the small, rectangular, black box. "Merry Christmas, Dani. I'm sorry I couldn't wrap it."

She accepted the box from him and looked at it. She opened it up and a gasp escaped her lips. "Peter, this is beautiful. How could you afford something like this?"

"Don't worry about it. You're worth it." He smiled while she took the silver necklace out of the box. She held the diamond pendant in the open palm of her hand. She looked at it for a long moment. "I love it, Peter! Thank you." She turned to show it to Officers Sanchez and Tillman.

"Wow, that's beautiful, Danielle," Officer Sanchez said. She took the necklace from Danielle's hand, and had her turn around. Danielle held her hair up off her neck and the officer clasped it on her.

She turned around and Officer Tillman said, "Wow, your brother has good taste." Danielle smiled and started to give her brother a hug until she noticed his grimace.

"Sorry, Peter, I forgot." She smiled again and said, "This is so nice. I wish I had something for you."

"Don't worry about it. You have a good excuse."

*****

Nine days later, they were released from the hospital. Four Marshals met them at their rooms and they all left together with Officers Sanchez and Tillman. Agent Davis was waiting for them in the lobby.

"I have some good news for you. Some of my officers went to your friends' houses and picked up most of your belongings. So now you won't just have to live out of your backpacks. I think some of your friends were even able to write letters to you. They were so relieved to know that you're okay."

"That's great news," Danielle said. "I can't wait to read the letters." She looked at Peter then back at Agent Davis and added, "Will we be able to see them at all, or at least write them back?"

"I don't think you'll be able to see them, Danielle. If we do get approval for you to write them, the letters will have to go through an editing process to make sure you are not giving any information concerning your whereabouts away."

"We would never do that, Agent Davis."

"I believe you would never do it intentionally, Danielle, but even details like saying that you've found a good church could lead to Gravano's people finding you."

A somber look crossed her face and she replied, "Oh, I never thought about that. I would totally write that, too. I'm sorry. I'm not very good at this."

"It's okay, Danielle, that's why we would have people edit your message, if my bosses even let you send it." He paused and a more serious look came over his face. "I'm not sure if you want to know this, but I also found out that your father is almost halfway through his court appointed rehab and reports say he's doing very well."

"That's good news," Danielle replied. "Isn't it Peter?"

"Not really. I guess it's good for him, but I'm just happy I'll never have to see him again."

"Peter!"

"Can we not talk about this, Dani?" Before she could reply an SUV pulled up to the curb and Agent Davis began walking them outside.

When they reached the curb, Davis said, "I guess this is goodbye for now. I will see you again once the trial starts." He put out his hand and Peter shook it. He offered his hand to Danielle and she paused for the briefest of moments, and then she wrapped him up in a big hug.

"Thank you for helping us, Agent Davis. I'm sorry we were such a pain."

He patted her back with one hand while looking around at the smiles of the officers. "That's not true, Danielle. It's Gravano's men that have caused all the trouble, not you guys."

"Well thank you, anyway." Danielle said and then she moved on to hug Officers Sanchez and Tillman. "Thanks for being our bodyguards while we were here. I hope you weren't too bored."

"No, we enjoyed watching you beat your brother at cards all the time," Officer Sanchez replied while she returned the embrace. "Take care of yourselves and stay safe."

"We will." Peter said and then he and Danielle stepped into the SUV the Marshals would be using to transport them to their temporary home. The vehicle pulled away from the curb and Danielle put her head on her brother's shoulder.

"Isn't it great how God protected us while we were on the run?"

Peter scoffed. "Protected us? Dani, I was shot... twice! I almost died in surgery. You wound up with double pneumonia and almost died. We're lucky to be alive. I think God's angels took the day off on this one."

"Or they were protecting us and that's the reason we're still alive. Pastor John always says it's not easy. God rarely saves us the way we think he should. Maybe there was a reason we had to go through all of this. Maybe we're stronger for it," Danielle replied. She knew God had saved them, she just hoped she could convince her brother. She remembered reading in James that trials help Christians grow in their faith.

"We'll have to agree to disagree on this one, Dani."

"You'll see it someday, Peter. You'll see." It looked like it might take more convincing than she thought, but she knew she would convince him.

"You really haven't lost your faith through any of this, have you?"

"No. If anything, I think it's even stronger."

*****

"We need to be prepared for the worst, Mr. Gravano," Rosenberg said. "With the trial due to begin, we still have no clue where the Donovans are." He frowned, knowing what his boss's reaction would be.

"This is unacceptable. Hire every hitter you can think of to take these kids out. They have to come back to New York for the trial. We'll get them on the way in or on the way out. Those kids cannot be allowed to survive." He slapped the dented, metal table for emphasis.

"After everything those kids have been through, they'll have an army watching over them once they get back to New York. I'll do what I can, but you should start making accommodations for your brother to come back from Toronto and hold your enterprises together until we can somehow get you out on appeal."

"I don't think we're there yet. Just get the word out. All our guys and any independents we can trust. Do you understand?"

"Of course." Rosenberg stood and packed up his briefcase. "I'll see you tomorrow, Sal."

"Bring me some good news when you come."

Rosenberg tapped on the door and the guards let him out. He was already on the phone with Vic relaying Gravano's instructions as he left the building. Matthew's bond had been revoked for witness tampering and somehow Rosenberg didn't seem to mind that development at all.

*****

"All rise!" the bailiff exclaimed. After everyone in the courtroom was standing he continued, "United states District Court for the Southern District of New York is now in session. The honorable Judge Harlon McCray presiding. Please be seated."

The judge looked over the courtroom and said, "Good morning ladies and gentlemen."

The bailiff then read the charges out loud, "Federal case number: 35872C-2F The People Versus Salvatore Gravano on the charge of murder in the first degree."

The judge looked down and asked, "Are both sides ready?"

Lance Stevens stood and replied, "The people are ready, Your Honor."

Rosenberg projected a confidence he did not feel when he replied, "The defense is ready, Your Honor."

"Will the clerk please swear in the jury?" The judge asked. The trial had finally begun. There was a heavy media presence for what was being billed: The Trial of the Decade. There was also a heavy police and FBI presence around the witnesses. After the opening statements were given, the details of what Sal Gravano was accused of were explained, and the video was played as evidence. The judge looked down from the bench and said, "The prosecution may call its first witness."

After a long pause Stevens stood, looked over at Gravano and Rosenberg, and said, "The prosecution calls, Peter Donovan to the stand."

Made in the USA
San Bernardino, CA
13 May 2015